FORBIDD

"Where are you taking me, Tall Cloud?" Christa demanded. "And why must we go so far from my cabin?"

"You ask too many questions," the handsome warrior answered. "Just follow. We will once more share our love."

Christa's heart leaped in anticipation, then she felt ashamed of her wanton reaction. "No," she said quietly. "I was wrong to let you make love to me the first time. It can't happen again."

In the shadows of a gigantic oak, Tall Cloud took Christa in his arms, ignoring her efforts to push him away. His lips met hers in a heated fury, and he moaned as he felt the softness of her breasts against his chest.

Christa felt the rapture she remembered so well spreading like wildfire inside her. His kiss was demanding . . . hot . . . possessive. His body was rock hard against hers, and even through the cotton fabric of her dress she could feel the heat of his muscled flesh.

All thoughts of right and wrong were cleansed from her mind as Tall Cloud began to caress her trembling form. A passionate shiver raced through her, and she didn't protest when he eased her down to the ground where a thick layer of soft fallen leaves became their bed of love. . . .

Other books by Cassie Edwards:

Beloved Embrace

Desire's Blossom

Elusive Ecstasy

Enchanted Enemy

Eugenia's Embrace

Forbidden Embrace

Passion's Fire

Passion's Web

Portrait of Desire

Rapture's Rendezvous

Savage Obsession

Savage Innocence

Savage Paradise

Savage Torment

Silken Rapture

CASSIE EDWARDS

SAVAGE HEART

ZEBRA BOOKS
Kensington Publishing Corp.
http://www.kensingtonbooks.com

ZEBRA BOOKS are published by

Kensington Publishing Corp.
850 Third Avenue
New York, NY 10022

All Kensington titles, imprints and distributed Lines are available at special quantity discounts for bulk purchases for sales
promotion, premiums, fund-raising, and educational or insti-
tutional use.

Special book excerpts or customized printings can also be created to fit specific needs. For details, write or phone the office
of the Kensington Special Sales Manager: Kensington Publishing Corp., 850 Third Avenue, New York, NY 10022, attn:
Special Sales Department, Phone: 1-800-221-2647.

First printing: February 2002

10 9 8 7

Printed in the United States of America

*In memory of my beloved mother,
Dorothy June Decker, who still
guides my heart . . .*

Acknowledgment

A thank you goes to Ann Willis, supervisor of the Tesson Ferry Branch of the St. Louis County Libraries, for her assistance in the research of the Suquamish Indians of Seattle.

And a sincere thanks to poet James A. Hanf of Bremerton, Washington, for sharing his knowledge of Seattle and the beautiful state of Washington.

I love you
For the part of me
That you bring out;
I love you
For putting your hand
Into my heaped-up heart
And passing over
All the foolish, weak things
That you can't help
Dimly seeing there,
And for drawing out
Into the light
All the beautiful belongings
That no one else had looked
Quite far enough to find.

—Croft

One

The pine stick was taking on an appearance of gold beneath the rays of the early morning sun as David Martin sat beside a window, whittling skillfully. The aroma of biscuits and sausage still hung heavy in the air, making it hard for David to leave the house to begin his morning chores.

But deep inside, where his fears were formed, David knew that his sister, Christa, was always the main reason for his lingering each morning. Though the Suquamish Indians of this Puget Sound land had proven to be peaceful enough, David had never let himself fully trust them. And how unnerving it was that they came and went from all the settlers' houses without even asking.

"A *nanitch*," the Indians always said when questioned about this annoying habit. "A look around" was all they wanted.

Up to now, the white settlers had learned to put up with the inconvenience of the Indians' sudden appearances in their dwellings, but none of them approved of the rude practice.

"And what are your plans for today, Christa?" David asked his sister, who had just emerged from the doorway. He stopped his whittling long enough to run the fingers of his left hand over the smoothness of his pine stick. No particular shape had been planned. For David, whittling was just a calming thing to do while idling away the time waiting and watching out for his sister's welfare.

David's gaze moved slowly toward Christa, and he was certain that the Indian braves recognized how beautiful and vulnerable she was at her age of nineteen. Surely they were in awe of her long blond hair and soft green eyes. Though her eyes were lovely, David would have much preferred that they did not have that slightly seductive slant. Christa was a shy and soft-spoken person, never a seductress.

But it was not only her hair and eyes that would draw the Indians to notice her. Christa's skin was as fair as a pearl freshly plucked from the womb of an oyster, marred only by a few dots of freckles on the bridge of her perfectly shaped nose and upper cheeks. And though she was petite, with a tiny waist and graceful hips, David feared the interest the Indians seemed to take in the ample swell of breasts that overly filled her dresses.

"Plans?" Christa asked, blowing a strand of hair back from her cheek. "What are my plans for the day? I believe I shall go search for wild cranberries for supper. You know that one barrel of cranberries is worth five yards of white cotton cloth."

She frowned as she once more observed the tight fit of David's shirt. "My dear big brother, I don't think I have to tell you how badly you need a new shirt."

David laughed softly, resuming his whittling. "That's just like you, Christa," he said. "You're always thinkin' about somebody else, never yourself. It's you who could do with a new dress. I'm sure you'd enjoy huntin' and pickin' through the bolts of cloth at Harrison Kramer's general store just for the right design of cotton for a new dress, now wouldn't you?"

"I can't deny that I would," Christa said, pushing aside the leftover biscuits and jar of molasses on the table to make room to knead and work her bread dough. "But I prefer not to speak of Harrison today, much less go to his store and come face to face with him. He's a most unlikable man. How many times do I have to tell you that, David? Please stop trying to play matchmaker. I could *never* marry such a man as Harrison Kramer. Not only do I dislike him, but he's old enough to be my father."

David rose from his chair and placed his pocket knife and pine stick on the fireplace mantel. Then he let his eyes absorb the drabness of this two-room cabin with its half loft overhead which he used for sleeping. When first he had dreamed of moving from Boston to this timbered world to be conquered and cut, David had known to expect hardships. The death of their parents from the ravages of cholera on the trail had been the first hardship faced. The second was having to make do in this log-sided, shake-roofed cabin with the room in which he now stood serving as kitchen, dining and living room, and the one other room, for Christa, only large enough for a feather bed.

Yes, David wanted more for himself. But his sister's needs were his main concern, and Harrison Kramer appeared to be his answer. Not only was he a wealthy and powerful man in the community, but he was also quite interested in Christa.

"It's not only the cloth you should buy at the store," David persisted. "I thought you were in need of saleratus, for leavening, and whole spices. Didn't you say that you also wanted ginger and nutmeg to grate into your puddings?"

"David, *please!*" Christa sighed, busily kneading the dough.

"Are you worrying about the cost, Christa? I have almost a thousand cedar shakes split. Those shingles can net us a quick three dollars and fifty cents."

Christa's gaze traveled over David, seeing his flimsy trousers secured with a cowhide belt, the legs tucked into high, cowhide boots, and she frowned once more at the tightness of his shirt. Then she glanced down at her own attire, seeing the faded flower design of her floor-length cotton dress, the yellowed fabric of her apron, and the torn lace that lined the deep vee of the bodice of her dress.

"I can do without extras like fancy spices," she blurted quickly. "We must concentrate only on our year's essential supplies. We must be sure to keep sugar and flour in the pantry."

"With our farm stocked with pigs, chickens, and cows, how can you worry so about sugar and flour?" he scoffed. "Why, Christa, I even know that you've already thriftily stored many wild berries and fruits in the cellar. You've churned butter and put it down in barrels of brine. You even made sausage and head cheese at hog-butchering time. And your garden grows from seeds you've saved from year to year."

"David, I know all of this—"

"The point *is,* baby sister, your argument against shopping at Harrison's store isn't valid," he said, stooping to lift his ax from the corner of the room where he had left it.

"David, say no more. I do have a mind of my own, you know. Please allow me to use it as I see fit."

David shrugged, lifting the ax to rest on a shoulder. "All right," he said, moving toward the door.

He gave her a sly smile from across the room. "For now," he quickly added.

Christa brushed her hands together, knocking flour from them. She went to David and grabbed his free hand, stopping him. "Where's this morning's bear hug?" she asked with a giggle.

With his ax still supported on his one shoulder, he swept his free arm about her tiny waist and hugged her fiercely.

"Ouch!" she scolded through her laughter.

"You said a bear hug," he teased. "I didn't want to cheat you none."

Christa playfully smacked him on a cheek. "Oh, go on,

David. Get to work," she said. "You're impossible this morning. I don't know what's got into you."

"It's the time of the full moon," David said in a ghostly fashion. "It brings out the mischief in me."

"I hope it brings out the muscle," Christa said, walking with him to the door. "You've many swings of the ax to take this morning."

"Yep. A busy day that started before daybreak," David said, pushing the door open. "The farm animals were fed even before I was."

"That's the way you want it, David."

"It's a nice way to spread the full day's work out," he said. "Stoppin' for meals takes the dreariness out of my duties."

"Be careful, big brother?" Christa said, standing on tiptoe to kiss him good-bye. "Sometimes you get reckless with the ax. *Please* don't be in such a hurry."

"You fret too much, Christa," he said, stepping out onto a stone-laid path. He turned to face her, frowning, still full of his own fears for Christa.

He glanced down at her apron pocket. "It's there, ain't it?" he said thickly, now looking up into her eyes which always reflected a quiet confidence in herself. This confidence was another reason for him to be concerned. Her trust ran so much deeper than his.

Christa patted the outside of the apron pocket, cringing as she felt the cold hardness of the lady's pearl-handled pistol which rested inside. "Yes, it's there," she said. "Loaded and ready, if needed. But I think it's foolish carrying the pistol with me at all times."

"The Indians, Christa . . ."

"I've seen a few white men that gave me more cause to feel the need to protect myself," she scoffed. "Though the Suquamish Indians are a nuisance, I don't feel threatened by them."

"You wouldn't, Christa," David said hoarsely. "No, you

wouldn't." He turned and looked in the direction of the forest. In its darkness, so much could be hidden. . . .

"David, we must get on with our chores," Christa argued softly. "I do want to pick wild cranberries, and I enjoy the time spent in the search. It's always nice to be able to get out of the cabin, if only for a short while."

David wanted to talk more about Harrison Kramer and what his riches could give Christa, but having already over-stated his argument this morning, he gave her a slow wink instead and began walking to his cedar wood pile, whistling.

"Be careful, David," Christa yelled, following him out of the house.

She relaxed then and absorbed the clean, fresh smells and sights of morning as she looked toward the huge body of water that was only a stone's throw from where she stood. Puget Sound was not only the city of Seattle's front yard, but Christa's and David's as well.

The Sound was a stout arm of the Pacific Ocean that twisted its way into the northwest corner of the land that was now the state of Washington. San Francisco was one thousand miles away by sea, yet it sometimes seemed to the fishermen and loggers of Seattle a continent away, for San Francisco was the only population center on the coast large enough to provide a market for the products of fisheries and forests.

Christa inhaled the pure, sweet smell of the breeze blowing in from the Sound and listened to the slap of fish breaking the surface in a rhythm almost as constant as the beat of the waves.

Gulls wheeled overhead on steady wings, turning their smooth heads slowly as they scanned the water for prey. Cranes flapped heavily into flight, dwarfed by the great mountain that rose in the east with white, cone-streaked peaks and blue-black ridges—Mount Rainier. It was a ghostly apparition on the horizon, often hidden by heavy, gray clouds which hung low over firs and hemlocks. But today the mountain rose magnificently into the sky, displaying its new coat of snow, a reminder that winter was not so far away.

The sound of the ax making contact with wood made Christa look away from Puget Sound and its displays of wonder. She turned to gaze at the small farm that had been cut out of the dense forest looming black to the left of her. Fruit trees had been planted close to the cabin, and slips of Mission Rose now grew beside a white picket fence that outlined this small section of land that Christa now called "home."

Anxious to get her bread baking in the hot coals of the fire, Christa turned and went back to the table. She powdered her hands with flour and once more began kneading the dough, silently looking around her at the sparse furnishings of the cabin. This table on which she labored stood in the middle of the room with two white enameled chairs pushed beneath it. A stone fireplace served as the source of heat and cooking, and two upholstered chairs sat before it, with kerosene lamps on tables standing beside each.

Christa tensed, hearing a creak in the bare, sanded oak planks of the floor. She turned around slowly and watched in keen annoyance as the Indians began inching their way into the cabin, looking around guardedly.

Christa wiped a stray lock of hair from her eyes, accidentally smearing flour on her forehead, and wondered just how much longer the Indians would continue to invade her privacy. If in Boston someone had told her that she would have to put up with such nonsense as this, she would have laughed and called the person a fool. She never would have thought that Indians would mingle so freely with the white men, especially not in this way.

Feeling the need to stay busy, to hide her frustrations at this intrusion, Christa greased and floured a pan and patted her bread dough into it, all the while keeping her eyes on the Indians' each and every move.

There were no Indian squaws present from this Suquamish, *Salish*-speaking tribe. Only the male Indians ever dared an uninvited visit to the white men's cabins. And as usual, Christa noted, those who were here today were attired in various modes of dress, but all were barefoot. Some had untailored, loose-fitting garments made of deerskin or plant fiber, and others wore only loincloths.

Feeling an intense pair of eyes on her, Christa let her gaze move to see which of the Indians was so mesmerized by her golden hair, green eyes, and fair skin *this* time. She had discovered that these Indians were fascinated by so many different things about the white men and women. Once, while Christa stopped in Harrison Kramer's general store, an elderly Indian had followed her around, looking at her stiffly starched bonnet so closely, she hadn't been at all surprised when Harrison told her that the elderly Indian had thought her bonnet to be a huge clamshell.

But this time she wore no bonnet, and it wasn't an elderly Indian giving her all the attention. Christa's heart suddenly seemed to float in a strange, sweet whirlpool as she discovered the source of her turmoil in the gaze of the one Indian who stood out from all the others. He was extremely handsome and towered over the others, holding himself proudly erect.

In his expressive, large gray eyes she could see intelligence, warmth, and something else. It was a look of immense appreciation of what he was seeing, an appreciation which went beyond the fact that her hair, eyes, and skin were different from his. There seemed to be the sort of attraction a man conveys when he looks at a woman because she *is* a woman.

Christa had had many men look at her in such a sensuous way, but never before had she let such a look affect her. She felt clumsy, shy. She felt as if her heart would pound right out of her chest if the Indian did not quickly avert his searing gaze.

She forced her eyes away from him, but she had already memorized his every noble feature. He was, oh, so finely proportioned, she thought, with his light copper skin, broad shoulders, and deep chest. And once more she looked at him out of the corner of her eye as she carried her pan of bread dough to the hot coals of her fire.

His hair was shoulder length, slightly wavy, and a deep brown color. It was drawn straight back from his forehead and held in place by a headband, with an eagle feather secured where the band was tied together in the back.

He was all muscle, more than likely through his many seasons of hunting, Christa guessed, which had made his arms and legs grow strong. His face was magnificently sculpted with well-defined Indian features, and he wore a necklace made of tusklike animal teeth.

Trembling, wishing that he would say something instead of just standing there mute, watching her every move, Christa knelt on one knee and slid the pan of bread dough in place. Then, as she turned to rise again, he was there. Directly in front of her eyes was his brief loincloth and outlined distinctly beneath the deerskin flap, Christa could see the strength of his manhood.

Blood rushed to Christa's face, flaming her cheeks and making her eyes grow hot. She swallowed hard and let her eyes move slowly upward, only to see him smiling down at her knowingly. She wanted to die from embarrassment. She was acting as if she had never seen a man . . . a man's . . . greatness before. Living in such close quarters with David, it had been impossible not to occasionally see him before or after a bath.

But seeing this Indian was so very different. It caused her insides to fill with a strange, liquid heat. And, oh! Why didn't the Indian at least try to say something to her in sign language? He was obviously enjoying playing such a wicked game with her. Well, she would show him that he did not affect her in the least!

Rising quickly to her feet, Christa pushed her way through the Indians. How many were there? She quickly counted them. Ten! This time there were ten!

She moved her hand inside her apron pocket to where the gun lay. Perhaps . . .

Her eyes grew suddenly wide as the handsome Indian strolled over to her table and began helping himself to the leftover biscuits and the jar of molasses. She gasped softly as she watched him place a table knife into the molasses and then spread the molasses on first one biscuit and then another. She tensed when he turned and nodded toward her, smiling back to her his approval of the taste.

"Just help yourself," she finally managed to say, sarcasm thick in her words. "Don't ask. Just take. Don't even bother thanking me for my hospitality. It's always here for the taking, isn't it?"

Surely she recognized a chuckle when she heard one, and she most definitely had heard him emit such a sound. This proved that he had understood what she had said and was indeed finding this situation quite amusing.

Gaining courage from her anger and her need to put space between herself and this Indian whose eyes seemed to mirror his soul, she went to him and jerked the knife from his hand.

"I would appreciate it if you and your cohorts would leave my cabin at once," she hissed.

Never having asked the Indians to leave before, Christa became weak in the knees. Her throat went dry. She didn't dare look toward the handsome Indian, not knowing what to expect from him. Had he truly understood what she had said?

The knife slipped in her hand, and the molasses was suddenly all over her fingers, threatening to stick them together.

She cast the handsome Indian an ugly look. "Now see what you caused me to do?" she cried softly. "Look at the mess on my fingers!"

Slamming the knife down on the table, she started to go to a stand where a wash basin sat filled with water. But suddenly the tall Indian stepped in her path, grabbing her by the wrist and lifting her hand to his lips.

"What?" Christa gasped. "What . . . do . . . you think you're . . . doing?"

Her breath caught in her throat as his lips were there, sensuously moving from finger to finger, kissing away the molasses, all the while watching her with his large and expressive gray eyes.

Embarrassed but unable to move away from him, as though cast under his spell, Christa looked slowly around him toward the other Indians. They were watching solemn faced, showing dislike for what their noble-appearing companion was doing. Yet none of them protested in any way. It was as if they had been commanded to stand their guard and to keep their silence. As with Christa, the handsome Indian appeared to have some hold—a power of sorts—over his fellow Indians. Or did it appear that way just because he was bolder? Christa wondered.

Christa's blood was spinning wildly through her veins. She knew that she should make the Indian stop, for not only was he making a fool of her, but it was being done with an audience! Yet something kept her from reacting as she knew she must, and it wasn't because of any fear of the Indians should she take a forceful action to make this one stop his gentle assault. No, it was because of the exquisite sensations that his kisses were causing between her thighs . . .

A loud shriek of pain surfacing from outside the cabin quickly jerked Christa from her hypnotic trance. Her gaze moved to the door as she pulled her hand away from the Indian, and her insides grew cold.

"David . . . ," she whispered harshly. "Oh, God, no! David!"

Forgetting everything but her brother, Christa swept the

skirt of her dress up into her arms and rushed across the room and through the door. As she ran down the stone-laid path, her heart wouldn't stop its pounding. Everything around her was much too quiet. The ax was no longer making contact with wood. David! Either he had injured himself or a warlike Haida Indian had attacked him. The Haida traveled from their home in the north to make occasional bold raids against the white men. It seemed that the Haida were enemies to everyone, the white men *and* the Puget Sound Indians, who were a mixture of both the Suquamish and Duwamish.

With her golden hair flying behind her and breathless from fear, Christa ran through the plowed garden, across the cow pasture, and finally reached the barn behind which David always labored, neatly stacking his shakes after he cut and shaped them into a product for selling.

The bright red color of blood caught Christa off guard as she made a quick turn around the corner of the barn. The blood seeped out on the ground where David sat looked dazedly down at his foot, which displayed a gaping wound oozing blood from jagged, ripped flesh. A bone was partially exposed, splintered.

Christa stopped dead in her tracks. Her hands went to her mouth, closing off a scream that had a need to surface. A light-headedness engulfed her and bitterness rose up into her throat. The blood-covered ax on the ground beside David was proof enough of what had happened.

David's eyes, glazed with pain and shock, lifted to plead silently with Christa, making her shake herself from the horror of what she had discovered.

"David . . ." she cried softly, falling to her knees beside him. "Oh, David, you're . . . you're . . . hurt so badly."

Her fingers gently touched his ankle above the wound. She could feel his flesh pounding beneath her fingers, and she looked up into his eyes, hurting with him.

"Make a tourniquet with my shirttail," he said, gasping

for breath as he struggled to rip his shirt in half. "We've got to stop . . . the . . . blood flow."

"Here. Let me do that," Christa said, taking the shirttail from him. She desperately wanted to hug him to her, comfort him, but she knew that would have to come later . . . much later.

With trembling fingers she finally succeeded at getting a length of material torn away and quickly tied it about his ankle. She searched around her for a stick, and, finding one, she secured it into the knot of the tied material and twisted it as tightly as she could.

"Hold it in place, David," she ordered softly. "I've got to ride into Seattle, to get Doc Adams."

Her face paled and her heart skipped a beat then. She realized that she couldn't leave him out in the open, helpless, for the length of time required to ride into Seattle to get the doctor. She had never before felt as helpless.

A shadow fell across David and Christa. And before Christa even had a chance to rise to her feet, the handsome Indian had swept David up into his powerful arms and was carrying him toward the house.

Christa hurriedly pushed herself up from the ground and rushed to the Indian's side, half running to keep up with him. She marveled not only at his kindness but also his strength. David was a powerful man, hard built with muscles, yet the Indian was carrying him as if he were a baby. There didn't seem to be much strain on the Indian's shoulders, arms, or leg muscles, and he wasn't even breathless as he reached Christa's bed and placed David upon it.

Christa fluffed a pillow beneath David's head then turned to face the Indian in whose eyes she saw so much as he gazed down at her from his towering six-foot height. Her pulse raced when his lips rose into a warm smile. She wanted to make him understand how much she appreciated his help, but she still wasn't sure if speaking the words would be enough. To be sure that he understood, she would use her skills with Indian sign language, which she had studied from a book on her long journey from Boston in preparation for life among the Indians.

Smiling slowly up at him, Christa held both hands shoulder high, palms facing out, and pushed them in a slight curve toward the Indian in an effort to say thank you to him. She watched as his expression became serious, his jaw tense, and his lips sealed tightly together. His eyes reflected a shadowy trace of passion as he circled his hands into tight fists, crossed his arms over his chest with his right arm close to his body, and pressed hard with his left arm.

A flame of color rose into Christa's cheeks, for she understood the Indian's way of saying "love." Strange, magical feelings overwhelmed her, but only for a moment, for when David let out a soft moan, she was once more thrown into a world in which her brother took precedence over everything else.

She glanced down at David, full of shame for having forgotten the importance of rushing to get the doctor. Then she looked back toward the Indian whose arms were no longer crossed but relaxed at his side. Something on the muscled curve of his upper right arm suddenly grabbed her attention as he turned to walk from the room. It was a tattoo, a tiny black tattoo in the shape of a raven.

"Christa . . ." David said, reaching out for her. "When you go into town, please be careful. Be sure to carry . . . the . . . loaded pistol."

Christa went and smoothed David's hair back from his brow. She leaned over and kissed him softly there. "I won't be long," she whispered. "And please don't worry. I can take care of myself. All that's important now is you."

She glanced over her shoulder, hearing the shuffling of many feet, knowing that the Indians were leaving her cabin. A part of her wanted to run to the door to bid the handsome Indian a pleasant good-bye, for she now feared that she would never see him again.

"Hurry, Christa," David said hoarsely, his eyes closing and his face laced with perspiration and a feverish flush.

"I'll be back before you can say scat," she encouraged. She gave him a last, lingering look, then went out to the horses and chose a black mare. She didn't attempt to attach her to a buggy or place a saddle on her. Time didn't allow it. She had already taken up too much precious time by acting ridiculous over the Indian. How foolish of her to believe, even for a moment that there could be anything between herself and an Indian. To many whites, Indians were savages, a word she personally detested. The Indians of the Puget Sound area even called themselves by that name, never having realized that it was a derogatory title. Only their inaccurate pronunciation of the word "savage" had caused them to call themselves *Siwashes* instead of savages.

After mounting the horse, with her dress and petticoat hiked up above her knees, Christa grabbed the reins and urged her horse toward Seattle. The underbrush which crept from the forest hugged the dirt road on the right side of her, and the cliff that overlooked the Sound was on her left. The wind whipped her hair up and away from her shoulders. Intermingling with the sea breeze, the smell of cedar created a fragrance that clung like rare perfume to Christa's face, bare arms, and exposed legs.

As the horse thundered down the road, Christa kept remembering the Indian—the way he had kissed her fingers, his tattoo in the shape of a raven, his gray eyes burning into her flesh, and his way of saying "love."

A movement in the blackness of the forest drew her eyes from the road. In the shadows she saw the handsome Indian standing alone, watching her. Christa didn't know whether to be thrilled, or afraid.

Two

Sitting on the edge of the bed, Christa once more bathed David's perspiring brow with a damp cloth. Three days had passed, the doctor had once again come and gone, and David's foot was now wrapped with a fresh, snow white bandage. Only a trace of blood had risen to the surface, leaving a threatening blotch of red as a reminder of the seriousness of the wound. David had fought hard against the fever which had robbed him of his senses for two days and nights, and now he was once more becoming his old, spirited self, ready to argue with and tease his sister.

"Doc Adams said it shouldn't be long before the Indians will be moved to reservations," he said, licking his parched lips. "Then maybe they'll quit makin' themselves at home where they don't belong."

Hearing the thickness of David's speech, Christa dipped her cloth into the fresh water of the wash basin, then squeezed drops of water onto his lips. "Do you forget so quickly that it was one of those Indians who so kindly carried you to this bed?" she asked, conscious of a strange quivering around her heart as she recalled the handsome Indian and how he had made her feel. If *he* ever chose to return, she would welcome him at her door. She now knew this to be true, and the thought brought warmth to her cheeks.

"He'll be back to get payment for his good deed," David

scoffed. "He wouldn't have helped unless he had somethin' in mind."

A pang of guilt struck a chord inside Christa's heart as she remembered the sensual moments shared with the Indian—innocent moments, though and with an audience. The guilt feelings were for having allowed herself to enjoy them, despite the fact that not even a word had been exchanged. Oh, how sometimes a look—a touch—could speak louder than words! she thought wryly.

"Yep. The treaty havin' been signed by the Indians in January of this year should clear up all these problems," David said, wincing and grabbing at his leg as a pain stabbed him where the bone had been splintered in his foot.

"The treaty hasn't even been ratified, David," Christa argued softly, once more bathing his brow. "And you know as well as I do that not all Indians agreed to the terms of the treaty. There are those who refused to attend the treaty conference. Governor Stevens didn't paint a picture glorified enough to fool those Indians. Schools and money, indeed! The ones who signed the treaty did so assuming they would have schools for their children. And they actually agreed to sell their title to their two million acres, to move to reservations, in return for one hundred fifty thousand dollars payable over twenty years in usable goods. Chief Seattle is not as smart as he should be to deserve to have the city of Seattle named after him."

David brushed Christa's hand aside and rose up slowly on an elbow. "Christa, what is this?" he asked, his eyebrows raised. "You . . . you sound as though you are defending the Indians. Why is that? Surely not because you feel that you owe them the courtesy for helping me the other morning."

Feeling a blush rising, Christa turned her face from David and rose from the bed. She suddenly realized what she had been saying. Until now, she hadn't thought much about the plight of the Indians, and now she had spoken openly of it. She could understand David's surprise at her doing this. She only wished that she could understand herself and why she was so caught up in thinking and dreaming of the Indian with the tiny raven tattoo on his arm.

She took the washbasin from the table beside the bed. "I didn't even realize that I was so heartily defending the Indians," she confessed, feeling awkward beneath the scrutiny of her brother's piercing green eyes.

"Perhaps you've been cooped up too much havin' to wait on me since my injury," David said, pushing himself up to a sitting position. "What you need is to attend the upcoming social event of the season."

To Christa, the conversation was going from bad to worse. She knew now to expect to hear Harrison Kramer's name spoken, possibly even with David's next breath. The social event of which David was speaking was the autumn dance planned by Harrison, at Harrison's plush mansion on Fourth Avenue, in Seattle.

"I'm fine, David," Christa said, heading for the door with the basin in hand. "Just please don't start fretting over me again. It's you who needs tending to. Not me."

"That's what concerns me," David said in a strained voice, which made Christa stop and swing around to face him.

"What do you mean, David?"

Her brother looked down at his bandaged foot, scowling. "Who's to know if I'll even walk again," he said then lifted his eyes to meet her look of surprise.

Christa laughed awkwardly. "Surely you don't think—"

"Exactly," he said, interrupting. "Maybe I'll never walk again. Perhaps gangrene will set in and I'll lose my whole leg. No one ever knows, from day to day, what the future holds for a body."

Christa hurried back to the bedside. She once more placed the basin on the table, then sat down on the bed and draped her arms about David's neck. "Shh," she encouraged. "Don't talk foolish. You're going to be all right. I just know it."

"But if I'm not, Christa?"

"You *are*," she said more firmly. She drew away from him, smiling. "Not tomorrow, but soon, David. You'll be as good as new."

"But we must be realistic about this," he argued. "We must make plans for the future. *Your* future."

Christa tensed. Her eyes took on a coolness. "Which, of course, includes Harrison Kramer," she said dryly.

She left the bed in a flurry, splashing water from the basin as she once more grabbed it from the table.

"If that man is all my future holds for me, I shall wish for no future," she said haughtily, rushing across the room to the door.

She gave David a sour glance from across her shoulder. "David, I'm leaving for a spell," she blurted. "You'll be all right. You're fed. You're comfortable. I shall return shortly."

"Where are you going?"

"To pick berries or maybe wild greens. Anything to get away from talk of Harrison."

"Aw, Christa, don't go on that account." David sighed. "I'm sorry. I'll watch my words."

"You, yourself, saw my need to get away, David. You said that I've been too cooped up. Well, I'm going to remedy that. I'm taking a walk."

"Christa, don't go too far."

"I never do."

"Take your pistol."

"I always do.

Leaving David, Christa hurried about the cabin, readying herself to leave, already hearing the soft rumble of his snoring. She had suspected that he needed a nap, though, in truth, he had awakened only a short while before as the first ripples of pale morning light traversed the bed, stirring him from his restless sleep.

It had been the same pale light that had awakened Christa on her small, feather bed in the loft. A tiny crack in the roof's shakes had allowed the light to steal its way onto a bed that was usually David's, a bed that would now be Christa's until David had fully recuperated and could climb the clumsy ladder leading to the loft.

With her hair tucked beneath her stiffly starched bonnet and her deep-pocketed apron still tied about her faded cotton dress with its long sleeves and revealing neckline, Christa eagerly left the cabin. She first went inside the barn to find a wicker basket, then she headed toward the bluff and walked alongside it. There was plenty of time for berry picking, she thought to herself. She would first enjoy the wonders of Puget Sound.

The bluff was golden in sunshine and crowned with madrona trees which leaned over the edge of the bluff toward the sun and blue water. Far out to sea, the Pacific swells seemed to rise out of the west like vast, cumbersome shadows. Aside from the sound of the surf, Christa now and then heard the croaking of a raven, the breathing of seals who rested below the bluff on sand bars, or the scream of an eagle.

Farther on, as far as the eye could see, the Sound was lined by continuing steep bluffs that dropped off suddenly to wet, gray mud flats, uncovered by the outgoing tide. Atop the bluffs and beyond the misty ooze of the mud flats lay the unbroken forest, with tremendous clouds rolling over its wooded shores.

This was a setting which so much reflected peace that Christa felt foolish to feel the loaded pistol weighing heavily in her right apron pocket.

Shrugging, she left the Sound behind her and began making her way along a small, winding stream with muddy banks and salt grass on the margin, which ran through a partial clearing in the woods.

Mottled trunks of alder overgrown with wild roses stood

among the evergreens. Bees and colorful butterflies darted from flower to flower, competing for space on each. Christa heard a breath of wind passing through the giant firs and the farther she moved into the forest the harder it was to see or hear the lapping waters of the Sound.

Fearing that she had traveled too far, she began to turn around, to search for berries and greens closer to her cabin, when a woman's scream rose from somewhere close by. Stiffening from fear, Christa's reflexes caused her right hand to go to her pistol and take it from its hiding place in her pocket. She began to edge backward, away from where she stood, then stopped when a sharp cry of pain once more pierced the air.

"Who . . . ? Where . . . ?" Christa whispered, wishing her knees would cease their trembling. But she knew what was expected of her. She couldn't ignore a cry for help, especially that of a woman. . . .

Looking in the direction from which she thought the cry had come, Christa made her way toward it. She feared the deeper forest where even the sun was hidden from sight and knew all sorts of dangers awaited those who ventured there. If she did not find a vicious animal, perhaps she would encounter Haida Indians, who were not only known to hate the white man but the Suquamish Indians as well, for the Suquamish had welcomed the white man to this land of trees and sparkling waters.

"But I must do what I must," Christa whispered, placing her forefinger on the trigger of her pistol and hoping she wouldn't be forced to squeeze it.

The undergrowth became thicker and tangled as she moved onward. Only silken threads of sunshine could now be seen at the forest's ceiling. Bluejays squawked and squirrels nibbled away at acorns on the limbs of the trees. A rustling of dried leaves just ahead and the whimpering of what now sounded like a young girl made the hair rise at the nape of Christa's neck. But determination and false courage made her take her next two steps. They led her to a clearing, flooded by sunshine, where a scene of degradation made Christa's breath catch in her throat and her stomach churn.

Strange that at such a time all she would see were the many designs of the tattoos on this dark-skinned Indian who was in the process of raping a young Indian girl. Tattoos on the man's hands, arms, wrists, shoulders, legs, and bare torso swirled eerily in front of Christa's eyes as she became suddenly light-headed from seeing a man in the throes of passion, plunging his manhood inside the girl and grunting with each eager thrust.

The tattoos took on the shape of live birds, flapping toward Christa. She felt the need to turn and run, but the renewed screams from the girl being assaulted brought Christa back to her senses, and, more alert now, she was filled with disgust and anger.

"Stop that this very minute," she finally yelled. "Stop or I will shoot."

She dropped her basket to the ground and with her left hand steadied the shaking hand which held the pistol. She aimed and held the pistol poised, ready to shoot if necessary.

Her voice had hit home. The Haida Indian jerked away from the young girl and jumped quickly to his feet, glaring, quite nude, toward Christa. He began to take slow steps toward her, his eyes dark with hate, his fully tattooed body tight with flexed muscles.

"I'll shoot," Christa hissed. "Take just . . . one . . . more step and . . . I'll shoot."

She had to believe that he couldn't understand her, yet her threat was real enough. Couldn't he see? Or didn't he believe that she would shoot?

Her heart thundered wildly against her ribs, and her eyes hazed over with fear. Yet when he took another step toward her, she had no alternative but to shoot him. She closed her eyes as she pulled the trigger, the discharge and explosion of the bullet giving her a start and sending her back against a tree trunk.

Moaning, she opened her eyes widely, just in time to see the Indian's body jerk as the bullet whipped into the flesh of his upper right arm. Blood flew from the wound, and the Indian yelped in pain, clutching at his arm. He then turned on a bare heel and began running, hollering, into the darkest recesses of the forest. Before Christa had a chance to move, she heard the whinnying of a horse and the clip-clop of its hooves. She listened stiffly until she could no longer hear the horse and she felt safe enough to go to the crumpled heap of the young girl who was hiding her face behind her hands, still whimpering, yet with her buckskin skirt now pulled down to hide the shame of what had just happened to her.

Dropping the pistol back inside her apron pocket, Christa rushed to the girl and knelt down beside her. With gentleness, she eased the girl's hands down from her face. Wide, tear-soaked gray eyes looked up at Christa and her heart ached when she realized how young the girl had to be. Surely she was no older than thirteen. And how beautiful she was with her pale copper skin and tiny facial features. Her dark brown hair had become half unbraided in her struggles with the Haida, and blood rolled from the corner of her mouth where a purple lump now marred her perfectly shaped lips.

The buckskin blouse the young girl wore was ripped, revealing tiny buds of breasts. Then something else caught Christa's attention. There was blood on the girl's skirt, and Christa wasn't sure if it was from the dripping, bleeding lip or from the Haida Indian's rape of the innocent child.

Before leaving Boston, Christa's mother had taught her, in much detail, the facts of life, for the older woman had not known whether or not she would be there later to tell her. And Christa knew what to expect the first time with the man she loved. It disgusted her to remember the Haida forcing himself upon this young, innocent Indian girl. Surely it would be different when two people cared for each other.

The girl's voice was weak when she spoke. *"Enati,"* she said, pointing in the direction of the Sound. *"Canin. Enati illahee. Kahpho tyee."* Once more tears flooded her eyes and her body shook with fierce sobs.

Christa dared a touch to the girl's copper face to smooth her tears away. She felt helpless, not understanding the Salish language. "I'm sorry," she murmured. "I just don't know what you're saying."

The young girl's eyes blinked nervously as she frantically began moving her hands, now communicating Indian sign language. Christa became keenly alert and watched, silently forming the words on her lips, one at a time, as she recognized the hand movements. First she recognized the word "name" and then "Star," and thankfully realized she now knew the girl's name. She watched silently as Star continued to talk with her hands.

Star made a complete circle with the fingers of her left hand and drew an imaginary circle with the right hand, around the left hand. Christa then understood the word "island."

Then Star once more spoke the word "Enati," desperately pointing toward the Sound.

"Enati Island?" Christa blurted, knowing of the island which lay across the Sound from Seattle.

Star once more spoke eagerly with her hands. She pointed the right index finger and moved her hand forward. Then she pulled her hand back, hooking her index finger at the same time.

"Take?" Christa whispered to herself, paling. "She wants me to take her to . . . to . . . Enati Island?"

Star continued. She crossed her index fingers in front of

her face and drew her hands downward and apart to describe the sloping walls of a tepee, or lodge.

"You make residence on Enati Island. You want me to take you to your village," Christa said, fear lacing her heart at the thought. Surely David wouldn't approve. But Christa felt that she had no other choice. Star appeared too weak and distraught to leave the forest on her own.

Again Christa watched while Star's hands moved as if she grasped an imaginary paddle, making paddling motions at the side of her body. Then she made a sweeping motion forward and up, with an open right hand, to indicate the curved prow of a canoe.

"Canoe . . ." Christa said, looking toward the Sound, now knowing just how she was expected to return the injured, frightened girl to her people.

With extreme care, Christa placed an arm about Star's waist and helped her up from the ground. Then she held Star close to her side, and together they made their way toward the Sound.

When they reached the bluff, Christa held onto Star even more strongly as they slipped and slid over the loose rock, down the slope of the bluff, until they finally had their feet firmly on sand. The canoe was only footsteps away, its bow and stern beautifully shaped and adorned with the teeth of the sea otter.

Christa's heart plunged as she felt Star's body go limp against her, as Star once more broke down into tearful sobs, seeming to be completely drained of energy. Christa watched as Star spoke once more with her hands, holding her hands open, backs out, at each side of her face, crossing them over her face to hide it.

Christa recognized the word "ashamed" and understood. She helped Star into the canoe and eased her down to lie on some bearskins on the floor; then, with trembling hands, she lifted the short, strong paddles and pushed the canoe out into the water.

In the distance, Christa could see smoke spiraling lazily from the chimney of her cabin. She kept her eyes focused on this as she paddled the canoe farther away from the land, needing this as a link to everything in life that was dear to her. She had no idea how she was going to be received by the Indians on Enati Island. But she had to grasp onto the hope that the Indians would be Suquamish, perhaps the tribe which housed the handsome Indian. But she knew that she was asking too much to expect this. Only in fantasies did such desires of the heart happen.

Never having commanded a canoe before, Christa found it to be a major battle. She groaned. She panted. Her arms ached with each stroke. A seagull circled down over her, eying her quizzically with his bold, black eyes, and waves splashed and sprayed water onto her face, leaving the distinct taste of saltwater as it dried on her lips.

When Star turned to her left side, snuggling deeper into the bearskin at Christa's feet, the shoulder of her right arm was exposed to Christa's watchful eye, and what she saw made her heart lose a beat.

"A tiny, black tattoo! In the shape . . . of . . . a raven," she whispered. Only one other time had she seen such a tattoo.

Three

Laboring, her shoulders and upper arms racked with pain from the constant paddling, Christa felt awash with relief when she realized that only a few, brief strokes would carry her on to the beach of Enati Island.

Stopping to take a breath of air, she ran the back of a hand over her brow, erasing dampness from it. Her bonnet had lost its stiffness and hung like a wet sack around her face, and her deep cleavage was wet with drops of moisture sparkling like sequins.

Now cupping her hand over her eyes, shielding them from the glare of the cloud-free sky, Christa let her gaze move slowly along the shoreline ahead. Cedar, fir, and madrona trees stood like warriors, guarding the slopes which led up to the Indian village. But higher up along the bluffs, something else could be seen, tall, elaborate, and even frightening.

"Totem poles," Christa whispered. "And . . . so . . . many!"

Ornamented with great, brooding figures, with their bright colors of reds and yellows, the totem poles glistened brilliantly beneath the rays of the late August sun.

Christa had read that totem poles were depictions of supernatural beings in animal, monster, or human form, who, according to lineage or clan tradition, had appeared to some ancestor of a particular Indian, or who, in some instances, had actually transformed themselves into human form and became ancestors. She had also read that the descendants of those ancestors inherited the right to display symbols of the supernatural being to demonstrate their noble descent and that the painted or carved motifs were referred to as "crests," a brand of sorts, which established legal ownership.

Squinting her eyes and looking even more closely at the totem poles, Christa now realized that the distinct shape of a raven was their main subject and that huge replicas of the birds, proudly perched at the very top of each pole, appeared to look down upon the Sound, dominant over everything in its sight.

"A . . . raven!" Christa whispered. Her heart began to beat faster as she let her gaze move to Star, once more observing the tiny raven tattoo on her arm and remembering the same on the handsome Indian. The raven signified something special to these Indians. It was obvious that it was an ancestral crest, but Christa didn't know if it was a family crest, or tribal.

Star stirred, moving up on an elbow to look around. When she saw that Enati Island was near, she once more burst into tears and turned her eyes away.

Christa wanted to reach out and comfort Star, but her need to get her feet solidly on soil urged her to lift the paddle and resume moving it laboriously in and out of the water. So many questions were racing through her mind. Perhaps soon she would know the answers, and hopefully none of them would create danger for her. Once on the island, she expected to be treated decently. She was returning one of these Indians' young maidens. And she had to believe that the handsome Indian would be there, welcoming her *and* Star with open arms.

Feeling the canoe scraping bottom, Christa jumped quickly from it, ignoring the water seeping through the soles of her shoes and wetting the tail of her dress and petticoat.

Thickly needled branches of towering pines amplified the breeze's whistle as it whipped through them and around Christa's sea-dampened face.

She huffed and puffed, dragging the canoe farther onto the sandy beach and positioning it among the many other fancy canoes beached there. She was happy to see that Star was finally composing herself, enough to climb from the canoe and help anchor it between two monstrous boulders rising from the rich bed of sand.

Then Star stood hugging herself, trembling as she let her eyes move to a narrow path that had been cut through the underbrush and led at an angle up the side of the incline. Christa could see fear in Star's eyes, and this fear quickly became contagious. If the young Indian girl was afraid to enter her own village, then shouldn't a white woman fear the prospect as well?

"*Kahpo Tyee,*" Star mumbled, moving toward the path. "*Chako Hyak.*"

It didn't take much thought to realize that Star was asking Christa to follow her. And Christa, not owning the canoe in which she had just arrived, and having no other way to return home, knew that she was at the mercy of the Indians who inhabited this island, be they friendly or hostile.

She felt trapped, yet the handsome Indian's friendly smile kept flashing before her eyes. She could almost feel the warm softness of his lips as they had kissed the molasses from her fingers. She prayed softly, over and over again, that he did make his residence on this island.

The incline was steep and the flattened grass on it slippery. Christa lifted the tail of her skirt into her arms with one hand and clung to overhead, curling exposed roots of a madrona tree with the other. She looked ahead at Star, marveling at how quickly she had regained her strength. But Christa knew that fear caused many things, a surge of strength among them.

The splotches of blood on Star's buckskin skirt caused

ripples of apprehension to race through Christa. It was as if the young girl were wearing her shame openly, for all to see. The Suquamish Indians would surely become enraged, but hopefully *after* Christa was safely in her own cabin, on familiar ground, doing familiar, everyday things. But for now, she focused her thoughts on hopes of seeing the handsome Indian again.

Winded, perspiring, and dry mouthed, Christa took the last step leading to solid ground where she was suddenly dwarfed by the monstrous, ugly totem poles towering over her. But these were no longer of interest to her. She was engrossed in seeing the Indian village which stretched out before her and the many Indians busy as bees in and out of flat-roofed lodges with cedar pole frames covered with mats of overlapped cedar boards and woven grass along the sides and on the roofs.

Christa observed it all—the sounds and the sights. Fragrant smoke of many lodge fires filled the air. There was the low drone of voices and the barking of dogs, the dull clop-clop of an unshod pony and the distant sound of a medicine song being chanted to the pulsating throb of a tom-tom. All these things were a part of a setting that had been carved from a forest of pine, cedar, elm, and the ever-present madrona tree with its gnarled roots growing in and out of the rich, dark soil of the island.

The Indians' skills at wood carving were in evidence everywhere Christa looked. Near most lodges several oblong squares made of thick cedar boards had been positioned and were painted with hieroglyphics and figures of different animals. Canoes were being constructed and elaborately carved. But of all the designs displayed, the raven stood out as a reminder to Christa of the man she sought. He would be found easily among these other, shorter Suquamish Indians. Oh, how tall he had stood, she remembered, dignified and proud, qualities she would expect to find in a chief . . .

Christa's gaze found an even more elaborately decorated

lodge, which stood out from all the rest. A totem pole had been built onto the front of the lodge with a large opening forming the doorway at the base. And again, the most prominent of the carvings was that of the raven.

In the blink of an eye, Christa saw a figure of a man stepping from the lodge and into the shadows at the doorway of this unique lodge. Her knees grew weak as the Indian who had been the cause of her sleepless nights stepped into view, his handsomeness marred by the dark frown on his magnificently sculpted face. Again he wore only a loincloth and his necklace of tusklike animal dentalia.

Seeing him again made Christa's insides take on a strange glow and her lips feel hot. She began to speak but was robbed of her words as she watched Star rush furiously into the Indian brave's solidly muscled arms.

Listening to Indian words being exchanged between Star and the brave, Christa began to grow cold inside. No translations were needed for her. She could recognize a scolding when she heard one. And it was quite evident by the brave's tone of voice that Star was not only being scolded but shamed as well.

Star's whimpering and lowered eyes as she stepped away from the brave convinced Christa to intervene, for she thought that an explanation was needed, and quickly. She moved to Star's side and began gesturing with her hands, speaking in Indian sign language to the brave.

The coolness of his steel gray eyes seemed to reach clear to Christa's soul, so severe was the injury to her pride. But she stood her ground, straightened her back, lifted her chin, and continued her efforts at communicating. She only hoped that she could find the courage to fully explain the rape. And could she even find the words to do so? It had been hard enough to witness, much less give details of how it was done.

Suddenly the brave took two wide steps, standing tall

over Christa, and took her hands in his, stopping her from making further words with her hands.

"Hand language is not required in my presence," the brave said in a deep, commanding voice. "I speak white man's language fluently. Hand language is for the weak mind or for young *la daila* such as my sister, Princess Star."

"Princess Star?" Christa gasped. "Your . . . sister?" She wanted to question Star's title, but the feel of this handsome Indian's flesh against her own caused a drugging passion to sweep through Christa, even as the threat beneath the scrutiny of his cold eyes unnerved her. It wasn't as before with him. In her cabin when he watched her, there had been a warm, friendly appraisal of her displayed in his smile and the sensuous kisses to her fingertips.

But now it seemed as if he were angry with her. And why should he be? She had just done him a service! She had even shot a man—the first time, ever, in her life she had done such a thing of violence. And what thanks was she receiving?

Then she realized something. He had just spoken to her in very clear English, yet when he had been with her before, he had failed to say even one word. He was so hard to figure out!

She watched as he released her hands and went to resume scolding his sister, which resulted in Star running away from him sobbing loudly.

This enraged Christa, for it did not seem the appropriate time for the young girl to be treated so harshly. What had happened to her had been a thing far beyond her control. Why didn't her brother see this?

Placing her hands on her hips, Christa went to Star's defense. "You are behaving much different from how I would expect a brother to react when hearing that his sister's been raped," she snapped.

The brave took Christa by a wrist and began leading her toward his dwelling, and Christa tugged and pulled at him, trying to free herself. She had dreamed of being with him again but never under such circumstances.

"What do you think you're doing?" she demanded hotly.

"Talk of my sister's rape is not good for my people to hear," he said. "It does not make me, Tall Cloud, chief of this tribe of Suquamish, appear capable of teaching my own sister right from wrong."

Heat rose into Christa's cheeks and her lips parted slightly. Then she stammered, "You're . . . a . . . chief?"

She had suspected it, but now that she had found it to be true, the realization overwhelmed her. She knew the power of a chief. She understood the respect shown such a great man. But she couldn't understand why he had shamed Star instead of immediately going in search of the true guilty party.

"Is my telling you that I'm a chief such a hard truth to grasp?" he growled. "Just because I differ so from the white man's great *tylee*—the chief in Washington—does that make me less important to my people?"

"No. I didn't mean . . . to . . . imply . . ."

Tall Cloud released her wrist. "Then come into my lodge willingly," he said in a quieter, less threatening tone. "We will share food, and talk. I do not wish to see such anger in eyes the color of soft moss. We will settle our disagreements peacefully, won't we, *Nahkeeta?*"

Christa's head jerked around. *"Nahkeeta?"* she questioned, color once more rising to her cheeks.

"Nahkeeta is a beautiful name, don't you think?" Tall Cloud asked, guiding her by her elbow into the lodge.

"Perhaps it is," Christa said softly. "But it belongs to someone else. My name is Christa."

"While with me, you will be called *Nahkeeta,*" Tall Cloud said flatly.

Somehow Christa felt threatened by his assumptions, though her insides were melting from being so close to him. "And what if I don't approve of such a name?" she dared.

"How could any *la daila* refuse a name which means beautiful maiden, gentle, pretty, and graceful as maidenhair ferns which grow in the forest," he said thickly, looking down at her, his eyes darkening with desire.

Christa's tongue suddenly wouldn't work. She couldn't speak. She knew that she had just been paid a compliment by this handsome Indian chief and here she was, awkwardly dumbstruck by the gesture. Out of the corner of her eye she saw his sleek, light copper-colored skin, broad shoulders, and tight muscles. She didn't dare a look lower, where the loincloth hung brief and barely concealing the strength of him, the man.

Then the picture of the Haida Indian raping Star flashed before her eyes, Star's screams sounded inside her brain, and the blood on Star's skirt sent fear into Christa's heart. If making love was supposed to be so rewarding and beautiful, why . . . why had . . . the Haida Indian made the experience so ugly and painful?

Christa now feared her first time with a man and hated the Haida for this as much as for his rape of the innocent Indian Princess.

"Come," Tall Cloud encouraged, helping Christa into the lodge, to sit on one of the ubiquitous checker-work mats of red cedar bark that lay before a pit in the dirt floor, where a soft fire burned.

Christa nodded a silent thank you to him as she eased down onto a mat, suddenly feeling strangely awkward in her drooping bonnet, limp dress, and her apron that was heavy from the weight of the pistol in the pocket. Untying her bonnet and lifting it from her head, she absorbed the decorated interior of his dwelling which displayed raised shelves along the walls that served for storage.

Drums of all sizes and shapes hung decoratively from the ceiling, and elaborately carved and painted backrests and neatly finished redwood stools added touches of color, contrasting with draped white deerskins, great flint blades, and strings of dentalia which could be seen in the dim streamers of light emitted from the smoke hole in the ceiling.

Berries and fish were hanging to dry from the crossbeams under the roof's rafters, and a big, black bearskin had been spread on the ground.

Once more Christa's eyes traveled to where this Indian's bed lay prepared for sleeping. Pillows and mats were there, made of colorful cedar-bark pads. She had to wonder if Tall Cloud always slept there.

Scarcely breathing, Christa watched Tall Cloud as he went to a shelf and removed a reed basket from it. He brought it to Christa and placed it on the floor before her. Then he brought her a dish made in troughlike form, hollowed out of blocks of alder. Some skillful person had modified the simple dish shape into the form of a raven, and once more Christa wondered if this "crest" design was for the entire tribe, or only for one family.

"We shall eat while we talk," Tall Cloud said, settling down opposite her with his own fancy dish positioned on his lap.

Christa gazed down into the reed basket, seeing something wrapped in leaves. "What is it?" she asked softly.

"Nothing as good as your biscuits and molasses," Tall Cloud said with a chuckle. "But it has a taste that should please you."

Christa avoided his eyes, having seen with a quick glance that they were no longer filled with anger. Instead, they showed the warmth that she remembered from her one other time with him. Strange that he could forget his sister's misfortune so quickly. Christa would *never* forget it!

She lay her bonnet aside. "But what *is* it, Tall Cloud?" she persisted, then smiled shyly up at him, realizing that she had for the first time spoken his name. Ah, how good it had felt on the tip of her tongue, so familiar, as though it truly did belong to her vocabulary of names . . .

"Berries," he said, leaning over to take a squarely wrapped skunk-cabbage leaf from the basket. "An assortment of berries. They have been cooked together to a pulpy mass, poured into rectangular wooden frames lined with these leaves, and dried into cakes."

He unwrapped the leaves from around the cake and placed it on Christa's plate. "Eat," he commanded in his deep, authoritative voice.

Christa gave him a nervous smile and gazed down at the purplish mass. She touched it gingerly with a forefinger, then placed the finger to her tongue and tasted. Her eyes brightened. The taste was sweet, yet vaguely tart. The prime taste was that of cranberries.

She shook her head yes. "It *is* good!" she exclaimed, relaxing her shoulder muscles. But although she had found the cake favorable, she had a need to talk rather than eat. She returned the cake to her plate, and her eyes wavered as she gave Tall Cloud a half glance.

"I believe you were wrong to shame your sister for what she had no control over," she blurted quickly. "How could you shame her so openly, when you should, instead, be nursing her wounded pride? She was used today in the worst way possible. It is something that neither she *nor* I will ever forget."

"I am grateful that you returned her to her village," Tall Cloud snapped. "But now you are interfering in tribal customs you do not understand."

Christa flipped her hair back from her shoulders. She leaned her face up into his, so close to him that she could smell the manliness of him. "Customs?" she argued. "What on earth do customs have to do with your sister having been horribly abused?"

She saw his jaw tighten and a throbbing begin at the curve of his high cheekbone. "You further show your ignorance of what the Suquamish intend for their girls changing into women," he grumbled, locking his arms fiercely about his upswept knees, glaring into the dying embers of the fire in the pit.

"My sister disobeyed the laws of our people. The spirits condemned her. They allowed the rape as her punishment. Now it is I, Chief Tall Cloud, who must punish her in my own way. She will now live the life of the shamed."

Christa frowned. "I *don't* understand," she murmured. "None of this."

"Nahkeeta, how can you not understand puberty rites? Don't the white men make restrictions on their young girls at the onset of their puberty? Surely you were made to go into seclusion at such a time in your life."

Clearing her throat nervously, Christa looked quickly away from Tall Cloud. She couldn't imagine talking of such a delicate subject with a man—and not only a man, but one who stirred her insides as one would stir hot, fiery coals on a grate. Yet she had this need to pursue the subject, to see why Star was going to have to live the life of the "shamed," as Tall Cloud had so coolly put it.

"I have never had restrictions of any sort placed on me," she said, slowly moving her eyes back to him. "None whatsoever, Tall Cloud, at any time in my life. My time . . . my time of puberty was a private matter, only known to me when my body . . . when my body began to perform its womanly functions."

Her face turned scarlet. She once more turned her eyes from him, feeling oddly brazen for having spoken so openly with him. But there was something about him that made her feel free to do so. She was becoming as comfortable in his presence as she felt in her brother's. To her, this was a thing of total puzzlement.

Tall Cloud's eyes lowered, seeing where her dress opened into a sharp vee in front, exposing to him her deep cleavage. A slow smile lifted his lips, for he knew that she had fully blossomed into womanhood and had left her days of puberty far behind her.

He hungered to touch, to kiss, the soft white of her breasts. Even though hidden beneath the cotton of her dress, the distinct outline of her nipples was visible to him, and an ache in his loins and the pounding of his heart made it hard to concentrate on anything but fully possessing her.

His voice was deeper when he once more spoke, his eyes now looking into the soft green of hers, reading in them what so highly pleased him. "My sister—*any* young girl who is entering into puberty—has to agree to our Suquamish puberty rites or she is shamed, and by being shamed herself she shames those of her family," he said. "And since I am chief, it makes it awkward for me, since my people will condemn me as well as her."

"What did she do that was so terrible?" Christa questioned. "By seclusion, does that mean that she had to stay hidden away in a lodge? I can see why she couldn't do that. That would be hard for anyone to do, especially a girl her age. Girls as well as boys like to experience. Was it so terrible that she crossed the Sound in the hope of being alone in the woods to enjoy nature?"

"At such a time in a girl's life, her presence is offensive to the spirits of the salmon of the Sound, of the many winding rivers, and of the game of the forests. She is prohibited to approach the waters of the Sound, the rivers, or to go to the forests away from this island. She is prohibited from eating fresh fish or meat," he growled. "She is restricted not only from travel but also by that which she eats. She was ordered to eat only a diet of very thin acorn mush. If one travels to the forest, the temptation of eating berries is great. Surely you know that."

"But what does it prove by forcing such restrictions?" Christa scoffed. "I was not restricted, and I didn't bring harm to *my* family."

"You are white. Star is Suquamish," Tall Cloud stated flatly. "Faithful obedience to the taboos set down by my ancestors would have meant that Star would have become an industrious woman and would have borne many healthy Suquamish children. By remaining in seclusion, by observing the rules and so avoiding offending salmon and other important fish and game, she would have protected the food supply of our family and would not have endangered the luck of any of our fishermen or hunters with her condemning presence."

"And now you fear that not only your family but your whole tribe will suffer because of your sister's disobedience, because you are the chief of all your people," Christa said softly, slowly understanding.

Tall Cloud's eyes widened. "Your heart tells you to be sympathetic to my feelings?" he asked thickly. "My people's customs are becoming more clear as I speak of them to you?"

Christa laughed, a quiet sort of laugh, and lowered her eyes as once more her face felt the heat of a blush. "I am trying to understand," she whispered.

She slowly lifted her gaze to his. "Your ways are quite different from mine. But, of course, you know this. You have been in my cabin. You have seen the difference." A smile touched her lips. "You have even tasted the difference." She giggled. "Did you not enjoy my molasses?"

Remembrance of how the taste of her had intermingled with that of the molasses when he had kissed her fingertips caused a strange rippling in the pit of Tall Cloud's stomach. His eyes absorbed her loveliness—the gold of her waist-length hair that was now fully free of her discarded, ugly bonnet, the seductive slant to her green eyes, and the childish freckles that dotted the bridge of her perfectly shaped nose and upper cheeks.

His gaze held at her lips that were slightly parted and so temptingly near, and he was visualizing her without her lifeless cotton dress and drab, bulky apron, knowing that beneath those things was skin as fair as the snow on the mountaintops. Her waist would be tiny, her hips graceful, and her breasts would overly fill his hands.

Christa became unnerved by his silence and open stare. She could see that he was studying her carefully, and she knew what a sight she must be. She unconsciously reached a hand to her hair, to sweep in farther back from her brow. She jumped when he reached and captured the hand, lowering his lips to begin kissing her fingers, one fingertip at a time. Desire gripped her. Her voice was strange to her when she spoke. It was a husky whisper.

"What do you think you're doing?" she asked, vividly aware of the expanse of his copper-colored sleekly muscled shoulders so close to her. Her body was turning into a strange liquid, melting, slowly melting, especially now that he was looking up at her with his wide, gray eyes. They were hollow pits of passion, and she knew that soon he would kiss not only her fingertips but her lips as well.

"Do you also feel it?" Tall Cloud asked hoarsely, now holding both her hands tightly, drawing her down next to him as he stretched out onto the layers of mats spread on the earthen floor.

Christa swallowed hard, her heartbeats threatening to drown her. "Do I feel *what?*" she murmured, being drawn into a spell created by the magic of him and his touch and kisses and the fire in his eyes.

"The need to be together, to share completely what a man and woman are meant to share," he said huskily, drawing her down closer and closer to him, seeing the beat of her pulse in the hollow of her throat.

"No," she lied. "I do not."

She began pushing at his chest, once more remembering the Haida Indian's grunting and groaning as he attacked Star, and hearing Star's scream of pain. She also remembered the blood.

"I must go," she cried. "I should never have . . . even . . . come. My brother. He must be frantic with worry."

Tall Cloud held onto her shoulders and placed her on the floor, then knelt down over her. "Forget your brother. Forget your fears, *Nahkeeta*," he said, setting her afire inside with his hands now traveling down her arms, barely grazing the outside of each of her breasts through her dress.

She felt herself slipping into a world where she no longer knew right from wrong. And as his lips lowered to hers, not only was her breath stolen from her, but her senses as well. Her head began a strange reeling, absorbed now as she was in this new, delicious feeling of lethargy, as if a rare, exotic potion had been offered her and she had consumed it eagerly.

Tall Cloud's kiss was gentle. His hands carefully traveled from her arms to her breasts, fully cupping each through her dress. Christa writhed in response, never having realized before that her breasts possessed such thrilling sensitivity. A warmth spread upward inside her, beginning at her inner thighs where she was experiencing a new feeling of sweet pain. Lost in rapture, she twined her arms about his neck, her fears ebbing, as if there had been no Haida Indian, no screams, no blood.

"I must fully have you," Tall Cloud whispered, showering kisses on her cheeks, the hollow of her throat, and the lobes of her ears. "Say that you are willing, *Nahkeeta*. My need is so great that my head is as many drums, beating hard inside my chest, paining me so."

Christa was becoming breathless as his fingertips probed sensuously down her dress, where her breasts lay hot with their nipples hard and dark. Desire coiled inside her, a feeling that had been unknown to her until this handsome Indian had come into her life, face to face with her. She wanted to believe her wanting him was wrong, but the thought of denying him, which also meant denying herself, caused a pulling sensation at her heart, and she knew then that she could not back away from what had begun between them any more than she had the power to deny the sequined stars their place in the velvet black skies of night.

"Then take me," she said, her face flaming hot with anticipation. She had to believe that with him it would be beautiful. It was not a thing being forced upon her. "Tall Cloud, I am ready."

She closed her eyes, swallowed hard, and doubled her fists at her sides, waiting for him to touch her "there," in her very secret place. Surely he would be quick about it. The pain was a part of this thing between man and woman. Her mother had told her this. But it was supposed to be brief; and then, later, the pleasure would be sweet and fulfilling.

She now waited, wanting to get the pain over with quickly, anxious to share in the later pleasure. She wouldn't think of David and the shame that she should be feeling. At no other time in her life had she done such a thing. And if she had not been so overcome by her feelings for Tall Cloud, she would not be doing such a thing now.

"*Nahkeeta,* why have you stiffened?" Tall Cloud asked, drawing away from her. "Why do you close your eyes and clench your fists so? Have I frightened you?"

Christa's eyes flew widely open in surprise that he hadn't taken advantage of the situation, despite her offering herself fully to him and even asking him to seduce her. "Tall Cloud, why do you question what I do?" she asked. "I have said that I am ready."

Tall Cloud rose to a sitting position and turned from her. He picked up a stick and idly began stirring coals in the fire space. "No. You are not ready," he said, a nervous strain evident in his voice.

Christa rose up on an elbow, full of wonder. "How can you say that?" she argued softly, feeling odd as she realized just what she was arguing over. When she had awakened this morning, she most definitely hadn't thought that she would be in this sort of situation only a few hours later.

That she was even on the Indians' island was cause for wonder, let alone her being ready to lose her virginity to an Indian.

"No woman is ready for lovemaking when she lies stiff as a board," Tall Cloud grumbled.

"What?" Christa gasped, paling.

Tall Cloud's head jerked around and his eyes were accusing. "A woman *shares* in lovemaking," he growled. "She must return love."

"Love?" Christa asked in a near whisper. "Are you saying that . . . ?"

Tall Cloud looked at her intensely. He crossed his arms over his chest, his right arm close to his body, and pressed hard with his left arm, his fists tightly clenched—the Indian sign for the word "love."

"My heart tells me it is so," he said huskily. "I watched you silently, from afar, for many weeks. When my heart wouldn't be still, I came into your dwelling to test how you could feel about me—an . . . Indian."

"And . . . ?"

"In your eyes, I saw the answer I was seeking."

"That I could—"

"Also love me no matter the color of my skin," he said, tossing the stick back into the fire space. He once more knelt over her, framing her face between his hands to guide her lips to his.

"Whaht-kay Nahkeeta," he whispered before crushing his lips to hers. His hands wove through her hair; his tongue softly probed between her teeth. His body ached with need of her, and he moaned longingly.

Christa's limbs were weak, her insides heating to an inferno, as she understood that she was meant to enjoy the seduction. She shivered with intense pleasure as Tall Cloud's hands moved to her breasts and softly squeezed them through the cotton of her dress. He hadn't yet, through all of their touches and kisses, and pressed himself fully against her, and now as he did she felt him emit a soft groan as his tight muscles made contact with the small pistol in her apron pocket.

Unable to suppress a giggle, she watched as he rose quickly away from her to question what had caused him this discomfort.

"Kahta?" he asked, lifting an eyebrow.

"If you are wondering what is in my pocket, you may be surprised when you find out," she replied with further giggles, reaching for the pistol.

When she withdrew it with the barrel pointed in his direction, he recoiled and jumped quickly to his feet, frowning.

"Mesachie!" he roared.

"I don't know why you're so upset," Christa said, easing the pistol down on the earthen floor beside her. "It's no threat to you. It's the pistol I carry to protect myself. If not for the pistol, the Haida Indian would have raped not only your sister, but also me."

The anger left his eyes and his shoulder muscles loosened. "It's not a usual thing for me to see a woman carry such a deadly weapon," he grumbled. "A man, yes. A woman? No!"

Christa's eyes sparkled with her own anger now. "Oh, I see," she snapped. "It's all right for a man to protect himself. But a lady must be at the mercy of men. Is that what you are saying, Tall Cloud?"

Tall Cloud went to his knees before her. With his right hand, he covered her mouth. "Harsh words are wrong at this time," he said.

His hands then went to the ties of her apron, loosened them, and tossed the apron aside. While watching her with a silent command in his steel gray eyes, he reached around and unbuttoned her dress. As he removed it, a shoulder at a time, he kissed her exposed flesh as it was revealed to him.

Closing her eyes, caught up in the rapture of his tenderness, Christa trembled as she felt her breasts being set free of all her confining clothes. She took in a shudder of breath and felt a splash of warmth invading her insides as she felt his hands on her breasts and then his lips on a nipple, sucking it, nipping it gently with his teeth. Opening her eyes, she touched his cheek, loving the smoothness of it.

"Tall Cloud," she said in a dreamy whisper.

Tall Cloud drew away from her, his hands traveling lower to where her dress and petticoat clung to her waist. Pressing his fingers into her flesh, he urged her to her feet as he continued to kneel before her. Once more he leaned toward her, curling his tongue into her navel, all the while skillfully disrobing her completely. She stepped out of her shoes, quivering sensuously as he trailed kisses lower, and she emitted a guttural sigh when his hot breath caressed her flesh.

A dart of his tongue where no man had ventured before made Christa's face burn with embarrassment. She blinked her eyes nervously as though awakening from a trance, then stooped to grab her dress, to hold it in front of her.

"No . . ." she gulped. "I just can't, Tall Cloud."

Tall Cloud rose to his feet and placed his thumbs inside the buckskin strap that held his loincloth in place. Slowly he lowered it, all the while watching her with fire in his eyes.

"*Mesika,*" he said hoarsely as he dropped his loincloth to the floor, displaying his readiness to her.

Christa's eyes slowly lowered. Her heart skipped a beat. She was feeling many things now, seeing him. Her desire for him was overwhelming, yet she feared his largeness.

Tall Cloud reached for her hand. "Touch it," he encouraged. "It is my gift to you, *Nahkeeta*. Use it. Feel the pleasures you will receive from having it inside you. It will come to life and become a teacher, teaching you the mysteries of man and woman."

Feeling as though hypnotized by his deep, smooth voice, Christa dropped her dress to the floor and fell to her knees before him. She reached a hand toward him then stopped to look up into the command of his eyes.

"Alta," he said thickly. *"Nahkeeta,* now.

Christa lowered her eyes and swallowed hard as her hands crept to him, and when she touched his swollen member, the coil of desire inside her grew tighter and her eyes grew hot with discovery. She enjoyed the smooth touch of him, and she enjoyed the pleasure that her touch was giving him. Slowly she moved her fingers over him and heard him groan. She saw him tense. When she looked up into his face, it was shadowed with ecstasy.

Feeling her hesitation and knowing that he couldn't hold back much longer, Tall Cloud eased her hand away from him. He placed an arm about her waist and drew her up to stand before him. Then he kissed her hard and long, fitting his body into hers. Her breasts pressed into his flesh, arousing him even more. He held her tightly and moved his largeness seductively against her abdomen, teasing, tormenting.

Then he led her to the spread, black bearskin and lowered her onto it. The softness was welcome to Christa's back. She fit herself comfortably into it, then held out her arms to Tall Cloud, ready to be fully taken by him.

He came to her, solemn, eyes hazy, and took no more preliminaries with her. With one thrust he was inside her, tensing when he heard her let out a soft whimper of pain. He kissed her softly, gently, then felt her relax against him as once more he began to thrust himself inside her.

Christa's fingernails dug into his shoulders, and she lifted her legs to wrap them around him. As though she had done this dance of love before, she lifted her hips and met his each and every movement inside her with abandon. The pain was now blending into a sweet lethargy, an euphoria so keen she knew nothing but the pleasure wrapping her in its lacy cocoon.

Tall Cloud's tongue became a hot spear as it searched inside her mouth, his hands magic as they explored her every curve. And then both bodies melted into the other as the full joy of release was reached, and spent.

With a pounding heart, Christa clung to Tall Cloud. The experience of first love had been even more than she had ever dreamed possible. She continued to feel heady even though he was no longer inside her.

He pulled away from her to stretch out beside her on the bearskin. He was panting and his eyes were closed.

Christa rose to an elbow and began tracing his body with a forefinger, giggling when she saw the sensual ripples of his flesh every place that she touched anew.

Then she found his tiny raven tattoo. She leaned over him and looked at it more closely. "Tall Cloud, your tattoo in the shape of a raven. Is it a family crest or the crest of your entire village?" she asked, placing a soft kiss on the tattoo.

"The crest design of the raven is my family crest," he said, taking her hand and kissing its palm. "I bear the crest on my flesh, as does Princess Star, because I am of high rank, and she is my sister."

"But the totem poles—everything of your village—represents your crest as though it were that of all your people."

"I am chief. They respect that I am and allow me my pride in my crest by displaying it in as many ways as possible."

Christa stretched out on her stomach beside Tall Cloud and rested her chin in her hands. "You are so young to be chief," she marveled. "Why, Tall Cloud, you can't be over thirty."

He chuckled. "So I look older than my years?"

A blush rose to Christa's cheeks, her eyes wide. "Are you saying that you are even younger than that?"

"Twenty-five years I have been on this land of green forests and sparkling blue waters."

"Is it a normal thing . . . to become chief so young, Tall Cloud?"

"It was not in my plans to be," he grumbled. "It just happened that way."

"The rest of your family. Where are they? Was your father . . . was he chief before you?"

"He was chief before the white man brought smallpox to Puget Sound land," he growled, rising quickly to his feet. He pulled his loincloth on and glared down at Christa. "Smallpox killed my mother, father, and older brother. Somehow Star was spared. I was spared."

Christa gathered her clothes in her arms and began dressing. "How is it that you speak English so fluently?" she asked. "Princess Star doesn't appear to know one word in English."

Smoothing his dark brown hair back from his eyes, Tall Cloud sat down and watched her dress. "I learned from Chief Sealth when I was a child," he said, getting a faraway look in his eyes. "My father and Chief Sealth were the best of friends. After Chief Sealth learned the white man's language from trappers and traders, he then taught me, and he was proud to do so."

"Then you were once a part of Chief Seattle's village?" She felt somewhat awkward speaking of Chief "Seattle" since Tall Cloud still called the chief by his true Indian name, "Sealth." She was reminded of how Chief Sealth had acquired the name Seattle. Unable to pronounce Sealth's name in the Salish tongue with its guttural inflection, the earlier settlers had altered the pronunciation to Seattle. Then when searching for a name for their new town, something distinctive that would set it apart from other prospering villages on Puget Sound, one of the area's most distinguished citizens, a man by the name of Doc Maynard, urged them to honor the chief of the local Indians who had been the first to welcome the white man to Puget Sound.

"Yes. I was a part of Chief Sealth's village until talk of treaties began," he growled. "Chief Sealth was for signing. My father was not. We then separated from him and came to this island which we named *Enati,* meaning 'across,' since it lies across from Seattle."

"Then you are among those who refused to sign the treaty?"

"Yes. And those who did sign were wrong to do so. I am going to try everything in my power to reverse their decision and see if the treaty papers can be burned. It is not fair to the Suquamish, this piece of paper sent to Puget Sound from the white man's *tylee*—the great white chief in Washington."

Christa settled down beside Tall Cloud and placed her hands on the thick muscles of his legs. "When did you, yourself, decide against the treaty?" she asked softly. "You are a man with a mind of your own. Surely you didn't let your father's decision become yours just because it was his."

"No. I traveled to the new city of San Francisco to see for myself the effects of the white man on a new community."

"And . . . ?"

"I didn't stay long," he grumbled. "That should be answer enough for you."

"And now you are in partnership with the Haida Indian, fighting against the treaty?" she asked, wincing when he jerked away from her, his eyes suddenly cold.

"How can you say that?" he roared. "You saw the Haida. Do you see me in him?"

"No!" she gasped.

"I am *not* like the Haida," he said, taking her hands, squeezing them. "They steal innocent girls and take them back to their camps to use as slaves. Princess Star would have been raped then taken to be a slave. And if her master had been killed in battle, she would also have been slain."

Christa brought her hands to her mouth. "Good Lord . . ." she gasped.

Tall Cloud drew her into his arms. "I failed to give you thanks for rescuing Princess Star," he murmured, weaving his fingers through her hair. "One day I will repay you. You will see."

"Having been with you is payment enough," she whispered, kissing his neck, inhaling the manly fragrance of him.

"But now you have to go?"

"I'm afraid so. . . ." She sighed. But the thought of seeing David made her become cold inside. She had lost track of time. She wasn't even sure now how long she had been gone. And would David be able to tell that she had been with a man in the most intimate of ways?

"I shall return you to your dwelling," Tall Cloud said, helping her up from the floor.

"Only as far as the shore," she said, placing her limp bonnet on her head and pushing her hair up beneath it. "David mustn't—"

"With the injured Haida somewhere out there, I will see you to your door," he ordered.

"But, David—"

"I will return you to your brother as you returned my sister to me," he said flatly. "Do not argue, *Nahkeeta*. Your brother will just have to get used to seeing me with you. I *do* plan to be with you . . . and often."

Christa cast him a glance of wonder as he slid his arm about her waist and led her to the door. Then he stopped and went back to get something. Chuckling, he brought her apron and handed it to her, heavy with the pistol in its pocket. "You don't want to forget this, my little warring *Nahkeeta* . . ."

Four

As she walked stiffly beside Tall Cloud up the stone-laid path which led to her cabin, Christa's apprehensions mounted. David would be furious enough with her for being gone so long, let alone for arriving with Tall Cloud as her escort. And the way her cheeks were flushed! Surely he would see right through her and somehow know that she had stepped into the realm of full womanhood.

Tall Cloud had been wrong to have said that she had left her puberty far behind her. Until this day when she had surrendered herself fully to this handsome Indian, each day since her early teens had been an extension of her puberty. Only now did she feel that she had truly attained the title of "woman."

A sense of shame swept through her, always having been taught that a woman did not give herself to a man until vows had been spoken in the presence of a minister.

But then she fought that shame by remembering the suddenness of her parents' death on the trail from Boston and realizing that life did not always extend far into the future. Only the present was a sure thing, and Christa wanted to live, *truly* live, while breath was afforded her.

They reached the closed door of the cabin. Christa stepped in front of Tall Cloud, blocking his way. "I don't really think you should," she blurted, pleading with her eyes. "David will not understand."

"Are you ashamed to be seen with me because I am Indian?" Tall Cloud growled, squaring his shoulders angrily.

Christa's insides melted as she remembered their sensual moments together. She didn't ever want to give Tall Cloud the impression that she thought of him with anything other than sincere love and admiration.

She reached a hand to his cheek, growing heady merely by touching him. "You know that isn't so," she murmured.

"Then I will go inside with you," Tall Cloud said flatly. "I will see how your brother is faring . . . see if the white man's doctor performed proper rites over his injured limb."

The sun was at a right angle in the sky, hazed over by a sheer layer of lacy white clouds, and the waves splashed softly against the bluffs. Seagulls soared peacefully low over the beach, absorbing sprays of seawater into their wings, and the breeze rustled in the trees of the forest, whispering low.

"All right," Christa blurted quickly as she stepped inside. "Come ahead. But again I must warn you. David will not understand. Please don't stay long."

"My *nanitch* this time will be very brief," he said blandly, then a slow smile lifted his lips as he touched the brim of her bonnet. *"Nahkeeta,* your hat. It is *klakowyum!"*

He untied and removed it and tossed it across her shoulder. "That's much better," he said thickly. His hands went to her hair and loosened it, to let it flutter to her shoulder and then down to her waist. "Pure gold," he whispered, kissing her softly on the lips. "It should never be hidden."

Flustered, Christa shoved him away from her. "Why are you doing this now, at such a time, when my brother is only a closed door away?" she whispered harshly. "Tall Cloud, do not tempt fate to such an extreme. If David should hear . . . if David should *see* . . ."

Tall Cloud jerked her to him. She could feel his breath hot on her face as he looked down at her. His muscled chest and arms pressed hard against her. His nearness, his eyes looking deep into her soul, were drowning her in a river of sensations. If he were to choose to take her now, even on her doorstep, she wasn't sure if she had the power to dissuade him from such a reckless deed.

"Do not forget that you are no longer your brother's," he growled. "You are mine!"

These words shook Christa from her slow surrender to him. She was at first stunned by his statement of ownership, and then she was angry. No one owned her—perhaps her *heart,* but not her.

"How dare you," she hissed quietly. "Just because you—"

Tall Cloud bore his lips down savagely upon hers. He held her as though in a vise then let her go so abruptly she teetered sideways. Her hands flew to the hot flush of her cheeks, and she rushed away from the cabin and went to stand behind the barn, breathing hard. It was impossible to go inside the cabin to face David now. She knew her outward appearance too well. Not only were her cheeks flaming hot, but her eyes felt the heat in them as well. Perhaps he could even see or *hear* the rapid beat of her heart!

"Why did you run away?" Tall Cloud asked, coming to her and lifting her chin so their eyes could meet.

"I can't go inside my cabin just yet," she confessed. But she would not tell him why. He already knew too much of her feelings for him. She knew quite well that this was a futile thing—love between an Indian and a white woman. The men in Seattle had taken Indian squaws as wives, but no white woman had ever taken an Indian as a husband. Women were scarce in Seattle. There were too many white men to choose from, as those concerned with her welfare would argue once the truth was known about her feelings for Tall Cloud. It was even said that there were ten men to every woman in the whole Northwest territory! Yes, it was hopeless. But, oh, how she loved Tall Cloud!

Softly sobbing, she fell into his arms and clung to him with her cheek against his chest, hearing the pounding of his heart and the nervous breaths he was emitting. She knew that he surely was experiencing the same doubts and fears as she.

"Hold me" she whispered. "Just hold me."

Tall Cloud held her close, smelling the sweetness of her hair as he pressed his nose into it. He was trying to understand this woman who scrambled his insides so strangely. "I will enter before you," he said hoarsely. "Your brother will think I am only there for another *nanitch*. You can come when your eyes have cleared of tears that I do not understand."

"But why must you go inside my cabin at all?" she argued softly. "There is no need."

Tall Cloud had many needs that he could not voice aloud to her. His reasons for needing her were many. And it was important to him that her brother see them together. Then what Tall Cloud would ask of David later would not come as such a shock.

"If you do not come with me I will go alone," he said flatly. "I will wait for you until you *do* come inside your dwelling."

Christa stepped out of his embrace. She looked up into eyes full of expression and intelligence. "You insist on doing this without explaining why?" she murmured, shaking her head, causing her hair to cascade farther down her back.

"One day soon you will know the reasons for everything I do," he said, clasping his hands onto her shoulders. "This heart of mine is full of you. Soon you will know just how much."

A sensuous thrill coursed through Christa's veins, hearing the huskiness of his voice and seeing the passionate haze growing over his eyes. She reached a hand to his magnificent pale copper face and stroked it.

"I will soon know everything?" she murmured. "Everything, Tall Cloud?"

"Konaway. Alki," he said, taking her hand and guiding her

toward the cabin. "Now be brave again as you were when you sent the Haida away from Princess Star. Step inside with me, and I will then leave you alone with your brother."

Christa laughed nervously. "That's what I'm afraid of," she said. "I will get quite a scolding once you are gone."

"For being with me . . . an Indian?"

"For being gone so long and for being what he will call reckless when he hears about what I did."

"What you did. It *was* an act of bravery."

Christa frowned up at him. "I'm afraid David will use a much different sort of word to describe what I did. He has warned me against traveling so far from the cabin. He may call me stupid for having done so."

Tall Cloud's eyebrows forked. "Stupid?" he said. "That word is unfamiliar to me."

The lighthearted moment of his innocence was welcomed by Christa. She gave him an adoring look. "Yes, that word would be one unknown to such a noble, wise chief as you." She sighed.

She glanced toward the closed door of the cabin which had once more been reached. She swallowed against a knot growing in her throat, yet more prepared now to face David with Tall Cloud than she had been moments earlier. Tall Cloud's soft words, his strong embrace, had given her the courage she needed. She looked up into his gray eyes, smiled at him, then focused her eyes straight ahead as she turned the doorknob and pushed the door open, flinching as it creaked noisily.

The shadows of Tall Cloud and Christa fell long and dark into the room where only pale light from the window filtered in through sheer, white, homemade priscilla curtains which hung there, delicate and unobtrusive.

Christa stepped inside, seeing how the coals had dimmed to glowing embers in the fireplace. There were no sounds except from outside, where an occasional rush of waves rose up noisily from the Sound.

Trembling, Christa made her way across the room, around the table which sat in the center, and toward the door which led to her tiny bedroom. Tall Cloud's bare feet were soundless, but Christa could hear him breathing, a reminder of what she soon would face with David.

"Christa? Is that you?" David suddenly yelled from the bed. "Christa? Speak up! I've been worried sick about you? What took so long? I've warned you—"

David's words caught in his throat and he quickly paled when Christa stepped into view and, beside her, a Suquamish Indian. David was not a man of violence and had been patient with the Indians. But an Indian with Christa? Had the Indian forced her . . . ?

"Christa," David said hoarsely, glancing from her to the Indian, "are . . . you . . . all right? Why are you with—"

"David, I'm fine," she blurted quickly, rushing to his bedside. She eased down onto the edge of the bed and touched his brow. "And you? Your temperature hasn't returned, has it? I didn't worry you into a fever, did I?"

David took her hand from his brow and held it tightly, looking from her to Tall Cloud. "What is he doing here?" he whispered harshly. "Were you . . . with . . . him?"

Tall Cloud stepped forward, standing tall and proud with his arms held tightly across his chest. "I have come to see how your wound is healing," he said, glancing down at the bandage, seeing the splotches of red blood that seeped through it. His eyes moved slowly upward, surveying the loose-fitted trousers and unbuttoned shirt of the white man and seeing him as no future threat.

"I see by the blood that your healing is coming slow," Tall Cloud quickly added, seeing how David's eyes were so much the color of *Nahkeeta's*. This color green seemed to him a mystical phenomenon, as did their shared golden colored hair. They were a unique pair, this brother and sister. Tall Cloud had to believe that they surely held much power of persuasion in the white community. Tall Cloud had chosen wisely.

"You are here on my behalf?" David asked, leaning up on an elbow, not believing this even for an instant. There was something unspoken between the Indian and his sister, and David's insides rippled cold with suspicions that he didn't want even to think on!

"I have seen. Now I must go," Tall Cloud said. Without looking at Christa and with no further words, he turned and left the room and then the cabin.

Christa started to rise from the bed, to go after Tall Cloud to inquire about his sudden departure, but the pressure of David's hand in hers reminded her that she already had too much to explain. Slowly she turned her eyes to David, seeing no smile, but instead a dark, heavy frown being directed toward her.

"Christa, I think you'd best explain what the hell's going on here," he said dryly.

Never having heard David use a curse word before, Christa gasped. She knew this reaction from him meant that he was angrier at her than ever before in her life, and she dreaded having to tell him.

"David, please don't be angry," she whispered, lowering her eyes.

"Where have you been besides picking berries and greens?" he said icily. "You've not returned with your basket, and you're missing your bonnet. Your face even has a . . . a . . . strange sort of aura about it."

Afraid that he might suspect the full truth, and not wanting him to know about her private, beautiful moments with Tall Cloud, Christa clasped David's hands and told him almost everything.

Freshly bathed and dressed in a crisp, newly ironed cotton dress, Christa added potatoes to the pot of stew simmering over the fire. Everything that had happened between her and Tall Cloud now seemed just a dream to Christa, though in truth it had happened only the day before.

She eased her apron from around her waist and settled down into a chair, pinning her hair back from her face as she watched the fire rolling up from beneath a log. The fire popped and crackled cozily, and she was glad David was taking a short nap, for he had not rested well after hearing the details of Christa's morning adventures. He had blanched to a sickening white when Christa had told him about shooting the Haida Indian and then taking it upon herself to escort the anguished Indian princess across Puget Sound to her village.

David had used a word much stronger than stupid when scolding Christa, and it hadn't offended her, but, instead, it had amused her. It had been good to watch David's face fill with color and see fire enter his eyes.

Christa smiled and sighed heavily. David was going to be all right. Soon he was going to be as good as new. But what about her? David had his own plans for her future, and it most certainly did not include her love for an Indian.

The creaking of the door behind her caused Christa's heart to jump. Who else entered without first knocking but the Suquamish Indians? Or could it be the Haida Indian?

Eying her apron where it now hung on a nail beside the door and realizing that her pistol in its pocket was out of reach, fear inched its way inside her. She had become careless.

"Nahkeeta?"

A sweet chord of ecstasy played a rhapsody inside her heart as she recognized Tall Cloud's now familiar deep, masculine voice. But her joy was short-lived. Her brother had warned her not to be so friendly, especially not to this particular Indian, and that the dangers were many. David had suggested that Tall Cloud's intentions may not be honorable, chief or not, and that he should not be trusted. Yet as David had preached to her, her mind had been elsewhere, recalling the moments on the bearskin.

Christa rose from the chair and turned to face Tall Cloud, now feeling the bond between them that being together intimately had formed. But how could she tell him that he could no longer come to her like this? And why had he returned so soon? Was he missing her as much as she was missing him?

Her eyes swept over him. He wore the same attire as before, still barefoot, but this time he was void of his dentalia necklace. "Tall Cloud," she said, taking a step toward him. Then she let out a quiet gasp when another Suquamish Indian entered the cabin. He was much shorter and older than Tall Cloud and had bowlegs and stiff facial features.

This Indian with Tall Cloud was dressed only in a loincloth except for the elaborately carved necklaces of bones about his neck and the decorations of shells in the pierced septum of his broad, flat nose. Hanging long and shaggy, his hair appeared never to have been cut or combed, as if wearing it that way was his badge of office. He carried in his hand a globular rattle carved in the shape of a raven, decorated with neck rings of shredded and red-dyed cedar bark—the insignia of his profession.

"Who is he?" Christa asked, still staring at the Indian who had a mystique about him quite different from the force which drew her to Tall Cloud. If not for Tall Cloud's presence, Christa would have been keenly afraid.

"This is the shaman for my tribe of Suquamish," Tall Cloud said proudly. "Dark Hawk."

"A shaman?" Christa softly murmured. She had almost blurted out "witch doctor," but, thankfully, she had caught herself before doing so. "Why did you bring him here?" she said then, already fearing that she had guessed the answer.

"Dark Hawk is here as a gesture of friendship, to thank

you, *Nahkeeta,* for helping Princess Star in her time of trouble."

"What does he have to do with *me?*" she asked, taking a step toward the bedroom door. She wouldn't let the Shaman enter her bedroom where David peacefully lay. She wouldn't!

"The white man's doctor has not been effective in your brother's struggles to be healed," Tall Cloud said, puzzled by the fear etched across her lovely, gentle face. A shaman was not to be feared! He was to be respected!

"So I have brought you *our* doctor, Dark Hawk," he continued. "He will perform over your brother. He will chase the evil spirits away. He will remove the contamination."

Christa tried to keep calm. She knew that Tall Cloud's gesture was from the heart. "I appreciate your kind offer. David will also when I tell him," she said quietly. "But, Tall Cloud, David is resting. I don't want to disturb him. I'm sure you understand that rest is as important for healing as any medicine prescribed by a white man's doctor *or* an Indian's."

She finally succeeded in reaching the door. Petite as she was, she made her point by being there.

David spoke suddenly from behind her in a groggy voice. "Christa, what's going on?" he said. "I awakened to voices. Who's there? Why are you standing at the door with your back to me?"

Christa stiffened. She had hoped that, somehow David would sleep through the disturbance. If he had not made a sound, perhaps Tall Cloud might have left, agreeing that sleep was important. But now, she was quickly losing control of the situation, for Tall Cloud and the shaman were approaching her.

"He is awake now," Tall Cloud said, taking Christa by an elbow, urging her from the doorway. "Dark Hawk will begin his rites."

Now more angry than afraid, Christa jerked away from

Tall Cloud and rushed past him and the shaman to stand protectively over David. If only she had her pistol! she thought. That would have dissuaded the shaman from bothering her brother in any way.

"Dark Hawk, your services are not required here," she said coldly, folding her arms across her chest in defiance.

David rose up slowly on an elbow, staring wild eyed toward the old Indian. "Christa, don't tell me that he thinks he—" he said, gulping hard.

"No. He will *not,*" Christa said hotly.

She gave Tall Cloud an icy stare. "Tell Dark Hawk to leave, Tall Cloud," she ordered. Her knees were trembling from her boldness. She expected Tall Cloud to explode in anger at any moment because of her behavior. But, instead, she saw a quiet amusement dancing in the pleasant gray of his eyes.

Tall Cloud went to Christa, took her gently by a hand, and led her from the bedside. "You've much to learn of the ways of the Suquamish *and* of politeness," he said, casting her a half smile. "Watch Dark Hawk for a while, and then we will leave him alone with your brother."

"Christa . . ." David said in a low, throaty drone.

"David, don't get upset," she said, hearing the soft hysteria in his voice. "Everything will be all right. You'll see."

Dark Hawk began shaking his rattle and chanting in a high-pitched voice as he stood over David, looking down at him. Then the shaman began a dance around the bed, tapping his bare feet against the floor in rhythm with the shakes of his rattle. A low, mournful song rose from his lips, and he bobbed his head up and down.

"We must leave now," Tall Cloud encouraged. "The spirits won't hear Dark Hawk if we are here."

"But David—"

"No physical contact will be made between the shaman and your brother," Tall Cloud reassured, suspecting her reason for apprehension and trying to understand. "Only spiritual contact will be shared."

Christa gave David a last, lingering look, relieved to see that he was as resigned to what would take place as he had been to all the other strange behavior of the Puget Sound Suquamish. He gave her a nod, a silent message for her not to worry, then settled back on the pillow, once more his quiet, gentle, patient self.

The sing-song effect of the shaman's chants trailed along after Christa as she continued to be led away by Tall Cloud. "To please the spirits we must leave your dwelling," Tall Cloud said, motioning toward the door with a nod of his head. *"Chako.* We will go to the forest. We will rest beneath a tree. Dark Hawk must have complete privacy to do his duty well."

"No. I must stay close to my brother in case he needs me," Christa argued softly.

"You did not stay close to him yesterday," Tall Cloud grumbled. "It's not necessary that you do so today."

His grip strengthened on her hand. Christa gave him an icy stare and stumbled over the threshold as he half dragged her after him. She tried to jerk her hand from his, succeeding only in inflicting pain on her wrist from the strain.

"Tall Cloud, you are impossible," she fussed. "Do you always get your way?"

"Halo," he said, shaking his head back and forth. "It is not written in the heavens that a man, even a chief, should always win."

He was thinking of the treaty. If the terms of the treaty were carried out, he would be the loser. But if he lost in his efforts to prove the treaty invalid, at least he knew in the end he would win *something.* He gave his *Nahkeeta* a sideways glance, smiling coyly.

"Then why did you see the need to do so today?" Christa fumed, lifting up the tail of her dress with her free hand as they moved through the brush at the outskirts of the forest. "And why must we go so far from my cabin?"

"You ask too many questions," Tall Cloud protested. "Just follow. We will once more share our love."

Christa's insides rippled sensuously, then she felt ashamed. She couldn't let herself be so wanton as to let Tall Cloud make love to her again, especially not while David was alone with . . . with an Indian witch doctor!

"No," she stated quietly. "This is *not* a victory you will boast of this day. I was wrong to have let you make love to me the first time. There won't be a second."

In the shadows of a gigantic oak, Tall Cloud took a quick step in front of Christa, stopping her further approach. He placed his arms about her waist and yanked her next to him, almost knocking the breath from her, so intent was he to have his way with her again.

His lips met hers in a heated fury, and his tongue speared its way inside the sweet softness of her mouth. He moaned as her tongue flicked against his and her breasts pressed hard into his chest.

Christa felt a spinning inside her head and rapture spreading like wildfire throughout her insides. She knew his skill in making her lose her senses and was torn by wanting him yet knowing that it must not be.

Splaying her fingers against his chest, she tried to push him away from her. She pulled her lips free and began to protest, but his hands were suddenly in her hair, pressing her lips back to his.

With a pounding heart and weakening knees, Christa felt her defenses against him crumbling. His kiss was demanding . . . hot . . . possessive. His body was rock hard against hers and even through the cotton fabric of her dress she could feel the strength of his sex pressed against her through his brief loincloth.

All thoughts of David, of a chanting shaman, of right and wrong, disappeared from her mind as Tall Cloud lowered a hand and cupped the full outline of Christa's breast. A passionate shiver raced through her, and she could not refuse Tall Cloud when he began to ease her down to the ground where a thick layer of soft fallen leaves became their bed of love.

Christa smiled warmly up at Tall Cloud as he eased away from her to remove his loincloth. She was seeing him through a hazy glow and let out a soft moan as he knelt down over her and kissed the hollow of her throat.

While his hands unbuttoned her dress, hers explored the smoothness of his skin. His chest was not marred by hair, and his nipples were hard and stiffly peaked. She worked with each, between her thumbs and forefingers, then she let out a soft cry and closed her eyes as his lips swept down and possessed one of her breasts that was now exposed. Quivering with ecstasy, she clung to him, her arms about his neck. She parted her legs as she felt his hand slipping up the skirt of her dress. When his fingers crept farther and pulled her bloomers down to explore where her legs softly parted, a rush so sweet engulfed her that she lifted her dress, placed her hands to his buttocks, and urged him down and inside her.

Tall Cloud wove his fingers through her hair and urged her lips to his, moving his chest against her breasts, feeling her hardened nipples digging into his flesh. He kissed her long and hard, savoring how she lifted her hips to meet his every thrust. She was a skilled seductress, though he knew that he had been the first with her. When watching her from afar those many times, before approaching her in any way, he hadn't guessed that he would find her so untamed. It seemed to him that he had unleashed a mountain cat in what he had thought to be a kitten.

He molded the silken flesh of her breasts in his hands, easing only a little away from her, slowing his pace inside her. He looked down at her, seeing the passion in her slanted green eyes, and smiled.

Christa placed a hand on each side of his face, feverish now with need for fulfillment. "I love you," she whispered. "I want you. I need you."

She drew his face down, ran her tongue over the outline of his lips, then fully kissed him. Her fingers raked through the coarseness of his shoulder-length, dark brown hair, not disturbing his headband and feather. Once more he plunged deeply inside her. She was so overcome with pleasure that her kiss turned into a bite, making Tall Cloud wince then chuckle as he playfully bit her back on her own lip. Then he pressed his face down and between the magnificent swells of her breasts, losing himself in the momentary, immense joy of release.

Christa felt his body tense and then jerk in spasms at the instant her own release came in a feeling so intense she was momentarily blinded with rapture. Clinging, kissing him softly, Christa made a slow descent from their shared heaven. She became aware of a scent so fresh and pure nearby, carried to her by a breath of wind, that she eased her lips away from Tall Cloud's to seek its origin. She spied a trail of wild pink roses climbing the trunk of the oak tree under which she and Tall Cloud lay.

Tall Cloud's eyes followed hers. He gave her a quiet smile, rose, and plucked some of the flowers for her. "A remembrance of today, my *Nahkeeta,*" he said, placing roses in her hair to shape a crown.

Christa giggled, then blushed, then became suddenly worried when she glimpsed his nudity and then her own exposed breasts and her hiked-up dress.

"My dress!" she gasped. "It was just freshly ironed. Now look at it. David will notice the wrinkles."

She blanched, looking through the trees toward the cabin. "Good Lord! David! I forgot," she cried, scurrying to her feet, buttoning her dress and slipping up her bloomers to cover the part of her that was still hot and tender from lovemaking.

But once she had her dress and bloomers secured, she groaned miserably, holding its skirt out, seeing the massive wrinkles. "Oh, what shall I do?" she cried softly.

Tall Cloud pulled his loincloth on, then quickly swept her up and into his arms. "There is one way to fool your brother," he said, chuckling.

Christa clung about his neck. "You're carrying me farther from my cabin," she said. "Why? Tall Cloud, I must return to David. I no longer hear the shaman's songs or chants."

"When Dark Hawk is finished, he will return to Enati Island without me. Do not fret so, my *Nahkeeta*. It takes your loveliness away."

"Nahkeeta!" she protested. "Why must you continue to call me that? I am called by the name Christa!"

"Do you not think the maidenhair ferns of the forest beautiful, gentle, and pretty?"

"Why, yes. I do—"

"As *you* are," he insisted. "I've told you before, *Nahkeeta* means beautiful, gentle maiden. Any woman should be proud to be given this name."

"As I would be if I didn't already *have* a name."

"What does the name Christa stand for?"

Christa blushed. "I don't truly know," she confessed softly.

"So you see?" he boasted. "A name without a meaning is a name of no importance."

Sighing exasperatedly, Christa squirmed in his arms. "Names? How did we get on the subject of names?" she fussed. "Put me down. I must return home."

"You no longer are concerned over wrinkles in your dress?"

She looked down at her dress and emitted a soft groan. "I forgot," she murmured.

"I did not, and I am ready to remedy that for you, *Nahkeeta*." Tall Cloud laughed softly.

"How?" she asked, looking ahead, now catching a glimpse through the trees of sparkling water from a creek.

"You will see," Tall Cloud said, now softly running past the tall trees, the maidenhair ferns and scarlet vines of climbing ivy. When he reached the creek, he ran on into it.

As the cold water splashed up onto Christa's face, she squealed and batted her eyes frantically. "Tall Cloud, what—" she said, but further words were stolen from her when he carried her into deeper water. He held her tightly to him as he ducked them both beneath the surface. His hands grazed her breasts which were thrusting out against her clinging dress. His lips found hers and he kissed her, continuing to do so as he raised her back out of the water.

Christa drew her lips away, coughing and wiping water from her eyes. "Why on earth did you do such a crazy thing?" she asked hotly.

"Your dress. It is wet. The wrinkles won't show."

She gave him an amused look. "What?" she gasped. "A wet dress will be even more questionable than a wrinkled dress."

"Not when you say that you accidentally tripped and fell into the water."

Once more his innocence caused Christa's heart to swell with love for him. She draped her arms about his neck, giggling. "Tall Cloud, at this very moment I don't care if my dress is wrinkled *or* wet. Just kiss me. my darling. Kiss me. . . ."

Five

David had been so relieved to have Christa safe inside the cabin with him, without the presence of any Suquamish Indians, he hadn't asked for lengthy explanations about her wet dress. She had never been one to lie, he knew. If she said that she had fallen into a creek, she had fallen into a creek. It was as simple as that. And he hadn't wanted to pursue the issue further, not eager to hear the details. He hadn't wanted to believe that the Indian was responsible in any way. It was best not to think of it. Christa was safe. He was safe.

A week had passed since any Indian had come to Christa and David's cabin. David was sitting before the fire with his leg propped up on a stool. Christa was restless. She found herself wandering to a window and pulling the curtain aside to peer out. Feeling eyes on her back, she slowly turned to challenge David's stare.

"What are you finding so interesting outside that window?" David asked, taking his knife and pine stick from his lap to resume whittling. "If you're not pacin', you're starin' from the window."

The air inside the cabin was close. Though it was the early part of September, it was still hot and dry. The lightning zigzags in the sky gave Christa relief for two reasons. One, she would welcome the rain and cooler temperatures. Two, it gave her a good excuse to go to the window, to watch the play of the heavens, but in truth she was watching for Tall Cloud in the direction of the Sound.

"It's the lightning," she said, turning once more to look up into the sky. She wiped beads of perspiration from her brow. "It's quite a sight to see, David. I've never seen such brilliant flashes." As Christa finished speaking the walls of the cabin shook with a rumble of thunder, and the room was lit with an explosion of lightning.

"First, there's too much rain; then there's not enough," David grumbled. "If you'd ask my opinion, I'd vote for the latter. There's always a threat of mudslides in Seattle where they've scraped the topsoil away, to build streets and houses."

"The crops and animals could do with watering," Christa argued softly. She removed her handkerchief from her apron pocket and dabbed it down, into her deep cleavage. She glanced over the scorched garden and then toward the cows. Since David's accident it had been hard for her to keep up with all the chores. But she had done her best. The calluses on her fingertips and the sunburn on her nose were proof of that. But with winter coming she needed David's help to ready themselves for it.

She leaned forward, trying to see across the Sound, still wondering about Tall Cloud, and his people. How did they survive the long months of winter? Where was he now? A full week! She hadn't seen him for a full week!

Christa jumped when a more fierce fork of lightning broke from the sky and appeared to go straight down into the waters of the Sound.

"Get away from the window, Christa," David scolded. "You know the dangers. Want a bolt of lightnin' to seek you out and strike you dead?"

Laughing softly, Christa walked away from the window. "David, I'm too mean to get struck," she teased. "Don't you know that?"

Her hair was swept back from her face and tied with a

green velvet bow, and her lowswept, pale green cotton dress twisted around her legs as she went about lighting kerosene lamps. The sky had darkened so, it appeared to be night instead of midday.

David watched his sister, seeing her gentle loveliness and still hating the drab cotton dresses that made up her wardrobe. "You're never mean," he said thickly. "Just awful pretty."

He paused then added, "Harrison's dance is next week. You're goin', aren't you, Christa?"

Christa sat down at the table, picked up a paring knife, and began peeling potatoes. "Now that you're unable to attend, I shall refuse the invitation also," she said, avoiding looking his way. "It just wouldn't be fair to you, David."

She shook her head, cutting a potato into fours, dropping them into a kettle. "No. I don't plan to go."

She hated that David was ailing, but she liked having an excuse not to have to be with Harrison Kramer for any reason.

"I plan on going," David said, placing his knife on his lap, smoothing his fingers over the pine stick.

Christa quickly looked his way. "You plan to go?" she gasped. "David, your foot. . . ."

"I can have me some crutches made by then if you'll bring me the necessary wood from the wood pile," he said. "I'm seein' to it that you get to that dance or die tryin'."

"David, it isn't necessary," Christa argued. "I have no desire whatsoever to go to Harrison's social function. I've told you that and *why* I feel this way."

"Christa, I'm more determined now than before," David said, once more whittling. "This thing with the Indians—the way they seem to have taken over our lives—has got to stop. If I can get you married off to Harrison, I bet no Indians would come around here any more."

A flush rose to Christa's cheeks and her heart fluttered nervously. "David!" she once more gasped. "Why on earth would you say such a thing? Why would I have anything to do with why the Indians come or go from our cabin?"

David gave her a pensive stare. "Christa, I'm sure they've not seen anyone as pretty as you, ever," he said hoarsely. "I'm beginnin' to think they only show up on our doorstep to watch you. Take that taller Indian . . . that one named Tall Cloud. He acts as though he owns you, now that you helped his sister."

He slammed his knife and pine stick on the table next to his chair. "No. I don't like it. You've got to get it out of your head that Harrison is not the proper man for you. I've got to see to it that you get moved into the city and married *soon.*"

Frustration and anger fused inside Christa. Since their arrival in this northwest territory, David had become almost unbearable in his persistence to rule her life. She loved him with all her heart and understood that his motives were guided by his intense love for her, that protective, emotional cocoon usually spun by an older brother.

Before, she had smiled and accepted his proddings about Harrison Kramer, thinking them innocent enough. But now wedding bells seemed much too close for comfort. She loved Tall Cloud. How could she agree to marry Harrison Kramer?

Christa was so angry, she couldn't even talk. She dropped the rest of her quartered potatoes into the kettle of water, rose quickly from the table, and irritably hung the kettle over the fire.

"Well? Don't you have anything to say back to what I just said?" David asked, lifting his leg gently, repositioning it more comfortably on the stool. "Anger is spilling out of your pores, Christa. You may as well get it fully out of your system by shoutin' at me."

"I have nothing to say," she said coolly, turning to go to the table, to rid it of potato peelings. "I've said it all before. But it seems you've got cotton in your ears or you're going deaf, because you've paid no mind at all, ever, to what I've said back to you, David."

"I'm only thinkin' of what's best for you, Christa."

She glowered toward him. "Or perhaps what's best for you?" she snapped. "If I said vows with a rich man, wouldn't you be better off yourself?"

David blanched. He leaned forward in his chair, staring blankly at Christa. "Surely you don't mean what you say," he said hoarsely. "I've never considered my feelings one way or another in this matter of Harrison Kramer."

Christa experienced a dull ache around her heart. Shame caused her to rush to David. She knelt down and wrapped her arms about his neck. "Sweet David," she murmured. "My adorable brother, I'm so sorry. I don't know what got into me. I shouldn't have said that. I'm sorry. Please forgive me?"

A loud clap of thunder shook the foundation of the cabin. "It's the approachin' storm," David said, patting her fondly on the back. "It's got you nervous. That's all."

Christa drew away from him. "No matter what, I shouldn't have accused you so unjustly," she said. "You haven't got a selfish bone in your body. You're just like our papa was—honest and big hearted. I know that, David."

The wind began to howl down the chimney and around the outside of the cabin. A sudden banging of the door reverberated throughout the cabin and Christa jumped, startled, thinking the fury of the wind had blown the door open suddenly. She turned quickly on a heel to shut it, then let out a loud gasp when she saw the tall outline of Tall Cloud standing there in the doorway, looking toward her intensely.

David's head jerked around and his insides grew numb, then cold. "You!" he said venomously. "Why have you returned? And do you once more bring your shaman?" He patted his leg. "As you see, his magic is no stronger than the white man's doctor."

A flash of lightning behind Tall Cloud made his presence

in the door appear an ominous thing. "The spirits of the mountains cause a storm," he said, stepping into the cabin. "The thunderbird's wings are flapping, causing the sound of thunder. The flash of the thunderbird's eyes is the lightning."

David sighed dubiously. "I'm sure you aren't here to explain why it thunders and lightnings today," he said. "Why *are* you here? Or is this just another *nanitch,* a time to stand around and watch what we are doing?"

Tall Cloud's expressive gray eyes swept over Christa, and he was engulfed once more by the nervous pounding of his heart that always occurred in the presence of her extreme beauty. He smiled slowly toward her, and she gazed back at him with wonder in the luminous green of her eyes.

"I have come for a distinct purpose," he said strongly, still watching Christa, seeing the flame of color rising to her cheeks under his close scrutiny of her.

"And what might that be?" David said cautiously, looking from Christa to Tall Cloud, seeing much that filled him with dread. He let his eyes travel up and down the full length of Tall Cloud, wishing he would wear more than a loincloth in Christa's presence. It unnerved *him.* He had to believe that it had the same effect on his sister!

"Mahlieh," Tall Cloud said proudly. "I wish to marry *Nahkeeta."*

"Marry? *Nahkeeta?"* David gasped. He forgot his wounded foot in this moment of utter shock. He started to rise from the chair. But as he placed his full weight on the injured foot and pain stabbed away at it, he let out a loud yelp and crumpled back into the chair, groaning mournfully.

Christa was too stunned to move. Even David's low groans of pain couldn't pull her from her trance, so startled was she by what Tall Cloud had just said. Marriage? He had actually asked for her hand in marriage! He loved her this much, this sincerely, that he would go against all the rules and step forward to profess his love for her in such strong terms!

Tall Cloud was not to be moved by David's reaction to his question. "I wish to marry *Nahkeeta,*" he said, setting his jaw firmly. "I wish to take her with me. Today."

Blanching, Christa emerged from her trancelike state. She swallowed hard, placed her hands to her throat, and looked quickly toward David. Now he would surely know that there had been more between Tall Cloud and herself than mere talk. Tall Cloud was calling her by her intimate Indian name. She was thrilled, even melting inside, to realize that Tall Cloud loved her so much, yet there was David to consider. She didn't want her brother to hate her!

David glared at Tall Cloud, his face red from intense anger. "Get out of here," he snarled. "What do you mean by coming here and asking for my sister's hand in marriage? And you even have the gall to call her by an Indian name? Get out. Now!"

Tall Cloud's face shadowed with hurt pride. He gave Christa a lingering look then spun around on a heel and rushed from the cabin.

A throaty sob rose from inside Christa. She gave David an annoyed look then hurried to the door. The wind caught her dress and whipped it around her ankles, and the ribbon in her hair became untied and began flapping against her neck. She was suddenly blinded by an onslaught of rushing rain.

Wiping desperately at her eyes, she looked toward the Sound, worrying more for Tall Cloud's safety than about David speaking her name from behind her. She could now see Tall Cloud fighting the giant waves beating against his canoe as he paddled his way toward *Enati* Island. The lightning danced overhead in erratic designs, and the thunder roared. She knew how dangerous it was for Tall Cloud to be in the water. If the waves didn't swallow him whole, the lightning might strike him.

"Christa, turn around and face me," David ordered in a tone of voice unfamiliar to Christa.

Weak-kneed, she closed the door then leaned her back against it, looking toward her brother. Breathing hard, she murmured, "Don't make me say it, David. You truly don't want to know."

David's gut twisted. He quickly looked away from her and hung his head in his hands. "No," he said weakly. "It can't be."

Going to him, Christa fell to her knees before him and eased his hands from his face. When their eyes met, she silently pleaded with him, forcing a weak smile. "It doesn't matter all that much that he is Indian, does it, David?" she begged.

"How can you ask such a question?" he said, choking on his words. "Christa, he *is* an Indian. A *savage*."

She threw her head back and closed her eyes, tightening her hands into fists. "Good Lord, how I hate that word 'savage'!" she shouted. "Would you also say that Tall Cloud has a savage heart? That he isn't kind? That he isn't gentle?"

"And you know firsthand that he is both kind and gentle?" David asked, dying a slow death inside, yet not letting himself believe that anything more than a fierce attraction had been exchanged between his sister and this Indian, Tall Cloud.

Christa settled down in a chair next to David. She leaned forward and met his challenge. "Yes, I know these things," she confessed. "And I do love him, David. I *do*. And it's not merely infatuation because he is 'different.' I love him because of how he makes me feel, and because he is a good, sincere man."

David began nervously raking his fingers through his hair. "Papa would have said at a time like this that I had failed in my efforts to do what was right for you," he worried, shaking his head. "When Papa and Mama died on the trail, I should have turned the oxen back in the direction of Boston. I shouldn't have brought you out here to this untamed wilderness. I have failed you miserably. It's all my fault."

Christa felt tears welling in her eyes. She rushed to David and knelt to hug him. "No. You haven't failed me," she sobbed. "You've been the best brother ever. You've always put me first in your mind as well as in your heart. It is I who have failed you." She wiped a tear from her cheek and beseeched David with her red-rimmed eyes. "But David, I can't help loving Tall Cloud." She sobbed. "It just happened. Please try to understand."

David refused to ask where this "love" had led Christa. She was old enough and mature enough to have the needs of a woman. And if anything *had* transpired between her and the Indian, it was obvious that it was not something forced on her. She would have agreed, willingly.

"Help me to bed, Christa," he said thickly, once more shaking his head. "I'm suddenly tired."

"David, is that all you're going to say about—"

"What else is there to say? Now, please, help me into bed."

Christa felt drained. Sadness overwhelmed her. With a lump in her throat and a pain beneath her breastbone, she helped David from the chair and began walking him toward the bedroom door, his weight heavy against her. She wanted to reaffirm his trust in her, yet her worries were mainly about Tall Cloud. Had he made it safely across the Sound? What was he feeling at this moment? Would he ever try to see her again?

Six

Gray clouds hung low and gloomy over Puget Sound, and there was a dampness in the air as Christa set about collecting eggs in the barn. While she carefully placed them in her wicker basket, her thoughts wandered. The last time she had seen Tall Cloud he had been battling the waters of the Sound. A chill rushed through her as she wondered if he were even still alive. She couldn't travel far from the cabin to go to Enati Island for David had positioned himself by a window to watch her each and every move. It wasn't that he didn't trust her; instead, it was Tall Cloud he feared.

With her free hand she wrapped her knitted shawl more securely around her shoulders. The barn was drafty, and the straw in the loft and at her feet was still spongy from the recent rain which had blown in through the cracks in the roof.

The smell from the chicken droppings and horse dung was sulfuric and burned her nostrils and throat. She hurried her pace, shooing chickens from their roosts, gathering up the last of the eggs, then leaving the barn and heading toward the cabin.

The giant firs and hemlocks of the forest reached up into the low-hanging clouds, their tips lost in the billows of gray. A brisk wind whipping across the Sound impeded Christa's walk on the narrow, stone-laid path. She turned her face from the saltwater breeze and clung to her basket with one hand and her shawl with the other, having to let the trail of her dress have its own way as it fluttered and thrashed around her legs.

A movement catching the corner of her eye made Christa look quickly back toward the Sound. She stopped so abruptly that an egg flew from her basket and splattered at her feet. But she was not aware of it. Her heart beat rapidly with the joy of discovery, her eyes brightened, and her lips lifted in a warm smile. Tall Cloud was still alive and he had not forgotten her. He was now walking toward her, tall and proud, and dressed much differently than ever before. He wore buckskin leggings, moccasins, and a fringed buckskin shirt trimmed with porcupine-quill embroidery. Around his neck he wore his necklace of tusklike dentalia, and his wavy, dark brown hair hung neatly to his shoulders, held in place by a magnificently beaded headband in which stood a beautiful eagle feather.

"Never has he been as handsome," Christa said, and sighed to herself. Then her eyes settled on his arms and what he held in them. From this distance, it was hard to make out. But his walk was filled with determination, and she had to wonder just what it was he held so closely to his breast.

Then a sudden dread filled her. She glanced quickly toward the house. "David," she whispered. "Good Lord! David! How will he treat Tall Cloud *this* time?"

She knew that David wouldn't harm Tall Cloud in any way. Tall Cloud was the chief of a Suquamish tribe of many Indians. If harm came to Tall Cloud, all of the white men and women of Puget Sound would be held accountable. But David could verbally assault him again, and sometimes words could cut deeper than a knife . . . , she thought silently.

Placing the basket of eggs on the ground and not caring that her shawl fell from her shoulders and blew away onto the dew-dampened grass, Christa rushed in the direction of Tall Cloud. She grabbed up the skirt of her dress in her arms and her waist-length hair lifted and swirled wildly about her face. She no longer cared about David. All she wanted was to be in Tall Cloud's arms, hear his words of love being whispered into her ear, feel the strength of him surround her. Her love for him was as fierce as that of the wolf for its mate. She realized that without Tall Cloud she had been only half alive.

"Tall Cloud, thank God you're all right," she cried as she met him face to face. Her breath was heavy, her arms aching to embrace him. But he wasn't responding in kind. In his large gray eyes which mirrored his varying moods she did not see warmth, but instead a cold sternness. This was cause for Christa's smile to fade and her heart to skip a beat.

"Tall Cloud, what is it?" she asked, her voice full of trembling which she hated but could not control. "Why are you looking at me . . . like . . . that?"

"I must speak again with your brother," he said flatly.

Dread filled Christa. "David?" she asked, her green eyes wavering. Though David was usually gentle and soft spoken, seeing Tall Cloud could make his personality change as quickly as the weather changed on Puget Sound, and he might even become as fierce—all for the sake of his sister.

"I have come bearing a special gift to offer your brother," Tall Cloud said flatly. "Take me to him, *Nahkeeta*."

"Gift? For David?" Christa murmured. Her gaze lowered. She studied the garment folded neatly in his arms. It had the appearance of a blanket, yet in its folds she could see many pearl-shell buttons sewn to it.

"Take me to your brother, *Nahkeeta*," Tall Cloud insisted, finding it hard to be near her without gathering her up into his arms to hold her tightly to him. His love for her was as dedicated as the stars which never set in the heavens. He now knew that his need for her was a complex need, and he hoped she would fully understand it one day.

Christa nervously lifted her hands to her hair and combed

her fingers through it. "You and David have already talked, Tall Cloud," she said softly. "You saw his reaction to your proposal."

She took a step closer, looking up into his eyes as she now touched the smoothness of his cheek with her hand. "When you were here last, you asked my brother for my hand in marriage," she said, her heart swimming in desire for him. "Did you truly mean it, Tall Cloud? Do you want me to be your wife?"

"You're my woman. You should bear the title of wife," he grumbled. "But it is important to me that your brother gives his consent. It would mean more to my people if he does. To carry you off without his approval would not be as effective for my Suquamish tribe of Indians."

Christa dropped her hand to her side. Her eyes squinted, trying to read the meaning of his words in his expressive eyes. But still he stood aloof from her, stubborn in his stance.

"Effective?" she questioned softly. "I don't understand."

"Come. Go with me into your cabin. Hear the words which I must speak to your brother today," he said. "Then you shall see why I have brought this special gift."

Christa glanced back over her shoulder toward the cabin. She knew that David must be frantic, wondering where she had gone in such a flurry. Unable to get about on his own, frustration and impatience had set in, causing him to be constantly in a fretful state of mind. And she knew that no matter how much she wanted to envision a future with Tall Cloud, it could never be.

With eyelids heavy with sadness, she once more looked up into Tall Cloud's magnificently sculpted, well-defined Indian features of soft copper coloring. "Tall Cloud, don't you know that it's useless?" she said sorrowfully. "You saw David's earlier reaction to your proposal. It won't be any different today."

"Today my approach is different. So shall his reaction be."

"I don't know what you have on your mind. But I do know that David will not agree to my marrying you. He sees a sort of life for me other than living in an Indian lodge," she said.

She swung around and gestured with the sweep of a hand toward her cabin. "He wants even more for me than a cabin such as I now make residence in."

Anger flashed in Tall Cloud's eyes. "What are you saying?" he growled. "That your brother has a man already chosen for you? A man who displays white man's riches, who has many white man's gifts to offer your brother for the bride price?"

"Bride . . . price?" Christa said in a near whisper.

"No white man's bride price could match what I offer today," Tall Cloud said, glancing down at the blanket in his arms, holding it even more snugly against him. "This Suquamish button blanket which I offer bears the design of my family crest, outlined by sewn pearl-shell buttons. This type of blanket is popular with my people for formal wear, and, when traded, the highest price is paid."

Christa paled. She took a step backward. "You plan to trade that blanket . . . for . . . me?" she gasped. She wished then that she hadn't sounded so astonished, for she saw a sudden hurt in his eyes.

"It is not enough?" he asked softly. "Then I shall return later with more gifts. I shall bring my valued bearskins. I shall offer your brother a totem pole to display proudly outside his door."

Shaking her head, Christa placed a hand to his lips, stopping further words. "No," she said. "Nothing else is required. It's just that you wish to trade me as if . . . as if I were a 'thing.' "

"It is the way of the Suquamish," he grumbled. "A bride price must be paid."

He looked toward the cabin, frowning. "And now that I am here, I will not turn back. I will spread out the blanket for you and your brother to see its magnificence; then I shall try to bargain with your brother."

"Bargain?" Christa whispered, hating the sound of the word and worrying about its meaning. She started to question Tall Cloud further but he suddenly stepped around her and proceeded toward the cabin, his shoulder muscles corded so tightly they rippled the shirt which covered them there.

Fearing the next few moments, Christa began to hurry toward Tall Cloud. When she reached her basket of eggs, she picked up the basket in such a frenzy several more eggs popped out and broke in a scrambled mess at the hem of her dress.

"Oh, no," she cried softly. "What else is going to happen to me today?"

She looked toward the door just as Tall Cloud stepped across the threshold. "Tall Cloud," she whispered, reaching out for him with her free hand. She bit her lower lip and walked ahead, each footstep matching the nervous beat of her heart. And when she entered the cabin she found Tall Cloud spreading out his prided blanket across the kitchen table, with David red faced though held in his chair by his injured foot,

Inching her way behind Tall Cloud, barely breathing, Christa placed the basket on the floor, far from the heat of the fireplace. She reached her hands to her face, wishing that it weren't so hot. But never in her life had she been so nervous. She could see the mistrust and hate being exchanged in cold glances between David and Tall Cloud. She was torn, wanting to be there for each of them, and ready to console if needed.

Yet she knew that the situation was beyond her power to change and that nothing would make a difference between these two men who were of almost equal importance in her life. It seemed the way had already been paved for an explosion to erupt in this room, and it would be much worse than any clap of thunder heard in this Puget Sound territory.

"I had thought to expect you again," David said, dryly, hating the disadvantage of his wounded foot. The Indian was tall enough without towering over him even more while David was forced to sit like an invalid. "Yes, I had thought you would return," David continued. "But I had hoped I was wrong."

David looked at the blanket spread across the table. Straining his neck, leaning up, he could make out a design of a raven, outlined by shells, against a pale blue background. "And why have you placed *that* on the table?" he asked hoarsely.

Tall Cloud gave Christa a guarded look as she stepped up to the table, remembering her earlier reaction to his mention of a bride price. He did not understand. And he wondered what the white man called his bride price.

But this was not the time to wonder. This was the time to impress his *Nahkeeta's* brother!

Folding his arms over his chest, Tall Cloud directed his full attention to David. "This button blanket is a gift I offer to you as an exchange for *Nahkeeta,*" he said in his deep, commanding voice. "It is proudly given to you as my bride price, paid for *Nahkeeta* so that I can not only call her my woman . . . but also my *wife.*"

David's hands were clenched so tightly to the seat of his chair that his knuckles whitened. His mouth dropped open; his throat grew dry. He looked quickly toward Christa whose eyes were wide with uneasiness.

Then he glowered back at Tall Cloud. "So you are now calling my sister not only by the Indian name *Nahkeeta,* but also your woman," he said in a strained voice. "And you wish to bargain for her to make whatever has transpired between you legal by making her your wife? Do you truly believe I would let her go with you because you offered me that . . . that thing which you have taken it upon yourself to place on our kitchen table?" A nervous laugh shook David's body. "Never. Under no circumstances will she go live the life of an Indian squaw!"

Tall Cloud forced himself to keep his anger at bay. He would not let this white man humiliate him into leaving *this* time. Tall Cloud had to guess that it was a ploy. No one had ever laughed at a button blanket before, especially one that bore his family crest!

Stiffening his back and shoulders, Tall Cloud lifted his chin proudly. "It is the custom of the Suquamish Indian groom to give a gift of value to the future bride's family," he said flatly. "If more gifts are required to make you happy, proud brother that you are, I shall bring more."

He gave Christa a reassuring smile, then once more talked directly to David. "It is also the custom of the Suquamish to assure the family of the bride that through the trade they will not lose all interests and rights in her, but can continue to be concerned about her welfare. You, proud brother, will be welcome at any time to partake in a *potlatch* with the Suquamish Indians on Enati Island."

"Potlatch?" David fumed. "I have no idea what that term means, and I don't care. Again I must order you from my cabin. This has gone far enough. I don't wish to hear any more about bride prices, trades, or button blankets. I just want you to leave me *and* my sister alone."

Tall Cloud's eyes wavered. Again he wasn't able to convince this stubborn brother of the way it must be! But Tall Cloud would not give up so easily this time. He went and bent his knees, to squat down on his haunches closer to David. Out of the corner of his eye he saw Christa creep closer. He could tell that she was uneasy. She was nervously wringing her hands before her, her beautiful, slanted green eyes still shadowed with uncertainty. Hopefully soon he could take her in his arms and show her just how right everything was going to be in their lives. But first he had this hurdle to cross—that of a brother not wanting to cut ties with a sister.

Tall Cloud clasped his hands together and rested his arms on the tight muscles of his knees. He looked forcefully into David's angry green eyes. "I will try to explain my intentions to you, proud brother," he said softly, trying to use this less aggressive approach. "You see, a Suquamish chief might seek to marry the daughter, or in *Nahkeeta's* case a sister of some important personage to create useful alliances. I feel the need to create this alliance between myself and the white man in the hope that by doing so I will have the means to encourage the white man to void the treaty which steals much from the Indians and which forces them to move onto reservations. Surely the white man won't cheat the husband of a white woman or force *her* to live on a reservation."

Christa's heart sank. Her hands went to her mouth as a gasp tore from her throat and a sick feeling invaded her insides. She couldn't believe what she was hearing. He had only wanted her to better his relationship with the white man! She had been made love to only because he needed her as a pawn! And that he had the nerve to admit to such a truth was more cause for her disbelief.

She watched as David tried to rise from his chair then fell back onto it in pain. "You have some nerve," David finally blurted. "You don't even know what you've done here, do you? You've made my sister appear a fool as you admit your selfish reasons for wanting her."

David laughed hoarsely. "But the laugh is on you, Indian. You've chosen the wrong 'important personage.' I am nothing but a farmer who makes a living by making and selling shakes to anyone who will buy them."

"In the Suquamish eyes all white men are of importance because it is all white men combined who are taking from the Indians," Tall Cloud growled. He looked toward Christa and her hurt-filled stare caused an agonizing ache deep within him. He hungered to go to her, to embrace and comfort her, but he couldn't touch her in the presence of her brother. Soon he would explain away her hurt.

He rose to his feet and looked solemnly down at David. He pointed toward the window. "Every part of this land is loved and cherished by my people," he stated. "Every tree, every hillside, and even the shell-paved floor of Puget Sound have known my people. And now my people's children are forced from the pleasures of knowing these things. Proud brother, I come to you in peace, to try and remedy this. If you have misunderstood, it is because I am ignorant of all your ways except for knowing to speak your language."

"At least you realize that with me and my sister you've failed," David said, sighing heavily. "Now please take your blanket and your offers and leave us in peace. I have no control over any other white man's decisions. What they do, they do as individuals. And you must realize the futility of arguing over a treaty that is already signed."

Tall Cloud turned to Christa. *"Nahkeeta?"* he questioned. "Do *you* not understand?"

Christa was so humiliated she felt the need to return the hurt. She went to David, stood behind his chair, and draped her arms around his neck. "Tall Cloud, I told you before that David has his own plans for me," she said blandly. "I am now voicing aloud to all who hear that I will marry Harrison Kramer. And soon. I will be moving into Seattle, to live in his mansion on Fourth Avenue."

It tore at her heart to hear those words surface from her lips, but for now it was her only defense against a man who had used her, a man who had taken her virginity away from her. Shame for what she had shared with him caused a sick feeling to invade her insides.

Tall Cloud's eyes grew wide with surprise then hot with building rage. He went to the table and hurriedly folded his blanket. "You wish white man's riches instead of Indian's love?" he growled. He tucked the blanket beneath his left arm and glared at Christa. *"Nahkeeta,* you are not the woman I thought you to be. I have seen such women as you surely will soon be. Diamonds worn about the throat lessen the goodness of the heart."

He turned on a heel, broke into a trot, and was quickly gone from sight. Christa and David exchanged glances, then Christa turned her head away to hide her distress, almost too numb to go through her usual daily routine. But she forced herself to pick up the basket of eggs and place it on the table. She began sorting through them, for candling, then stiffened when David began to speak.

"Christa, go get me that wood from the woodpile," he said, smiling strangely at her.

"Wood? What wood are you speaking of, David?"

"For the crutches. I've got to get those crutches made. We're going to make that appearance at Harrison's. Just imagine the expression he'll get on his face when we tell him the news."

"News?"

"That there can be a wedding, and soon. We'll show that Indian a thing or two, won't we?"

An egg slipped from Christa's hand and fell into the basket, and as it broke others broke with it. The wide cracks on each resembled Christa's aching heart.

Seven

Christa had managed well enough to help David dress smartly for Harrison Kramer's autumn social function, which not only afforded the best of food but also a rare opportunity to dance. The cut required in the one leg of his finely pressed trousers through which to slip his heavily bandaged foot was hardly noticeable. David looked so spanking fresh with his wheat-colored hair combed to perfection, his nose shining from a good scrub, and his frock coat's handsomeness accented by a ruffle gathered down the front of his white shirt. It was nice, Christa had thought as she removed David's Boston clothes from storage, that he would once more dress as he had always dressed in Boston. The only difference was that his labors on the farm had put more muscle on him, making these clothes fit him much too snugly.

The buggy creaked and rattled over the pitted road which had dried rock hard beneath the strong gusts of wind whipping across the Sound. On this day in mid-September, the setting sun was an orange disc which seemed to be sinking into a Sound laced white with the spume from the rolling waves.

Handling the reins while David held his leg partially up from the floorboard of the buggy to keep his foot from suffering from the continuing bouncing, Christa was the epitome of womanhood. She had fussed for what seemed hours to her, brushing and twisting her long strands of hair into a fancy swirl atop her head and setting this off with a stylish bonnet made of wine-colored velvet, tied beneath the proud tilt of her chin with a matching satin bow.

Her gold silk gown, worn beneath a wine-colored, double-faced velvet cape had a meticulously tucked bodice with a plunging neckline which displayed the splendid, soft, white upper lobes of her breasts and a pearl necklace which had been her mother's. The floor-length gown was gathered at her petite waist and beneath its skirt she wore many layers of delicate, lace-trimmed petticoats.

David glanced over at Christa. In her eyes he could see so much that she had not spoken. It was as though the spark had been removed from inside her since Tall Cloud had stated his true reason for pursuing her.

Not wanting to inflict more hurt, David had left his questions unspoken. He was just relieved that she had made the wise decision to marry Harrison Kramer. The Indian wouldn't dare approach her once true vows had been exchanged and she lived in the Kramer mansion on Fourth Avenue.

Christa could feel David's eyes on her and could imagine what was uppermost in his thoughts. He expected her to accept Harrison's proposal of marriage this night. And the announcement would probably be made before Harrison's whole group of guests. Christa wasn't sure if she could bear it; but now, having seen the true side of Tall Cloud's nature—a revelation that had left her feeling so cold inside—it didn't matter much who placed a ring on her finger. In her heart, there would always be passion only for one man, a man who had toyed with her and used her in the worst way possible. Yet in using her, Tall Cloud had taught her how to love a man, to love him with a love so strong that it could not easily be turned to hate.

Now, ahead of Christa and David, Seattle spread out over the hills, and on each side and behind the city the thick woods

were black with the impenetrable darkness of early night.
The road on which the horse and buggy continued to travel
ran alongside the lowland where the hills of the city flattened
out and ran into the tide flats area called the "Sag." Yesler's
Mill stood quiet this time of evening, as the buggy passed
it by, but through the day it was a thriving business. Yesler's
Mill was the first steam sawmill for Seattle, and, no matter
the weather, the ox teams labored each day pulling logs along
Mill Street to the mill.

Clustered about the mill on the tide flats were the mer-
cantile establishments which served the ships that traveled
back and forth between Seattle and San Francisco and all
smaller ports along the coast between the two busy seaports.
Brigs, clipper and lumber schooners now lined the shore
where they had dropped their anchors, waiting for the next
morning and a turn to load lumber at the docks. The sea
sounds were soft this early evening, intermingling with the
cries of the gulls, the creak of the lines as the moored ships
gently swayed, and the slap-slap of the waves against the
pilings.

Still without a word shared between Christa and David,
the buggy moved on to Front Street, which was lined with
saloons, fish stores, hardware stores, boardinghouses and
various other establishments. Men on horseback traveled
through the mud of the street; others wandered along the
planked walks. Most were dressed carelessly in slouch hats
over bearded faces, patched hickory shirts, and fading blue
jeans tucked into cowhide boots.

The buggy strained as the horse began its ascent up First
Street toward Fourth Avenue. Christa had grown to dread
these streets that appeared to rise straight up from the
Sound, though when she dared a look back over her shoulder, her fear of the steepness always lessened because the
view it afforded of the Sound and its turquoise water was
such a breathtaking sight.

"We're just about there," David said, breaking the silence. "How are you feeling about things, Christa?"

"I'm sure you know," Christa returned with a pout. "It's nice to be dressed in my favorite gown which I wore last in Boston and until today has been hidden away in our travel chest. But no matter which gown I wear or the hours spent fussing with my hair, I cannot feel good about what might transpire tonight."

"You're talking about an announcement that is forthcoming from Harrison?"

"He doesn't have any idea yet that I have decided to marry him."

"And will you tell him tonight?"

Christa guided the horse and buggy onto Fourth Avenue and past attractive, freshly painted houses. Most were framed, one-story houses of wood. The evening had a sting of cold to it and light blue wood smoke rose up sluggishly from the chimneys of each.

"Do I have any choice, David?" Christa snapped, giving him a sour glance and noting that he was becoming only a shadow in the fast-falling dusk of night. "You know that we cannot go on the way we have."

"Am I wrong to want the best for you, Christa?"

"You're wrong not to include the word 'love' when you speak of what's best for me, David."

"Love will come later."

Christa's brows lifted. "Later?" she gasped. "How do you mean?"

"Respect usually turns to love," David said. "Once you see how well Harrison treats you, you will respect and then love him."

"Never," Christa hissed, tensing when the horse and buggy reached a winding, gravel drive which led to a magnificent, two-storied house standing far back from the street on a hill. It was whitewashed plaster, one of the few two-storied mansions of Seattle, with three tall columns gracing the front and shutters and doors painted a bright green. A high, white picket fence surrounded the estate grounds, which were a showcase of various trees, and Douglas firs, hemlocks, and blue spruce filled the air with the sweet smell of pine.

Christa guided the horse to the side of the house where a long hitching rail was already wrapped with secured reins. Inching her buggy between two grand, black carriages, Christa's heart pounded, for she dreaded the next several hours awaiting her.

Yet, the thought of mingling with people actually thrilled her. It was the time spent in Harrison's company that was so undesirable. She realized that everyone tolerated him only because of the wealth he possessed and the power this wealth gave him in the community. But to share a bed with him as his wife . . .

Brushing the thought aside, Christa left the buggy, secured it, then went around and got the homemade crutches from the back of the buggy and handed them to David. She flinched when she heard David emit a loud groan as he accidentally hit his foot with one of the crutches.

"Can I help you?" Christa asked, smoothing her cape away from her arms.

"I'm not totally helpless," David grumbled. Then realizing how he had snapped at Christa, he gave her a half smile. "Christa, I'm sorry. I continue to be hard to live with. It seems my accident—not to mention that Indian—has unsettled me just a mite."

Christa laughed softly. "Yes. I believe you have been unsettled. *Just* a mite," she said.

David struggled with the crutches then finally managed to get himself squarely on the ground, puffing. "Shall we, little sister?" he said, nodding toward the house.

Hearing a tune being played by a string ensemble somewhere inside the stately mansion, and recognizing the song so many were humming now, Stephen Foster's "My Old Kentucky Home," lightened Christa's mood.

"Yes, we shall." She giggled. Then she placed a hand under David's arm, helping him over the gravel of the drive, and headed for the granite front steps of the mansion.

The crackling of a twig to Christa's right side and a swooshing sound as though someone had moved quickly through the thickness of the trees made her jerk her head and look in that direction. Her pulse raced, thinking she had caught sight of a headband and feather. Surely Tall Cloud wouldn't—

Swallowing hard, she turned her head away, trying to quell an overwhelming desire to see him again. She knew the only reason he had made love to her. And it would never happen again. . . .

As she helped David up the steps, the sound of the crowd inside the house blended with the symphony being played by the string ensemble. To Christa it had begun to sound like a grand, exciting social function. Perhaps she could enjoy it!

After knocking on the door, Christa turned and let her eyes scan the dark shadows of the night. Was Tall Cloud out there somewhere? Had he followed her?

The oak door opened and a Negro servant invited Christa and David inside to the foyer. Christa was helped off with her cape and bonnet and then guided along with David down a narrow hallway lighted by wall sconces holding tapered, flickering candles inside clear, blown-glass chimneys.

Christa had been in the house only once before, but she had had time enough to learn that it was so huge it required at least six servants. The rooms were large with high ceilings and beautifully waxed hardwood floors. Each room was heated either by fireplaces or highly ornamented stoves. The living room furniture was formal, in plush, pastel upholstered pieces, and the drop-leaf and lamp tables were crafted from solid maple woods and highly figured black-cherry veneers.

There were upstairs as well as downstairs living rooms.

Imported furniture, such as pedestal tables with British lion and Russian double-headed eagle carvings were among what could be seen in the various rooms of the mansion. The woodwork and stairs were of particularly fine workmanship, and bouquets of fresh flowers were situated throughout, giving the house the aroma of a garden.

The sounds of people and music became louder, and suddenly Christa was faced with a room filled with beautifully attired women and their handsomely dressed escorts. The room was well lighted by an immense chandelier which hung from the center of the ceiling, displaying at least a hundred burning candles. The flames reflected on crystal prisms hanging down like huge teardrops, breaking up the light into beautiful rainbow colors.

All of the furniture had been moved from the room except for an occasional high-backed chair along the outside wall. On a platform at one end of the room, the string quartet continued to play its magical music, and those guests who weren't standing in small, conversational groups were dancing.

Christa watched women as they circled gracefully about the room with their escorts, the skirts of their elegant gowns sweeping along behind them, their heads tilting, their faces shining with pleased smiles. It was an enchanting sight, one which Christa hadn't seen since leaving Boston.

"Christa! David! I was beginning to think you weren't coming!"

Christa stiffened, recognizing the dreaded voice of Harrison Kramer. With a forced smile, knowing that she owed him at least that much for having included David and her on his guest list, Christa swung around and faced the man that she loathed with a passion very different from that which she felt for Tall Cloud.

Her gaze fell upon a man who had been a widower for ten years now, and she noted his stocky build and the thick head of coiffed gray hair that matched his heavy eyebrows.

He was smiling broadly from a face which displayed a sharp-beaked nose, narrow lips, and dark, penetrating eyes which revealed a hungry lust for Christa as he took her right hand and pressed his lips against it.

"My dear Christa, I thought you'd *never* get here," Harrison said in a voice which reflected a southern drawl. "I want you at the head of the table with me when dinner is served, and you've arrived just in time. My guests are just now being instructed to move to the dining room."

"The roads we travel never allow us to set a precise time of arrival at a particular destination," Christa said in a cheerful tone while skillfully easing her hand from his. "You are, I am sure, quite aware of that, Harrison," she added. She hated the dampness of his pudgy fingers, and she recalled that he had the misfortune to be one who perspired profusely even when the temperatures were at the freezing level. Even now she could see a circle of wetness beneath his arms on his smartly tailored, gray frock coat. His expensive men's cologne could not hide the perspiration odor about him, and Christa was not only embarrassed for the man, but herself offended as well.

"Yes, it *is* hard to make plans to arrive on time when one lives out in the wilderness," he said. "But that could be remedied. You know that this house in Seattle could be yours at any time. You'd never have to travel far again for anything. It would all be here within walking distance should you choose to be so daring on the slopes of these Seattle streets."

Harrison directed his attention to David. He gave him a quick once-over, eying the homemade crutch and the bandaged foot. He then smiled broadly at David, offering a handshake.

"Now isn't what I offer too good to refuse?" He chuckled. "David, I hope by now you've convinced your sister that I'm sincere in all that I've offered her."

David leaned his full weight on his left crutch and managed to reach his hand out to accept Harrison's handshake.

He flinched when he felt the dampness, understanding why Christa didn't wish to be with this man. Yet deep inside his heart, he knew that this house, this wealth, and the man who owned all these things, would be best for Christa's future.

"Yep, your offer *is* too good to refuse," David said, smiling. "But I never speak on Christa's behalf. As you can see, she's a mature woman, quite capable of speaking her own mind."

Christa blushed as both pairs of eyes turned to her. She was relieved when Harrison's twenty-five-year-old daughter, Delores, came up to them, her sky blue eyes brilliant with excitement. Delores had only recently arrived from Kentucky, where she had been mourning the death of her wealthy husband. Christa had on one occasion met Delores, but David had not yet had the pleasure.

"Christa!" Delores exclaimed in her Kentucky drawl, taking Christa's hands and squeezing them fondly. "We meet again. I'm *so* glad." Her eyes lowered and she smiled coyly. "You have to know that Papa here speaks of no one as affectionately as he does you."

Christa laughed throatily. "It's good seeing you again, too," she murmured, ignoring the comment about Harrison. She slowly took possession of her own hands again, drew them away, and dropped them to her sides. Then she became aware of something strange happening before her. It was David! He seemed almost in a trance as he watched Delores, as if she were the first woman ever to step before his eyes.

Christa smiled knowingly, realizing that her brother was coming alive in a way unique to those feeling an attraction to the opposite sex.

Delores's gaze slowly moved up and captured David's full attention as she smiled ravishingly at him from her five-foot height of voluptuous proportions. David's heart gave a leap as her blue eyes seemed to penetrate into the depths of his soul. Never had a woman had such an effect on him.

He returned her warm smile, admiring her waist-length

auburn hair drawn severely back from her face and held in place by combs which sparkled with tiny diamonds, matching those around her throat and on the lobes of her ears. Her dress was long sleeved and cut low at the bodice, its fabric an expensive, rose-colored satin which rustled enticingly as she stepped closer to him, offering her hand.

"And you must be David?" She sighed. "David, I've heard so much about you."

David's insides melted as she fit the tininess of her hand in his and pressed warmly. "And you're Delores," David said in a hoarse whisper. "Harrison's daughter. It's a pleasure, ma'am."

With a slow sweep of her eyes, Delores took in the full length of David. He was handsome, she thought, and his eyes bespoke a gentle personality. She saw this as a unique quality in a man and most refreshing!

She eased her hand from his, letting her gaze settle on his bandaged foot. "Oh, my, but you do appear to have had an accident recently." She sighed, clasping her hands together before her. "I do hope it doesn't pain you much."

"No. Not much, ma'am," David said, feeling awkward at her close scrutiny and her closeness. She had to be the prettiest lady he had ever laid eyes on! he thought to himself.

"Delores, maybe you can escort David into the dining room," Harrison suggested, smiling as he observed Delores and David becoming enamored with each other. Though she would be surprised to know it, Harrison was glad to see Delores's attention to this particular man, despite the fact that he was anything but wealthy. In Harrison's mind, the only wealth David possessed was his beautiful, alluring jewel of a sister! Perhaps a relationship between his daughter and Christa's brother could pave the way for his romancing Christa at a much quicker pace. Yes, he would encourage this thing between his daughter and David! There was surely more to gain than to lose.

"Escort this gentleman into the dining room? I shall be

delighted," Delores announced, placing an arm through David's. "And, David, if you have any trouble whatsoever, all you have to do is lean against me. I may be small, but I have much strength in these tiny bones of mine."

Christa suppressed a giggle as she let Harrison take her elbow and guide her into the dining room. She enjoyed seeing David's captivation with this lively, tiny creature grow. She sensed that from this point on she would not be the only person on her brother's mind, and she was glad. For many reasons, she was glad.

Now entranced herself, but for a different reason, Christa let out a soft sigh when she captured the enchantment of this dining room with a quick sweep of her eyes. Long, tapered white candles were the only light in the room. They had been placed at intervals along the full length of the magnificent oak table set with fine linen, silver, glassware, and delicate, expensive china. Wine already sparkled in tall-stemmed glasses, and a low hum filled the room from the conversations of the many guests positioned along each side of the table. Red roses spilling from crystal vases added a final touch of elegance to the scene, and, in the background, the string ensemble which had moved from the parlor, now played softly in a corner. One of the violinists strolled along behind the guests, serenading each one individually.

"Beautiful!" Christa admitted with a sigh. "Absolutely breathtakingly beautiful, Harrison."

"Romantic . . ." Delores said, clinging to David.

"Let's be seated," Harrison suggested, easing Christa into a chair that was just to the left of where he would sit at the head of the table. Christa watched as Delores and David seated themselves opposite her, then looked up at Harrison who had positioned himself at the head of the table yet was still standing to offer a toast to Seattle and its continuing growth.

Glasses clinked, the wine was consumed, and after Harrison seated himself, the servants began serving the meal's many courses. Most impressive was the main course of filet of beef, mushrooms, string beans, Belgian carrots, romaine salad, all of this complemented by a dry white wine.

The conversations around the table were varied. Those who discussed the literary world spoke of new works such as Thoreau's *Walden,* Longfellow's *The Song of Hiawatha,* and Whitman's *Leaves of Grass.* Harrison, always interested in politics, directed his attention to David. "And what are your feelings for our president, Franklin Pierce?" he asked, capturing a mushroom on the tip of his fork, holding it poised before him as he awaited David's response.

David cleared his throat nervously. "He's a personable enough president," he said, toying with his food, feeling Delores's intense stare of interest. He had almost forgotten the thrill of a woman's attention. . . .

"I agree," Harrison said, placing the mushroom in his mouth, eagerly chewing and speaking at the same time. "Though he is a Democrat and the youngest president ever to be in the White House, his personal good looks and brilliant speaking manner impress all who meet him."

"It was quite a battle for him, fighting against three other strong candidates, but he was, for sure, the winner," David said, giving Delores a nervous smile as she continued to watch him.

Harrison gulped down a glass of wine then smiled smugly as a servant quickly refilled the glass. "President Pierce gained his support because he strongly favored the Compromise of 1850, which sought to settle the slavery dispute," he said, stuffing his mouth full of food again.

"Yep," David agreed. "He said something like if the compromise measures are not firmly maintained, the Constitution will be trampled in the dust."

"And what's your feeling about the damn savages here in Seattle and on the islands across from Puget Sound?" Harrison quickly interjected, unsuccessfully trying to stifle a burp behind his hand. "The treaty, though not yet ratified, still offers the Indians too much freedom. So many of our people who live out away from Seattle—like you and Christa, David—are complaining more and more about the Indians pestering them. You know. The Indians call what they do a *nanitch*. Are you and Christa bothered much, David, by the Suquamish?"

Christa's insides splashed cold, yet she could feel heat rising in her cheeks. She tensed and gave David a quick glance, only to find that he was looking back at her, worried wrinkles forming about his eyes and mouth. She pleaded with her eyes. She didn't want Tall Cloud's name mentioned.

Oh, please, David, don't! she prayed silently to herself, She took a slow sip of wine, awaiting his response.

"I'm sure no more than anyone else," David said blandly, placing his fork on the table. He didn't wish to draw attention to Christa or himself where the Indians were concerned. Enough trouble had been caused by the Indians, without letting them be a part of his daily conversation.

"If it were up to me, all savages would be done away with," Harrison growled as an ugly frown creased his brow. "To hell with fooling with reservations. We should get the president behind us and completely rid this community of Indians. What we didn't shoot, we'd hang. The ones who escaped us would surely run up to Canada and leave us to make this city of Seattle the greatest in the country."

Christa's insides twisted with a silent rage. Never had she heard such coldhearted statements. She realized now that no matter what, this was *not* the man with whom she would share her life, much less her bed. She looked at him with distaste and felt the need to direct the discussion away from the Suquamish Indians, for if Harrison so much as spoke Tall Cloud's name in ridicule, she would most surely be forced to stand up and pour a bottle of wine directly over his head!

"You were speaking of President Pierce before bringing

the Indians into the conversation," Christa said coolly. "Isn't it a dreadful shame how his wife, Jane, suffers so?"

Harrison gave Christa a look of admiration. He reached a hand to cover one of hers and held it tightly on the table as he talked. "Now isn't this something?" he said, smiling. "Here's a woman who knows about politics as well as the skills of cooking and being lovely."

Christa cringed beneath his possessive hold, but she didn't dare budge. All eyes were on her now, watching, listening. "It's just that it's so sad about Jane Pierce," she said softly. "She not only lost her son Benjamin in a tragic accident, but she suffers with tuberculosis as well."

"Yes. It was unfortunate that Benjamin had to die in that railroad accident at his young age of eleven," Harrison said, squeezing Christa's hand affectionately. "And only two months before the inauguration. Jane didn't even attend Franklin's inauguration."

"It's a shame how she secludes herself even now in an upstairs bedroom most of the time," Christa sighed. "Washington gossips call her 'the shadow of the White House.' It's unfair. Why can't people keep such cruel comments to themselves? A woman should be able to do as her heart dictates without being gossiped about."

"Ah? And do you speak from experience?" Harrison asked, chuckling. He leaned closer to her and spoke in a bare whisper. "Does your heart guide you in ways forbidden to you, Christa?"

A blush rose quickly to her face. "My word, Harrison," she blurted. "What a thing to say!" Her thoughts went to her intimate moments with Tall Cloud. Oh, how could she ever erase them from her mind? Why had he only pretended to love her? She would never forget him.

Harrison leaned away from her, laughing boisterously, then rose from the table, suddenly ready to offer another toast. "To my beautiful Christa, who blushes as do the roses in the garden when touched by the kiss of the sun," he said thickly. He looked down at her. "And to the woman I hope soon to make my wife."

Christa's eyes flashed up at him in anger, and she seemed to die a slow death inside. "How dare you!" she furiously whispered up at him. She lifted her glass then purposely spilled it and rose quickly from her chair.

"Oh, how clumsy of me," she said, stepping back from the table with wine splotches wet along the front of her gown.

Delores came to her quick assistance. "Oh, how terrible!" she cried. "Come with me. Let me help you remove that from your gown. When we return, we will join everyone in the parlor for dancing."

"Not I," Christa murmured softly as she walked beside Delores from the room.

"Oh, but you mustn't let a simple spill of wine on your gown dissuade you from dancing with my father," Delores said quickly. "Christa, you know how few dances there are in this poor excuse of a city. Why, in Kentucky, after the races, we always danced into the wee hours of the morning."

"Yes. As we also danced in Boston." Christa sighed.

"Then don't you see? You must enjoy the evening. You *must* dance."

Christa gave her a guarded glance. "As you will also do?" she said, wondering if Delores's interests in David would be short-lived since he obviously couldn't dance.

Delores giggled. "No. I don't think so," she said. "I've promised to show David around the grounds. We've such a lovely garden."

Christa smiled to herself. David had not lived for himself for so long now, and she was glad to see the attention being paid him by Delores.

She looked toward the front door as she passed by it, and her thoughts were directed elsewhere. Had she seen Tall Cloud hovering about earlier? Surely not. It had probably been a puff of wind stirring the trees . . .

Eight

The moon was at its highest point in the sky, lighting the garden with a pale white coat which gave the many varieties of flowers a luminous cast. The path made of brick led along a neatly trimmed hedge, behind which the earth had been freshly spaded around rose bushes, velvet-blossomed snapdragons, and other, more exotic flowers imported from other countries. In the center of the garden, a fountain splashed its water into the air, where it burst into shining crystal droplets which floated back down into a circular pond where giant goldfish swam.

David and Delores were a part of this enchanting setting. David affixed his crutches more securely beneath his armpits as he felt Delores slip her arm through the curve of his, at his right side. Being in her company made a scramble of his thoughts, and there was no denying that her petite loveliness stirred his insides in a way no other woman had ever before. And it was because of this that his words seemed to come out all wrong each time he spoke to her.

"Isn't it just too gorgeous, David?" Delores sighed.

"Yes. Quite," David said stiffly, clearing his throat self-consciously.

Delores lifted her chin and inhaled deeply. "Ah, the aroma of the roses. Isn't it just too grand?" She sighed again.

"Yes. It's quite nice," David replied, giving her a nervous, sideways glance, thinking her even more lovely in the moonlight. He had a very strong urge to kiss her, but he forced himself to be a proper gentleman. After all, he had only just met her.

Delores spun away from him, causing her skirt to give off a sensuous swoosh of satin as she circled around to stand before him. "You aren't a man of many words, are you?" she asked, her eyes innocently wide as she looked up at him. "While alone with me, you've said no more than twenty words, I am sure. Is it me? Am I such miserable company that you do not wish to make conversation with me?"

A slow flush rose to David's cheeks. "No. It's not that at all," he gasped.

"Then *what?*" she pouted.

"You're . . . you're so lovely, you render a man speechless," he managed to say in a rush of words.

Delores's delicate fingers went to her cheeks, for now she was devoid of words herself. She was in the company of quite an unusual man. At first he said nothing much at all to her and then when he did, his words were so *sweet*. It caused a rapturous warmth to begin weaving itself around her heart. This man would be hers. She couldn't let him get away. In a sense, he was the answer to all of her dreams. Harrison would not get a chance to discourage this relationship as he had done in the past when a young, handsome man had caught her fancy. She had been forced into two loveless marriages by her scheming father. It would not be allowed to happen again!

"You truly think me lovely?" she asked softly, placing her hands on the muscled strength of David's forearm.

"I'm sure I'm not the first one to tell you that," David said thickly, his gaze lowering to capture the full swells of her breasts. Petite as she was in every other way, this part of her anatomy had been generously endowed. There was no denying that such a sight was firing his insides!

"No. You are not the first to tell me that," Delores murmured, turning on a heel to step away from him and standing close to the pond with her back to him. "As you must know, David, I am twice widowed."

David inched his way over to stand beside her, his crutches causing a strange echoing ring against the bricks beneath them. "I'm sorry," he said hoarsely. "You're so young. I'm sure it's not been easy for you."

Delores turned her eyes up to him. "Both marriages were mockeries," she blurted. "They were both arranged by my father."

"Oh . . ." David uttered, an eyebrow forking.

"My father never seems to have enough riches," she said bitterly. "So he saw to it that I married into wealth despite the fact that both gentlemen were more than twice my age."

"Good Lord!" David gasped.

Delores placed a soft hand on his cheek. "I didn't love either of them," she murmured. "I've been waiting for the perfect man with whom to share my love, David."

David's heart began to thump wildly inside him as she looked up at him in her ravishing beauty "And when you . . . uh . . . find this man, what will you do?" he asked in a mild stammer.

"Marry him," she said matter-of-factly.

"Marry . . . ?"

"Yes."

"But what about Harrison?"

"I've already told father that he will never, never interfere in my life again. I am twenty-five. I've a mind and a heart of my *own*."

As though a magnet pulled him, David slowly lowered his lips to hers. His head began spinning as he took his first taste of her sweetness. When she smoothly twined an arm about his neck, he moved closer to her, kissing her more ardently and reached a hand to fully cup a breast through the satin of her dress. His loins became enflamed, his throat dry. But when a low groan rose from inside him, he became aware of what he was doing and quickly broke free of her.

"I apologize," he said thickly, nervously raking his fingers through his hair. "For a moment I forgot my manners. Surely you must think me less than a gentleman."

"Oh, David!" Delores giggled. "You've no need to apologize. It's not as though I'm your *sister.*"

"But, still, I want to do what's right," David said. "You deserve to be treated like a lady. And ladies . . . don't . . . uh . . . get pawed. Again I apologize."

Delores cocked her head to one side, studying David closely. "I've never met anyone quite like you before," she said. "And, David, no other woman is going to get the chance to have you. You're going to be *mine!*"

"Oh? Is that so?" David chuckled.

"Yes. That's so," Delores said, swinging her skirt around as she once more locked her arm through his. "And I think that decision calls for a glass of bubbly."

"Glass of what?"

"Bubbly. Champagne," Delores said, laughing softly. "Shall we return to the house? Now that I've gotten you to say more than a few words, we've *much* to talk about."

David was flattered. No—he was more than that. It was possible he was falling in love!

Repelled by Harrison's awkwardness and seeing the perspiration thick on his brow, Christa couldn't bear the thought of having to finish this dance with him much less begin another. Smiling politely at those who looked her way, she lifted the skirt of her dress as Harrison once more guided her around the room.

"Harrison, do you think we could stop to get a breath of fresh air?" Christa asked, glancing toward the opened

French doors that led out to the terrace. "You have absolutely winded me."

It had been hard to speak to him in a civil tongue after his bold announcement. But she had decided that she could force herself to stand him just a while longer, for in truth this would be her last time with him, ever. David would just have to set his sights elsewhere for her husband!

"Certainly," Harrison said, waltzing her across the floor until the French doors were reached. Then he placed an arm about her waist possessively, escorting her onto the moon-splashed terrace and then away from it, seeking the privacy of a spot where many towering blue spruce trees were fused together by intermingling branches, forming a wall of sorts.

Christa quietly protested, jerking away from him. "Harrison, I asked for a breath of fresh air, not to be taken to the wilderness," she snapped. "Either you return me to the terrace, or I shall go alone."

Harrison grabbed her by the wrists and yanked her to him cushioning her against his massive chest. His lips were wet, his tongue a crude invasion inside Christa's mouth. When Tall Cloud had kissed her, she had tingled with aliveness. Now, with Harrison, she felt dead inside. Nothing stirred except for her keen dislike of him.

Shoving at his chest only seemed to worsen the situation. He held her closer, his one free hand traveling possessively over her as though she were already his.

Finally able to struggle free, Christa raised a hand and briskly slapped him across the face. "Who do you think you are?" she hissed.

"The man you are going to marry," he snarled, grabbing her wrist, once more pulling her to him. He lowered his lips to the hollow of her throat as his free hand fully cupped a breast through her dress.

Christa shivered with disgust. "I could never marry you," she hissed. "You are sometimes even less than human."

Harrison laughed hoarsely. "I'll show you just how human I am," he said, forcing her downward.

"Stop! Immediately!" Christa cried. "I shall scream."

"And cause a scandal?" he said, having managed to lower her to the ground. He began to lower himself over her.

"A scandal, yes," she argued. "For you, Harrison, it could mean ruin. I would tell everyone that you forced yourself on me."

"And lose the opportunity to live a life of leisure in my mansion?" He laughed. "No woman could stick her nose up to the wealth I offer. You are just trying to play hard to get. And, Christa, I find this refreshing in a woman."

Feeling the full weight of him upon her, Christa began pounding at his chest with her fists. "You are just fooling yourself," she fumed. "I don't want any part of you *or* your money."

"We shall see . . ." he said huskily, slipping a hand up her dress.

The crackling of a twig close by drew Christa's head around. The moon revealed a tall silhouette moving from the shadows of the trees. Christa's breath caught in her throat when she saw the distinct features of Tall Cloud's face as he stepped to the back of Harrison, and towered over him, again dressed in only his loincloth. The shine of the barrel of a rifle swam before Christa's eyes as Tall Cloud brought its butt down onto the back of Harrison's head.

A sickening thud rose into the air as Harrison's body flinched with the blow and he emitted a painful groan. Before his body had a chance to crumple completely down onto Christa, Tall Cloud grabbed him and tossed him aside as if Harrison were no more than a feather.

"Tall Cloud . . ." Christa whispered, too stunned to rise from the ground.

Tall Cloud reached a hand to her. "Did he hurt you, *Nahkeeta?*" he asked, his concern evident.

"No . . ." she murmured, still numb from what had transpired here. She looked from the lifeless form of Harrison to Tall Cloud. "No. I am . . . not . . . hurt."

She took a second look at Harrison. The moon was reflecting a glistening of blood on the back of Harrison's head. "Good Lord, Tall Cloud," she gasped. "Is . . . he . . . dead?"

"And if he were? Would that matter to you?" Tall Cloud growled. He stooped to place an arm about her waist and helped her up from the ground.

"I dislike the man as I've never disliked anyone in my life," she said, now trembling. "But I don't wish him dead."

She steadied herself on her feet and stared up into Tall Cloud's serious face. "Tall Cloud, why are you here? Why did you do this?"

She wanted to fall into his arms, have him so close to her that not even a whisper of a breeze could pass between their bodies. She wanted to thank him for rescuing her from what had been surely leading to rape. But she was remembering too much. She could not forget why Tall Cloud had wanted her to become his bride. And how could she thank him for killing Harrison, if Harrison were indeed dead? Explanations to David, Delores, and the whole community would be hard. Yet, Harrison *had* been forcing her. Harrison was fully at fault here!

Tall Cloud dropped to his knees beside Harrison and placed his cheek over Harrison's mouth. When he felt Harrison's warm breath escape from between his lips, he nodded.

"He is not dead," he said, looking up toward Christa, relieved himself that the white man was alive.

Though death was what this rich merchant deserved, it would only cause more trouble for the Indian community if it were known that an Indian had taken the white man's life. It was best this way. But it wouldn't stop the evil white man from trying to attack *Nahkeeta* again! It seemed to Tall Cloud that even many warriors watching *Nahkeeta* would not be enough to assure her safety while she persisted in being a part of the white man's community!

Christa uttered a quivering sigh as she clasped her hands together before her. "Thank goodness," she said. Then she felt a flush rise to her cheeks when she saw Tall Cloud's gaze sweep over her as he rose slowly from the ground. She now realized that he had never seen her in anything but cotton, and her hair had always been loose and long.

Subconsciously her fingers went to her hair and slipped some stray, fallen locks back into place and then went to the skirt of her dress and smoothed out some wrinkles which had been caused by Harrison's assault upon her. As Tall Cloud now stood over her, still looking down at her intensely, she gave him a slow, nervous smile, invaded herself by emotions which only surfaced in his presence. Suddenly it no longer mattered why she had been angry at him or that he had hurt her. All that mattered was that he was here and that he had saved her from a fate that would have been worse than death. Tall Cloud's presence was even making her forget the clamminess of Harrison's hands upon her flesh and the vile wetness of his kisses. But Tall Cloud's silence was quickly unnerving her.

"You dress as rich white women dress," Tall Cloud grumbled. "Is this what you want of life, *Nahkeeta?*"

He gestured with a hand toward Harrison. "Is he the man you chose over me?" he asked in a softer tone.

"Would I have been struggling with him had I wanted him as my choice?"

"But you were with him. You *did* tell me that your plans were to accept another man as your husband. If not this man, *who?*"

Christa's gaze lowered. "Tall Cloud, there is no other man in my heart but you. Surely you . . . know . . . that."

"But you *and* your brother sent me away."

Christa's eyes rose to meet the challenge of his. "And you really don't know why?" she murmured.

"Should I?"

"You were bartering for me," she accused softly. "You wanted me for the wrong reasons."

"Wrong reasons? My love for you is a wrong reason to want you with me?"

A low groan rose from Harrison. Christa tensed, looking down at him. She saw his hand move. Then she looked quickly back at Tall Cloud. "You must go," she urged, reaching to touch his arm, flooded by fiery sensations. "If he awakens—"

Tall Cloud grabbed Christa and pulled her behind another stand of trees. He drew her brusquely into his arms and kissed her ardently, then released her and fled into the woven web of darkness.

Christa was left breathless. She placed her fingers to her lips, still tasting him. Her knees were weak, yet her heart pounded soundly. She watched him until the night seemed to swallow him whole, then her attentions were once more drawn to Harrison as he emitted another, almost soundless groan.

Hating to, but knowing it was expected of her, Christa fell to her knees beside Harrison just as his eyes slowly began to blink open. She stiffened her shoulders as he stared up at her.

"What . . . happened?" he mumbled, reaching his hand to the back of his head.

Christa's heart skipped a beat. Should he find the blood . . . She had to think of something, and quickly! No one could ever discover that Tall Cloud had inflicted the wound. Her thoughts began spinning as she tried to come up with an answer, one that would draw attention from the man she loved. Harrison hadn't seen Tall Cloud. And since he seemed disoriented, perhaps he didn't remember being struck over the head. All these thoughts raced through her mind as, with a racing pulse, Christa knelt down closer to him. "Harrison, you suddenly fainted," she said, hoping that the slight tremor of her voice wouldn't give her lie away.

"Fainted?" he stammered hoarsely. He once more groaned. "I guess I struck my head when I fell. There seems to be a knot, and I even feel a wetness."

He drew his fingers around before his eyes, and the blood showed bright red beneath the brightness of the moon. "My God," he gasped. "Blood! I'm bleeding!"

Christa recoiled. She bit her lower lip nervously. Then she reached for his arm. "We must get you to the house immediately," she encouraged.

She tugged at him, quite aware of his weight when he pushed himself up and leaned heavily against her as he rose from the ground.

"Yes. I still feel faint," he said, wobbling as Christa began helping him toward the house. His breathing was harsh and his chest heaved wildly in and out with the exertion of walking.

"We'll get you to your bedroom; then Doc Adams can take a look at you," Christa said, then regretted the suggestion. What if the doctor could distinguish between a wound caused by a fall and a wound caused by a blow from a rifle?

Harrison shook his head frantically. "No. No doctor," he growled.

"Oh?" Christa said, lifting an eyebrow as she cast him a quick, questioning glance.

"I don't want to know why I fainted," he said. "If my heart is the cause, I don't wish to know."

"You . . . don't?" Christa asked, glad but confused.

Harrison hung his head. "I'm afraid to know," he murmured. "I don't want to know if I don't have . . . long . . . to live."

Christa's mouth dropped open. This was a much different Harrison from the one she had known. *This* Harrison resembled a helpless little boy. Yet she couldn't care for him any more than before. This little boy could turn back into a cruel, unthinking man at the blink of an eye—a man who had tried to rape her!

Growing tired from her effort to help him, Christa breathed heavily. The steps which led up to the veranda were a welcome sight. She struggled with Harrison as she helped him up, first one step and then another. And when the veranda was reached Christa flinched as he jerked quickly away from her.

"I shall now make it on my own, thank you," he said dryly.

Clearing his throat and straightening his frock coat, Harrison walked away from her, sluggish in his movements. Christa didn't follow along behind him, not wishing to be a part of what was soon to transpire in the large parlor. She steadied herself and listened as several people rushed toward Harrison, full of questions about his welfare, since he did not appear to be himself at all. The gasps and low mutterings followed along after him, and suddenly the four-string ensemble ceased to entertain with its music.

Christa stepped to the doorway as Harrison's voice rang out over the crowd, explaining that he was ailing and had to retire for the evening, then excusing himself. Christa watched as the crowd began to disperse. She couldn't help but wonder what Tall Cloud would do next in his campaign to claim her as his.

Nine

There was a crispness in the air as September passed into October. Christa was gathering the last of the string beans from her garden and dropping them into a wicker basket hung over her left arm. The stiff breeze whipped at her bonnet and the ties of her apron, and Christa was glad that she had chosen to wear the high-necked dress with wide collar and long sleeves which protected her from the early morning chill. She had left her shawl behind, always hating having to fight it as it slipped and slid around her shoulders each time she stooped to pick a handful of beans.

Placing a hand to the small of her back, Christa moaned softly as she straightened herself, stretching her spine. She looked toward the Sound as it was her habit to do, full of thoughts of Tall Cloud. It seemed years to her since the night of the dance, when in truth it had only been two weeks. Strange how Tall Cloud would seem to forget her completely, and then suddenly appear again when least ex-pected. She would never forget how he had saved her from Harrison's attempted rape. . . .

Looking toward the house, Christa could see that David had given up his vigil at the window. He was convinced that Tall Cloud would not come again. Too much time had elapsed since that day Tall Cloud had offered gifts. Oh, if only David knew the truth about Harrison's strange, sudden illness and Tall Cloud's timely appearance that night!

Giggling, Christa resumed her chore of picking beans, amused about the many trips David had made into town, with all sorts of excuses, yet always ending up at Delores's house. Since David couldn't man the horse and buggy himself, and since he wouldn't ever think of leaving Christa alone at the farm, she had had to go with him, which in turn meant that she had also been forced to meet with Harrison. But she had made herself tolerate him for David's sake. It had been heartwarming to watch the developing courtship between her gentle brother and his chosen. David had spent the past several years "fathering" Christa. It was only right that he now allowed himself the pleasures of courting Delores.

Christa cried out when her fingers caught hold of a cocklebur instead of a green bean. She placed her basket on the ground and put her throbbing finger to her lips and sucked on it, unaware of movement behind her. When she felt an arm swing around her waist, she let out a soft scream. And as she tried to turn to see who it was, she found herself scooped up from the ground and into strong arms and staring unbelievingly into the deep gray of Tall Cloud's eyes.

"Tall Cloud . . ." she gasped, having no other recourse than to cling to him around his neck as he began to run toward the Sound with her.

"What on earth do you think you're doing?" she protested, wriggling furiously. Each time he decided to approach her again, she mused, his way of doing so was different and full of surprises. His methods were as complex as the man—this chief of a band of Suquamish!

The pistol in Christa's apron pocket hung heavily down away from her and slapped hard against Tall Cloud's bare thighs with each lift of his foot. His loincloth flapped wildly in the wind and his breath came in shallow rasps as he continued to ignore what she was saying. His eyes were focused straight ahead, his jaw and mouth set firmly.

"Tall Cloud, put me down," Christa ordered, not giving

up her fight for freedom so easily. She wanted to be with
him, but something seemed amiss here. She watched as he
scrambled down the slope's steep face of rock and mud
which led to the waters of the Sound. And as they reached
the beach and he continued to run soundlessly along it,
Christa caught her first sight of his fancy canoe moored at
the edge of the water.

She gave Tall Cloud a quick look. "Tall Cloud, you're
not—"

"You are going with me to Pahto Island," he said flatly.

Christa paled. "Pahto Island? Where is . . . ?" she asked
in a bare whisper. Then she spoke more boldly. "You're
surely not abducting me, Tall Cloud," she said, though his
intent became startling clear as he splashed into the water
and eased her from his arms into the waiting canoe.

"It is the only way to get your brother to agree to your
becoming my wife," he said.

When he saw her rise quickly to her feet with protest
written all over her lovely face, he gave the canoe a quick
push away from the shore, jolting her back on the seat.
Swiftly he jumped into the canoe, lifted the paddle, and
plunged it into the water.

He had the canoe out in deeper water before Christa
could manage to get to a standing position again. Instead,
she found herself clutching tightly onto the seat while the
wind whipped wildly about her face. Her bonnet flew from
her head. Even the bow came untied in the fierce turbulence
as the canoe slid smoothly through the water.

"My bonnet . . ." she cried softly as it fluttered away
from her to land in the water. Her hair now whipped more
freely about her face, across her shoulders, and down her
back.

Clouds stretched low and gray over the water. The chill
penetrated Christa's flesh, causing mountains of goose
bumps to rise on arms covered only by the thin layer of
cotton of the sleeves of her dress.

"Tall Cloud, this is insane," she cried, looking back over her shoulder. Her cabin became smaller and smaller as the canoe rushed on through the silvery foam of the water.

"Take me back, Tall Cloud," Christa urged. "This is no way to get David to agree to our marriage. You'll be hunted down and shot, or hung!"

Tall Cloud's shoulders corded and the muscles of his powerful arms flexed as he pulled the paddles through the water. "When I go to your proud brother and explain to him the way things must be, he *will* agree," he said dryly. "No harm will come to me. You'll see."

Christa's green eyes sparkled with rising anger. She contemplated jumping into the water and swimming for shore, but two thoughts dissuaded her. The shoreline was much too far away, and the water was severely cold.

Flipping her hair back from her eyes, she shouted at Tall Cloud. "Even if David should agree to the marriage for whatever reasons are forced upon him, I won't speak vows with you. Tall Cloud, you do not want me. You only want alliance with the white man. And, Tall Cloud, I do not appreciate being taken by force!"

Tall Cloud gave her a frown from across his shoulder. "I want you for *you*," he said flatly. "The alliance becomes of less importance to me each day I am without you. To have you has become an obsession. Surely you know that now, my *Nahkeeta*."

A spray of saltwater fell upon Christa's lips. With the back of a hand she wiped her lips free of the briny taste, then spoke more softly to the man who set her insides afire just by his nearness. "You can say these things and not mean them," she argued. "But I know that a chief's first obligations are to his people. A white woman is *not* a part of such responsibilities to his people unless this white woman can somehow benefit them. You said as much earlier, Tall Cloud. Don't try to deny it now."

"You will see," he said. "I shall show you the truth by actions, not words."

Christa began to defend herself again, but he turned his head around to stare straight ahead where the Sound seemed to stretch endlessly before them. The clouds had now lifted, enabling Christa to see into the far distance. On either side of them the scenery was spectacular. The narrow beaches rose to shallow shelves which folded into raw, clay cliffs. The sheer, fog-dampened walls of the cliffs glistened with moisture, and at their tops stood tangled jungles of fir trees.

Sea otters and porpoise rose and fell in the water's playground, and fish of all sizes and shapes moved like shadows in the deep, clear water. Christa could even see them weaving between the underwater sand and stones and the seaweed waving in the depths of the water. A bald eagle soared overhead, its wings wide and majestic, and ducks scooted along the water in a vee formation.

Christa sighed, sensing the peaceful aura of this northwest country, yet inside she was a mass of nervous tremors. Abducted! How could he? This was a deed which would not only cause Tall Cloud harm, but his people as well. She now doubted his worth as a chief, and she feared his people would also.

"His people . . ." she suddenly whispered, glancing quickly around her in the direction of Enati Island. She now remembered that Tall Cloud had mentioned that he was taking her to a Pahto Island. This was an island unfamiliar to her! Was it also one unfamiliar to his people?

Then she realized his purpose in taking her to an island other than the one on which he made his residence. If the authorities came searching for her on Enati Island, she wouldn't be there! Tall Cloud had planned this quite well. And would he have her all to himself? Surely he didn't have *two* islands of Indians!

Christa became aware of the sudden change in the direction of the canoe. A bend in the Sound was challenged and left behind as Tall Cloud now began paddling toward a sharp rise of land in the distance. She clung to the sides of the canoe, watching the island drawing nearer. The shore line went up rapidly to high hills, taller and much more impressive than those of Tall Cloud's Enati Island.

Sea gulls swept up and around the canoe as it continued onward. And then Tall Cloud beached it where the receding sea laced over the damp, steel gray sand. Christa looked up at the walls of rock. A shiver coursed through her as she wondered what awaited her at the top. The island appeared to be so cold. It most surely was isolated!

Tall Cloud hopped from the canoe and secured it on the beach. He went to Christa and lifted her from the canoe into his arms and carried her through ankle-deep water. As they reached dry sand, he removed her from his arms then dragged the canoe behind some boulders, to hide it from possible passersby.

"Tall Cloud, you're wrong to do this," Christa said, hugging herself as she trembled beneath the strong chill of the sea breeze.

Tall Cloud stepped back and eyed the spot where the canoe was hidden, seeing if any part of it was visible. When he concluded that it was concealed well enough, he turned his full attention to Christa.

"While you are here with me, I will see to it that you are comfortable," he said hoarsely.

He saw that she was shivering and went to her to draw her snugly into his arms. He held her tightly, consumed by his heartbeats as he felt her breasts crushed against his bare chest and smelled the sweet fragrance of her windblown hair.

"You're cold," he said. "Let me warm you with my body for a moment, then we will go and make a fire in my lodge."

"Your lodge? You have residence also on this island?" Christa murmured, enjoying for the moment the warmth she was absorbing from his closeness, yet not wanting to get caught up in the mindless rapture he so easily induced.

But she knew that it was a futile effort to fight her feelings. She knew that while they were here alone, much would be shared between them. She hoped that her love for him was stronger than any hurt he could inflict by being with her again.

"This island named *Pahto,* which means 'standing high,' has belonged to my tribe of the Suquamish Indians for many moons," he said softly. "My people followed my grandfather from this island when my father was a small boy. He hoped to find a better life across the *whulge,* which you and all white men call Puget Sound."

"And?" Christa asked, drawing away from him, looking up into his expressive gray eyes and seeing a faraway look in them.

"You have seen," he grumbled. "The white men came."

"Why did your people move to Enati Island? Why didn't they come back to this island?"

"All along my people thought the move to Enati Island would be temporary," he said. "They all thought they would soon return to the land that has now been named Seattle. Pahto Island was left for our ancestors' spirits to claim as theirs."

"And you bring me here . . . to . . . disturb your spirits?" Christa asked, glancing up at the wall of rock that towered over her. She shivered involuntarily when a low, whistling sound rose eerily from somewhere close, and she had to wonder if she and Tall Cloud were truly alone. Perhaps there *were* spirits! But a strong gust of wind made her laugh to herself, for she realized that the wind had fooled her. Its whistle seemed to originate from somewhere far off, beginning softly and building to a crescendo as it echoed against the floor of the beach.

"It is only right that my woman, my future bride, come

to Pahto Island for my ancestors' spirits to smile upon her with approval," Tall Cloud said, proudly lifting his chin.

He placed an arm about Christa's waist and began leading her down the beach, stopping where steps had been carved into the side of the rock wall. Tangles of morning glory vines decorated the steps with dots of blue flowers, leaving hardly a place free to step without crushing the lovely, opened velvet petals.

Oblivious to this, Tall Cloud helped Christa up the steps, which were slippery from the dew-laden vines, and urged her upward at a steady pace. The steps were so steep, Christa knew that if she looked down and behind her she would grow dangerously dizzy, and she welcomed the strength of Tall Cloud's arm still wrapped possessively about her waist as she desperately lifted the skirt of her dress which constantly threatened to trip her.

Becoming breathless from the endless climb, Christa gasped for air, but she was too stubborn to ask him to let her rest for a moment before venturing onward. Surely they would reach the top soon. She knew one thing for sure. She wouldn't look up to see how much farther they had to go. The threat of toppling backward was an ever-present fear.

The higher they climbed the more life was found on the sides of the cliff. A nest of bald eagle babies was within reach on a small shelf of rock; cedar trees had somehow managed to grow out of the rock to point straight and statuesquely tall toward the sky; and thick beds of moss grew in heavy patches along other outcroppings of rock.

The wind howled, the ocean splashed incessantly, and a pungent smell of dampness invaded Christa's senses. But above all, her bones were taking on an unbearable ache. Just as she felt that she couldn't take another step, they reached the top.

Christa let the skirt of her dress fall from her arms and ripple down to hang once more about her ankles. She was

not surprised to find a totem pole close by, remembering
the many she had seen on Enati Island. Then her gaze traveled farther, away from the edge of this dangerously steep
cliff where she still stood. A village of huts made of poles
covered by mats stood deserted and crumbling. Vine tangle
grew in and out of most of the doors, windows, and smoke
holes in the roofs, and the silence was almost overwhelming.

Tall Cloud took a step forward. He outstretched his arms
and raised his eyes to the sky. *"Ah-tah lah 'tah lah!"* he
chanted. *"Wakush tiyee a winna!* It is good to come home
to the island of my ancestors to pause from the cares of
leadership! Oh, powerful spirits, welcome me and my
woman, *Nahkeeta.* Much stands in our way of becoming
wholly as one."

Christa felt tears stinging her eyes. This scene that Tall
Cloud enacted before her was so touching it made goose
bumps rise on her flesh. He was a unique man, and it was
this uniqueness—his continuing mystique—that made her
attraction to him grow stronger now as they were alone
together, away from the interference of any man, white or
Indian.

But she had to remind herself why she was here. It was
not under favorable circumstances. And no matter how
much she wished to be with him, she couldn't let him think
she approved of being taken hostage.

Tall Cloud went to the tall totem pole and looked in silence at the carved figures which decorated it, most of
which were replicas of his ancestral crest, the raven. Many
moons had passed since this mortuary column had been
erected in memory of his great-grandfather. Tall Cloud's
grandfather had placed the totem pole on this sacred ground
as a part of the ceremony of assuming his predecessor's
title and prerogatives.

Tall Cloud could feel the presence of his great-
grandfather's spirit like an embrace as the wind moved

gently against and around him. He closed his eyes and silently absorbed the moment, knowing that if he moved only a few steps to the right, he would see the bones of his great-grandfather, preserved beneath a thin layer of rock where his skin-wrapped body had at one time been placed in a canoe which had been pointed toward the setting sun to light his way to the land of the dead. When his body had faded away to bones, the canoe had been removed and the bones left beneath the shallow rock to rest, hopefully undisturbed for eternity.

A slight sneeze behind him jerked Tall Cloud from his reverie. He turned on a bare heel and saw his *Nahkeeta* rubbing her nose as another sneeze erupted. Feeling the cold dampness in the air on this sunless day, Tall Cloud went to Christa and once more draped an arm about her waist possessively.

"Come," he said. "I will take you to a dwelling that I have prepared for your arrival."

Christa's eyes shot upward, seeing so much written in his stern expression. "You actually came here and prepared for my arrival ahead of time?" she asked, lifting the skirt of her dress as it became tangled in the briers of the tall grass through which they were now making their way. "How long have you been planning this abduction, Tall Cloud?"

"Since the day my bride price was refused," he grumbled.

"As it will be again," she said icily. "Surely you know this."

"You are my bride price," he said dryly. "To get you back as a sister, your brother must agree to my terms."

"And if David doesn't?"

Tall Cloud's silence and sudden set jaw was answer enough to fill Christa with a strange coldness. Surely he wouldn't harm her if David didn't agree to let her marry him.

A hut in more repair than the others was finally reached. The clinging vines had been removed from the rush-mat walls, roof, and windows, leaving only a few dried roots that had clung stubbornly to the hut's side. The door was open in an invitation to enter.

"My dwelling is your dwelling," Tall Cloud said, gesturing with an arm for Christa to go inside ahead of him.

Lifting the skirt of her dress even higher, Christa went inside, scarcely breathing, hoping at least for cleanliness, since she would be making her residence there for whatever time Tall Cloud required. She let out a rush of air when she saw that her fears for the most part had been unfounded.

The interior was semi-dark, with light filtering downward from the smoke hole and along the floor from the two opened windows. From what Christa could tell, this hut was not unlike the one in Tall Cloud's village on Enati Island. The main difference was the lack of skins spread out on the floor and hung along the walls.

The floor was lined with what appeared to be newly bound rush mats, and the shelves along the walls had a supply of food placed on them. There was no bed made up on the floor, but a roll of blankets along the far wall made her believe that a bed would be made from them.

Tall Cloud went to the fire space where he had already placed an abundance of wood and twigs for a fire. "I will soon fill our dwelling with warmth," he said, moving to his haunches, already working at starting the fire. "Then I will prepare a feast for you, my *Nahkeeta*. I want to make you *want* to stay with me. Let me show you all my skills that you would benefit from when you become my wife."

Christa trembled from the cold. The draft was severe through the opened windows and the rush mat door was only half hanging on what appeared to be twines of rush fiber. She dropped the skirt of her dress to drape snugly around her ankles and crept closer to the fire space when a quiver of flames became visible among the scattered twigs. She knelt down beside Tall Cloud and held a hand over the crackling and popping of twigs, gathering the warmth of the fire as best she could against her palm. Then she tensed as Tall Cloud reached to wrap his fingers about her hand and looked imploringly into her eyes.

"We shall share much together while alone here on my ancestors' island," he said thickly. "Let yourself enjoy . . . partake *in* the joy of togetherness."

Christa could feel the web of enchantment weaving the magic that had bound them together before in moments of sensuality. She had to gain control of her senses as well as the situation to prove to Tall Cloud that the way he had chosen to approach David this time was totally wrong.

Jerking her hand away, she rose quickly to her feet. There was no denying the pounding of her heart or the rush of need miserably burning her insides. With nervous fingers she smoothed the wrinkles from her skirt as she placed her back to him.

Filled with angry humiliation, Tall Cloud followed after her. He placed his hands on her shoulders, digging his fingers deeply into her flesh as he roughly turned her to face him. "You are being foolish," he growled, his face marred by a frown of disappointment.

"Just because you say I am doesn't make it so," Christa argued.

"You love me. Why deny me?" he demanded.

She winced beneath the tightness of his fingers. "Tall Cloud, you're hurting me," she cried softly.

"To love, one must sometimes feel pain," he retorted.

"I have experienced enough pain caused by you," Christa said, boldly challenging him with her eyes and a set jaw. She commanded herself not to feel the throbbing where his fingers were punishing her.

"I will right that wrong," he insisted. "But you must *accept,* not reject the way in which I choose to do this thing."

"How can I when you so unwisely bring me to this . . . this . . . island occupied solely by your ancestors' spirits?"

she fumed. A tremble traveled through her, visible to Tall Cloud. "How can I sleep one night here when . . . when I won't know what or who may slip in through the door or window to hover over me . . . to . . . watch me . . . or worse?" she questioned hotly.

"Each wind is the breath of some being who lived here before me," he defended, dropping his hands to his sides. "This is how the spirit world will come to us. In no other way, *Nahkeeta*. There is no need to be afraid."

He tried to draw her into his arms, to comfort her, but again she worked herself free. "Please don't, Tall Cloud," she murmured, lowering her eyes for fear he would read her need for him in their depths. "I only wish to be returned home. David will be frantic."

"I will go to David. I will tell him the way it must be," he said, once more working with the fire. "I will go soon, before he involves other white men in our personal struggles."

"Oh, Tall Cloud!" Christa sighed. "Why don't you see how useless this is?"

He refused to listen. He had promised her food. He would fulfill this promise then hurry on to speak to David. Tall Cloud knew that time was in his favor because of David's injury. David couldn't travel to town without complete assistance, so the waiting, alone, could do him good. Perhaps David's worry for his sister building up over a period of hours would make him come to a much quicker decision to say yes to all that Tall Cloud would suggest.

Smiling, he set about preparing a warm, nourishing meal for his *Nahkeeta*. He placed several small, round rocks in the sand under the fire in the fire space and waited for them to get hot. While waiting, he chose a water-tight basket made of sewn spruce tree roots and filled it with water that he had brought earlier to the hut. Wild onions and carrots and *wappatoe* roots, which were round, red, egg-sized potatoes, had been dug by a Suquamish woman for Tall

Cloud's use, and he now placed them in the water. Then he added the heated stones to make the soup warm and pleasant to the stomach.

When it was finished, Tall Cloud poured a good portion of the soup into an intricately carved wooden bowl. Nodding toward the rush-mat flooring, he said, *"Nahkeeta,* sit and let me offer you nourishment before I leave Pahto Island to go speak with your brother."

He reached for two spoons made of mountain goat horns and placed one before Christa and then himself.

Christa had watched his preparation of the soup. Up to the point where rocks had been added to the liquid, she had thought it had looked appetizing enough. But now . . .

"Nahkeeta, you must eat now," Tall Cloud growled. "I may not return for many hours."

"But . . . the rocks?" she said softly, easing down beside him.

"I understand that the Suquamish way of heating food is different from the white man," he said. "We do not use iron pots and pans as you do. We use our own sewn baskets which would burn if placed directly in the fire. The heated rocks are the source of heat to our food."

"But rocks are normally dirty," Christa said, visibly shuddering.

"They are as clean as your tongue which tastes all the food that enters your mouth," he argued. He held the bowl out toward her. "Here. Eat."

"Aren't you hungry? There is only one bowl."

"You will share my bowl," he said. "With the Suquamish, it is a mark of great favor to be offered food from the chief's bowl. With you, my *Nahkeeta,* it will be a mark of great favor to *me,* to share it with *you."*

"I *am* hungry," she murmured. "And I am cold. Perhaps the soup will help me with both these complaints." She smiled nervously up at Tall Cloud as she accepted the bowl from him. She even let him place a strange sort of spoon between the fingers of her right hand.

"It is good," he encouraged. "You will see. And it is quite nourishing."

Sinking the spoon into the liquid and capturing some solid pieces of carrot and wild onion she slowly lifted it to her lips and tasted. Her eyes widened in wonder. The taste was bland but surprisingly pleasant. She swallowed the first spoonful, then another, then offered the bowl to Tall Cloud.

"Thank you," she murmured. "It *is* quite good."

"So you approve of my skills as a cook?" He chuckled, relaxing his shoulders now that she was becoming more relaxed in his presence.

"Well, I can't say that anyone would hire you to cook in Seattle's restaurants." She giggled. "But for now . . . for *us* . . . you'll do."

"Smoked salmon is the main food of the Suquamish," he said. "The salmon is to the Suquamish what the buffalo is to the Plains tribes of Indians. The sea also provides a tremendous quantity of edible mollusks. My people have always said that when the tide goes out, the table is set."

"David and I depend on what we plant in our garden and the supplies I store in my food cellar, which we buy in Seattle or gather from the forest," she said. "But you have seen what we eat and how I prepare the food."

"You will be taught many different ways to cook my people's food to please me," he said hoarsely, taking several spoonfuls of soup, watching her all the while. He eagerly absorbed her loveliness and ached to have her, but he knew their moments of fulfillment would come much later.

"I surely won't be here that long," she said. "You will come to your senses and take me home. When you speak with David, he will convince you what must be done."

Tall Cloud placed the bowl back in her hands and rose to his feet. "I must go now to prove you wrong," he said. "Marriage is a social contract, not merely between man and wife but between respective families. Your brother must give his approval or else."

Christa's eyes shot upward. "Or else?" she murmured.

Tall Cloud gave her a long, bland stare then turned on a heel and left her.

The food no longer was pleasant to her tongue, and the silence in the hut became forbidding. Christa placed the bowl on the rush-mat flooring and rose quickly to go after Tall Cloud. But when she stepped from the hut, she discovered he was already gone.

Hugging herself, she looked slowly around her. She was alone, but she felt the eerie presence of many. . . .

Ten

Feeling the need for reinforcements should Christa's brother refuse to cooperate, Tall Cloud first traveled to Enati Island and banded together several canoes filled with his most fierce-looking warriors.

The Chinook canoes, hewn out of red cedar logs which had been beautifully carved with designs of ravens, eagles, whales, and human faces and burned on the outside to eliminate splinters, now traveled silently over the waves. The short, broad paddles moved gracefully in and out of the water, sending the canoes swiftly along. The wind-hurled spray of the Sound was cold and invigorating as it settled onto Tall Cloud's sleek body. He inhaled deeply, puffing his chest out proudly as his gaze moved from canoe to canoe and from warrior to warrior. It had been too long since they had had a purpose to travel the Sound as one mind and one body. Those who had disagreed with his choice of wife had stayed behind. They were Tall Cloud's most faithful followers who accompanied him this day on his journey of the heart. Most of these warriors were his same age and had shared stories of their puberty rite experiences when they had gathered around evening campfires many moons ago. It had been good, the sharing, Tall Cloud recalled silently.

The Suquamish Indians were known as "canoe people," unlike the tribes of Indians who traveled solely on horses.

Tall Cloud let his mind drift back to the time when he had been told by his father that ownership of a canoe was a religious responsibility, and in order to become a canoe owner, he would have to fast and meditate in the wilderness for days. Tall Cloud had been taught a song to sing as he walked through the woods, seeking a tree to bless him with the ownership of a canoe. If his prayers were answered, a tree would choose him to be a canoe owner, and it would sing back to him. Then he would make a camp at the bottom of the tree and stay there to learn all the responsibilities of canoe ownership.

When the tree was satisfied that he was worthy of having a canoe, it would teach him how to fell it and how to trim its branches. Then the tree would teach him another special song, and, as he returned to his village singing the song, the tree would follow him down the mountainside to the village, where it would be made into a canoe.

Tall Cloud smiled to himself. As a young boy he *had* been blessed. A western red cedar tree had chosen him, and he traveled in it now; it had been carved to perfection to fit his image of chief. His crest in the shape of a raven was prominent over all other designs on his personal canoe, for even as a child he wore the raven crest tattooed on his arm to represent his family of chiefs.

Tall Cloud's thoughts were suddenly filled with the duties of the moment, for through the beginnings of a softly falling rain he could make out David's cabin outlined by the cedars, pines, and oak trees rising tall behind it. A faint quivering of lamplight glowed from the house, and smoke rose gray and spiraling from the chimney.

Determined to get his way this time with this proud brother of *Nahkeeta,* Tall Cloud sank his paddle more deeply into the water, catching it and forcing it beneath the canoe.

The canoe rode high in the water, then shuddered as a large wave crested and fell against it. The sky was a hazy gray and thunder rumbled ominously from valley to valley and mountain to mountain. Yet only a cold mist of rain continued to fall.

With the shoreline now close enough to beach the canoes, Tall Cloud shouted commands to his warriors until all were out of the canoes and standing about David's house. The shine from a rifle barrel could be seen at the side of each Indian, and their faces were solemnly directed at Tall Cloud as he towered over them.

Proud of his warriors' attentiveness to him, Tall Cloud stood before them and spoke in his deep, commanding voice. "You will not be required to enter the white man's dwelling unless you see the need," he said in almost a whisper so David wouldn't be alerted that they were near. "Watch through the window and door. If the white man threatens me in any way, make your entrance."

Doubling his right fist and raising it into the air he leaned his face closer to his men and spoke more harshly. *"Nah! Skookum Kanaway,"* he said. "I *must* make alliance with the white man. It's best for you and your families, my brave warriors."

Grunts and affirmative nods were the responses. He nodded his own head, lowered his arm, then turned and went to the door. In one jerk, he had it open to find David sitting beside the fire, anguish etched across his pale, white face.

David's heart seemed to plummet to his feet when he heard the door open. He looked quickly toward it, and, this time, instead of being angry at Tall Cloud's rude, unannounced entry, he was glad. Tall Cloud's feelings for Christa would be reason enough for him to go in search of her. It was surely the Haida Indians who had abducted her. It was common knowledge that women were kidnapped and used as slaves in their camps.

Trying to rise to his feet, then finding the pain in his foot too severe to do so, he settled back into the chair. "Tall Cloud," he blurted. "Thank God you've come."

Tall Cloud was taken aback. His eyebrows arched. Never had he expected to be greeted so eagerly by this white man, especially now! "You welcome me with open arms, proud brother?" he mumbled. "I have to question why. I know of your true feelings for me."

David leaned up in his chair, tired of being rendered helpless by his injured foot. Mounting a horse was impossible as was the chore of securing a horse to a buggy. Since Christa's disappearance, he had died a slow death inside, being incapable of going for help to get a search party together. Perhaps Tall Cloud was the answer!

"It's Christa," David explained. "She's been abducted and surely by the Haida, Tall Cloud. You've got to go find her. Bring her safely home. I've heard horrible tales of what is expected of a woman taken captive by the Haida."

David's words were absorbed inside Tall Cloud's brain. It hadn't occurred to Tall Cloud that David would suspect anyone other than himself for his *Nahkeeta's* disappearance. The thought somewhat amused him, and a wry smile lifted his lips before he once more grew serious, for this was not a time to think on tormenting this white man.

"Nahkeeta is safe," he said with a serious expression on his face, though he would have enjoyed taunting David for awhile by pretending he also believed *Nahkeeta* was held captive by the Haida and that he, Tall Cloud, refused to help the white man with stubborn eyes.

David's mouth dropped open. His fingers tightened on the arms of the chair. "How do you know that she is all right?" he said hoarsely.

"I have seen her," Tall Cloud said, taking his time to reveal the full truth to a man who was responsible for Tall Cloud's abducting *Nahkeeta* in such a way.

"You . . . have . . . seen her?"

"Yes. I have seen her. And she is well, proud brother."

"How? Where?" David persisted.

"Isn't it enough to know that she is well?"

David ran his fingers nervously through his hair. "Tall Cloud, will you quit playing word games with me?" he growled. "My sister. Please tell me where she is, if you have, indeed, seen her."

Tall Cloud moved, barefoot, to tower over David. "Would you be pleased to know that the Haida do not have your sister?" he said dryly, folding his arms across his bare chest.

David blanched. "If not the Haida . . . then . . . who?" he gasped.

"Nahkeeta is safe. I have seen to that. But I cannot say any more until you cooperate fully with me and agree to what I ask of you."

"You!" David snarled. "I accused the wrong Indians! You are the one responsible for her abduction!"

"Yes," Tall Cloud said dryly. "She is held hostage by me, but she is safe *and* comfortable, proud brother."

With his shoulders slumped and with a keen sense of defeat, David settled back into the chair. "I guess I should be relieved to know that Christa isn't with the Haida since at least you do have feelings for her," he said. "But how can I? The future you want for her could be as questionable as if she were held by the Haida."

"You are wrong, proud brother."

"Am I?" David said, lifting an eyebrow as he looked up into steel gray eyes. "A life with *any* Indian is not best for a white woman. Surely you see this, Tall Cloud. What can I do to convince you of the wrong you have done here?"

"As I will continue to argue with you how wrong you are," Tall Cloud said stubbornly.

"Tall Cloud, I plead with you. Bring Christa home. Forget her. Don't you have any squaws in your village who are better trained to be a chief's wife?"

"Nahkeeta is my choice over all women—white and Indian. And she returns my love. The only thing standing in the way of her full commitment is *you,* proud brother."

"I can't believe she would want to live your way of life,"

David argued, slowly moving his hand down to the side of the chair out of Tall Cloud's view. He had placed his shotgun there, loaded and ready. He knew the risks of using it on this particular Indian, a revered chief, but if worse came to worse. . . .

When his hand made contact with the cold steel of the shotgun barrel, he rested it there, ready.

"Her love for me is strong," Tall Cloud said, his chin lifted proudly.

David paled, once more aware of the true meaning of the Indian's words. For him to believe she loved him so intensely, Christa would have had to share intimate moments with him. It made a sick feeling grab at his gut, as he realized that his sweet and innocent sister had been deceived into making love with the Indian. Now, even if arrangements could be made between Harrison and Christa, Harrison would realize that she was no longer a virgin and believe that he had married a loose woman.

Such a thought kindled the anger inside David, and his fingers circled the barrel of the shotgun. His heart pounded wildly, and he hoped that he had the courage to do what was going to be required of him if Tall Cloud didn't back down and agree to bring Christa home.

"I will ask you once more to return Christa to her rightful place in the world," David snarled, leaning forward.

"My reason for being here is not to be ordered to bring *Nahkeeta* back to you," Tall Cloud argued. "I have come to tell you that you must agree to let me have *Nahkeeta* as my wife. Once you agree she will return home, but only long enough to hear you personally give her your blessing. It is important to her and to me that you fully agree to this marriage."

David tossed his head as he laughed sarcastically. "It is as it was from the beginning," he said. "Your crazy notion that marrying my sister would make you favored more by all white people?"

"I want her only because my heart is empty without her," Tall Cloud defended. "Anything else that comes with the marriage is only a bonus."

"I hate to disappoint you again, Tall Cloud," David laughed. "But you can't have my sister or any bonus acquired by marriage to her. Now you go to your island and return her to me, or I will get the law after you."

"To send the white man to my island would be foolish," Tall Cloud growled. "It could mean a sure, swift death for *Nahkeeta*. If I can't have her, no one can. I will kill her first."

Rage tore through David like tornadic winds unleashed. He grabbed the shotgun from where it leaned against the chair and pointed it threateningly toward Tall Cloud. "Sorry, Tall Cloud," he said, hating that his voice was trembling. "But I must kill you before you get the chance to return to your island to give orders to kill my sister."

A rush of feet sounded and the cabin filled with Indians armed with rifles, startling David so much that he dropped his shotgun onto his lap. He was numb with fright as Tall Cloud grabbed the shotgun from him and tossed it to one of his Indians who stood across the room.

"My warriors protect me well, don't you think?" Tall Cloud laughed.

"I should have killed you that very first day you showed interest in my sister," David growled, then swallowed hard as all of the Indians' rifles were lifted and aimed at him.

"If you wish a speedy death, continue speaking harshly to me in front of my warriors," Tall Cloud said. He gestured with a hand toward his men. "They haven't tasted the thrill of killing a white man for many moons."

Taking a step toward David, Tall Cloud touched the gold locks of David's hair. "It has been a long time since a scalp has been taken," he said thickly. "You see, it is I, their proud chief, who has discouraged such actions. All I would have to do is give the word. . . ."

David recoiled, his face flaming with a mixture of fear and humiliation. "And what *do* you plan to do with me?" he asked shallowly, moving his gaze slowly from Indian to Indian. Most were short and squat in comparison to Tall Cloud. But they were all dressed the same, in only a brief loincloth.

"Leave you to have time to think more clearly," Tall Cloud said, already moving toward the door. He gave David a stern look from across his right shoulder. "I will return again. And remember what I said should you decide to include any other white men in our discussions."

David was speechless. Since the day his Papa had made the decision to travel to this northwest country, nothing had been the same. . . .

"Newhah!" Tall Cloud ordered his warriors. *"Hyas-hyak."*

David watched as the Indians filed from the cabin one by one. When he was left alone in the ensuing silence, a nervous sob tore from deep inside his throat. Hanging his head in his hands, he silently wept.

The rain had finally ceased. Christa saw her first true opportunity to move from the hut to assess this dilemma she now found herself in. She knew David well enough to be sure he wouldn't agree to anything that Tall Cloud might suggest to him. She only hoped that Tall Cloud was as gentle as she thought him to be and wouldn't hurt David in any way. But she didn't know which approach Tall Cloud would take to persuade the man who kept refusing him what he persisted in wanting.

Placing her hand in her apron pocket and touching the cold steel of her small pistol, she was reassured of her own safety for now, while she remained alone. Glad to see a faint ray of sunshine breaking through the clouds as the sun was lowering in the sky, she stepped from the hut and looked toward the edge of the cliff, which dropped sharply off to the waters of the Sound. She hurried toward it, chilled from the incessant, brisk breeze that blew across the top of the high rise. When she was at the cliff's edge, she kept one hand clutched around her pistol while the other fought her skirt as it whipped up and away from her ankles.

Her eyes swept the magnificence of the horizon. The shores of the Sound were lined with tall evergreen trees, and behind them stood two great mountain ranges. To the east, Mount Rainier glowed soft and orange colored beneath the fiery disc of the setting sun. To the west, giant rain forests blanketed the Olympics, which were white with early snow and appeared as long, graceful waves breaking in the sky.

Christa gazed downward at the luminous gray waters of the Sound. The water was a ballet of motion as though every crested wave were alive. Then her breath was stolen momentarily when her attention was directed to another movement in the water. It was a side-wheel steamer which had been making pleasure excursions up and down the waters of the Sound, since it first had made its appearance in Seattle in July of 1850. Hope sprang forth. If she could draw the attention of those on board the steamer, they could rescue her and deliver her to David before Tall Cloud returned.

Stepping so dangerously close to the edge that rock began to crumble beneath her feet, Christa cupped her hands over her mouth and began to shout for help over and over again, her own voice echoing back to her in many different octaves. Then she paused and watched for any scrambling of activity on board the steamer which would indicate that she had been heard, but there was none. The wind whistled around her still form and her hair thrashed about her face, tangling. The steamer continued to plunge its way through the water.

Her hopes shattered, Christa watched wistfully as the

steamer slid by beneath her. It was double-ended and had a tiny, flimsy cabin aft where benches faced a table on which passengers spread their lunches. Since the boat lacked a galley and sleeping accommodations, passengers always brought their own blankets and lunches. It was said that a pair of young Suquamish fishermen had been hired to go along, to help keep the craft headed in the right direction. Christa wondered if these Suquamish were of Tall Cloud's tribe.

"Nahkeeta . . ."

Hearing Tall Cloud suddenly there behind her, Christa turned around so abruptly she lost her footing. She felt herself falling backward. She screamed then felt her head spinning just as Tall Cloud's firm grip on a wrist jerked her back to safety and into his arms.

Breathing hard, still terrified of what had almost happened, Christa clung to his muscled chest, sobbing. Her cheek lay where his heart swiftly pounded, and she knew that her moment of danger had given him the same fright that it had given her.

"What were you doing so close to the edge?" Tall Cloud softly scolded. "The earth and rock could have given way. The strength of the wind could have blown such a tiny thing as you from the ledge as though you were no more than the eagle feather that I wear in my headband."

Christa now realized her foolishness in venturing so carelessly close to the edge of the cliff and in thinking that she could yell for help. The wind had carried not *her,* but her *voice* away like a feather, taking it perhaps to the high trees across the Sound, but not downward to where the steamer had so slowly traveled. And now, in Tall Cloud's arms, did she even care that she hadn't been rescued? It felt natural. It felt delicious. It felt as though she truly belonged.

Then she made herself remember why she was with him and where, and she slipped easily from his arms and began to move in the direction of the huts.

"Nahkeeta!" Tall Cloud yelled after her.

Christa stiffened, hearing his footsteps behind her. Then once more his fingers were upon a wrist as he stopped her and forced her to turn to meet the challenge of his anger-filled eyes. Her heart raced. As always he looked so noble, as one would expect a chief to be, with his broad shoulders, deep chest, and fine proportions. His light copper skin glistened from moisture acquired on his recent voyage by canoe, and his loincloth whipped in the wind, threatening to expose the part of him that she had found could give her such intense pleasure.

The magnificent muscles of his shoulders, arms, and thighs were tightly corded as he stood there, towering over her. His large, expressive eyes were once more faithfully mirroring his mood of angered hurt.

"You are still pretending to be angry with me?" Tall Cloud grumbled.

Christa forced a mock laugh. "Ha!" she said. "Pretend? Do you truly believe I only pretend? Oh, how wrong you are."

Then her eyes wavered and she swallowed hard. "David? Did you see him? Did you talk with him?"

"Is that not the reason I left you?" he said dryly.

"Yes. . . ."

"Well then, you must already know the answer to your question."

Christa's mouth dropped open, stunned by his cool aloofness. Then she began trying to work her wrist free. "Let me go, Tall Cloud," she fussed. "You're impossible to talk to. I don't even know why I try."

"This is the reason you try," he said, yanking her to him, crushing his mouth down upon hers. He released her wrist and swept his arms about her slim waist, drawing her so close to him he could fit his hardness solidly against her. His mind filled with a drugged sluggishness as he began slowly gyrating himself even more into her; he had desper-

ately missed such moments of complete togetherness. His tongue sensuously explored and his lips quivered from the intense joy of being with her in such a way again.

Awareness of what Tall Cloud was doing with his body and feeling the hardness of his manhood grinding into her sent Christa's senses reeling. Her heart became erratic. First it thundered, and then it seemed to skip a beat. As he slipped a hand between their bodies and cupped a breast through her dress, she couldn't stop a hungry moan from surfacing from somewhere deep inside her.

Tall Cloud withdrew his lips only a fraction from hers. *"Nahkeeta,"* he whispered huskily. "My woman."

He swept her up into his arms and held her tightly to him as he carried her toward the hut. Christa was oblivious to worries of David, of tomorrows. Her heart told her that there was only Tall Cloud. Oh, how she had ached to be wholly with him. While in the throes of their shared rapture, all else completely vanished from her mind.

Stepping inside the hut, Tall Cloud carefully placed her down on the rush mats beside the softly glowing fire in the fire space. His fingers trembled as he proceeded to disrobe her, bending to touch his lips to each freshly exposed area of flesh.

Christa lay breathless, enjoying his devoted attention, unconcerned by the steady, cool breeze blowing in through the opened windows and door. His lips . . . his hands . . . were firing her insides. She lifted her hips as he pulled her dress and underthings down and away from her then she saw the dark passion in his eyes as his gaze moved slowly over the unclad beauty reclining daintily before him.

"My love for you is like the winding, rippling rivers," he said hoarsely. "It is endless, *Nahkeeta*. It shall be forevermore."

With a fluttering heart, Christa moaned softly as he knelt over her and placed his lips to a breast and inhaled its nipple between his teeth. His hand sent fleeting touches across the flatness of her abdomen, and lower, where soft tendrils of hair protected the core of her womanhood.

With tenderness, Tall Cloud combed his fingers through this hair then buried his forefinger deep inside her. He moved it sensually, caressing her, touching the warm wetness of the inner walls of her love cave. His mouth left her breast. He let his tongue taste the sweetness of her flesh as it made a path downward. And when he reached the small triangle of hair where his finger still skillfully played, he kissed the pulsing mound in which all her feelings now seemed to be centered.

Tossing her head back and forth, becoming more mindless by the minute, Christa closed her eyes and released a guttural sigh as his lips now fully possessed her there and his hands moved beneath her buttocks to lift her even closer to his mouth.

His tongue flicked. His lips sucked. He seemed unable to get enough of her. The ache in his loins was becoming too painful, though, to deny himself full release much longer, and he began another trail of warm wetness with his lips, this time upward.

Christa's insides throbbed, the painful ache between her thighs so sweet she felt as if she were floating above herself, drifting in space. Never had she been engulfed in such lethargy as at this moment, and as his lips possessed first one breast and then the other, she begged with her eyes for him to take her fully.

Rising to his feet, Tall Cloud placed his thumbs over the waistband of his loincloth and began slowly slipping it down over his thighs then let it drop to the floor. He stood there for a moment, his arms tightly at his sides, his chest held proudly out, letting her see the powerful strength of his manhood. Surely no other man could display to his woman such hugeness, such readiness. His virility was one of his greatest assets, and all women before *Nahkeeta* had gladly, eagerly, announced their willingness to become his bride.

But *Nahkeeta* was the first white woman. Perhaps that was the difference—the reason why she was being so stubborn about what the future could hold for them, if they shared it together . . .

Christa rose slowly to her feet as though drawn there by the silent command of his eyes. She went to him and twined her arms around his neck and fused her body to his. She curved a leg about him tingling with desire as his lips lowered slowly to hers. His hands gently framed the soft lines of her face; his kisses were sweet and undemanding. But inner fires burned higher between them as once more Tall Cloud sensuously and deliberately pressed his manhood against her.

Christa withdrew her lips. "Now, Tall Cloud," she whispered. "Love me now."

Her hands slipped down to lightly caress his muscular buttocks with her fingertips. Her body turned into a warm liquid as his mouth fastened gently on a breast and released it just as quickly as he once more lowered her to the rush mat.

She moaned with pleasure as he held her in tender bondage beneath him, and he found her open and ready to take his manhood fully inside her. His lips pressed against her throat, and he tasted the familiar sweetness of her as he thrust himself inside her, over and over again.

Writhing in response, Christa lifted her hips and locked her legs about him. She clung to him. Her soft cry of passion mingled with his thick, husky groan, and then the silent explosion of their desire consumed them, leaving them lying side by side, breathless and fulfilled.

Tall Cloud possessively placed a hand on her left breast and moved his thumb gently over its stiff, brown peak. He then leaned up on an elbow and gazed intensely into Christa's eyes. "How can his be so stubborn when yours

are such a soft green," he said, tracing the slant of one of
her eyes with a forefinger.

"What . . . who are you talking about?" Christa asked,
sighing. She turned to lie on her side to face him as he
once more stretched out on his back.

"Your brother," Tall Cloud grumbled. "He is such a stubborn man. His eyes reflect his stubbornness."

Guilt splashed through Christa. Her face flushed with
shame that she hadn't even asked about David's welfare
when Tall Cloud returned. How had David taken her absence? Was he all right? She should have asked. But her
passion had gotten in the way . . .

"What did David say to you?" she finally asked, rising
to a sitting position, now uneasy in her nudity. She reached
for her underthings and began slipping into them. "How is
David? Did you quarrel?"

Tall Cloud teasingly slipped a strap of her petticoat from
her shoulder after she had placed it there. "Do not hide
yourself from my eyes," he said, leaning over to slip the
other strap from her other shoulder. He kissed first one
breast and then the other, then drew her next to him.

"We are alone," he said huskily. "Night is upon us. Let
us be as one all the night through. I can think of no better
way to spend time with you while waiting for your brother
to come to his senses."

As his fingers worked magic on her body, Christa's mind
became hazy with rapture again. She feared this, for she
did not want to be put completely under his spell again.
From his announcement, she knew that David had not been
agreeable to Tall Cloud's request. She also knew that David
would never willingly agree to her marriage to Tall Cloud.
She couldn't understand how Tall Cloud could be so blind
to this.

Rising quickly to her feet, she dressed. A shiver raced
across her flesh. The night hours had brought with them
even more dampness and brisker winds. She stood there

trembling as Tall Cloud slipped his loincloth on and then added more wood to the fire.

"We will have nourishment, and later we will share a blanket for sleeping, *Nahkeeta*."

"I will sleep alone," she said dryly. She had to show more self-control with him. Soon she wouldn't be with him at all.

Tall Cloud smiled wryly. "We will see," he said. "We will see just how long you will stay alone on a blanket."

She didn't respond. She had heard his smugness. And what she hated was the fact that he probably knew her better than she knew herself.

Tall Cloud went to his food supply, placed something in an intricately carved dish, then settled down beside Christa in front of the blazing fire. He gave her a lingering look then offered her the dish.

"Eat," he ordered quietly. *"Pemmican."*

Christa leaned over and studied what appeared to be some sort of cakes. "What *is* it?" she murmured.

"Pemmican. It is pounded cakes of lean meat," Tall Cloud said, pushing the dish onto her lap. "It will give you strength."

He reached for a pitcher and cup which were also carved from wood. "And clam juice will wet your tongue," he encouraged, pouring some into the cup. "When milk is scarce among my people, the clam juice fills the need."

Christa ate and drank her fill, then felt peacefully drowsy. She watched as Tall Cloud spread two blankets and crawled upon one, placing his back to her. Disappointed that he hadn't put forth more effort to have her sleep with him, Christa sulked and stretched out on her own blanket. She tossed and turned. She watched the fire cast dancing shadows on the walls and ceiling of the aged hut. She felt the coldness seeping into her flesh as the hours lengthened into deeper night.

An eerie screech surfacing from somewhere outside the hut made her jump with fright. Then she heard it again.

Gulping hard, she moved her blanket next to Tall Cloud's and fit her body against his back. Her arm crept about him, and when his hand circled hers and squeezed, she smiled and dreamily closed her eyes.

"My *Nahkeeta,* you have nothing to be frightened about," he said softly. "What you heard was only a screech owl."

Christa's eyes flew open, then she smiled slowly. "Tall Cloud, *I* knew that," she said giggling softly.

Eleven

A full week passed. Tall Cloud came and went as he pleased, yet Christa remained a prisoner on Pahto Island. For Tall Cloud it had not been time wasted. When he hadn't been making love to his *Nahkeeta,* he had been making himself a new bow to use for hunting.

For Christa, it had been a time of mixed emotions and frustrations. Her sensual moments with Tall Cloud would always occupy a special corner of her heart, where memories of love were stored. Yet her worries over David and what he must be going through plagued her other waking hours.

And in the end, Christa thought, wouldn't Tall Cloud pay for what he was doing? It amazed Christa that so far no one had come for her. This Pahto Island wasn't so far from Tall Cloud's Enati Island that it couldn't be found. And surely someone could follow him here!

Christa sat cross-legged by the fire, watching Tall Cloud construct his bow. His fingers worked with speed and skill. As she contemplated the man before her, a part of her wanted to be rescued and a part of her wanted to stay with him forever. She hadn't known what bliss was until she had been isolated on this island with the man she loved. Surely heaven could be no lovelier!

With a love so strong that it frightened her, Christa continued to watch Tall Cloud. This day he wore trousers, moccasins, and a fringed buckskin shirt trimmed with porcupine-quill embroidery. His headband lay beside him, and his dark brown hair hung neatly to his shoulders. He was fully absorbed in the craft of bow making, oblivious to her eyes upon him.

With a set jaw and squared shoulders, Tall Cloud watched his knife as he whittled away at the short, rather heavy stave of yew. At this point he was working it down to a cylindrical grip at the middle, after which he would string it with a heavy cord of twisted sinew. He recalled how he and *Nahkeeta* had walked for what had seemed like hours in the forest which reached out beyond this village of huts, looking for a tree which had the proper bend in its grain to make a good bow.

Suddenly Tall Cloud's eyes rose and caught Christa studying him. His lips lifted in a warm, slow smile as without words he returned her studious stare.

A slow blush rose to Christa's cheeks, for she wondered if he truly approved of the way she looked. But of course he should, for she wore the buckskin dress that bore designs of paint and beads, which he had brought to her from his village. Even her hair was worn in the fashion of his choosing. He had braided it for her so that it hung in one long, golden braid down to the small of her back. She knew that her cheeks were bright with color. Fulfillment in lovemaking was, indeed, the cause of this. Even now, as his wide, gray eyes silently appraised her, she felt the coil of desire tightening inside her.

"Tall Cloud!" She giggled. "Please stop looking at me in such a way. It's as though you're looking right through me."

"In Indian clothes you are even more beautiful," he explained. "It is only right that you wear them. It was meant for you to. Don't you realize that while you were in your mother's womb, your destiny was already charted to include me and the Indians' way of life?"

"Your beliefs are not as my own," she argued gently. "A man *and* a woman make their own destiny by their deeds and actions. Right now, you are in full control of mine, it seems."

"Are you not happy with me?"

"I *love* you. Of course I am happy with you. But I do not like being forced to be with you. I like to be in charge of my own self."

"Men are the leaders of the world, not women," Tall Cloud growled, resuming his whittling.

Flecks of anger sparkled in Christa's eyes. "Tall Cloud, you are no different from most white men," she argued, rising quickly to her feet. "You see women as helpless and mindless. Soon we will show you all! A woman will even be President one day!"

Swinging around, she rushed outside, gladly accepting the bright rays of the sun, the crystal-clear blue sky, and the sweetness of fresh air. The strong odors of food cooking over the fire had become overpowering in the close confines of the hut. Yet she knew the pheasant that she had endlessly turned on a spit over the fire, dripping its fat into the flames, and the biscuits of dried, ground fern roots baking near the hot coals would be a pleasant evening meal.

Stretching her arms over her head and yawning, she let the sun caress her upturned face. The past several days had been gray, cold, and rainy. She would enjoy this day to the fullest, even while wondering which day Tall Cloud might decide to deliver her back to David, for she realized that her Indian would not be the winner in this undeclared war between brother and lover.

Tall Cloud stepped up beside her and took one of her hands in his. "Come. We will enjoy the wonders of nature together this day while the sun blesses us with its presence," he said, already guiding her away from the village of huts.

They moved to the edge of the bluff and settled down on a thick bed of moss. Tall Cloud pointed to the distinct outline of the mountain which stood tall and clear to the east of him.

"Long ago mountains were people," he said thickly. "But now only powerful spirits live on the tops of the highest peaks. The spirits of *Dahkobeed,* Mount Rainier as the white men now call the great mountain, must not be angered. This is why Indians never climb above the snow line of *Dahkobeed.*"

"What would happen if you did venture there?" Christa asked, looking toward the mountain. White spirals of moisture which looked like smoke rose intermittently from the crevices of the mountain, truly seeming to be apparitions dancing and weaving in the wind, so ghostlike were these images.

She could understand why the Indians could be frightened. At times the mountain did seem to take on a supernatural, ghostly appearance. Even to her the mountain was a thing of mystery!

"There is a lake of fire on top of the mountain," Tall Cloud said softly. "In the lake lives a mighty demon. If you should reach the top, the demon would seize you and kill you and throw you into the fiery lake."

He gestured with a hand. "Do you not see the smoke even now as it rises into the sky?"

Christa knew not to argue with him for she understood that his spiritual beliefs were deeply ingrained.

"But the four 'Great Chiefs,' each of whom rules a segment of the universe, watch over us all," he said, picking up a pebble. He tossed it over the side of the cliff and leaned over to watch it glide downward and into the water.

"Dokitbatl, Doquebuth, Xelas, and *Mikamatt* are the Suquamish Great Spirits. But they are not worshiped as you do your great white chief in the city you call Washington."

Christa gave Tall Cloud a quick, surprised look. "Tall Cloud, we do not worship the President," she quickly corrected. "He is no god. Surely you don't believe that."

"It is he who has great power over all the white men," Tall Cloud argued. "It was he who made the decision that the Indian policy in the northwest, as elsewhere, would be a 'reservation' policy."

"President Pierce did not act alone on this decision," Christa said softly. "Many men—"

Tall Cloud interrupted her. "Once the Indians move to reservations, then the reservations will be gradually reduced in size," he gruffly predicted. "By this means not only will the white man get legal title to the remaining land but we Indians will be forced to give up our hunting and fishing economy which requires much land."

"I understand," Christa murmured, lowering her eyes. She hated to hear the bitterness in his voice. She was reminded of his initial purpose in pursuing her to become his wife. A planned alliance. That was all she had meant to him at first, and perhaps that was still the only reason for his confessions of love to her.

"No one but the Indians understand," he said solemnly. "The fish we eat, the animals we skin, the very hills we climb are cousin and brother to the Salish of Puget Sound."

Christa jumped with alarm as he rose to his feet and offered her a hand. "Come. Let's walk, not talk," he said. "My burdens should not become yours. It is for men to make council over. But I am afraid that too many chiefs have already been fooled by the white man's treaty papers. There are not enough like me who disagree."

They walked on into the forest. The smell of cedar was heavy in the air, and the yellow leaves of the maple and the red of the oak trees banded together to form a canopy overhead.

A flapping of wings, the shrill call of a bluejay, and the click-click sound of a chipmunk reverberated about Christa as she stepped high over the dense underbrush tangled along the floor of the forest. Ferns and wild rose bushes were beautifully profuse where the sun broke through the thick cover of trees, and poison ivy vines had turned a scarlet red from the cooler, brisker temperatures of night.

Suddenly the memory of another time in another forest flashed before Christa's eyes. She would never forget the helplessness of Princess Star nor the fierceness of the Haida warrior as he had attacked her.

"How is Princess Star?" she blurted suddenly, realizing that up to now she had been too caught up in her own private concerns even to inquire about the wronged young Indian princess.

A dark shadow seemed to settle over Tall Cloud's face, and his usually handsome features became marred with frown wrinkles. "She is twicefold shamed," he grumbled.

Christa gave him a questioning, unbelieving look. She had thought that by now Tall Cloud surely would have come to his senses and would no longer blame Star for that which she had had no control over. It was at times like this that she realized just how little she knew about him as the man, the chief, the brother of Star, though as a lover, she knew him so very well.

"What do you mean, Tall Cloud?" she asked, not really believing that she would understand the reasons that he would give her.

"Her shame is doubled because she now carries the child of the hated Haida warrior. The child will always be a reminder that my sister cared so little for her people. She should never have left the village. She should have remained loyal to her puberty rites."

"She . . . is . . . with child?" Christa gasped. "How terrible! How miserable her life must be now."

"No Suquamish brave will ever take her as a bride," Tall Cloud said in a voice filled with anguish. "She *and* her child will be my responsibilities. That is not good. In my heart I only want to make room for *one* woman."

He stopped and clasped his hands onto Christa's shoulders and turned her to face him. His eyelids were heavy, his lips aquiver. *"Nahkeeta,* I want only you to share my dwelling with me. Tell me that this will become a reality. Without you, life means nothing to me. Without you, I'm afraid I will be too saddened to perform the duties of chief as I am expected to do."

"I want to be with you," she murmured, placing a hand on his copper cheek, once more feeling its utter smoothness. "But our people would not understand this love that we feel so strongly for each another. Once you accept this and realize that we—you and I—*must* learn to live apart, you will be a better chief for it."

"And you?" he growled. "You would marry that pompous fool who wrestled you to the ground the other night? You would put up with him just to live the life of a fancy white woman?"

His words stung her. "You know me so little?" she replied. "You think I'm capable of such deceit as to give myself to a man for the riches he possesses?"

Dropping his hands to his sides, Tall Cloud looked away from her. "No. I guess that isn't so," he murmured. "If you wanted wealth . . . if you wanted a man of power . . . you would fight your brother to be my wife. In my people's eyes *I* am the richest. *I* have the power."

He swung around and faced her again. "But perhaps you don't see or understand this. To you I am just another Indian, no more or less to you than my brothers Duwamish and Suquamish."

Christa felt a pulling at her heart. "You are much more to me than *any* man on the face of the earth, be he of white or copper skin," she softly cried. She fell into his arms and fiercely hugged him. "Oh, God, if only there was a way, Tall Cloud. I love you so."

Heavy hearted, he drew her away from him and took her hand. "We must walk again," he said. "Let us meditate while we walk. Somehow the future will be ours. We will make it so."

Feeling his sadness, Christa walked beside Tall Cloud down a gentle slope until they came upon a creek meandering through the fringe of vines, around maple, alder, and ash trees. They then followed the stream through denser vegetation and thick stands of conifers—Douglas fir, spruce, red cedar, yew, and coast redwood—until they reached the shore. Here a strong northerly current prevailed and the great Puget Sound swells broke and thundered at the foot of the back side of the island.

Christa stood alongside Tall Cloud, watching the angry waves splash onto the shore. A thin mist of sea breeze continuously blew in from across the water and with it came a chill so sharp that Christa couldn't help but shiver severely.

"We must return to our dwelling," Tall Cloud said, placing an arm about Christa's waist. "It is not good that you become so chilled."

He started to guide her away but stopped with a start as he caught sight of a movement other than that of the waves out on the thrashing waters of the Sound.

"Klaksta?" he said suddenly, leaving Christa as he trotted down to the rock-strewn beach.

Christa stood her ground, watching Tall Cloud as he began flailing his arms wildly and shouting out to sea, where a canoe was now visible, making its way toward the island.

"Newhah!" Tall Cloud shouted over and over again, recognizing one of his tribe's majestic canoes and wondering why his men had disobeyed and were coming to the island against his orders. But now that they had, he thought it best to direct them to this stretch of beach where he was more accessible, rather than have them travel around to the other side where the steep steps were a challenge.

"Newhah!" he continued to shout then sighed with relief when one of his braves saw him and instructed the others to change their course. Now they headed directly toward Tall Cloud who had waded knee-deep into the water to greet

them. He knew that something had to be terribly wrong for his men to come to Pahto Island in such a way.

Tall Cloud's insides did a strange rolling. What if *Nahkeeta's* brother had not heeded his warning and had eluded the Suquamish braves who had been ordered to watch his cabin? Had he sent many white man to Enati Island looking for *Nahkeeta?* What if several of his people had been slain in the search for her . . . ?

Christa hugged her arms about her chest, now trembling from the cold *and* from fear. The sudden arrival of Tall Cloud's braves surely didn't represent good news. All sorts of thoughts and conclusions were spinning around inside her head and most led her back to her major concern— David and his possible part in this.

With her teeth chattering noisily, Christa watched as the intricately carved canoe came alongside Tall Cloud. He remained in the water as the ten braves took turns talking with him. And just as abruptly as they had arrived, they traveled away again.

Tall Cloud splashed out of the water, his expression dull and clouded as he came to tower over Christa.

"What is it, Tall Cloud?" she asked in a faint voice, now certain that the news was not good.

He took her by an elbow and began guiding her quickly back the way they had just been walking. "It is the Haida," he growled. "They are making raids upon the white settlers who live on land outside the city of Seattle. Some homes have been burned, but so far only few settlers have been killed. There could possibly be a war."

It was as though someone had pierced her heart with an icy arrow, the pain of anguish and dread was so severe for Christa. She stopped and spun around to face Tall Cloud, breathless.

"David . . ." she said. "He is unable to defend himself. I must go to him, Tall Cloud. Please. I must go to him now."

"Nahkeeta, from the moment I took you as my hostage,

my braves have been watching your cabin in case your brother tried anything foolish," he said flatly. "My braves just informed me that he has not done this and still waits, unharmed, in your cabin until I return you to him."

"But will your braves continue to watch him? Will David truly be safe?"

"My Suquamish braves would squash any Haida who approaches my *Nahkeeta's* dwelling," he vowed. "I know the bond between you and your brother. Though aggravating to me, I know that it is a special one to you."

"I still wish to return to my brother," she argued. "If you love me, Tall Cloud, you will do this for me."

"Nahkeeta, my plans *are* to take you home," he said thickly. "Tomorrow, as the sun rises orange on the horizon."

Christa's lips parted softly, her eyes wide. "You will take me home?" she gasped. "So easily? Without any further prodding from me?"

"Tomorrow," he said flatly.

"Why tomorrow?" she dared to ask. "Why not today?"

"This one night more must be mine to have with you," he said, drawing her gently into his arms. His heart ached as he realized their time together had come to an end. He hadn't won this time. But he would. One day he would! For now, he had his people's welfare to think of. Should the white man rebel against all the Indians because of the misdeeds of some, then his people would be prepared. It was important that he had a clear head so that he would be fully capable of leading his people.

Together Christa and Tall Cloud traveled back to the hut. "Prepare yourself for me," he said. "I will return soon. I first must pray beside my great-grandfather's mortuary column. The days ahead could be hard for my Suquamish Indians."

Christa watched him leave then slowly disrobed. She knelt down before the fire and leaned her full weight on her bent legs, waiting. She felt a strangeness in the air, a foreboding of sorts. But she had to believe that it was because the word "war" had such a frightening ring to it. Thus far, her and David's existence in this Northwest Territory had been peaceful enough. But now what did the future hold for them? And what part would Tall Cloud play in that future? She felt as though tonight could be their final good-bye.

A plaintive tune being played somewhere close by drew Christa slowly to her feet. She knew that it was Tall Cloud playing a simple little flute that he had found in one of the deserted huts. He had told her that the braves carved these flutes and used them to serenade their ladyloves.

As a moth being drawn to the flames of a fire, Christa stepped from the cabin into the fast falling dusk and followed the sadness of the music until she came to Tall Cloud standing tall and proud, overlooking the Sound which stretched out far below him.

Christa reached her forefinger to his back and began running it down the straight line of his spine. And when he spun around, she saw in his eyes a deep, dark passion. With one hand he swept her to his side and began walking her back to the hut, and with the other he continued to hold the flute to his lips, blowing into it softly.

Tears filled Christa's eyes. She was already missing him.

Twelve

The fire had died in the fire space, but desire was running hot through Christa's veins as Tall Cloud's lips were once more awakening her senses in the early morning light. She coiled her arms about his neck, her body like silk against him as he fully possessed her, entering gently from below. Spirals of warmth spun inside her, setting her aglow from her toes to her brain. She squirmed passionately beneath his meltingly hot kiss and emitted a soft moan as his right hand captured her breast. His thumb and forefinger squeezed its hardened tip, then his hand gently kneaded it while he continued to move skillfully inside her.

The realization that this could be their last time together seemed to kindle the flames of love to burn even higher. Christa opened herself eagerly to him and met his thrusts with raised hips. She clung to him as if there were no tomorrow.

Tall Cloud's lips moved from hers and sent sweet kisses along the gentle slope of her jaw, then lower to the pulsing hollow of her throat. He pressed his lips against her there while his fingers dug into her hips to lift her closer . . . closer.

With a thudding heart and dizzy with need, he drove harder inside her. Perspiration glistened on both their bodies, and their heavy breathing filled the silent morning air.

It was as though both were mountain climbers, laboring, moving higher, seeing the peak within reach.

A few more thrusts amidst wild, hungry kisses and together their goal was met as they made that final step into a realm where their bodies and souls fused into joyful bliss.

It was the faint color of orange on the ceiling above them that made them aware that the time had come to say their good-byes. The sun was rising in its brilliance from behind the distant mountains, and the world was unfolding into another day. To Christa it seemed the world would never be the same again. Without Tall Cloud there would be no world for her. The thought of parting made her cling to him fiercely.

"Tall Cloud, I don't think I can bear it," she cried softly as she buried her face into the flesh of his chest.

His fingers combed through her unbraided hair. He smiled to himself. In the eyes of those who learned that she had been returned to her brother, he would appear to be the loser in this battle of the heart. But he knew he had won a *most* important victory. He was certain that his love-making had been skillful enough to seal her heart with endless love—love for him alone.

"My *Nahkeeta,* I promise you that our time together will come," he said huskily. "We must practice patience. We both have duties other than to ourselves now. You have your brother . . . I have my people."

"I wish we could all be of one mind," she whispered, running her hand along his tight chest and down to where his need of her was so strangely shrunk and lying placid against his body. She circled her fingers around it and felt it slowly springing back to life, a thing that was of keen amazement to her each time she witnessed this strange phenomenon.

"Perhaps one day the white man and the Indians *can* live as one. But for now the Haida have decided to make their own mark in history," he said thickly, feeling the heat once more rise inside his loins. This thirst for her seemed to be unquenchable! But he knew it was not the time to renew passions. The sun was rising much too quickly in the sky.

He gently brushed her hand aside. *"Nahkeeta,* we must dress and leave," he said. "We have delayed what must be done long enough."

"Yes. I know," she murmured. "And I should feel ashamed for not being any more eager than I am to leave a place where I have been held against my will."

"Did you not enjoy our peaceful time together?" Tall Cloud asked, fitting his loincloth in place. "Can you really call this a time of being held prisoner?"

Christa rose to her feet, sliding up next to him and splaying her fingers against his chest. She looked up adoringly into his expressive gray eyes. "I will always be a prisoner no matter where I am," she murmured. "Tall Cloud, I'm a prisoner of your heart."

"A savage heart?" he asked thickly.

"Never," she replied vehemently. "The word savage is not a pleasant one, you know."

"My people are only now realizing this," he growled, drawing away from her. "As they are now learning much that displeases them."

"Yet they have remained peaceful Indians," she said, hurrying into her undergarments and then her dress.

"Under my guidance they have," Tall Cloud said proudly. He positioned his headband and feather on his head then hung his necklace of dentalia about his neck. "I practice what my forefathers practiced before me. The only warring done by the Suquamish is against the Haida."

Tall Cloud's insides did a strange rolling as a thought came to him as a result of this last statement. His Indians had always hungered for a fight with the Haida enemies. Wouldn't this be a perfect time to allow his warriors the fulfillment of battle and at the same time prove to the white man just how much of a friend the Suquamish could be to them? Perhaps this could pave the way to the same sort of alliance that he had sought by marrying *Nahkeeta!* If he and his warriors fought side by side with the white man against the Haida, surely the white man would reconsider forcing the treaty papers upon *them!* The land could still belong to the Suquamish. The valleys, the mountains and all the wildlife that roamed there could still be theirs to hunt freely. The nasty word "reservation" could be erased from his people's aching hearts! Yes! He would fight off the Haida for the white man and, while doing so, avenge the reputation of his shamed sister!

Suddenly laughing, seeing that this was the answer that he had been seeking, Tall Cloud went to Christa and lifted her into the air. He spun around on a heel, in circles, carrying her with him.

Breathless, Christa giggled. "My word, Tall Cloud," she said, her head spinning as he continued to turn in a merry circle. "What . . . do . . . you think you're doing?"

"The future is suddenly brighter for my people." He laughed. *"Nahkeeta,* all tomorrows are laced in sunshine. My people will never have a need to frown again."

"What has happened to make you say that?" she asked, glad to have her feet solidly on the rush mat flooring again as he stopped spinning and released her. She placed a hand to his cheek, studying the sparkle in his eyes.

"In time you will see," he said. "It's best to remain silent. My actions will be my words."

He stooped to pick up his new bow, finished now with many miniature designs of the raven on its handle, and slipped it over his shoulder. "For now, my *Nahkeeta,* we must concentrate on getting you safely to where your proud brother waits for your return."

"Yes. David." Christa sighed, flipping her waist-length golden tresses away from her shoulders. "My sweet David. I'm sure his days and nights have been spent much differently than mine."

Her thoughts wandered to Delores Kramer, and she was certain that Harrison had not allowed his sister to wander out into the wilderness to go to David. Most of the white settlers feared the Indians, even the peaceful Suquamish, and Christa suspected that Harrison's harsh words about the Indians stemmed from fear more than hate.

The steep steps leading to the beach were left behind and the canoe made its way through the diamond glitters of the water. Only a few puffs of clouds skitted along the horizon but there was always a threat that these could change quickly into thunderheads, bringing Seattle a typically gloomy mid-October day.

Christa clung tightly to her seat, watching the gracefulness with which Tall Cloud maneuvered the paddle of the canoe. It seemed no effort at all for him to propel it at a quick rate of speed, though the canoe itself was heavy with its intricate, carved designs.

Tall Cloud lifted the paddle. He pulled. His shoulder muscles corded. Christa listened intently as he occasionally emitted a laborious groan when a sudden wave splashed harder against the moving craft, turning it into a shuddering mass of wood. And then it wasn't long before he had it beached only a short distance away from Christa's cabin.

Tall Cloud stepped from the canoe in to ankle-deep water. He went to Christa, lifted her up into his arms, and carried her to the shore; yet he hesitated at letting her go. Christa clung to his neck, feeling the pounding of his heart against her cheek which lay pressed against his chest. It beat with the same rhythm as hers, and she knew they shared the same feelings of sadness at their parting.

Christa lifted her cheek from his chest and gazed with longing into his eyes. "I shall always love you, Tall Cloud," she murmured. "Always. With every beat of my heart."

"You're truly not angry with me for taking you away from your white man's way of life?"

"I should be, but I'm not. You *have* returned me. David will be forever grateful."

"Now that you are away from me, he might send the white man's posse after me."

"Never!" she said firmly.

"It had not been a main concern of mine," he said hoarsely. "I knew that you would not allow it. And given the chance, I will give your brother reason to be thankful that he did choose to accept you back with him without causing harm to me for having taken you."

"I won't question you about the meaning behind your words," she said, glancing over her shoulder, seeing the gray smoke spirals rising from her chimney. "I must hurry to David. We must make plans. We may have to go into Seattle, at least until the Haida are dealt with, though leaving here is something that I do not wish to do."

"And the Haida *will* be dealt with," Tall Cloud growled.

Christa heard the venom in his words. She looked searchingly into his eyes but left her questions unasked. There was a private side to his nature that neither she or her words had yet succeeded at penetrating. She squeezed her arms more forcefully about his neck and lifted her lips to his.

"Just hold me tightly a moment longer," she whispered. "I love you. I love you."

Tall Cloud's arms held her more closely to his chest. His lips bore down upon hers, kissing her with the wild passion she had known before. Her heart seemed surrounded by liquid fire, and the ache between her thighs became torture. And then she was on her feet, looking up at him, trembling as their fingers remained laced together.

"I will leave you here," he said huskily. "But I will watch you from the canoe until you are safely inside your cabin."

"When will I see you again?"

"We *will* be together. That's all that matters. Time? It is just a word. One day blends into the next. Soon many moons pass. I promise you that when many moons are passed for us, you will be not only my woman, but also my *wife*."

He unlocked his fingers from hers and went to his canoe. In a blink of an eye he was paddling away from her.

"Go to your cabin," he shouted. "I will watch you from here."

"My heart is yours," she shouted back. "Please remember that, Tall Cloud."

She watched as he placed his paddle on the floor of the canoe. Then, in Indian sign language, he acted out the word "love" by crossing his arms over his chest, with his right arm close to his body, and pressed there with his left arm.

With a pleased smile, Christa turned and began struggling to climb up the muddy slime of the embankment. She lifted the skirt of her dress into her arms and determinedly kept climbing until finally she had her feet solidly on the grass-covered ground.

She stopped and caught her breath then broke into a run, her eyes never leaving the cabin. It seemed an eternity since she had last seen David, and now she fully understood his importance to her. But she also knew that one day a complete break would have to be made . . . and that would be the day she would leave to be with Tall Cloud forever!

Finally at the door, Christa stopped once more to catch her breath, then she rushed into the cabin, almost running directly into David as he stood there, supporting himself on his crutches.

"Christa . . ." David gasped, paling. He let his left crutch fall away from him and wrapped his one arm about her as she moved quickly into his embrace.

"David, you're all right!" She sighed, hugging him tightly. "When news reached us of the Haida . . ."

David's whole body stiffened. He eased her away from him. "Us?" he said dryly. "Of course you mean you and Tall Cloud."

His gaze swept quickly over her. His free hand touched

her here and there, as though testing her for injuries. "He seems to have taken good enough care of you," he said hoarsely. His eyes narrowed as he saw the glow of her pink cheeks and the peace in her eyes. Yes," he added quietly. "When you're with him, you seem to come even more alive."

Christa swung away from him, embarrassed, realizing the implications of his words. She began moving about the cabin, seeing its clutter of unwashed dishes and scattered vegetable peelings on the floor. She laughed nervously. "It appears that I've been missed," she said, already stooping to clean the mess from the floor. "You never were the neat one, David, and with your lame foot, heaven knows how this cabin would have looked had I been gone longer."

She glanced quickly toward his foot, then let her gaze meet his watchful, silent stare. "Your foot? Is it much better, David?" she asked softly. "You do seem to be getting around quite well on the crutches."

"My foot is fine," he said, patting the thigh of his leg. "Should be as good as new quite soon. But it won't be soon enough, Christa. A rider came by this mornin' urgin' us to move into town until the Haida scare lessens."

She tensed. Straightening her back, she went to fuss over the clutter of dishes on the table, now avoiding his eyes. "And, David, when the rider was here, did you by chance explain my absence to him?" she asked cautiously, almost fearing to hear the answer.

David bent and rescued his other crutch, slipped it beneath his arm, then hobbled over to the table and spoke directly into Christa's face. "If you mean to ask did I tell him that Tall Cloud had abducted you, no, I did not do that," he grumbled. "I didn't have the chance. Tall Cloud's braves came into the cabin immediately upon the arrival of the rider. To the rider it was the Suquamish entertaining themselves with another *nanitch,* nothing else. But to me, it was a warning . . . a warning not to mention Tall Cloud's name in any way to the rider."

"Tall Cloud told me that he had his braves watching our cabin," Christa said, stacking dishes. "It was for two reasons, David, one of which was to see that you were safe from the Haida."

"I could defend myself," he grumbled, working himself down, stiff legged, into a chair before the fire. He reached for his rifle and ran his hand over the shine of its barrel. "I was ready. I'm not helpless, you know."

"Where's your shotgun, David?" Christa asked, looking around the room.

"Tall Cloud made short work of it the one time he was here," he said, his face coloring as he remembered how swiftly Tall Cloud had moved that day.

Christa blanched. Her hands went to her throat. "Don't tell me that you . . . you tried to shoot Tall Cloud," she gasped.

David's silence and set jaw were answer enough for Christa. She went to him and fell to her knees before him. "David, always . . . *always* remember that Tall Cloud is a friend," she cried. "Never would he harm anyone but the Haida."

"He abducted you," David shouted. "Doesn't that mean anything to you?"

"He also brought me back," she murmured. "Will you also condemn him for that?"

David's eyes wavered. "That's unfair, Christa," he said.

"You're unfair, David," she argued. "You must know now that I'm in love with Tall Cloud, just as he's in love with me. Doesn't that—the fact that I love and that I'm loved in return—mean anything to you? Tall Cloud only took me to his island with him to prove a point to *you*. Had you agreed to our marriage—"

"Never," David said harshly beneath his breath.

Christa felt numb. She rose to her feet and gently placed

a log on the fire. "David, your hatred of Tall Cloud seems deeper than your happiness to have me home again," she murmured. Brushing her hands on her skirt, she swung around and faced him. "Why, you didn't even greet me as if you had missed me."

David lowered his eyes. "I knew you were safe," he said. "And I knew you were being returned this morning. Tall Cloud's braves told me last evening. So my thoughts dwelled elsewhere . . . on the fact that this Indian suddenly seemed to have control over our lives, as though *he* were shaping our destiny. I feel bitter, Christa. So very, very bitter."

"What are your plans, David?"

"What do you mean?"

"You aren't going to contact the authorities about Tall Cloud now that I'm safely home, are you?"

"I think we have more important decisions to make now," David said, placing his rifle aside. "Many have moved into Seattle, into a blockade that's been erected for the safety of those who seek refuge from the warring Haida. Do you wish to risk staying here, or do you wish to go to the blockhouse?"

An involuntary shiver shook Christa as she went to the window to scan the darkness of the forest. "Just how dangerous would it be to stay here, David?" she asked, now studying their grazing cows, horses, and their many chickens. "Surely we would lose everything by leaving." She also suspected that Tall Cloud would see to it that his warriors would be close by, watching her, protecting her.

"Each individual weighs danger in a different sort of way," David said. "With you to protect, I might say that the dangers of stayin' behind, here at the cabin, are too much a risk."

"How many houses have been burned, David? How many lives have been lost?"

"Reports vary," he said, shrugging. He looked over his

shoulder toward Christa. "Christa, what are you gettin' at? What are you tryin' to tell me?"

Christa went to David and once more knelt before him on her knees. "David, everything we own is right here in this house and on our farm," she murmured. "All of our memories of Mama and Papa . . . our family mementos . . . are in this house. How can we leave, to let the Haida steal or burn them? Can we stay, David? Can we at least give it a try? Christmas isn't that far away. When Christmas arrives, I want to be able to celebrate it with the decorations Mama and Papa made for our trees when we lived in Boston."

David frowned. He raked his long, lean fingers nervously through his hair. "A dispatcher *has* been sent to Washington asking for military support," he said contemplatively. "Surely the Haida will receive word of this and will be frightened off. Perhaps we could be safe."

"Then we can stay?" Christa asked, yet once more remembering the fierceness of the one Haida that she had come in contact with. Even now his tattoos seemed to be alive, fluttering toward her. Once more she was experiencing the fear she had known right before she had pulled the trigger.

Something grabbed at her heart as her hands fell to her waist and she felt the void there where her apron was usually tied. "Oh, no," she groaned. "My apron. My pistol. I left them in Tall Cloud's hut!"

David let out his own groan. "It will just give him a reason to return here to see you quite soon," he grumbled. "You won't be without it long, I assure you, Christa."

Christa concealed a flicker of a smile as she rose to her feet and walked away from him. "I shall collect all the firearms in our possession and ready them for use just in case the Haida do decide to pay us a visit," she said. "I'm sure we'll be safe enough, David. If not, I will be to blame for whatever happens, for it is I who has made the decision to stay."

David worked himself up out of the chair, leaning heavily on his crutches. He went to Christa and placed his hand on the pink of her cheek. "No, Christa," he said thickly. "If anyone is to blame for anything that has transpired or will transpire in the future, it is I. I should have turned back after Mama and Papa's death on the trail. How many times will I have to pay for that wrong decision?"

Christa's thoughts went to Tall Cloud. Had she not met him, she never would have known the bliss of his love.

Smiling at David, she covered his hand with hers. "David, never regret coming here," she murmured. "I don't."

Thirteen

It was Christmas Eve. Only a dusting of snow accompanied Christa and David as they walked into the outer edges of the forest in search of a perfectly shaped Christmas tree. A cedar tree was their preference because of the heady fragrance that type of tree emitted.

The air was brisk and cold; the forest quiet. David hobbled along on one crutch beside Christa. He was dressed in warm underwear, heavy trousers tucked into the one cowhide boot on his uninjured foot, and a flannel shirt. Instead of a jacket, he had a folded blanket around his neck, crossed in front and secured with a cartridge belt. A slouch hat was pulled down low over his forehead, and in his left hand he carried a pistol so that he would be ready for any sudden disturbance in the brush.

Christa had tied a heavy knitted shawl about her shoulders over her high-necked, long-sleeved cotton dress. Her stiffly starched bonnet accentuated the loveliness of her face and the slant of her green eyes which were wide and searching in the slowly fading light.

In her left hand she carried an ax, and in her right a loaded pistol, which was already causing an ache to grow in her wrist because of its heaviness. Her thoughts went to her small, personal pistol and where she had carelessly left it. She couldn't help but wonder if Tall Cloud would ever return to Pahto Island, to the same hut in which they had shared such beautiful moments, moments that were still so much a part of her dreams at night.

But she doubted that he would. He had no reason to, since Enati Island was now the home of his people.

Almost two months since I've seen him, she thought despairingly to herself. Again she couldn't help but feel used. David had seen Delores even more than she had seen Tall Cloud! It had only been recently that her brother's trips into Seattle had ceased. The need to stay close to the farm and protect what was theirs had taken precedence over David's desire to be with Delores, though the fear of losing her to another had caused him many a sleepless night, of that Christa was certain.

"I'm not sure just how wise it is to be so far from the cabin," David said, nervous perspiration beading his brow.

"So far we have been safe enough," Christa said, her breath leaving her mouth like bursts of fog along with her words. "The Haida seem to have wandered back north, don't you think? We haven't received any more warnings to move to the stockade."

"I'm sure you're right." David sighed. "If the danger were greater, Harrison Kramer would surely have come to rescue you personally, Christa, his love for you is so strong."

Christa gave David a disbelieving look. She laughed cynically. "David, that statement proves that you don't know Harrison very well. Haven't you noticed that he has not attempted to court me since the beginning of the Haida scare? He wouldn't leave the safety of Seattle. I would even bet that he was among the first to flee to the stockade when it was suggested that everyone go there. He's not only a very dislikable and undesirable man, but a coward as well."

David laughed softly. "A *wealthy* coward, Christa," he said. "You'd never want for another thing if you'd marry him."

"How can you persist in wanting me to marry that man?"

Christa fumed. "You know how I detest him. It isn't like you, David. You never before placed such emphasis on wealth. Why must you now?"

David swallowed back a lump in his throat. "Until Mama and Papa's death, seeing how happy and in love they were, I had thought that 'love' was the magic word in marriage," he said. "But with their deaths occurring when they were so young, I've changed my mind. One must take in life what one can, for who knows about all the tomorrows?"

He looked down at his bandaged foot. "Take my foot, for instance. Who'd have ever thought that'd happen? With one false swing I half crippled myself!"

Christa looked down at David's bandaged foot. "Your foot is better, isn't it, David?" she asked, hoping to leave the subject of Harrison behind her. "You're getting by now with the use of only one crutch."

"It's about time, wouldn't you say?" David grumbled.

"When the new year arrives, you'll be as good as new," Christa reassured. "And the Christmas holiday should help to lift your spirits a mite and pass the time faster."

"First we've got to find a proper tree," David said, slowing his pace as he looked from tree to tree. "We can't choose one that'd be too large for our cabin. It's got to be just right, Christa."

"David, remember the trees we had in Boston?" She sighed. "Papa always brought home trees so tall they touched the ceiling. And they were so fat, it took string after string of popcorn to wrap around them."

"It makes for good memories," David said thickly. He gave Christa a wistful look across his shoulder. "I know how much you miss Papa and Mama. This Christmas won't be the same without them. But let's make the best of what we've got, Christa. Just having each other is a blessing out in this wilderness, you know."

Christa dropped her ax to the ground but held onto the pistol as she went to hug David with one arm. "I love you,

David," she murmured. "I'm sorry I've given you fretful moments these past weeks and months. You do mean so much to me, big brother."

David became choked with emotion. He couldn't hug her back because of the burden in his arms, but he placed a gentle kiss on her cheek. "I only want what's best for you," he said hoarsely. "And if I so heartily disagree with you over, uh, some matters as I have, it's only because I love you so much."

Tears turning cold on her cheeks made Christa aware of the temperatures of the day, and she saw the need to resume the search that had taken them to the forest.

Sweeping away from David, she bent and once more took possession of the ax. She looked from tree to tree. They were all shaped beautifully. Snow lay lightly on their branches, as if they were weaving apparel of fine, white lace.

"Which one, David?" she asked.

It would be the first time she had cut down a tree to be used for Christmas decoration. David couldn't swing an ax and support himself on his crutch at the same time.

"Hmm," David said, still not sure. He smiled toward Christa. "You choose. You're the one who'll be doin' the cuttin'."

The aroma of cedar hung sweet and heavy in the air, intermingling with a most identifiable heady scent from roses which grew wild and pink along the forest floors. So stubborn were these flowers that they caught the crystal snowflakes on their velvet petals and persisted to bloom on even into the cold days of Christmas.

"Okay, David," Christa said, giggling. "I'll gladly do the choosing."

She glanced down at the pistol in her possession then frowned toward David. "But should I part with the pistol for even that long, David? What if the Haida—"

"My rifle is loaded and ready, Christa," David reassured

her. "You just concentrate on gettin' us that tree so we can get back to the cabin."

Christa nodded her head and placed the pistol on the ground. She walked studiously around some trees, then smiled as she finally made her selection.

"This one," she said, admiring the perfect shape of one of the trees and its thick branches. "This one will do perfectly."

"Cut away, Christa," David said. "But be careful with the ax. You know the dangers well enough."

"Yes, I know," she murmured.

Wanting to clear her arms of extra weight to enable her to get good swings of the ax, Christa brushed back her shawl. She shook the snow from the tree, firmly grasped the ax handle, then took her first swing and several others.

The sound of the ax making contact with wood echoed ominously throughout the silent forest, bouncing from tree to tree, bush to bush. David tensed, suddenly realizing just how far sound could travel on a cold, hushed, winter day in the forest. If Indians were near, how easy it would be for them to follow this sound. . . .

The burning of Christa's fingers caused her to lean the ax against her legs as she rested from her labor for a brief moment. She now realized that she should have worn gloves. But she had thought they would cause her to be less accurate with the pistol should she have to use it.

David leaned down and inspected the trunk of the tree where sap oozed in sticky grays from its inflicted wound. He shook the tree, loosening it from its base even more. "Only a couple more strokes with the ax ought to do it," he said.

Straightening his back, he looked across his shoulder and from side to side, having heard a faint sound from somewhere close. Seeing nothing he shrugged, thinking it had probably been a bird or squirrel. But he placed his finger on the trigger of his rifle just in case.

Christa sensed David's wariness. She understood the need to complete her chore and lifted the ax. With one more blow the cedar tree toppled quickly to the ground.

Chuckling, David moved to her side and kissed her on the cheek. "Little sister, you've just cut down your first tree," he said. "You're a lumberjack for sure."

Wiping a bead of perspiration from beneath her nose, Christa took a step backward. She dropped the ax and exhaled heavily. "I'm sure to have mountains of blisters on my hands tomorrow," she said, rubbing her hands together.

"But won't it be worth it? We should have the tree decorated by then."

"Yes. By this evening we should have the corn popped and strung."

"Then what are we waiting for?" David said. "Let's get back to the cabin."

Christa eyed her discarded pistol, the ax, and the felled tree. "How on earth am I expected to carry all these things back to the cabin at once?" she wondered aloud.

David grunted as he bent to scoop the pistol into a hand. "I'll take care of the pistol," he said, thrusting its barrel down inside the waistband of his breeches, leaving its handle readily accessible.

"Sounds good to me." Christa laughed. She lifted the ax with one hand and stooped to grab the sticky mire of the tree's trunk with the other. "Shall we, big brother?"

"After you," David said, smiling, gesturing with his rifle.

Anxious, Christa began dragging the tree, already smelling the corn that soon she would be popping. Then her steps halted and fear grabbed at her heart when as if from nowhere several Haida Indians appeared, surrounding her and David. Though it was intensely cold, they wore only brief loincloths, and Christa could see tattoos which covered their bodies. In their dark eyes hatred seethed, and in their hands they displayed loaded, aimed rifles.

David awkwardly dropped his rifle when one of the

fiercest-looking Indians jumped directly in front of him and shoved the barrel of his rifle into his stomach. And when the Haida spoke in Indian to David and nodded toward the pistol thrust inside David's waistband, David understood and slowly reached his hand to it.

Casting a quick glance toward Christa, seeing her eyes frozen wide with fear, David knew that he couldn't just give in to these Indians without trying to defend his sister. He let his gaze count the number of Indians standing in a circle about them. Ten. He wouldn't have a chance to kill them all.

Once more he looked Christa's way. He hoped that she would read the silent message that he was going to relay to her. Their chances were small, but their future would be bleak if the Haida took them as hostages. Perhaps death would be better than being captured by the pirating Haida! He didn't want to think about what the vicious Indians might do to Christa. She would be at the mercy not of one Indian this time, but many. And none of them seemed to have even a trace of the decency that David had begun to recognize in Tall Cloud.

With his eyes, David implored Christa to look toward the rifle which lay only a few feet away from her, where he had dropped it. His heart pounded wildly as she followed his lead, looking at the rifle, then upward to where his hand was almost ready to touch the handle of his pistol. When her gaze moved up and their eyes met and momentarily held, David knew that she understood what was expected of her. His hand trembled as he touched the handle of his pistol, and his breathing came in snatches as he watched Christa drop first the ax and then the tree.

Then suddenly loud war whoops filled the air, and Tall Cloud and several of his warriors, fully dressed in their buckskin attire, came rushing forth to pounce on the Haida Indians. The Haida were wrestled to the ground, and Indian language rose angrily into the air as fists tore into the faces of the Haida.

David stepped back, waiting with his pistol poised and ready. Christa lunged for the rifle and, trembling, held it before her, watching Tall Cloud bodily lift from the ground the Indian he had been fighting and toss him away from him. Christa could tell that Tall Cloud was ordering the Haida away from him by the way he was shouting and gesturing with a hand.

Christa looked toward this particular Haida and saw so much familiar about him. Was it his tattoos? Were they so different from his companions'? Or was it the way he looked at her—that look of recognition, that look of deep hate?

Was this . . . the same . . . Haida? Was this the one responsible? Had . . . he . . . raped Princess Star?

Slowly Christa let her gaze move to his upper right arm. She tensed when she saw the scar for which she was personally responsible.

She began to speak, to tell Tall Cloud, but a shot fired behind her made her turn, startled. She gasped when she saw David holding his pistol in the air, smoke curling from its barrel.

All of the Indians, Suquamish and Haida alike, ceased their scuffling to look wide eyed toward David. Christa couldn't believe it herself, never imagining that David would have the courage to intervene.

"Clear out! All of you!" David shouted, another bullet from his pistol belching up into the air.

A look of amusement flashed in Tall Cloud's eyes as the Haida scampered away.

"You are not only a proud brother but a brave one as well," Tall Cloud said, going to David to place a hand heavily on his shoulder. "Your voice of authority was recognized by the pirating Haida. That is good. Perhaps they won't return another day to finish what they started here with you and your sister."

David leaned into his crutch and moved out of Tall Cloud's reach. "I owe you thanks for showing up when you did," he said thickly. "But, Tall Cloud, I would much prefer that you and your Indians also go on your way. Christa and I can defend ourselves. We could have done so even if you had not arrived when you did."

David didn't truly believe this, but he didn't want to show any obligation to this Indian chief whose full attention was now on Christa.

Christa's pulse raced as Tall Cloud stepped to tower over her. She was once more swallowed whole by deep feelings of love for him. "David's thank you is not sincere enough," she murmured.

She reached a hand to touch the smoothness of his cheek. "If not for you, I'm sure David and I would no longer be alive. Thank you, Tall Cloud," Christa said, swallowing hard. "Thank you for being here when needed."

She looked into the abyss of Tall Cloud's eyes, seeing so much in them that set her insides fiercely aglow. She wanted to tell him how much she loved him. Yet still she wondered why he had stayed away for so long this time. She had begun to believe that her usefulness to him was a thing of the past.

Tall Cloud took her hand in his. *"Mika whahtkay.* No thanks is needed," he said hoarsely. "What I do for you and your brother is done in love."

"Why were you here . . . now . . . when you have neglected to be here for several weeks?" Christa asked softly giving David a guilty, downcast glance for being so open with her affections for the man David did not wish her to marry.

Tall Cloud lifted the tail of his fringe-edged, buckskin shirt. With his free hand he slipped Christa's small pistol out of the waistband of his trousers. "I have brought you this," he said, offering the handle end to her. "It is yours, is it not?"

Christa let the rifle rest against her leg and accepted her pistol. She looked at it for a moment, recalling the circumstances during which she had removed it from her person in Tall Cloud's hut on Pahto Island. The moments . . . the hours spent with him. . . .

"Thank you, Tall Cloud," she murmured, now smiling up into his eyes.

"I would have brought it sooner, but my duties to my people have been many." He cast David a guarded look, then once more looked down at Christa. "You are cold. You must go back to your cabin. I will go with you. There is much I want to tell you."

David hobbled to Christa's side, his lips set in cold frustration. "Tall Cloud, this was to be a special day for me and my sister," he said dryly. "We will want privacy."

"Special day?" Tall Cloud said, forking his eyebrows. "Why special?"

"It's Christmas Eve," David said. "Christa and I are going to trim our Christmas tree and spend a quiet evening together. Surely you understand."

"Christmas tree? Christmas Eve?" Tall Cloud puzzled. "No. I do not know anything of such a custom."

Christa gestured toward the tree. "The reason we came into the forest this day was to find and cut a tree for trimming," she said.

Noting the lingering blank look on Tall Cloud's face, she looked toward David. "David, please let's show Tall Cloud how we trim our Christmas tree?" she softly begged. "What harm can there be? You must admit that he did risk his and his warriors' lives to defend us today. Couldn't we thank him in this special way?"

"Christa, now really . . ." David said hoarsely. He cast Tall Cloud an ugly frown, then let his gaze capture the many warriors who stood close by, silently observing.

"I gladly accept the invitation," Tall Cloud said, squaring his shoulders proudly. He turned to his men and gave them brief instructions in his scrambled Suquamish language, then took it upon himself to carry the ax and Christa's rifle as he headed away from her and David, in the direction of their cabin.

David gave Christa a disgruntled look. "Why on earth did you do that, Christa?" he scolded. "You know how I feel—"

Christa interrupted him. "You also know how *I* feel, though you choose to act as though my feelings do not exist or amount to a hill of beans," she hissed.

She stomped through the snow, once more placed her hand on the oozing stickiness of the tree's trunk, and began dragging it away from David. She gave him a quick glance over her shoulder. "Coming, David?" she said, giggling beneath her breath.

David's face flamed with color. He watched as Tall Cloud's warriors moved back into the forest and were soon lost from sight as if they had magically disappeared from the face of the earth. Then grumbling low beneath his breath, he followed along behind Christa. He knew that he was losing her slowly, yet completely, to Tall Cloud, and he felt helpless, so very helpless.

The cabin smelled deliciously of popped corn and melted sorghum molasses. Half of the corn had been strung on thread, and the other half had been formed into popped-corn balls, sealed together with the stickiness of the sorghum molasses.

After attaching the tree's trunk to boards nailed together to form a stand, David had placed the tree across the room from the fireplace, in front of a window.

While Christa had been explaining the meaning of Christmas to Tall Cloud, Tall Cloud had enjoyed his first taste of popped corn and popped-corn balls, liking the latter to a much greater extent because of his love for and fascination with molasses.

Tall Cloud now watched as Christa began to wind the strung popped corn on the cedar tree's branches, while David hung miniature figures which had been carved and painted by their papa.

"It is a strange custom to cut a tree and bring it into the dwelling," Tall Cloud said, laughing. "Strange also that you hang your popped corn and carved figures onto the tree."

"No stranger than most of your customs, I'm sure," David said, giving Tall Cloud a sour glance.

Tall Cloud went to Christa and helped her wind the strung corn around to the back of the tree. *"Nahkeeta,"* he said in a lower voice. "I haven't yet explained why I have been gone from you for so long."

Christa paused to look up at him, still not believing that he was really there with her and that David had not actually forbid it. Yet, surely David had known that nothing would hold Tall Cloud back. Hadn't he always walked into the cabin, unannounced, whenever he saw fit?

"What *did* delay you, Tall Cloud?" she asked, resuming her labor of love at the tree.

"My people," he grumbled. "I had to move them all to Pahto Island. Because of the disturbances caused by the Haida, all Duwamish and Suquamish were ordered to make camp at Port Madison where they were supposedly to be looked after by an appointed special white man's agent."

Christa blanched, understanding Tall Cloud's feelings about such things, how he never wanted his people to be under the authority of anyone other than himself, their chief.

"No," she gasped. "How horrible, Tall Cloud."

"I refused the white man's orders," he growled. "I would not force my people to live under restraint and under the command of a white man." He proudly thrust his chin into the air. *"I* am their leader. I led them home to my ancestors' island. No white man will venture there. It is too far. It would be of no use to the white man. It will be where my bones will be placed when I die. My spirit will live forever even when my sons are elderly and have sons, even grandsons, of their own."

Christa placed the last of the strung corn on the tree, then moved closer to Tall Cloud, speaking softly. "The move is made?" she asked. "The people are now settled on Pahto Island?"

"Every seed of grain . . . every thing movable was taken from Enati Island," he said. "We left nothing there for the white man or the pirating Haida to steal and take as their own."

Christa had the strong need to wrap her arms about Tall Cloud, to hug him to her, to say that she was sorry for what he was going through and that she truly understood why he had not come to see her. But under David's watchful eye, she couldn't even touch Tall Cloud, much less hug him.

"I'm sorry, Tall Cloud," she whispered. "So sorry."

"My people are better off on Pahto Island," he said dryly. "When the great black ship arrived on the *whulge,* with the muzzles of many cannons poking out of the gun ports on her sides and with its three towering masts, my people's fears became many."

David's ears perked up. He limped over to Tall Cloud. "Ship? What you described was a warship," he said. "Why would a warship be in the Sound?"

"The ship is called by the name *Decatur,*" Tall Cloud said, turning to look down at David. "It is a sloop of war requested by the white men in Seattle, to help protect your people from the Haida. There are also those called marines who have come to Seattle to help with the possible attacks from the Haida."

David paled. His eyes filled with alarm. "Then the threat of the Haida is as real in Seattle as it was a while ago for us in the forest. I had hoped—"

"Do not worry," Tall Cloud growled. "You are safe. My warriors will stay close by as long as you remain here in the cabin." He gave Christa a pensive stare. "You would be even safer if you would return with me to my island. You and your brother, *Nahkeeta,* would be safe while with my people."

David saw the web of desire spinning between Christa and Tall Cloud as they looked so intensely into each other's eyes. He cleared his throat nervously and noisily thumped his crutch against the hardwood of the floor as he made his way back across the room to stand before the fire.

"We will remain here until warned further by the authorities," David insisted. "Everything we own is in this cabin. Also, we've many farm animals to care for. It's out of the question for either of us to leave, Tall Cloud. At times like this, family must stick together, and Christa and I are all we each have left of family."

"I understand family ties," Tall Cloud said. "But with the Indians of my tribe of Suquamish, we are all family. You would become a part of that large family if you came to my island."

Christa saw David's frustration and building anger in the flashing of his green eyes. She placed a hand on Tall Cloud's arm. "Tall Cloud, you are more than generous with your kind offer," she murmured. "But you can see that David is determined to stay here and protect what is ours, just as you have moved your people and possessions to protect what is yours. Please understand."

"Perhaps it is best," Tall Cloud said coldly as he headed for the door.

Christa was numb as she saw him open the door and turn to give her a solemn look. She reached a hand out to him but in vain, for he was gone.

With desperation rising inside her, Christa looked quickly at David then back toward the void at the door, then broke into a run after Tall Cloud. Forcing herself not to hear David shouting at her or to feel the stabbing of the cold wind upon her face and through the thin cotton of her dress, she rushed on toward the Sound, catching a glimpse of Tall Cloud as he began his descent down the bluff to the rocky beach.

Winded, with her hair lifted and flying in the breeze, and with her side aching from the hard run, Christa shouted Tall Cloud's name over and over again. Tears rose in her eyes when she saw him stop and swirl around to see her making her way toward him. She rushed onward, then stumbled into his arms.

"Tall Cloud, why . . . why did you do this to me?" she cried softly, panting. "Why did you leave . . . so . . . so abruptly?" She was seeing only a blur of him through a haze of tears as she looked up at him.

"All was said that needed saying at the moment," he said bluntly, only half holding her. "My people need me more than you do. You have your brother. What else can I say? I said it all . . . as did both you and your brother."

"But you didn't have to leave angry," she said, wiping her eyes with the back of a hand. She shivered as the wind whipped in from the Sound, damp and cold.

Tall Cloud's gaze traveled over her, seeing her light attire. "You are cold," he said. "You must return to your cabin. Now."

"When will I see you again, Tall Cloud?"

"It is hard to say."

"Please don't wait for long," she pleaded. She lowered her eyes. "And once more I want to thank you for coming to our aid today."

"The Haida give *all* Indians a bad name," he growled. "That is too bad."

Christa suddenly remembered the one Haida whom she had recognized as the one who had raped Princess Star. Her eyes, now void of tears, sparkled anxiously. "Tall Cloud, I have something quite important to tell you," she said. "The one Haida that you, personally, were wrestling? He's the one responsible for your . . . your . . . sister's condition."

Tall Cloud's body stiffened. "Striped Wolf," he growled, his jaw set hard. "That was Striped Wolf. Are you sure he is the one?"

"I wounded him, don't you remember?"

"Yes . . ."

"Well, Tall Cloud, the wound is now only a scar. It was him. I'm certain."

Tall Cloud doubled a fist to his side, swung around to look silently across the Sound, then once more turned to Christa. "One day I will seek proper revenge," he said dryly. "But not now. There is already too much to do."

His eyes devoured her, then suddenly he swept her into his arms and crushed his mouth down upon hers. Christa's head began to spin with the thrill of the kiss. But just as quickly he released her and began making his way down the steep incline.

"I love you, Tall Cloud," she said beneath her breath then turned and fled in the direction of her cabin. She doubted that she would ever understand Tall Cloud's moods.

Fourteen

In January, winter began to show its ferocity. The temperature hovered just below freezing. The wind blew hard and cold as snow spit fitfully from the low-hanging gray clouds, adding more accumulation to the two inches that already blanketed the ground.

David placed more wood on the fire. He was now able to maneuver about without the aid of a crutch, though he still found it too painful to fit his foot into a boot.

Christa went to a window. She moved her hand in a circle over the window pane, wiping it clean of enough moisture to take another concerned peek outside.

"It's so eerily quiet this morning," Christa worried aloud. "Though the wind is blowing hard, it isn't emitting so much as a whistle around the corners of the cabin."

"It's the snow," David said, settling down in a chair to whittle idly. "It always muffles sounds, even the wind. You know that."

An involuntary shiver enveloped Christa. She clasped her arms across her chest and hugged herself, watching the snow being swept up from the ground by the wind, swirled around, and deposited in higher drifts alongside the cabin.

"I just don't like it," Christa argued. "Somehow I feel helpless. And what about our animals?"

"You succeeded at gettin' them into the barn," David said, casting her a sideways glance. "They're safe enough."

His face shadowed into a frown. "I'm the one who feels helpless, Christa. You've been takin' on the chores for way too long now. Why is it takin' my foot so long to heal completely? I still can't get into my boot."

Christa swung herself away from the window, whipping the skirt of her cotton dress around her ankles. She went to the table and patted flour onto its surface, readying it for making bread. "I admire you for the patience you've shown up to now, David," she said, smiling warmly toward him. "It won't be much longer."

With the back of a hand she smoothed a fallen lock of hair from her eyes. "You'll see," she encouraged further. "When spring comes, you'll be out planting crops. You won't even remember these months that you were incapacitated."

A sudden knock on the door startled Christa so, she knocked her canister of flour from the table. As it tumbled to the floor, flour dust rose like smoke into Christa's nose, making her sneeze.

The knock on the door persisted. Christa tensed. She looked toward David who had dropped his knife and pine stick and was now holding a loaded, aimed rifle. He rose slowly from the chair, pointing the rifle toward the door.

"Go on. See who it is," he said blandly. "One thing for sure; it's not the Indians. They don't bother to knock."

He gestured with the barrel of the rifle. "Go on, Christa," he urged. "I've got you covered. No one will get the chance to harm you."

Smearing flour on her nose as she tried to hold back another sneeze threatening to surface, she inched her way toward the door. Her heart beat erratically and her knees were weak. Never before had she so dreaded opening the door to a stranger. She still held inside her a strange foreboding that something terrible was going to happen this day.

With trembling fingers she placed her hand on the door

latch. Standing back so David could have clear aim, she swung the door open with a jerk, and the sight of who she found herself face to face with made her mouth drop open and a gasp of disbelief rush from her lips.

"Delores?" Christa once more gasped. "Delores Kramer?"

Though Delores was decked out in men's attire, even to the boots on her feet and slouch hat pulled low over her eyes, Christa fully recognized the lovely face upturned to her.

"I've come to get you and David," Delores said, brushing past Christa. She spied David standing beside the fire, his eyes wide with surprise and his rifle lowered to his side. She hurried to him and took his free hand in hers, the glove on Delores's hand keeping their flesh apart.

"Delores, what are you doing way out here all alone and in such terrible weather?" David blurted. His eyes traveled over her, seeing the loose-fitted men's trousers and the heavy, red-plaid flannel jacket. Her auburn hair was hidden beneath a hat, but loose tendrils peeked out here and there.

Her cheeks were a blistery red from the harshness of the temperature and the viciousness of the wind, but her blue eyes held in them their usual lively sparkle as she looked up adoringly at David.

"And dressed in such a manner?" David continued. "As a man, Delores?"

"Never mind the way I'm dressed or the weather," Delores said hurriedly. "You must go with me. Now. You and your sister must go into Seattle and join everyone else at the stockade."

"But why?" Christa asked, shutting the door with a bang, stepping high over tracked-in snow as she made her way to the fire, to erase the chill that had engulfed her in the open doorway.

"The Haida Indians," Delores said, easing her hand from David's, feeling the need to warm herself beside the fire.

She turned her back to David and leaned her hands low over the flames. She wouldn't reveal her numb toes and fingers or the fact that her throat ached severely from breathing in the cold air while racing her horse and buggy through the snow.

She wouldn't confess to her buggy getting stuck in high drifts those two times either. She would do nothing to dissuade David from taking the journey into Seattle on this blustery, cold day. She had seen the reflection of fires in the sky. She had known that the Haida were wreaking havoc throughout the countryside and had assumed the Indians considered the settlers more vulnerable when they also had the snow and wind to fight.

David grabbed Delores by a wrist and swung her around to face him. "Don't tell me that you've come all the way out here, alone, while the threat of Indians is so strong that everyone is being urged to go to the stockade," he growled. "Weren't you born with brains, Delores? And where's Harrison? Why didn't he stop you?"

"Harrison is concerned about Harrison." Delores sighed, blinking her eyes nervously. "David, surely you know that is Harrison's nature."

David gave Christa a half-downcast glance, smiling sheepishly when she gave him a I-told-you-so look.

Delores crept closer to David and spoke softly up into his face. "I *had* to come, David," she murmured. "Don't you know that? I've been worrying myself sick over you. It's been forever since I've seen you, and then there was this scare about the Indians. I couldn't stay in Seattle, wondering about you."

"You knew why I couldn't come, didn't you?" David asked thickly.

"Your farm. Yes, I knew," she said, nodding her head. Then she stepped back away from David. "I dressed as a man, thinking I would be safer." She laughed. "But most men traveling alone do so by horseback instead of a woman's buggy, don't they? I'm not sure I fooled anyone, yet I am here, safe."

"We heard nothing. No horse or your buggy," Christa interjected. "But of course we wouldn't. The snow muffles all noises."

Delores clasped her hands eagerly before her. "We truly have no more time for idle chatter. Get your wraps on," she urged. "Quickly. I've come to take you back to the stockade, and it must be done in haste."

Delores's gaze moved to David's freshly bandaged foot, then back up into his eyes. "How is it?" she murmured. "Is it no better?"

"It's better. But not well," David grumbled, raking his fingers nervously through his hair.

"Then we shall wrap it snugly in blankets for the journey back to Seattle," Delores said from across her shoulder as she moved toward the bedroom. She gave Christa a quick glance. "We must hurry, Christa. The Indian war is now a reality."

"We can't just . . . up . . . and leave," Christa argued, following along after Delores into the bedroom. She watched, mortified, as Delores whisked a blanket from the bed and brushed past Christa, back into the outer room.

"As I see it, you have no choice," Delores said, jerking David's flannel jacket and hat from a corner coat rack. "It's either leave . . . or . . . die . . ."

Christa's mind filled with thoughts of Tall Cloud. But surely his warriors had given up their vigil long ago because of the cold temperatures and snow, and because it had appeared for a while that the Haida Indians had retreated to their villages, perhaps also from the cold.

"Christa," Delores begged, shaking Christa from her deep thoughts. "Please. Time is passing. The ride back to Seattle will be arduous enough without our having to fight off the Indians or the darkness of night."

Christa went to David and clung to his arm. "David,

surely you're not leaving just because Delores is asking us to," she cried. "We had decided to stay, to protect our possessions."

"The time has come to place sentimentality behind us," he said hoarsely. "Don't you realize, Christa, that the situation has to be pretty bad or Delores wouldn't have risked her neck to come for us?"

Christa looked wildly at Delores. "And our animals? What are we to do with them?" she asked.

"Of course they will have to be left behind," Delores said, kneeling to help David into his one boot. "Christa, we don't have time for anything but getting in the buggy and heading the horse back in the direction of Seattle."

Frustrated, sad, and angry, Christa grabbed her rabbit-furlined cape. She swung it about her shoulders, secured it at her neck, and placed its hood on her head. "Perhaps we won't be gone long." She sighed. "The Haida have come and gone quickly before. Perhaps it will be the same again."

Delores placed an arm about David's waist. "Help me with David," she encouraged. "Then once we get him to the buggy, I'll wrap his foot snugly with a blanket."

First Christa rushed around the cabin, snuffing out the kerosene lamps and sprinkling ashes onto the flames in the fireplace to extinguish that fire. Sorrowfully, she looked about her then went to David, easing her arm about his waist. His arm swung about her shoulder and together with Delores they left the cabin and quickly boarded the buggy.

Refusing to look toward the barn, not wanting to think of the fate of her farm animals, Christa directed her eyes straight ahead, where snow covered everything in sight except the blue waters of the Sound. David sat hunched between the two women, with his rifle perched ready on his lap.

Christa braced herself as the horse and buggy lurched forward. Clouds of what appeared to be smoke snorted from the lone horse's nostrils as he plowed his powerful hooves straight on through the snow where no road was visible to the eye.

Delores snapped her reins and yelled a series of "hahh" sounds, keeping a close eye on the deeply shadowed forest at her one side.

Christa's breath caught in her throat as she got her first glimpse of fire reflected in the low-hanging clouds. "Good Lord . . ." she gasped.

"The Haida are burning houses," Delores said, casting Christa a nervous glance. "I didn't tell you earlier. I didn't want to alarm you that much."

"It's really that bad?" David said thickly.

"Most of the valley is deserted by now," Delores said. "I guess no one came to warn you again because you failed to heed the earlier warning."

David smiled crookedly at Delores. "You amaze me." He chuckled. "Who'd have thought a tiny thing like you would be filled with so much spunk."

"I should have come sooner," Delores apologized. "But Harrison just wouldn't allow it. This time I did what I felt had to be done."

"And it's appreciated," Christa said, though hating to admit this to Harrison's daughter. Once in Seattle, Christa knew she would once more be pursued openly by the man she despised, Delores's father! He would have some nerve doing so, after showing so openly what a coward he was by letting his daughter come out into the wilderness when he should have come. And, oh, how Christa dreaded the thought of the Haida burning everything that was so precious to her!

The wind whipped the snow into frenzied spurts which were almost blinding as they blew into the buggy. Christa trembled, feeling the cold penetrating her clothes and her flesh like stabs of icicles. She scooted closer to David and wrapped her arm and cape around his shoulders, glancing down at his blanket-wrapped foot. It looked snug and dry enough and safe from frostbite. Her own toes and fingers didn't feel that secure, though. They burned from the cold.

"Hahh!" Delores shouted at the horse when a thick snow-drift loomed before them. The buggy's wheels creaked and slid ominously; the horse snorted and shook his head. But then he was through and the snowdrift was left quickly behind.

The first signs that they were nearing Seattle were the log pilings left by the loggers, which began to appear in the waters of the Sound. And then the outline of moored ships in the distance gave an indication of safety ahead.

"The sloop of war *Decatur* is ready for the Indian attack on Seattle," Delores said. "But most say the Indians won't come this close to the city."

"Ha! I wouldn't count on what most say after seein' the signs of fire everywhere I look in the sky," David scoffed. "Looks like they mean business this time."

Their entry into Seattle was very different from previous arrivals. The streets were deserted. The wharves were empty of passengers coming and going from the moored ships. The warship *Decatur* looked menacing with the muzzles of its many cannons poking out of the gun ports in her sides. It was there that the first signs of life were evident in the marines milling on the ship's deck, waiting.

Christa then got her first look at the stockade which had been erected along the waterfront. Its tall fence covered only a small area. Above this fence she could see the second story of the blockhouse with many gun ports in its side. This made the war real for Christa, and true fear inched its way inside her heart.

"We must hurry inside the stockade," Delores said, guiding the horse and buggy toward a huge, closed gate.

After Delores announced herself and the horse and buggy moved on inside the blockade, Christa felt as if she were entering a different country. Blue-uniformed sentries stood guard, and everywhere she looked people milled about, shivering in the snow. And when she was directed to the blockhouse with Delores and David, she saw why most were outside. The large room was filled with cots, some with sleeping figures on them and others piled high with personal belongings. The strong aroma of fried fish filled the open spaces of the room, emanating from a fireplace at the far end where women huddled, cooking for the masses.

"I see you made it safely enough," Harrison's voice boomed from behind Christa.

She turned on a heel and saw him rushing down a set of stairs at the far end of the room, dressed in splendidly pressed trousers, a lace-edged shirt, and a maroon velvet frock coat.

Setting her jaw and flashing anger back at him, Christa prepared herself for his presence. "No thanks to you, sir!" she snapped. She cringed when the damp palm of his hand touched her cheek.

"You're cold," he said, ignoring her waspish remark. "Come upstairs. All of you. It's less crowded. Mainly military, you know."

"And you place yourself in that category, do you?" Christa laughed scornfully, flipping her hood from her head, revealing golden rivulets of hair cascading across her shoulders.

"My money helped build this blockhouse and is paying many volunteers to guard it," Harrison said icily. "Or do you forget the power of my wealth in this city, Christa?"

Her eyes rolled back in her head, showing her disgust. "Need one be reminded of that?" She sighed and grudgingly accepted the arm he offered her, accompanying him up the stairs. Over her shoulder she saw that David was doing well enough in the company of Delores, and she felt the smallest twinge of jealousy, realizing that her brother no longer belonged solely to her.

The upper floor contained a pot-bellied stove glowing orange in the center of the room and around the edges stood sentries on guard beside the gun ports, ready to shoot their rifles at a moment's notice. Several windows admitted what daylight remained. On this floor cots had been placed in a circle around the heating stove, and Christa noted they were unoccupied.

"Take any of your choosing," Harrison said, gesturing toward the cots. "These were placed here at my suggestion, for your use."

"Harrison, you should be horsewhipped for lettin' Delores come alone to our cabin," David growled.

"Of late, she does as she damn pleases," Harrison retorted. "But you would be the one to notice that, I am sure."

David watched Delores remove her hat and shake her auburn hair to hang long and free down her back. And when she removed her bulky coat to reveal the magnificent outline of her breasts against her clinging cotton shirt, he was glad that *he* was the cause of this change in her. He melted inside when her sky blue eyes smiled back at him.

Christa removed her cape and tossed it on a cot, then she knelt before David to inspect his bandage. It was wet and needed changing. She rose to her feet and stepped away from him as Delores began fussing over him.

"Hear *that!*" a male's voice called suddenly from behind Christa. She spun around and watched the two uniformed sentries as they removed their rifles from the gun ports and leaned closer to the openings in the walls to listen.

"Owls? Is that what you heard, Ed?" the other sentry asked, his whiskered face screwed up in puzzlement.

"That ain't owls, dummy," Ed scoffed. "That's Injuns. Those sounds of hootin' in the woods is damn Injuns. They're probably gatherin' and signalin' to one another."

"If'n it's a fight they're after," the whiskered man said, "it's a fight we'll give 'em."

Christa's insides knotted. She couldn't help but think of Tall Cloud when Indians were mentioned. What if his warriors were somehow mistaken for Haida and were fired upon by mistake? But then she realized the foolishness of such a thought. Tall Cloud and his people were safely on Pahto Island and had nothing whatsoever to do with this fight.

Still, she wanted to see for herself, so she strode to the wall and peered from one of the windows, seeing quite clearly into the outer reaches of the forest which outlined the city of Seattle in a frame of white. The snowfall was now only an occasional sparkle slowly drifting from the clouds, and the winds had died to almost nothing.

"You shouldn't be so close to a window," Harrison warned as he stepped to Christa's side. "Come. Sit by the fire with me. It's been a while since we last talked."

Christa glared at him. "You have no more say over what I do than you do over your daughter," she hissed. "Now, Harrison, just leave me be!"

Harrison's nose seemed more sharply beaked, his lips more narrowed, and his eyes more dark and penetrating as he took in Christa's words. His face grew ashen in color as he tried to control his rage. He had always known why she wouldn't agree to marry him. It was his age. A young, handsome gentleman was the fantasy of most unwed women. It was no different for Christa, and if not for his wealth, Harrison knew he would feel quite inadequate beneath the scrutiny of this lovely, very available young woman.

"None of us are going anywhere for a while," he said thickly. "When you are in need of conversation, Christa, I will be only a footstep away."

Christa's lips parted softly as she watched him turn and walk away. She couldn't believe that a man could take such verbal abuse from a woman and then actually ask for more of the same. It tired her, just thinking of having to be so near him for what might be many days. And to sleep in the same room with him. . . .

Distressed, shaking her head sadly, Christa once more

focused her attention outside, watching what seemed to be a building up of activity.

And suddenly the activity reached a crescendo as the harsh howl of the Haida's war cry rang out, and many Haida ran from the forest carrying flaming rush mats. One by one these mats were tossed over the cedar stockade fence to land among the crowds of Seattleites who had not thought themselves to be so vulnerable.

Christa's hands flew to her mouth as she watched the people scatter wildly in all directions, screaming.

The loud command, "Fire!" reverberated about the block-house's upper room. Christa looked toward the sentries who were now intent on killing Indians. The room dimmed with blue powder smoke, and the sound of continuous gunfire was sickening.

"Look at them Injuns scatter!" Ed laughed mockingly. "And I'd heard of a man tattooin' his body before, but those Injuns take the cake. Look at 'em. Their whole bodies are covered with tattoos, from tip to toe!"

"The tattoos are makin' it easier to see 'em against the snow," the other sentry said with a laugh.

Ed grew serious. "Ain't you thinkin' what I'm athink-ing'?" he said, aiming and shooting again.

"Huh?"

"Don'cha wonder why they're not freezin' with only those damn loincloths on?"

"Hell no. They're savages, ain't they? They've got no feelin's."

Christa's face flamed with color after hearing those last remarks. Anger coursed through her. No one on the face of the earth had such deep feelings and compassion as Tall Cloud, and *he* was an Indian. The Suquamish were not the same as the Haida. And just as she was about to speak in their defense, a ball of smoke blossomed from the side of the *Decatur* in the bay as the Marines lobbed a howitzer shell into the woods. The sharp report of the howitzer continued intermittently, and the settlers rushed from the stockade courtyard into the safer confines of the blockhouse. Then just as suddenly as the gunfire had erupted, everything was quiet and peaceful again.

David limped to Christa's side, leaned against the window facing, and looked out. "For a while there it did sound like a war," he murmured.

"Strange as hell," Ed said, leaning his rifle against his knee, idly scratching his brow. "The Injuns didn't even fire back at us."

"They're waitin' to attack," the other sentry grumbled. "Jist you wait an' see. They'll come in hordes and burn us to the ground. I feel it in my bones."

David stepped closer to Christa and eased his arm about her waist. "Come on over by the fire," he encouraged softly. "You're tremblin'. Hon, things are goin' to be all right. With the *Decatur* out there and its howitzer and cannons, no Indians can take us by force. It's virtually impossible, Christa."

Christa accepted David's comforting arm and his words. But she could not confess to him that her fears were not for herself, or even for him. She was concerned over Tall Cloud's welfare. Something deep inside her—a small voice, it seemed—told her that Tall Cloud would not remain on his island while so much excitement was occurring in Seattle. And if he came to the city, he could be mistaken for a hostile Indian.

An involuntary shudder engulfed her. If only she had a way to warn Tall Cloud not to come to Seattle. But it was useless. In a sense she was a prisoner, as were all the white settlers crammed within these reeking walls.

The howitzer shot another round and Christa tensed. She looked across her shoulder toward the window while she walked alongside David, who led her to the stove. The room once more became a haze of blue powder smoke as the two sentries opened fire again.

"Feel crazy as a loon shootin' at thin air," Ed yelled above the fire. "Cain't see the Injuns now for the dark of the forest."

"Maybe they have hightailed it outta here," the other sentry shouted. "Cowards. All of 'em, cowards."

Smoke curled up into the sky from the edges of the city. Christa could see it from where she stood. She grabbed David's arm. "Good Lord," she gasped. "David, they're setting fire to the city!"

"The *Decatur* can't do any good there," David growled. "And the Haida know that. They've decided to wreak havoc there while all Seattleites are *here.*"

Silence settled upon the blockhouse after all the sentries left to pursue the Haida on foot.

"I've just got to look," Christa said, wrenching herself away from David. She grimaced when Delores and Harrison fell into step on each side of her, but she understood their interest. Both had nothing to gain at the hands of the Haida but everything to lose, so she tolerated their presence at the window.

All of the excitement appeared to be centered now on First Street where warehouses constructed of wood lined each side of the street.

Suddenly Christa's breath caught in her throat when she looked in the direction of the Sound. Coming *en masse* were what appeared to be a hundred canoes, and leading these was one she recognized instantly.

Tall Cloud! she gasped to herself, growing faint. No. He can't. He'll be killed!

But Tall Cloud and his warriors continued along their way, now within shooting range of the *Decatur,* yet the warship didn't attempt firing upon them. Instead, it ceased firing altogether as the canoes were beached and emptied of Indians whose faces were painted with bold red stripes and who carried rifles and had bows slung across their shoulders. Dressed fully in buckskin, they were easy to distinguish from the Haida.

"What are *they* up to?" Harrison said, now watching Tall Cloud and his warriors as they ran stealthily along the snow-covered ground, past the stockade, toward First Street. "I'll be damned if we need *two* tribes of Indians to set fire to our buildings and houses."

Christa was confused into silence. Why would Tall Cloud . . . ? Then a small ray of hope began to shine inside her. Tall Cloud hated the Haida far more than he did the white man! Could it be possible . . . ?

With a pounding heart, she focused her full attention on the tallest and handsomest of the Suquamish who wore a fancy headdress of brightly dyed feathers which reached behind him to the bend of his knees. If anyone had looked into her eyes then, he would have seen the intensity of her love and her pride in the man who so bravely led his warriors. Never had she loved him more than at this moment when he might be going to his death, and it tore at her heart to stand idly by, helpless, unable to tell him so.

Clenching her fists at her sides, she waited. She uttered one soft, silent prayer after another. And as Tall Cloud and his warriors moved from within viewing range and the noise of a sudden eruption of gunfire reached their ears, she felt as though her gut would twist from her insides, so severe was the pain of her worry. And there was nothing for her to do but wait.

Fifteen

A full day and night had gone by, and still Christa did not know the fate of Tall Cloud. It was growing dusk now on what had been an uneventful day with no gunfire from Indian or white man. The Haida seemed to have disappeared into thin air, and only Tall Cloud's warriors stood guard at the edge of the forest which outlined Seattle on three sides.

"But where is Tall Cloud?" Christa whispered to herself as she stood on tiptoe and strained her neck to get a better view of the open courtyard. Suddenly there was some sort of commotion. Christa had watched many marines leave the decks of the *Decatur* and move in the direction of the stockade, and the volunteers who had fought side by side with the marines were now crowding about in the courtyard.

Breathless, standing alone, glad that the sentries had left the room and that Harrison, David, and Delores were in heavy conversation behind her by the stove, Christa continued to watch as the marines now marched into the courtyard and lined up in single file, row after row, with the volunteers doing the same opposite them. A lone aisle had been left between them, down which the distinguished-looking marine commanding officer in his navy blue full uniform strode square shouldered, looking from man to man.

The sun was now behind the distant mountains, leaving only streaks of orange smeared across the quickly darkening sky. The courtyard was not yet lighted, and Christa was finding it harder and harder to see what else was transpiring outside, below her.

Squinting her eyes, peering hard, she watched the gates of the stockade swing open widely. Her heart skipped a beat when she recognized Tall Cloud, standing proud and even taller than most of the white men who still stood at attention. All eyes followed the Indian chief as he was guided by the commanding officer to stand in the midst of the silent group of men.

Christa's hands went to her throat, and she felt the wildness of the pulsebeat there. She watched as the men began filing, one by one, in front of Tall Cloud, shaking his hand. She knew that he was being paid the highest honor by these white men and was eager to know *why*.

But whatever the reason, this demonstration of friendship and admiration for Tall Cloud was making a slow lump rise in Christa's throat. She knew how long Tall Cloud had strived for such recognition. Perhaps now he could attain what he had wanted from the first, what he had thought to gain by marrying her—an alliance with the white man. That had been his goal, and now it seemed within reach.

Christa felt a desperate need to go to Tall Cloud, to throw her arms about his neck, whisper her love to him, and tell him of the pride she shared with him during this ceremony of honor.

Casting a quick glance over her shoulder, Christa knew that she could not achieve an unnoticed escape. And when she looked back down at the courtyard, the crowd had dispersed and Tall Cloud was nowhere to be seen.

Tears formed in Christa's eyes, and she wondered when she might have a chance to see him again. The world seemed to have been turned upside down by the Haida Indians.

But are they gone now? she wondered to herself. And is Tall Cloud possibly the reason . . . ?

Kerosene lanterns being lighted behind Christa and the

strong aroma of fried salmon drew her away from the window to a cot beside the stove. She settled down on its edge, accepted a plate of fish, and ate her evening meal in silence, then eagerly sipped the hot cup of coffee Harrison offered to wash down the greasy, foul-tasting salmon.

Small talk began, and it seemed everyone except Christa was oblivious to or uncaring of the special attention given to Tall Cloud. Now that the sentries had returned to the room, the main topic of conversation was the Haida giving up the fight and running back to their villages like scared rabbits.

"Tomorrow, after we're sure it's safe, we can return home, Christa," David said, sipping a tin cup of coffee.

"Shortest damn Injun war in history, wouldn't you say, folks?" the whiskered sentry asked, laughing wildly. "We showed 'em. Yep, we showed 'em."

During the rest of the evening, the laughing and the talking became a blur to Christa. She couldn't join in the talk of victory. All she could think about was Tall Cloud, why he had been in the courtyard, and why no one bothered to acknowledge that he had been there or that his warriors had somehow had a part in this victory against the Haida. It was as if Tall Cloud and his tribe of friendly Suquamish Indians had ceased to exist.

Much later, relieved finally to be lying in her own assigned cot in the darkened room and hearing muffled snores surfacing from Harrison who lay much too close to her on his own cot, Christa crept to her feet and went to the window which directly faced the Sound. She watched the moon's reflection spilling into the water.

It was as if there were hundreds of lighted lanterns positioned beneath the surface of the water, twinkling, often blending into one smear of white as the waves rose and tumbled toward shore. Christa sighed heavily, absorbing the peacefulness of the setting, glad to be able to enjoy the distant cry of a single loon instead of hearing the explosion of many guns.

Her thoughts turned to her home and belongings. Had they remained untouched by the Haida, or had the things she held dear to her heart been destroyed? Tomorrow. She would know . . . tomorrow.

Yawning and stretching, realizing that she was probably the only one awake at this late hour, Christa decided to go to her cot and try once more to get some badly needed rest. She knew that the next few days could be draining, not only mentally, but physically as well.

Before turning away from the window, she once more looked toward the Sound. Her heart gave way to a feeling of dismay when she saw the familiar outline of Tall Cloud, who was now standing at the water's edge, looking toward the stockade. Did he know that she was there? Had some of his warriors still been standing watch when Delores had come with the news which had prompted Christa and David to flee to safety in Seattle? Had Tall Cloud's heart been filled with her when battling the Haida?

Christa touched the pane of the window, wishing she could somehow communicate with Tall Cloud, tell him that she was all right and that she ached so to be with him.

She longed for him even more deeply as she saw him stand there persistently, looking her way yet not seeing her. "I must go to him," she whispered to herself, curling her hands into tight fists at her sides. "I must, somehow, manage to go to him. *Now.*"

Spinning around, she looked about the room, seeing the many sleeping figures. It could be easy . . . slipping from the room, she thought. And to steal across the courtyard without being caught could be managed if she wore her black, hooded cape. The only true obstacle was the closed gate. But after the evening's celebration, perhaps the sentries would be fast asleep, since the Haida had been dealt with so successfully.

Soundless, stepping as lightly as possible across the floor, Christa grabbed her cape. She swung it about her shoulders and moved stealthily across the room and breathed much easier when she reached the staircase.

Slowly, lightly, she stole down the steps, through the crowded, lower room of sleeping settlers and sentries, and finally stepped out into the snow of the courtyard.

Looking cautiously about her, she saw that the walls of the stockade cast high, dark shadows which would give her cover from the bright rays of the moon. She slipped the hood of her cape onto her head and, with the tail of her cape and the skirt of her dress lifted up past her ankles, Christa leaned close to the cedar posts of the stockade wall, inching herself along. Her eyes finally caught sight of the gate, and, to her amazement, she discovered that someone had been careless enough to leave it partially open.

She reasoned that with the scare of the Haida eased, there were probably many who had left the confines of the stockade and blockhouse to return to their homes, fearing vandals or, worse yet, that their homes had been burned by the Haida. Perhaps she was just one of many making such an escape this night. But only she would be going to the comforting arms of a handsome Indian.

Appearing as a soft shadow in the night, an apparition, Christa fled through the opened gate, ignoring the cold seeping through the soles of her shoes as the snow pressed into them. The brisk air nipped at the flesh of her face, and her breath came in short gasps as she hurried toward the sparkle of the Sound. If Tall Cloud were gone, so would be her heart. And who could say when the opportunity to see each other would once more be theirs? And seeing would not be enough for Christa. Touching, kissing, embracing—that was what she desired. The fear of losing him made her love for him even greater than before.

The outlines of the moored ships at the wharves fell upon the ground in silent grays against the whiteness of the snow.

The sleek hull of the warship *Decatur* carried its own silhouette in the moon-reflecting waters of the Sound, and on the *Decatur*'s decks strolled sentries unaware of Christa's presence as she crept past it toward the place where she had seen Tall Cloud standing tall and proud from her vantage point in the blockhouse.

Squinting her eyes, trying to distinguish between many shadows in the distance, she felt her heart perform a strange fluttering dance when she saw that Tall Cloud was among them. He hadn't fled into the darkness of night. He had waited as though he had known that she would come to him.

With an eager spring in her steps, Christa hurried onward. And when Tall Cloud saw and recognized her, he began to run toward her. Arms circled and lips met as they came together in a joyous reunion.

"Mika . . ." Tall Cloud said huskily as he withdrew his lips from hers and looked down into her eyes. His hands brushed her hood from her head; his fingers wove through her hair which lay thickly upon her shoulders.

"I had worried so about you, *Nahkeeta*," he added. "My warriors saw you leave your dwelling. They followed you until you were safely in the white man's stockade. But once you were there, I did not know what had become of you."

"Surely you knew that I was safe," she murmured. "That's why we went to the stockade."

"There are dangers in the white man's dwelling for you almost as bad as the Haida," he growled. "The white man named Harrison Kramer—is he not a threat to your peace of mind?"

Christa giggled. "Oh, is that what you meant?" she said. "Yes. I can understand your concern. But, Tall Cloud, I am very capable of handling Harrison Kramer. Never concern yourself about him."

She shivered as a gust of wind blew across the waters of

the Sound. It seemed ice filled, almost cutting through the tender flesh of her face.

"You are cold," Tall Cloud said, frowning.

"Slightly," Christa said, laughing softly. She looked in all directions, trying to think of a place where they could go to be together and be warm while they were.

Then her eyes brightened. She felt devilish, but she did have in mind a place to go. They could even sit beside a cozy fire. The chance of being caught would make their being together even more exciting.

Grabbing Tall Cloud's hand, she urged him to follow along beside her. "Come with me," she said, casting him a coy look.

"Where?" he asked, raising an eyebrow.

"To a house the like of which I am sure you've never seen before," she said, lifting her hood back onto her head as the wind tore through her hair and once more sent chills up and down her spine.

They went past the stockade, across an unusually quiet First Street, ascending the steepness of the streets to Fourth Avenue, Christa's destination. She observed that only a few buildings in the city had been set afire by the Haida, and the rest had thankfully been spared.

As they passed blocks of houses, spirals of smoke rising from an occasional chimney indicated that some Seattleites had returned to their homes, hoping the Indian war, brief though it was, was indeed a thing of the past.

Smiling to herself, Christa heartily welcomed the sight of smoke from the chimneys. When she lighted a fire to share with Tall Cloud, its smoke wouldn't draw the sentries from the stockade. No one would think to separate one smoke spiral from another or question which house each was rising from. Now Christa's only fear was that someone would awaken in the blockhouse and discover that she was gone. But the darkness of the room where she was supposed to be sleeping most surely was her protection against wandering eyes in the night.

When they reached Fourth Avenue and Harrison Kramer's mansion, Tall Cloud stopped abruptly. He jerked his hand away from Christa's, very aware of whose residence this was, and he wanted no part of it.

Christa swung the skirt of her cape around, spraying snow onto Tall Cloud's moccasins. "What's wrong?" she asked. "Why have you stopped?"

"Why have you brought me here . . . to that man's house?" he growled.

Christa looked up into his face, even in the darkness of night savoring his closeness, marveling anew over his handsome Indian profile.

"He . . . Harrison Kramer isn't here," she reassured him. "He's back in the blockhouse, asleep. I've brought you here to be alone with you. Harrison is too much of a coward to return home until he's positive there are no more threats of Indian retaliation. It's all right, Tall Cloud. Please come inside with me."

"I want no part of that white man's world," Tall Cloud stated, setting his jaw firmly, remembering how he had discovered Harrison with Christa. Jealousy coiled inside him like a snake. Yet he knew she hadn't wanted that man's touches. There was no reason to be jealous. But there *was* a reason to hate the man who pursued his *Nahkeeta.*

Christa took his elbow and began tugging at it. "Tall Cloud, please do as I ask, for a little while?" she encouraged. "I can only stay for a short time. Someone might discover that I'm gone."

The soft pleading in her voice ate away at Tall Cloud's heart. He touched her face gently. "For a short while," he said huskily, envisioning them together as they had been before. His loins already ached with intense need of her. And couldn't it be a way to avenge Harrison Kramer, making love to *Nahkeeta* beneath the white man's own roof? His lips lifted in a smug smile.

Christa laughed. "Then let's go," she said, moving up the steps that led to one of Seattle's finest homes. But when she got to the door and tried the knob, her heart sank. Why hadn't she realized that it would be locked? How foolish she had been to think that she could make a grand entry into such a house without the owner's consent!

Sadly, she turned to Tall Cloud. "It's locked." She sighed. "A key is needed, Tall Cloud. I should have known."

Now as anxious to go inside this house as Christa, Tall Cloud stepped close to the door. "A locked door?" he said. "In my village, locks are not needed. Our people respect the privacy and belongings of other tribe members. There is no cause for locks on doors."

He tried the doorknob, then gave Christa a questioning look. "This lock would never keep me out of a dwelling. Do you still wish to go inside?"

He respected the privacy and belongings of others as he did his own people's. It had been instilled in him as a child. But since he didn't respect Harrison Kramer, how could he be expected to respect anything that belonged to him? Breaking into his house would be a pleasure. Doing so would even enhance his moments with *Nahkeeta*.

Seeing a strange, anxious glint in Tall Cloud's eyes, Christa tensed. "What do you mean?" she asked. "What do you intend to do?"

"Do you still wish to go inside?" Tall Cloud questioned flatly, eying her intensely.

"Why, yes . . ." she murmured.

Tall Cloud clasped her shoulders and gently eased her aside. He took a step away from the door and then lunged for it with the muscles of his right shoulder.

Christa's hands flew to her mouth, and she gasped as the door burst open beneath the forceful weight of Tall Cloud's body. The explosion that was made by the door crashing against the inside wall echoed outwardly, reverberating down the steps and into the snow-covered expanses of the estate grounds. Then once again everything was quiet.

"No door is a barrier to our love, *Nahkeeta,*" Tall Cloud said taking her hand and moving with her over the threshold, into the dark recesses of the stately mansion.

Then Tall Cloud pulled her into his arms and looked down into her eyes with a building passion. "We will make love, won't we, *Nahkeeta?*"

Consumed by a rush of ecstasy, Christa twined her arms about his neck. "Yes," she whispered. "We will make love, darling. Why else would I bring you here?"

"To show me what I can never . . . *will* never give you," he grumbled. "Perhaps you have decided to marry the rich white man and you wanted to show me the reasons why. Surely his possessions are an attraction to all white women. How can I expect you not to want the same?"

Christa giggled softly. "You silly," she said. "You *are* only jesting, aren't you? You have to know that my love for you is much stronger than a few foolish pieces of crystal and china."

"At times I have doubted this," he argued softly.

"If you will remember, I only behaved angrily toward you after I had thought that your feelings for me were not sincere, when I thought you wanted me only for the chance to form an alliance with the white men."

"I am here with you now. Is that not proof enough that you were wrong?"

"What do you mean?"

"I have successfully made that alliance with the white man," Tall Cloud boasted proudly. "I was rewarded today for helping the white man remove the Haida from Seattle. The alliance between the Suquamish and the white man is now complete. And you see? I am still here with you. I still want you."

His arms drew her closer and his lips bore down upon

hers. Christa's head began spinning; her pulse was erratic. She clung to him, now realizing that his love for her was true. His words had been sincere, and what he had just said dispelled all of her earlier doubts about why he had chosen to be with her.

A crisp breath of air blew in through the opened door behind Christa, lifting the tail of her cape and the skirt of her dress to expose the calves of her legs, reminding her that they were not yet any warmer than before. Though inside a house, they still hadn't built a fire.

Hating to, but knowing that it was best, Christa splayed her fingers onto Tall Cloud's chest and gently pushed him away from her.

"Tall Cloud," she said, realizing how breathless she sounded from his kiss, from just being with him, "let's get a fire started. Then we can do . . . whatever . . . you wish."

She lowered her eyes at those words, feeling heat rise to her cheeks. With Tall Cloud she had become so unbelievably brazen. At times she hardly knew herself. . . .

Tall Cloud swung around, peering into the dark recesses of the house. "Where is the fire space?" he asked, showing his innocence, something that made Christa love him even more.

"Fire space?" Christa said, turning to close the door. "This type of dwelling has what is called a fireplace where the family fires are built. You know, like the fireplace in my cabin."

She started feeling her way around the foyer, trying to recall the arrangement of the house. "Follow me," she encouraged. "This house has *four* fireplaces. But the one we want is upstairs. We shall make a small fire in one of the bedrooms."

Still feeling around her, Christa sighed with relief when she found a kerosene lamp on a table and, thankfully, matches alongside it. Pushing her cape back from her arms she raised the glass chimney from the lamp, screwed the wick up only slightly, then set a struck match to it.

The fire slowly traveled across the tip of the kerosene-soaked wick, casting flickers of light along the walls and ceiling. Shaking her hood from her head, Christa smiled toward Tall Cloud, seeing the look of love in his eyes as he fully absorbed her standing there in the soft light.

Beginning to feel awkward beneath his steady stare, Christa laughed nervously. "Tall Cloud, why are you looking at me like that?" she murmured.

"You are a vision of loveliness," he said thickly.

Lowering her lashes, once more blushing, Christa stepped around Tall Cloud, feeling the need to break this spell, but only momentarily. "Let's go upstairs," she said, taking first one step and then another. She knew that she should feel guilty being inside Harrison's house, never having done anything like this before. Had it not been Harrison's house, she would never have been so bold. But since it was Harrison's, she did not regret the intrusion.

Suddenly realizing that Tall Cloud wasn't behind her, Christa stopped and looked down at him. She was stunned. He hadn't taken one step. "Tall Cloud, why aren't you coming?" she said in a loud whisper, wondering why she felt the need to whisper with no one there but Tall Cloud.

"This house and its stairs are strange to me," he said. "Do you say that there is a room used for sleeping at the top of these stairs?"

"There are many rooms on the second floor," Christa said, trying to understand his hesitation.

"As you know, *Nahkeeta,* the Suquamish dwellings do not have even a separate room for sleeping. To have them stacked one upon the other, do you not feel as though you are in the clouds while making love?"

Christa threw her head back in a soft laugh. Then she rushed down the stairs, took Tall Cloud by an arm, and earnestly began directing him upward. "I must admit to you, Tall Cloud, that no matter where you and I make love, I always feel as if I am in the clouds." She giggled. "And since I have made love with nobody else, I'm not sure if it could be different in an upstairs bedroom."

Her smile faded as she watched him look backward and then upward. It was as though he were afraid. This was a new side to Tall Cloud that was being revealed to her. Then she scoffed at herself. She was being ridiculous. Tall Cloud was not afraid of anything.

Tightening her hold on his arm, she hurried upward, glad to finally reach the second floor landing. The lamp reflected light along the hallway as Christa led Tall Cloud to a closed door. She opened it and stepped into the bedroom.

Again she saw his hesitation as she held the lamp higher, revealing more of the room as the soft yellow glow from its fire spread along the ceiling and walls.

"This is what the rich white men offer their women each night?" he said thickly. He moved into the room and began touching the smoothness of the oak furniture and the brocade of the draperies at the two windows.

Feeling the tension in the room, Christa focused her eyes on the fireplace, relieved to see logs, kindling, and wadded paper already positioned inside it on the grate. She went to the fireplace, removed the chimney from the lamp, then held the fire to several pieces of the paper and watched the flames take hold. When she turned to see what Tall Cloud was doing, her mouth dropped open and she laughed softly. He was stretched out atop the bed, appearing to be quite comfortable and enjoying himself. His eyes twinkled as their gazes met and held.

"This is much better than the bear rug and rush mats I offered you in my dwelling," he said, laughing throatily. He held his arms out toward her. *"Newhah,* my *Nahkeeta."*

Understanding that he was asking her to come to him, Christa felt a sensuous flutter at the pit of her stomach, making her anxious to respond. She glanced over her shoulder at the progress of the fire. Seeing that slow flames were lapping upward toward the logs, she set the kerosene lamp on the dresser, removed her cape, and jumped with exuberance onto the bed.

With one sweep of his arms, Tall Cloud had her atop him and guided her lips downward to his. The feather mattress groaned under their weight as Tall Cloud skillfully rolled Christa around to a position beneath him.

His tongue probed between her lips and his hands kneaded her breasts through the thin cotton material of her dress. His heart raced; the blood in his temples pounded. Using a knee, he nudged her legs apart, yet he found that the skirt of her dress and her petticoats were like shields, protecting her from the fire raging inside him.

Christa placed her hands on his face as she let herself become lost in her fascination with this Indian whose lips and hands always possessed the skill to make her mindless. She stroked his cheeks with the inner sides of her thumbs, feeling the sleekness of his soft copper flesh. His tongue explored inside her mouth, causing rapture to rise like a glowing light inside her. Feeling the gentle warmth wrapping her in a soft, mellow cocoon of sensuousness, she welcomed his fingers at the back of her dress as he slowly began loosening the buttons.

Withdrawing his lips, he looked down at her with heated passion in his expressive gray eyes, and Christa leaned up on an elbow and let him slip her dress and underthings over her shoulders. A deep shudder coursed through her when he bent his head and circled one of her nipples with the hot wetness of his tongue then paused to set his lips firmly over the nipple and began a gentle sucking.

Sighing, Christa closed her eyes and savored his lips and tongue as they worshiped each of her breasts until both throbbed from pleasure, yet the sweet pain between her thighs was becoming almost unbearable.

"Enough . . . enough . . ." she cried softly. "Tall Cloud, please. . . ."

Tall Cloud leaned away from her, smiling as though beneath the spell of a drugged passion, then pulled her gently from the bed as he, too, rose from it. His hands busied themselves in undressing her further until she stood perfectly nude, gently curved, and smiling before him.

Without any words he began disrobing as Christa watched, spellbound. And when he, too, was nude, tall, proud, standing finely proportioned and sleekly muscled before her, she could stand it no longer and rushed into his arms, tingling deliciously wherever his flesh made contact with hers.

Twining her arms about his neck, she lifted her mouth to his and tasted paradise in his kiss. She clung about his neck as he swept her up from the floor and placed her gently on the bed where he proceeded to shower her body with more kisses, beginning at her toes, moving sensually upward. And when her inner thighs were reached, he lingered only momentarily there, sending a spasm of delight through Christa when his hot breath bathed her flesh. Then he continued on to her breasts and onward still, until he finally reached her lips.

Weaving his fingers through her hair, he urged her lips even harder against his while his knee nudged her legs apart and he placed the throbbing hardness of his manhood at the core of her soul.

Gently, he entered her, hearing her lethargic sigh as she lifted her hips to welcome him inside her. Rhythmically they worked together. She clung about his neck; he rained her face and throat with hot, demanding kisses.

"I love you. . . ." Christa whispered, feeling feverish as his cheek pressed against hers so that his lips could whisper in her ear.

"You are *tsee.* You are my woman. Soon you will be mine forever."

"I want that." Christa sighed. "Oh . . . how . . . I want that."

"We will make it so. *Alki.*"

"But for now, love me fiercely, Tall Cloud," Christa said, parting her lips seductively and closing her eyes while he wrapped his arms about her and held her tightly against him.

She felt as if she were swimming in a warm pool of water, weightless, as together they reached the peak of pleasure, sharing the intenseness of the moment. Afterwards they clung to each other, breathing hard, wondering once more at the passion that had been woven between them.

The crackling and popping of the fire diverted their attention to the fireplace and to the present and to whose bed they had used.

Christa was the first to speak. She eased away from Tall Cloud and from the bed. "Let's sit by the fire and talk a while, and then I must return to the blockhouse," she said, already slipping into her clothes. "I want to hear all about today. I want to know exactly why you were honored this evening by the marines and volunteers. I was watching from the window."

She smoothed down the skirt of her dress and looked adoringly at Tall Cloud. "I was so proud for you, Tall Cloud. I know just how much that recognition meant to you."

"Yes, my people were also proud," he said. "And it heightened my importance in their eyes. I proved to them that I deserve to be their chief . . . that I *am* wise in my ways."

Tall Cloud stepped into his fringe-trimmed buckskin breeches, moccasins, and then his shirt. He placed his headband and feather on his head, then he settled down next to Christa on a braided, oval rug in front of the fireplace. He placed his arm about Christa's waist and drew her close to him, staring into the fire. He felt as content as he might in his own dwelling, perhaps more. This white man's dwelling had no drafts with its many paned glass windows to protect its inhabitants from the harsher elements.

Then he felt guilty for enjoying anything of the white man's life. *Nahkeeta* was the only exception. But soon even she would not be of the white man's life. He would transform her into Indian.

Feeling the warmth of the fire as an extension of the caresses she had just experienced with Tall Cloud, Christa cuddled up close to him, trying not to worry about the passage of time. But she knew that the longer she stayed away from the blockhouse, the riskier it became. If they were discovered in their game of love, the most danger would fall upon Tall Cloud's head. He was guilty of breaking the white man's law this night. He had broken into a white man's house illegally. She worried more for *his* safety than for her reputation.

Momentarily dismisssing this from her mind, Christa looked up eagerly into his eyes. "Tell me, Tall Cloud," she said anxiously, "why were you treated so grandly today? Why did everyone shake your hand? I've never seen an Indian so honored before, though I've heard many speak of Chief Seattle and how he gets along so well with the white people."

A deep frown shadowed Tall Cloud's face with minute wrinkles. "As a young boy I looked up to Chief Seattle as a great leader," he said. "But since he was one who agreed to the white man's treaty and even encouraged all the Suquamish and Duwamish to sign the treaty, which, if passed, would take away our hunting grounds, I have lost all respect for the man. He betrayed us, as surely as I am sitting here with you, my *Nahkeeta*."

"But, Tall Cloud, you have your Pahto Island. No one can take that away from you, can they?"

"By treaty it could belong to the white man," he growled. "All land but that designated for reservations would belong to the white man."

"How terrible . . ."

"If the white man chose to use Pahto Island for a seaport, I would have to fight, *Nahkeeta*. No man but the Suquamish can be allowed to live on the land of my ancestors."

"Surely no one will try to take Pahto Island," Christa argued softly. "It would not benefit them. It rises too high from the ocean. The bluffs are too steep for it to make a good seaport."

"This is in my favor. I know that," Tall Cloud said, picking up a fallen twig that had popped from the fire and landed at his feet. "But the alliance I have succeeded at forming today with the white man is more in my favor than anything else. Now I am sure to be able to convince them to tear up the treaty papers and be fair to the Suquamish. I have proven my worth. I have proven *all* Indians' worth!"

Christa moved out of his embrace and settled down on her knees before him, placing her hands on the thighs of his crossed legs. "You still haven't told me all about it," she said. "Exactly what did you do, Tall Cloud, to make you so sure about this alliance?"

He tossed the twig back into the fireplace then placed his hands on hers. "Did you not see my warriors fighting side by side with the white man?"

"Yes . . ."

"My warriors outnumbered the white man's warriors," he bragged. "It was my warriors who chased the Haida back to their camps. This is why I, the chief of the brave Suquamish warriors, was honored. Now when I go to your leaders to ask that the treaty papers be torn in two, I am sure they will do this for me. They owe me this, *Nahkeeta.*"

Christa's exuberance waned. She knew that Tall Cloud was expecting too much to happen in return for his help in fighting the Haida. But she refused to say anything to discourage him from hoping. She didn't want to do anything to spoil their last moments together.

A sudden noise caused Christa to rise quickly from the

floor. Alarmed, she gave Tall Cloud a worried look. He had also heard and had jumped to his feet. Christa rushed to the window and looked outside and down, seeing a marine standing at the foot of the steps which led up to the porch.

"Is there another?" she whispered, growing cold with fear. She turned with a start as Tall Cloud placed her cape around her shoulders for her.

"We must escape. Now," he said, taking her by an elbow, guiding her hurriedly through the bedroom door.

"We'll have to leave through the back door," Christa whispered. "There's a marine positioned at the front. There may even be another already in the house."

Tall Cloud knew not to take any chances which might spoil the alliance he had just formed with the white people. If he were caught in a white man's house with a white woman, not only would he be hung, but his people would forever pay for his unwise acts. Almost anything would be worth being with his *Nahkeeta,* but to destroy his people in the process would mean that his spirit would never be allowed to rest in the land of the dead.

Stealthily, side by side, Christa and Tall Cloud moved down the staircase in the dark. The kerosene lamp and the fireplace still glowed warm in the bedroom they had left behind them. The bed was still disheveled, showing signs of its use, but none of this was important. Anyone could be blamed for these things if Christa and Tall Cloud managed to leave the premises unnoticed.

"This way . . ." Christa whispered, tugging on Tall Cloud's arm.

She led him down a long hallway, through the dark kitchen, and opened the door onto the back porch which was shadowed by tall pine and cedar trees. Cautiously she peered through the darkness, and, seeing nothing, she and Tall Cloud raced down the steps and into the cover of the trees.

Christa sighed heavily. "I believe we're safe now," she

whispered. "And from this point on, I'd best travel to the stockade alone. Enough risks have been taken."

"I will see you safely through the streets of the city and *then* bid you farewell, *Nahkeeta,*" Tall Cloud insisted.

"No. I must do this alone," Christa argued. "If I am seen, I can say that I was only in need of fresh air. If I'm with you, nothing I could say would be explanation enough."

Tall Cloud suddenly drew her into his arms and kissed her feverishly. Then he released her and stepped back. "I will come for you soon," he said thickly. "Now your brother will willingly agree to our marriage. Everyone looks up to Tall Cloud. Even . . . your . . . brother."

"For now, I must go and quickly," Christa said. She slipped the hood of her cape over her head and gave Tall Cloud a lingering look as if to memorize his every feature beneath the soft light of the moon. Then she turned and began to run through the snow toward the Sound. When she reached the end of the Kramer estate grounds, something compelled her to turn and look up at the window in the room where she and Tall Cloud had made such passionate love.

Her insides froze when she saw a silhouette at the window, outlined by the light from the lamp and fireplace flames. Her eyes shifted downward, seeing the marine still standing at the front of the house. There *had* been someone in the house while she and Tall Cloud had been making their escape. That same person was still there now. She and Tall Cloud had come so close to being caught. . . .

Sixteen

Melting snow was running in a steady stream down the middle of the road, making a mirey slush for Harrison's fancy carriage to travel through as it made its way along the shore of the Sound. Christa sat beside Delores on one side of the carriage, opposite David and Harrison. She avoided looking Harrison's way as much as possible, seeing in his eyes a gleam that she knew was caused by her presence.

She smiled to herself, remembering his rage after being told by the marines that someone had broken into his house and had spent time in his bedroom. Smugly, she sat there recalling her time with Tall Cloud brief as it had been. If she could, she would once again go with him as she had the previous evening. If she could, she would go to him and live with him forever. Somehow, that would have to be managed.

But today her main concern was returning to her cabin to see if everything was intact after the brief Indian war with the Haida. Somehow, she feared the knowing.

The sun beat through the window onto Christa's face, giving her a taste of what the early mornings of spring might be like in only a few more weeks. If David's foot were completely healed by then, perhaps she could tell him that she was going to leave, to be with Tall Cloud. David didn't need her. Didn't he now have Delores?

Christa gave Delores a sideways glance. She sat erect and beautiful, her eyes never leaving David. Surely it was love that Delores felt for him, for David didn't have any wealth to offer. Knowing Delores's past experiences with older, wealthy men, both of whom had died, widowing her twice, Christa judged there was reason enough for Delores never to have such a thing happen to her again. David was young. David was vital. And David was, indeed, handsome!

"And now that the Haida have decided that Seattle is no longer their playground, do you believe they will remain in their villages, David?" Harrison asked, slapping his hand on his knee. He was dressed in a tan, double-breasted frock coat, a black satin vest, and a black cravat on his high shirt collar. His fawn-colored trousers hung down over his boots, touching the floor in back, with a strap under the foot. His black top hat was slightly flared, and he carried a fashionable walking stick and had a monocle in his vest pocket. He looked as if he had stepped directly from a catalogue, whereas David wore only his plain cotton clothes, with a jacket of red-plaid wool over his shirt.

"I don't think we ever had much to fear from the Haida Indians in the first place," David scoffed. "So, yes, I think they're gone for good."

"And you feel safe enough staying out on your stretch of land alone with Christa?" Delores spoke up, her sky blue eyes twinkling, revealing her feelings for David in them as she looked his way. Her auburn hair had been pulled up beneath a bonnet with bavolet and lacing around the inside of the brim which matched her black velvet coat edged with ribbon and decorated with silk embroidery and jet beads. Caps accentuated the shoulders, and the split sleeves were caught at the wrists. The coat partially covered a dress of bright red, full and long in the back supported by many layers of petticoats.

"I feel that Christa and I will be safe enough," David

said. "Soon spring will be upon us. I have no other choice but to be on our farm. I've much to do."

Christa moved her face closer to the window and peered out. "David, I wonder how our animals are faring," she worried. "It seemed so cruel to up and leave them like we did. Just think how they must be feeling. The cows must be suffering so with the need to be milked."

David looked from Delores to Christa, comparing them. His insides ached from wanting the same things for his sister, seeing how elegant Delores appeared in her clothes shipped directly from New York. He had to continue encouraging Christa to marry Harrison. And she must—soon!

"Two days is bad, I know, Christa," he murmured. "But we had no other choice. You know that. We're lucky to be able to return today. It could have taken many weeks to rid our community of the Haida. As it is, even now, it seems unbelievable that they left so suddenly."

Christa toyed with the button at the neck of her cape, wanting so to tell them how she felt about Tall Cloud and how he had helped with the war. She lifted her hand to her hair, smoothing a curl back from her face, then readjusted the hood of the cape that lay bulkily around her neck.

"Yes," she said softly. "I guess we are lucky at that."

"The Suquamish Indians think they are responsible for the victory against the Haida," Harrison scoffed, tossing his head as he spoke. "Who does that Indian chief, Tall Cloud, think he is coming into the stockade like he did, accepting handshakes from all the marines and volunteers? And why did they do such a thing? Don't they know they are only adding fuel to fire? Next it will be the Suquamish breathing down our necks, wanting Seattle all to themselves. They'll say that we owe it to them for fighting against the Haida. Ha! I know why they did. And it won't work!"

Delores leaned forward, closer to her father. "Father, what are you talking about?" she questioned. "What won't work?"

Christa was quietly fuming, her lips set tightly together,

knowing that she mustn't say what she was feeling. She gave David a sour glance, seeing him watching her. She knew he sensed her anger and darn well understood why! It would take all she had inside her not to defend Tall Cloud. Hopefully, Harrison would soon shut his mouth and say no more about what he knew so little!

"The treaty, damn it," Harrison growled, tapping his walking stick on the floor of the carriage. "Don't you know the gossip? Chief Tall Cloud is one of the few Suquamish who is not agreeable to the treaty drawn up between the Indians and the white man. He wants it destroyed. Don't you see? He only helped us in this war against the Haida to try to persuade us to tear up the treaty. It doesn't take much intelligence to figure that out."

"And . . . ?" Delores persisted while David and Christa sat silently by, listening.

"There is no way that will happen." Harrison laughed. "Those savages are so dumb, they don't know their hind end from their front end. The treaty will soon be ratified. No one is going to destroy it merely for one Indian chief."

Christa closed her eyes and doubled her fingers into tight fists on her lap. *Savage!* How she hated the word! And the mockery! Harrison was actually mocking the man she loved!

Biting her lower lip, Christa succeeded at not saying anything and was glad when David pointed out the bend in the road which meant that they were almost home. Soon she would be away from the hateful, ugly Harrison Kramer. Then she would never agree to go near him again. And as soon as David was well, wouldn't Harrison get the shock of his life? Her choosing to marry an Indian instead of him would destroy all of the pride that he gained as one of Seattle's most respected rich men. It would sorely please her to take him down a peg or two.

Sighing with the peacefulness of the setting, the cool, lapping waters of the Sound on one side of the carriage and the tall pines and cedars on the other, Christa felt glad to be almost home. Only then could her future begin to take shape.

"Good Lord!" Delores suddenly gasped, looking past Christa, out the window, through the break in the trees, spotting the ruined remains of the cabin before anyone else.

"What?" Christa said, then looked through the break in the trees herself to see what had caused Delores to become so alarmed. Christa's insides knotted and her hands went to her throat as she saw what Delores had seen. Only charred timbers remained of their cabin and barn, and no signs of life were evident anywhere. The animals—where were the animals?

"God . . ." David said, leaning his head close to the window to look at the devastation. "Nothing is left. Nothing."

His words had become choked, as were his insides.

The carriage pulled up before what was once the cabin. In its ashes could be seen traces of glowing orange, suggesting that the house had only a short while ago been set afire. Skeletal remains of an iron bed rose ghostlike from the ashes, and the fireplace chimney pointed upward into the sky, mockingly it seemed.

Christa's hand went to the door handle of the carriage, but David's hand was quickly there, grasping onto hers. "No," he said thickly. "You mustn't. I'm not even going to get out to take a look around. It's gone, all of it, Christa. It's no use. Don't you see? It's no use."

"Even the animals, David?" Christa said, swallowing back a lump in her throat.

"Probably slaughtered and burned with the barn," he said, scowling.

"Even Mama's bible?" she said, emitting a low, soft sob as she covered her mouth with a hand.

"Everything, Christa," David said, shaking his head back and forth sorrowfully. "The damn savages."

Christa's head jerked around, and she stared with disbelief

into David's eyes. Not only had he cursed, but he had used that hated word, "savage," as Harrison Kramer so often did. It was not at all like her brother, but at a time like this, could she blame him for what he said?

She slid to the edge of the seat and placed her free hand on David's cheek. "I'm so sorry, David," she murmured. "This farm was your future. You know that . . . it . . . was never mine. My future lies elsewhere."

"Harrison," David growled, "please direct your coachman back to Seattle. Christa and I must find a suitable dwelling for ourselves until I can figure out what to do. I had . . . never . . . thought this could happen. I never should have left Boston." He dropped his head into his hands, defeated.

Delores caught Harrison's attention and used her eyes and a nod of her head to encourage him to exchange seats with her so that she could sit beside David and he could sit beside Christa. He complied, but before doing so he ordered his coachman back to Seattle. Then he settled down beside Christa and took one of her hands in his. To his chagrin, she just as quickly pulled it away.

Frowning, unable to understand her and how she could treat him so unjustly, he looked toward David, smiled coyly as he watched his daughter slip her hand into David's, and felt glad that David was not as cold in heart as his sister, for David readily accepted the comforting that Delores offered him.

"There will be no need to search for a place to stay," Harrison said, clearing his throat nervously. "Our house is your house, David. You and Christa will please be so kind as to accept my invitation to be my house guests for as long as you wish. It would so honor me, David, if you would say yes to my suggestion."

Christa's insides splashed cold with the thought of living even for one minute under the same roof as Harrison. She knew that he would not let her rest without flaunting his wealth over her, pestering her, talking about marriage. And might he even try to force himself upon her again when David wasn't looking? Such a thought made Christa feel as though she might retch.

David liked the suggestion Harrison offered him and Christa. Staying in the Kramer mansion might be a way of speeding up the marriage between Christa and Harrison. And marriage would place his sister's thoughts of Tall Cloud behind her. Surely she now saw the need to be taken care of by the proper man. Everything that had meant anything in her life was now ashes, gray, smoldering ashes.

And wouldn't this also give him the time with Delores that had been denied him of late? Things had come full circle now, and soon he hoped that he would get the courage to talk to her at length about marriage. Too many things had stood in the way of their total happiness. But now? Perhaps things would change for the better, for all concerned.

"It would not be an inconvenience to you?" David asked, his hand growing warm inside Delores's.

"None whatsoever," Harrison said, tilting his chin, half glancing toward Christa as his thoughts raced. Perhaps winning her brother over could be the way to finally win her. He smiled warmly toward David. "In fact, I must insist, David, that you do this. No boardinghouse could offer you what my house and servants offer. You will be quite comfortable, I assure you." He glanced down at David's bandaged foot. "And it will give you the chance to stay off your foot completely while it finishes healing."

David looked down at his foot. He was sure now that within a day or so he would finally manage to get his foot back into a boot. He patted his leg and met Harrison's watchful challenge as he looked toward him. "Then, Harrison, I can say that you have yourself two house guests," he said, fearing to look Christa's way, knowing how she must be feeling and sensing her icy stare.

"But, Harrison," he quickly interjected, "we will stay only long enough for my foot to heal. After that, we will make residence in a boardinghouse while I find work at the mill. I will pay my way. I want you to know that. I will even pay you back for the kindness you are offering me and my sister."

Planning to ask David once again for Christa's hand in marriage as soon as they were settled in his house on Fourth Avenue, Harrison relaxed his shoulder muscles and settled back comfortably against the thick cushions of his seat. The Haida Indians had done him a service. Yes, indeed, by destroying all of David's and Christa's belongings, the savages had done him a service. In the obligation he would feel for accepting Harrison's kindness, David would be more willing to encourage Christa to marry—and marry a man with riches!

"But, Harrison," David said, "I won't give up so easily. As soon as I get enough money together, I plan to return to my land and rebuild everything that was taken from me, this time in *brick*. Even if I have to have the brick shipped from Europe, I shall have a house that no Indians can take from me. A brick house. Yep. I plan to have me a brick house as soon as possible."

He crossed his arms and forced a smile, trying to act as if he weren't as disturbed inside as Christa was to lose everything that had meant "family" to them. Losing all their Mama and Papa's possessions that had been brought from Boston was almost the same as having to bury their parents all over again. The loss wasn't as great, but the pain was almost unbearable.

Christa sat wordless beside Harrison, her insides numb. If only she and David had stayed behind to protect what was theirs instead of going, like cowards, to the stockade! Except for Tall Cloud, she felt at this moment as if she had lost everything. To be obligated to Harrison for any reason was the same as owing her soul to Satan. How *could* David!

He had the same as bargained with the devil in agreeing to stay in Harrison's house. Now Harrison would most certainly force the issue of marriage.

No matter what, she wouldn't marry him—not for her brother, not for anyone. But she would have to learn to live her life one day at a time.

Seventeen

A fire glowed warm in the fireplace in the Kramer's grand sitting room where Christa, David, Harrison, and Delores sat about the hearth. They all hoped it would be a time for celebration, for David was just about to try his luck at placing his healed foot inside a highly polished leather boot. Christa's heart pounded. If David could wear his boot, then they could quickly leave the Kramer mansion! Two weeks had passed, and it had been two weeks of dodging Harrison at every turn and blink of the eye.

Eagerly watching David move his foot to the boot, Christa clasped her hands together anxiously on her lap. She hoped that he would stand behind his promise to leave this horrid place. But she was afraid that David had become fond of the fancy clothes, the grand furniture, and the gourmet food that had been offered him on Fourth Avenue. Even now he seemed the epitome of wealth in his expensive double-breasted frock coat of medium gray and a red satin cravat displayed against a white shirt with ruffles at the chest. His trousers were of a darker gray and fit him snugly in the right places. He had combed his hair to perfection and it lay neatly against his neck and parted at the side.

Yes, he did remind Christa of her papa and the way he had dressed in the days when he had strutted around their stylish house in Boston. Surely David remembered and wanted this sort of life as well, now that he had gotten a taste of it.

Christa looked down at herself and the way she was dressed. Harrison had made sure that she hadn't wanted for a thing. The dress she wore this day was a dark pink satin, trimmed with a lighter shade of pink lace down the low-swept, tight-fitting bodice, flared from the waist to cover her many petticoats.

Her golden hair had been pulled behind her ears, with the sides waved and the back coiled and held up with a slide. She hadn't wanted to accept the jewelry offered her by Delores, but after much insistence she had placed a diamond necklace about her neck and wore matching teardrop earrings clipped to her ears.

Without even looking into a mirror, Christa had known she was at least a little bit beautiful. But the wrong man was having the advantage of seeing her this way. Oh, how she longed to see and to be with Tall Cloud.

Noticing ribbons of orange clinging to the wall as the evening's sunset shone in its brilliance through the window, Christa knew that one more day had passed without her managing to draw Tall Cloud's attention to where she was. There had been no way to send word. She hadn't even been able to go for a stroll by herself. Eyes constantly seemed to be watching her. But tonight she would get the chance. Harrison had said that he was to attend a town meeting. Christa knew enough about David's needs to know that he would grab this opportunity to be alone with Delores in the way lovers dreamed about.

Nervous perspiration beaded David's brow as he felt a slight twinge of pain after barely placing his foot inside the boot. He had silently feared that he might be left with a limp, and he would soon find out when he took his first step on the healed foot since the day he had been careless with the ax.

With a limp, would Delores give him a second look? In

her eyes, would that make him half a man? Now that he had come so close to having her and planning as he was to propose this very night, he knew that it would be hard to learn to live without her.

And even if his foot were normal, would she want to live in the type of house that he planned to build once he had the money to do so? Even though his house would be made of brick, it would never match the greatness of the Kramer mansion. It would take years to accumulate such wall decorations, fine crystal and china, and furniture. And his house would be a one-storied house, not two-storied like her father's, to which she had surely become accustomed. She seemed to take such delight in making a grand entry down the staircase, sweeping her skirts up into her arms, revealing the daintiness of her feet and offering glimpses of the slight curves of her legs. And in her eyes, there was always such sparkle, such life!

Looking Delores's way, smiling, David paused, then once more he absorbed himself in fitting his foot in place. One tug and then another and his boot was finally on. He wiggled his toes. No pain. He moved the muscles that reached down into his toes. Only a slight pain.

But now came the true test. He glanced quickly over at Christa, seeing the anxiousness written across her flushed face and in the green of her eyes. He knew just how much this meant to her. She so desperately wished to be free of Harrison's presence. He understood but wished she would feel differently. Time. Perhaps more time. He would just have to fake by not appearing well enough yet to place his full weight on his foot. Then given a few more days, Christa would surely grow more used to this way of life and say yes to the man who must, in the end, be her husband.

"Well, David?" Christa said, moving to the edge of her chair, watching his foot as David set it flatly onto the floor. "Does it hurt? Do you . . . think . . . you can walk?" Her words came out in a soft whisper, so anxious was she to see him walk across the room, and then to boast that he was once more able to be his own man—without taking from another and learning to depend on this taking more each day.

David rose from the chair, steadying himself on its arm as he looked around the room from person to person. He could tell already that he would be fine, that he could walk as freely as the next man if he wished, but fake it he must. Looking down at his foot, he first put his good foot before him. He swallowed hard. With a forced groan he moved onto the other foot and made himself crumple back into the chair, his eyes closed, his groans more agonized as he tossed his head back and forth.

Christa blanched. She started to rise, to go to David, but stopped when she saw that Delores was already there, on her knees before David, framing his face between her hands.

"David," Delores gasped. "Darling. I told you that you weren't well enough just yet. Darling, does it hurt so terribly? Please tell me that it doesn't. I will die if I know you are in terrible pain."

Christa's eyes rolled back in her head, for she was disgusted with this display. But her disappointment in seeing that David wasn't well enough to leave took precedence over all her other feelings. As she heard David saying that the pressure on his foot was just too great at this time for him to wear the boot, Christa rose and rushed to look out the window, knowing that if she glanced toward the others at this time, they would see tears forming in the corners of her eyes. She felt as if she were a prisoner who had just been given a death warrant.

Yet she felt instantly ashamed for such thoughts. Here she was feeling sorry for herself, and all the while she should be worrying about her brother. But at this moment she could not show her concern outwardly. If she were to say a word, her voice would surely crack.

Harrison came to her side. He placed his chubby arm

about her waist, trying to ignore her recoiling at his touch. "Come back by the fire, Christa," he said. "I have something to say to your brother, and I want you there to hear."

Christa closed her eyes and clamped her lips tightly shut. She could just imagine what he had to discuss. He had waited these two weeks, which had surprised her. Though he had persistently tried to be with her, he had yet to discuss marriage. And now that the time was ripe, with David obviously still unwell, he most surely was going to grab the opportunity.

"Christa?" Harrison insisted.

"Harrison," she said icily. "Please just go ahead and talk with David without me. At this moment, I don't feel like conversing with anyone or hearing whatever you might have to say."

She gave him a sour glance. "You see, I thought my brother was well, and now I find that he is not. I'm sure you can understand my feelings. You know how much I love my brother."

Harrison dropped his arm from about her waist, his face scorched red from humiliation and frustration. "Then what I have to say I will speak quite loud so that you can hear me even from this vantage point," he said angrily. "For you see, Christa, it is for your hand in marriage that I am about to speak."

Christa flinched as if hit, though she had always known to expect it, and only a moment ago had realized that this would now be his plan. But hearing it from his lips had almost been the same as a slap in the face.

She turned her head away from him, unable to speak, then heard his heavy footsteps as he returned to stand before the hearth. With a nervous heartbeat she heard Harrison discussing her with David as though she were a prized hen to be bargained over.

"David, you know that I have been patiently waiting for the day that I can make Christa my wife," Harrison said quite sternly. "Now is the time to talk quite seriously about this. David, I will gladly share my wealth with both you and Christa. I will see to it that your house is rebuilt. It will be as grand as mine. You can choose to build in Seattle or back on your own land if you feel that it is safe enough. But understand that I am willing to do anything for both you and your sister, to have Christa's hand in marriage."

Christa began to tremble, knowing that what he was offering would be hard for any man to refuse. But surely David loved her too much to go against her wishes.

David looked over his shoulder at Christa. He could see her plight in the very depths of her eyes, and he knew that no answers about her future could be given yet. He couldn't bear to lose her respect.

Looking boldly up at Harrison who was nervously clasping and unclasping his hands, David said, "Harrison, I truly appreciate your generosity," he said. "But let's wait a while longer."

He tapped his foot with his fingers. "First I have to see to it that I can fend entirely for myself," he added. "I don't like to think of living on someone else's profits, and not my own."

Harrison's face reddened. Perspiration laced his upper lip. "Are you saying that you cannot at this time give me your answer as to whether or not you approve of my proposal of marriage to Christa?" he bellowed. "David, what must a man do to get you to agree? I've been more than generous with you already. I plan to be even more generous in the future. How can you refuse?"

"No matter what you say or do, I cannot give you an answer about Christa," David said thickly. "She is her own person. She will make her own decision about her future."

Christa sighed with relief, but her insides splashed cold when she saw the mask of hate on Harrison's face. She sensed that Harrison had just changed his feelings about

David. And would Harrison now stand in the way of David's and Delores's happiness?

Harrison glowered from David to Christa, slowly growing to hate them both. He would get even with them, one way or the other. They both had played him for a fool. And as long as he, Harrison Kramer, was alive, Delores would never be allowed to marry David Martin!

"I must leave now," Harrison muttered. "I have to attend the town meeting." He left the room in a huff.

Delores went to Christa. "Christa, I have to ask. If father had chosen to ask you directly, would you have agreed to the marriage? You know that he was doing what he thought was proper, asking David first."

"Surely you know the answer to that without having to ask," Christa said coldly. "Delores, I have never wished to marry your father. I didn't even want to be here in the same house with him for this length of time." Christa watched as a flame of color rose to Delores's cheeks. She instantly took one of Delores's hands in hers, feeling the need to explain.

"I don't love your father," she quickly explained. "That is the reason I have said these things about him. I knew that being in the same house with him for this long would only encourage him to pursue me further."

She studied Delores's expression, seeing that Delores still didn't understand. "It's nothing against your father," she lied. "It's just that he is not my choice for a husband."

"Oh?" Delores said. "There is someone else? Does my father know this? Surely if he did, he would step aside like a gentleman."

Christa lowered her lashes, hiding the truth that glowed in the depths of her eyes. "No," she once more lied. "There is no one else. But in time I am sure there will be."

Delores went to David and leaned over to kiss him. "At least we've no problems facing us," she whispered. "I love you, David. Oh, so very much."

Christa felt as if she were an outsider. Knowing that her brother and Delores needed to be alone and hearing the carriage carrying Harrison away from the house, she realized that she finally had the opportunity to leave herself.

Without a word, she left the sitting room, grabbed her cape, and ran out of the house into the orange-tinged dusk of evening. How free she felt, at last.

Eighteen

Christa shook the hood of her cape from her head and let the breeze lift her hair from her shoulders. She began to enjoy this moment of freedom away from the clutches of Harrison Kramer. She was almost overwhelmed with disappointment at having to linger longer at the Kramer mansion, and she wasn't even sure if she could stand to do so.

Walking alongside the Sound, away from the wharves, she saw that only a thin layer of snow remained on the ground and that bits of broken ice were floating through the crystal-clear blues of the water at her side. The breeze had a touch of warmth to it and, though it was not yet time for spring, this tiny taste of it made her hunger for its speedy return to this northwest country of Washington.

She stopped to look across the Sound, at a rise in the water in the distance. It was like a mirage, it was so hazy and overhung with clouds. Though it appeared to be only a speck, being so far away from where she now stood, Pahto Island was where her heart lay. Tall Cloud, she thought silently, oh, how I've missed you. . . .

Glad to be away from the activity and noise of the wharves, Christa moved onward along the shores of Puget Sound. Seagulls swept down from overhead, watching her with their large black eyes, their wings widespread and orange shadowed against the setting rays of the sun. Their call was friendly, their sleek bodies beautiful. Then another sound caught her attention. She turned and caught sight of many fish splashing up from the water then just as quickly disappearing again into its depths.

The smell of roses lured her a few steps away from the water, where a pink rose bush lifted its flowers toward the sky, the blossoms still holding traces of snow in the deep folds of their petals.

How do they still grow through snowstorms and such cold temperatures? she wondered to herself, stooping to pick one. But that is only one miracle of this beautiful northwest country, she mused silently. If not for the Haida, everything could have been so perfect.

Pricking her finger with a thorn, she flinched, involuntarily dropped the rose, and placed the bleeding finger between her lips. Frowning, she sucked on the finger then swung around when she heard the sound of a horse approaching, its hooves muffled somewhat on the remaining layer of snow.

In the deepening dusk, Christa couldn't make out who the rider was, and she became somewhat frightened, now realizing just how far she had wandered from the wharves and the city. She had been seeking privacy to be able to sort through her thoughts, but she had probably gone too far, for safety.

Placing the hood back on her head, she began to run along the water's edge, becoming breathless and slipping occasionally, almost falling. She didn't dare take the time to look back to see if she had left the rider behind. And with the snow still muffling the horse's hoofbeats so well, there was no way to tell if she was being pursued, or if she was just being foolish in thinking that she was.

Suddenly she distinctly heard the horse approaching behind her. She had not been foolish to believe that she was in danger. And what if it was a Haida Indian? She would be taken as a slave and used as a sex object probably from man to man, until she died from sheer exhaustion, or worse. . . .

Gasping for breath, glad to finally see signs of life ahead at the wharves, Christa started to scream, but her voice caught in her throat when she felt strong arms reach down around her waist and grab her up quickly onto the horse.

Blinking her eyes nervously, consumed by frightened heartbeats, Christa swung her head around to protest being held this way, but her mouth dropped open when she found herself face to face with Tall Cloud.

"Tall . . . Cloud . . ." she gasped, her limbs aching from running so hard and from being jerked so quickly onto the horse.

Tall Cloud didn't smile down on her, but instead he spun the horse around and headed away from the city, desperately holding onto her around the waist.

Christa didn't fight him. She was too numb and full of wonder even to think of it. Why had he abducted her in such a way? And on a horse? She had never seen Tall Cloud on a horse before. He had told her that his people were called "canoe people" since most of their traveling was done by canoe, not by horse.

Clinging to Tall Cloud's arm, feeling the rush of the wind upon her face as it whipped the hood of her cape from her head, Christa looked away from Tall Cloud and over his shoulder to see another horse with a man in its saddle in pursuit of both Tall Cloud and Christa. Christa thought fleetingly that the dull existence she had had while in Harrison Kramer's house, had somehow changed to one of bold excitement.

Yet she was afraid. Tall Cloud hadn't seemed glad to see her. Was he once more using her for some end that he hoped to achieve? Was she once more just something to be bargained over?

Watching the lone horseman approaching closer behind

Tall Cloud, Christa gulped hard, for she saw that the man had pulled his pistol.

"Tall Cloud!" Christa cried, wriggling in his tight embrace. "We're being followed. And the man has just drawn a pistol!"

Tall Cloud looked over his shoulder and saw the threat. He placed his knees deeply into the horse's sides and urged it quickly onward, but nothing kept the bullet from whizzing by, close to his head.

Grumbling, Tall Cloud led the horse to some cover of trees and released his hold on Christa. "Hide yourself," he ordered. "Quickly. Get behind the trees. I will deal with this crazy white man who doesn't care if he shoots even you, *Nahkeeta.*"

Still stunned by what was happening, Christa rushed behind a tree and stood, trembling, as she heard Tall Cloud's horse racing away from her again. Unable to bear the suspense, she peered around the tree just in time to see the other horseman whirl his horse around and ride in the opposite direction with Tall Cloud now in pursuit.

Placing her hands over her mouth, she watched as Tall Cloud went alongside the horseman. With fear lacing her heart, she saw Tall Cloud jump from his own horse and knock the other rider to the ground.

A struggle ensued. First Tall Cloud was on top, then the other man. And then a gunshot erupted and both Tall Cloud and the other man ceased fighting, leaving Christa to stand, barely breathing, not knowing which man had received the bullet.

"Tall Cloud!" she shrieked, rushing from behind the tree. Her legs would not carry her fast enough. Her heart seemed to be racing ahead of her as her eyes explored the two men still lying prone on the ground. Neither had stirred. Which was shot? Her fear ate away at her insides.

Coming up to the two bodies, Christa fell to her knees beside Tall Cloud, tears blurring her vision. But when she saw that his chest was heaving in and out, she understood that the reason he was lying so quietly was because his struggles with the other man had fully winded him.

"Oh, Tall Cloud," Christa cried, falling down upon him, placing her arms about his neck. "I thought you had been the one shot. Thank God you are all right."

Tall Cloud eased her away from him. "We must leave here," he said dryly. "At once. The gunfire surely will draw men from the wharves."

"But . . . who . . . was the man chasing us? And why?" Christa asked, rising to her feet and brushing snow from her skirt. "Was it because he saw you grab me in such a way?"

Her gaze fell upon the silent figure in the snow who was spread out on the ground, face down. There was so much familiar about the clothes—their fanciness—and about the shape of the man—his bulkiness. His top hat had fallen from his head and his thick gray hair was revealed in its true colors. Christa felt something grabbing at the pit of her stomach as she began to realize just who it had been in pursuit not only of Tall Cloud but also herself.

"Harrison . . ." she gasped. "Harrison Kramer?"

Tall Cloud placed his hand firmly on her shoulder. "It doesn't matter now who it was," he grumbled. "What matters is that we leave."

Christa squirmed away from him. "I never liked the man, Tall Cloud," she said in a strained whisper, "but I can't leave him just lying there without first checking to see if he is—"

A low groan rose from Harrison as his head moved slightly from where it had been lying so quietly.

Christa lifted the skirt of her dress and the hem of her petticoats into her arms, rushed to Harrison's side, and fell hurriedly to her knees. She ignored Tall Cloud's low grumblings as she tried to move Harrison from his stomach to his back.

Finding that he was too heavy, she leaned down into his face. "Harrison," she said softly. "How are . . . you . . . faring?"

Blood was running from his nose and mouth and from this vantage point, Christa could see the splatter of blood on his waistcoat. The bullet had entered just below the heart, and by the sound of the rattles in his throat, she knew that he was probably taking his last breaths. Death rattles. She had heard the terrible death rattles just before her mama and papa had died. . . .

"I was . . . watching . . . you . . ." Harrison said in broken speech. "I suspected . . . that . . . you . . . would meet another . . . man. I didn't . . . ever . . . suspect it could . . . be . . . an . . . Indian."

Christa flinched when his body jerked wildly and his eyes locked into a steady stare. She could not believe that he was dead.

Feeling a strong, vile taste rising in her throat, Christa turned her face quickly away and swallowed hard. Then she once more felt a strong arm about her waist and felt herself being carried toward Tall Cloud's horse.

"I said that we must leave," he growled. "There is no time to mourn over this particular white man. Do you not know that when he was shooting at me, he could as easily have shot *you?* He was not a wise man. And he was not the man for you. Only I am, *Nahkeeta.* And now I will take you and never bring you back again."

Not comprehending his words—and feeling it was wrong to leave Harrison Kramer lying dead in the snow, she began to fight against his hold. "Tall Cloud," she cried. "I want to be with you just as you wish to be with me. But this is not the way. Why are you doing this? Let me go. I would have come to you in time, of my own volition. But please let me go. We mustn't leave Harrison this way."

Tall Cloud looked toward the city, relieved that no one had heard the gunfire, but still sensing the mortal danger that he and Christa were in by being there. He ignored her pleas and thrust her onto the horse, taking his place behind her on the horse's bare back.

"Tall Cloud, please. . . ." Christa argued, cringing when his hold tightened about her waist. "David will be so worried. And when Harrison Kramer's body is found and I am gone, a posse will be formed to find me. You will be in danger, Tall Cloud. Release me now. I will go back into town alone. I won't tell anyone about you and Harrison. I will leave an anonymous message at the sheriff's office so that his body can at least be found and taken back into the city for proper care."

"When his body is discovered, there will be no reason to suspect me," Tall Cloud said, thrusting his knees hard into the horse's sides and flipping the reins. "By then you will be with me on Pahto Island, and soon you will become my wife. I will no longer wait for your brother's approval. I have waited long enough."

"But David will be distraught over my absence," Christa explained. "I don't want to worry him so, Tall Cloud. Let's do this in another way."

"There *is* no other way," Tall Cloud insisted. "And I must show the white men that they cannot play tricks on Tall Cloud by first being friendly and then not. They do not reward me properly for helping to rid the city of the Haida. They refuse to tear up the treaty papers. Well, I will show them. I will take you instead. I will show them that I do not lose at everything I attempt. When they find out where you are, it will be too late. You will already be my wife. And they will do nothing about it. They wouldn't harm a white woman's husband, now would they?"

Christa's heartbeats floundered in a cold iciness. His only motive for what he was doing was to prove something once again to the white man. Why hadn't it been for the right reason—for his sincere love for her? Why did he always have to hurt her so by using her!

Twisting violently against his hold, Christa began to beat her fists against his chest. "Release me at once," she screamed. "I don't want to go with you. I don't ever want to see you again. Tall Cloud, your thoughts are filled with only one thing—with vengeance. I am only a pawn, to be used. Let me go! Let me go!"

Tall Cloud pulled his horse to a halt and dragged her with him to the ground. He held tightly onto her wrists and glared down into her eyes. "You know that what you speak is not true," he growled. "*Nahkeeta*, my heart is warm with love for you. I will make you my wife for all the right reasons. Does it matter to you that this marriage will also benefit me in other ways? If your love for me is as strong as you have more than once professed, then you will want what is best for me. Say it. Tell me that you want what is best for me, my *Nahkeeta*."

Christa felt herself weakening as his gaze burned down at her, his eyes branding her, it seemed, with the intensity of his passion. And when she once more began to protest her being there with him, his mouth smothered her words as his lips bore down upon hers and his arms crushed her to his chest. Though the place was wrong and the timing poor, she couldn't help but feel the usual intoxication of his kiss. Her senses reeled in pleasure as the kiss lingered and his hands searched beneath her cape until they found the curve of her breasts and claimed them fully as his.

Then, abruptly, he released her and took her by a wrist and began guiding her toward the lapping waters of the Sound. "My canoe is moored here," he said thickly. "We will go to Pahto Island now, and soon you will become my wife, *Nahkeeta*."

Sensuous, anxious shivers raced along her flesh, for she wanted this, yet feared it. She knew that as a white woman, her decision to live the life of an Indian would be a true test of her love for Tall Cloud. And, to begin her new life this way, sneaking behind David's back, lessened the thrill she knew she should be feeling.

She hesitated as she was shoved gently toward the great canoe that she recognized as Tall Cloud's. She glanced at the horse standing idle beside the road then back at Tall Cloud. "The horse?" she asked. "Whose—"

"I borrowed it to ride into Seattle to use in capturing you," he said, lifting her up into his arms and forcing her into the canoe. "I knew that a quick escape would have to be made. A horse was the only way."

"Then you had planned it?"

"First I had to find out where you stayed," he said gruffly. "And when I found out, that made my determination to get you at this time even greater. I was afraid that the evil man, Harrison Kramer, would force himself on you again. If I hadn't found you today beside the Sound, I would have stolen you away in the middle of the night from that man's dwelling. It was my plan to watch until the lights were snuffed out; then I would have stolen into the house and searched room by room if need be, to find you and then take you away."

Tall Cloud placed Christa on a thickness of bearskin that had been positioned on the seat of the canoe. "In everything that you planned, there were so many risks." She sighed, gathering the skirt of her dress up and straightening it beneath her, tired now of her fight to escape from him. In truth, she relished the thought of being taken away forcibly by the man she loved. It seemed much more exciting this way, and it would always mean a great deal to her that he risked his own life to have her.

"For you? Anything!" Tall Cloud said huskily, settling down, facing her, and taking up his paddle into his hands.

"For you, also," she corrected. "You know that you are feeling good about having proven something else to the white men by stealing me away from them."

"I told you that already," he growled. "Why must you labor over that?"

"Because it would have been nice to have been stolen, instead, merely for love, nothing else," Christa pouted.

Tall Cloud pushed his paddle into the sandy bottom of the Sound, shoving the canoe out into the deeper water, then he began paddling back and forth powerfully, and soon the land was far behind them.

"Your life with me will be good," he said flatly. "You will see. I will make you happy, *Nahkeeta*. You and I have already had a taste of this sort of happiness and know that what lies ahead will be good. Why argue that? Isn't happiness together reason enough for what I do? Think only of that, *Nahkeeta*."

Night had finally fallen, and its total darkness made Christa tense. She looked toward shore but now could see only dark, heavy shadows which she knew to be the trees that rose high into the sky. Then she looked over her shoulder, where Tall Cloud was directing his canoe. She could see nothing but black where the waters of Puget Sound blended into the darkened sky. They seemed one patch of velvet, indistinguishable from each other.

Goosebumps rose on her flesh as a cool spray of water settled on her face and hair. She licked her lips free of the salty taste and risked loosening her fingers from the sides of the canoe long enough to place the hood on her head.

Then unsure of herself in this shimmering canoe which was whipping along beneath a starless sky, she once more gripped onto the sides, watching the muscles of Tall Cloud's shoulders flex with each stroke. In his fringe-trimmed buckskin shirt and trousers he evoked visions of other moments they had shared together when he had been dressed in the same way. Christa's thoughts caused a scorching flame of sorts to shoot through her. Were they truly so close to a time when they could share such intimate embraces again? Would he undress slowly before her feasting eyes as he had done in the past? Would she even be patient enough to watch without begging him to ravage her, to carry her with him once more to paradise?

Feeling that he could read her thoughts as his eyes continued to watch her, smothering her by his nearness, she felt a blush rising to her cheeks and lowered her lashes to look away from him. She felt a twinge of guilt for letting her thoughts wander when in truth she should have been worrying about David and what he would think when he found her gone. He had been through this before, when he had been unable to do anything about her disappearance because of his injured foot.

Even now, his foot was unable to tolerate the touch of a boot upon it, so again he would have to depend upon someone else to go in search of her. Would they find her before the vows were spoken between her and Tall Cloud? Or would it be later when she was already living the life of the Indians . . . ?

They finally reached Pahto Island and its high, dark cliffs. Tall Cloud helped Christa from the beached canoe and then let her walk ahead of him up the steep steps to the top, where his ancestors' village was once more occupied with the people of Chief Tall Cloud's tribe of Suquamish Indians.

The steps were damp and slippery, which sent fear into Christa's heavily pounding heart. And each time her foot slipped, her knees grew weak and threatened to buckle beneath her. But always there was the strength of Tall Cloud's grip rushing around her waist that kept her moving upward. And finally, breathless, pale, and tired, she took the final step upward to solid ground where she regained her full footing.

Looking about her, Christa saw many differences in the Pahto Island she remembered from the last time she had been there. The huts had been repaired and smoke spiraled from each of their smoke holes in the ceilings, and the light from the fire spaces glowed warm through the windows and door spaces of each.

A communal fire was burning large and bright in the center of the village. Several Indian women were there, turning a spit which displayed the carcass of a fairly large animal melting its fat into the flames and smelling enticingly good to Christa, for she had not eaten well these past few days. She had been upset at being pursued by the man she now presumed still lay dead on the road for someone to discover.

Tall Cloud once more placed his arm about Christa's waist and began guiding her toward the village. They had not taken more than two steps when a squaw came rushing toward them excitedly telling Tall Cloud something in the Indian language. One word that Christa was able to understand was the word "Star." And she had to wonder if the squaw was talking about Tall Cloud's sister. Strange how Tall Cloud always seemed to avoid any mention of her. But Christa remembered the shame he had felt upon discovering the wrong Star had done his people.

Christa hadn't understood the strange customs of the Suquamish at that time and knew little of them now. She had much to learn, and she feared the learning. If she did something wrong in Tall Cloud's eyes in her ignorance of his customs, would he also look on her with shame?

Tall Cloud swung around and clasped his hands on Christa's shoulders. "It is my sister," he said thickly. "She is not well. It seems the child that she is carrying is ready to come into this world early. I must go to her, *Nahkeeta*. Though she lives the life of the shamed, I know the dangers of early childbirth."

A low gasp surfaced from Christa's lips. "Tall Cloud, let me help you," she encouraged, though she did not know the first thing about birthing a child. But she had to show him that she could at least try to help. It was important for her to appear strong in his eyes in every way.

"A midwife sits at her side," he said. "I must give permission for a shaman to perform over her. My people knew that she was living the life of the shamed and were afraid to let a shaman enter my dwelling without first receiving my permission to do so."

"I will help if you will also give me permission," Christa encouraged.

Tall Cloud nodded his head. "Yes. Perhaps you can help," he said hoarsely. "Star would welcome your presence at her side. She has spoken so often of you since you rescued her from the Haida."

He dropped his hands from her shoulders and took one of her hands in his. "Come. We will go to her together. Once I see you to my dwelling, then I will go for the shaman."

Frightened that she might do or say the wrong thing, Christa couldn't stop the tremors that had begun in her hands and knees. Despite this, she walked proudly beside Tall Cloud until they reached the hut in which they had once made such passionate love.

Christa gasped when she saw Star lying on the familiar bearskin beside the fire. Her face was flushed crimson and soaked with perspiration, and her stomach appeared swollen to a strange proportion. She was naked and her body glistened in a wet, copper sheen.

Embarrassed, Christa turned her eyes away then felt Tall Cloud's fingers beneath her chin, urging her eyes upward to meet his.

"That is the way she must be laid out to have the child," he said softly. "Go. Sit by her. Do not let her nudity dissuade you, my *Nahkeeta.*"

Star moaned softly and her eyes fluttered only partially open. She began speaking in Suquamish to Tall Cloud, raising a hand, beckoning him down beside her. Tall Cloud dropped to his knees and placed her head on his lap where he cradled it while crooning softly to her.

A lump rose in Christa's throat, seeing Tall Cloud's gentleness and understanding the guilt that he must be feeling for having rejected his sister for so long. It was quite obvious that Star's body was being racked by a fever and that her life was surely in danger as well as that of the unborn child lying peacefully inside her womb.

Christa's gaze moved to the midwife who sat stiffly on the other side of Star, her arms clasped tightly across her chest and her eyes staring forward, oblivious, it seemed, of Star's plight.

Seeing this made Christa move into action. She knelt down beside Tall Cloud. "Tall Cloud, you must see to it that water is brought into the hut," she encouraged. "Don't you see how your sister is suffering from a high fever? She needs to be bathed, continuously, to get the temperature down. Maybe then she might have a chance."

Tall Cloud gave Christa a pensive stare then gently placed Star's head back onto the bearskin. He flew to his feet, ordering the midwife up from her silent vigil, speaking to her in Suquamish. Christa saw that what he had said had put fear into the older Indian's eyes, and the squaw rushed from the hut, returning soon with a basin of water and a soft doeskin cloth, both of which she handed to Christa.

"Thank you," Christa murmured then settled down beside Star and began bathing her gently.

Seeing that his order had been obeyed, Tall Cloud hurriedly left the dwelling, heading toward the shaman's hut and hoping it was not already too late. Guilt lay heavy in Tall Cloud's heart. If his sister died. . . .

Christa tried not to feel self-conscious when she moved the cloth over Star's large, milk-filled breasts, keeping her eyes only on Star's beautiful, inflamed face.

Struggling, Star managed to form the word "friend" in sign language, breaking into a soft smile before once more frowning, then groaning with a renewed pain.

Christa's eyes traveled to Star's abdomen and could see

it tightening with a contraction. Fear swept over her again, and she began dreading the next hour or so, not knowing what might happen.

She smiled down at Star when the Indian girl once more became passive and momentarily free of pain. "Friends, Star," she murmured. "We are friends forevermore. Please remember that."

To Christa's surprise, Star formed the word "friends" on her lips and managed to say it. Then she fell in to what appeared to Christa to be a fitful sleep.

Feeling a tugging at her heart, Christa continued with her soft application of the wet cloth, praying that God would find it in his heart to spare this sweet girl who had never yet had the chance to find the true meaning of love and life.

Nineteen

Loud knocks on the front door of the Kramer mansion drew David quickly from Delores's arms. He leaned up on the bed on his elbow, startled, for this was their first time together in such a way. It had been the natural conclusion to their setting a wedding date.

But he dismissed worries of being discovered when Delores brushed her lips softly against his. He placed his arms about her, drew her to him, and seemed to melt inside when she began to kiss him with more passion. Once more they were drawn apart by frantic knocks on a door, but this time it was the closed bedroom door that was the recipient of the blows.

"What . . . the . . . ?" David said, gently lifting Delores aside to rush from the bed. He forgot that he was still supposed to have an ailing foot as he went to the door and opened it a crack to peer at the intruder.

"What is it?" he asked, looking cautiously at the Negro servant who stood with her eyes appearing as dark pits against her even darker skin. He made sure not to let the servant get a glimpse of Delores in his bed. The gossip would spread like wildfire to the rest of the household employees and that would make it quite uncomfortable for both him and Delores in the future.

"I've looked all ovah the place for Miss Delores," the servant said in a tiny, fragile voice. "I can't find her nowheres.

A man just came and insisted to see her. He's mighty upset. Maybe you'd bes' come down and see him, Massa' David."

"Didn't you find out what he wanted?" David asked, combing his fingers nervously through his hair.

"You knows a nigga's place in the household," the servant said solemnly. "So's no, I don' know more than ah've ahready tol' you. Will you see the man or should he be sent away?"

David gave Delores a nervous glance, and, seeing that she was already dressing, he once more looked toward the servant. "I'll see if I can find Delores," he said thickly. "Surely you didn't check each room well enough. You know there are many. When I find her, we both will come down and see what all the commotion is about."

"Yassa," the servant said, lowering her head as she walked away quickly.

Delores frantically fastened the back of her dress. "It's Father," she said, frowning with worry. "Why else would someone be here to see me at this time of night?"

"It's not all that late, Delores," David softly argued, slipping into his breeches and then his shirt.

"When the sun sets in Seattle, it is late, David," she argued back, stepping into her shoes. "It will probably be that way for a while since the Indians put such a scare into the people of this city."

"Harrison probably just stopped by somewhere for a drink after the town meeting was adjourned," David said, starting to slip his boot onto his ailing foot and just remembering in time that he had to pretend for a while longer that this was an impossible task.

"That's not at all like Father," Delores whined, now fussing with her hair before a mirror. "He doesn't mix with riffraff, David. Surely you know that. He is a man of class. He would never lower himself to take a drink with scum on the waterfront."

David's eyebrows rose as he gave her a questioning look,

then he shrugged as he followed her out into the hallway and down the stairs. Within the next few moments he had heard the news of Harrison's untimely death and had also discovered that Christa was nowhere to be found in the house.

Delores rushed to her bedroom, crying violently as she threw herself across the bed. David tried to console her, yet his mind was on his sister. Eying his spare boot, he knew that the time for pretense was past. He had to go in search of Christa, and now. It didn't seem to make sense that Harrison had been found dead at the same time that Christa had gone so mysteriously.

Thrusting his foot into his boot, David looked sadly toward Delores. He knew that he should stay with her, to console her, but he had loved Christa much longer than Delores, and his loyalty was now to her.

Delores turned on her side on the bed and looked up at David with red-rimmed eyes. "Where are you going?" she sobbed. "Please don't leave me now, David. I need you. Just think of it. My father is dead. And he was murdered! It's like a nightmare. Who could have done such a thing?" Once more she buried her face in her hands and resumed weeping, moaning loudly.

David went to her, sat down on the edge of the bed, and scooped her up and into his arms. "Darling, I want nothing more than to stay here with you, to comfort you," he said hoarsely. "But perhaps you haven't noticed that Christa is gone. I fear that something as terrible has happened to my sister. I must go find her. Please understand."

"Christa?" Delores said, blinking more tears from her eyes. "You . . . say . . . that she . . . is gone . . . ? I had no idea, David."

"You were . . . you are . . . too distraught to notice," he said. "I understand. Now you be just as understanding that I must leave. I hope to find Christa wandering along the Sound, safe."

"Then go. Find her, David. I will be all right."

"While I'm away from the house, I will go and see to Harrison's arrangements."

Delores threw herself back onto the bed, crying frantically once again. David's heart was tearing to shreds. He ran his fingers over her hair, then he rose from the edge of the bed and hurried from the room, frightened that his hopes of finding Christa were futile. This all seemed the work of the Haida Indians. Perhaps they hadn't all decided to return to their villages after all. And if not, and if they had captured Christa, what would her fate be? he wondered miserably.

David's thoughts went to Tall Cloud. No, none of this could be Tall Cloud's doings. He had proven his friendship to the white men. Hadn't he fought side by side with them? No. If Christa had been taken hostage, the Haida would be responsible.

Placing a gun belt about his waist and feeling its heaviness, for he never liked to wear weapons of any sort, David left the house, determined to find all the answers.

Only patches of light could be seen at the ceiling of the forest as the posse made its way north, toward Haida Indian country. When no sign of Christa had been found, a posse had been formed, not only to find her but also the one responsible for Harrison's death. The ride had already been long. But the riders hoped it would be a profitable journey in the end. And David had vowed to find Christa, or die trying.

Silence prevailed among the fifty or so men riding with David. The last mile or so had given them cause to keep their hands on their gun belts, for they had heard mysterious bird calls emerging from the dark depths of the forest.

Watching keenly for any signs of movement in the brush, David's back stiffened. He had never been a man of violence. Should the Indians show themselves for attack, he hoped that he would have the skills to fight back. He so vividly remembered the times that the Suquamish Indians had casually ventured into his cabin unannounced, and he had let them, for fear of what they might do if he showed them the barrel of a gun.

But now it was different. He had Christa to think of. He had to find her, no matter what.

Suddenly all hell seemed to break loose. There were loud chants from the many tattooed Indians jumping from the brush, dragging the white men from their horses, plunging knives into their chests, while still other Haida aimed their rifles, ready to shoot.

Dumbstruck for only an instant, David jumped from his horse and rushed with several others into the cover of the trees. He raised his pistol and began shooting. Indians began to fall right and left, and others rushed back for safety into the recesses of the forest.

Then just as quickly as it had begun, it was over, quiet again. The air was filled with a sulphuric aroma from the gunblasts. Several white men and Indians lay stretched out on the ground, bloody and lifeless, and through the silence came the heavy breathing of the remaining men at David's side and back. Anxious and afraid, they wondered just how safe it was to emerge from where they had taken cover.

David straightened his back and looked slowly from side to side. He spoke to no one. Instead, he kept his thoughts focused on Christa and his need to find her before it was too late.

With this in mind, he boldly stepped out into the open and stealthily began working his way from body to body. A sickness invaded his senses when he saw the blood gushing from the wounds of those men who had so valiantly volunteered to ride with him. Now they lay dead, their eyes locked into steady stares.

David continued on his way, checking to see if any of

the Indians were only wounded and could tell him what he needed to know about his sister. Luck was with him. He came upon a Haida who showed signs of breathing.

Falling quickly to his knees, David turned the Indian over to lie on his back, cringing when tattoos stared back at him in the many shapes of birds and animals and also eyes, dark and accusing. Blood curled from the wounded Indian's nose and mouth. His right arm had been partially shot off and his left was smeared in even more blood. David did not fear the Indian, seeing that he had been rendered useless by his wounds.

"Indian, I need to know some answers," David said, lifting the Indian's head from the ground, placing his pistol into his face.

The Indian clamped his lips tightly closed, but his eyes continued to stare openly at David, revealing in their dark depths the hatred he felt for the white man.

David leaned down closer to his face. "Indian, you're going to die," he threatened. "So before you do, you might as well give me the answers I seek. I'm looking for my sister, Christa. She has been abducted from Seattle. Who among your tribe of Indians is responsible?"

In the dark shadows of the forest, within hearing range of David, one Indian lurked who had not been wounded or frightened away as all the other Haida had. Instead, he stood rubbing an old wound, the scar on his upper right arm, a constant reminder of the day he had been disgraced by a white woman. She had deprived him of the beautiful Suquamish Princess Star whom he had wanted as his private slave as well as his lover.

Leaning closer, within earshot of the white man who hovered over his wounded fellow Haida warrior, Striped Wolf listened, proud that he had at one time had the opportunity to be taught some English words by a white trapper that he had befriended and later killed. It made it possible now for him to understand what the white man was saying and why he was being so insistent about it.

Striped Wolf wanted to defend his warrior friend, but he knew the futility of the effort since he was the only remaining Haida in the area besides the warrior who appeared too stubborn to respond to any questions from the white man with the golden hair. Most of the others had run away, unlike Striped Wolf, who found glory in the fight.

Only recently had such feelings of glory begun to fade. Striped Wolf blamed Chief Tall Cloud and swore he would one day get his revenge.

David grabbed onto the wounded Indian's shoulders, growing angrier by the minute. "I know you understand what I'm saying," he growled. "Most Indians in this area can speak some English. What I am saying to you is not that hard to understand. Sister. My sister. Your Indians have her. Where? Tell me which direction to go."

The Indian began to shake his head slowly back and forth and gave out a soft laugh just as his eyes became locked in death, and he grew limp against David's hold.

Groaning, feeling defeated, David released his hands from the Indian's shoulders. He rose to his feet as a member of the posse came to his side.

"Get any information?" the man asked.

David raked his fingers nervously through his hair. "None," he grumbled. "I'm afraid that whoever has Christa is long gone from here. We . . . may . . . never find her."

With shoulders slumped, he walked away and found his horse wandering aimlessly on the edge of the forest. Throwing his leg over the saddle and mounting, he waited for the rest of the men to follow his lead. He watched sadly as some placed the dead bodies of the others onto their saddles and rode back in the direction of Seattle.

Somehow David felt responsible for these deaths, but he knew the foolishness of such guilt. He hadn't killed Harrison. He hadn't abducted Christa. The Haida—they were responsible for all the wrongs done to Seattle's white settlers, and, by God, somehow he would make them pay!

"Hahh!" he shouted to his horse, snapping the reins. He held his head high, refusing to look back, knowing that he would ride forever, if need be, to find his sister.

Striped Wolf's lips were set in a hard line, and he still did not believe what he had just heard. But shouldn't he have recognized this white man from the very first? It was the brother of the white woman who had acted as bravely as a man when she had used a gun against Striped Wolf.

Striped Wolf had watched from a distance as Christa and her brother had left for Seattle just before he had set fire to their cabin and personal belongings. If not for Tall Cloud's warriors guarding Christa like the giant, protective wings of an eagle, Striped Wolf would have had her as his slave long before this.

But now? He would risk anything to have her with him, because it would be a way to seek a twofold vengeance. In one brave act, he would abduct Christa, and in doing so, not only would he have revenge for her shooting him and depriving him of Princess Star, but at the same time he would be paying back Tall Cloud for having formed an alliance with the white men of Seattle!

Smiling, Striped Wolf now knew how to achieve this vengeance that he sought. Striped Wolf knew that no Haida Indian was responsible for Christa's abduction. She hadn't been abducted at all! It was obvious to him that Christa was with Tall Cloud, on Tall Cloud's Pahto Island!

With determination, he worked his way through the brush, finding his horse well hidden inside a dark, cool cave. Taking the horse from the cave, Striped Wolf decided not to chance riding out in the open, so he led the horse, while remaining on foot for a while longer.

Later, feeling safe enough, he rode in the direction of his

village. There he left his horse behind, ran to the river, and boarded a canoe. He had decided he would do this deed alone. Only by doing so would its rewards be as great in his heart.

Ah, how proud he would be to return with Christa at his side, not only to be his slave but his woman!

The moonlight settling into the water seemed to make a path for Striped Wolf to follow. His shoulder muscles flexed as he drew his paddle through the water, and he kept his eyes focused straight ahead, waiting to make that bend in the river which would direct him into the waters of Puget Sound. A full day and night of travel by canoe and he would be there. Neither food nor sleep would delay him. In his mind's eye he could already see Pahto Island, and he passed the time planning how he would scale its steep walls without being discovered.

Knowing the history of Pahto Island and its people, he knew that the island would be watched over by the spirits of Tall Cloud's ancestors. He also knew that the island had been abandoned until only recently when the white man had drawn up the hated treaty papers.

Striped Wolf had thought that he and Tall Cloud could become friends when the news of the treaty had reached all the Indians in the northwest territory. It was well known that Tall Cloud hated the terms of the treaty just as much as the Haida, yet, strangely enough, Tall Cloud had sided with the white man when Striped Wolf had led his people in revolt because of the treaty.

"I will never understand him," he grumbled. "He has chosen the white man over the Indian. How could he?"

Then Striped Wolf's thoughts went to another Indian, to Chief Sealth, and how Chief Sealth had befriended all white men since their arrival on the shores of Puget Sound. He vividly remembered the day that he, Striped Wolf, had stood at the edge of the throng of Indians, listening to General Isaac Stevens, the white man called Governor of the state of Washington, as he explained why the Indians should sign the treaty. General Stevens, a small, swarthy man who had distinguished himself in the Mexican War, had spoken in confidence, saying that the Great White Chief in Washington, D.C. loved the Indians as much as if they were the children of his own loins. Because of this love for them, General Stevens was going to have the Great Father buy the Indians' lands, and he was going to give them fine reservations and the blessings of civilization, such as schools, blacksmiths, and carpenter shops . . .

Shaking his head, Striped Wolf thought it useless to try to understand how the Suquamish Indians, Tall Cloud, *or* Chief Sealth had been tricked by the white men and their flowery words. He, Striped Wolf, would never give up his wish that the land once more be filled only with Indians instead of whites. If blood had to be spilled over and over again, then that was the way it would be. It was in his heart and soul to fight. And he would fight to the end.

But first, he had to taste the lips of the white woman called Christa. Then he would make her his slave and torture her whenever she gave him cause. Laughing wickedly, his strokes became swifter as he grew more determined than ever before.

Twenty

The Suquamish shaman remained outside Tall Cloud's hut as requested, chanting as he spun on his heel in a dance then sprang into the air from a squatting position. The night was filled with the sound of the rattle he shook, made of mountain sheep horn and baleen, steamed and folded over and fastened to its wooden handle. While he performed, the fire in the communal fire space cast his shadows onto Tall Cloud's hut, and they looked not at all human as his arms and legs flailed in his continuing spiritual dance.

Inside the hut, Christa labored over Star, still bathing her with a cool, dampened deerskin cloth. Christa's heart ached almost as badly as her back, for she now felt that there was no hope for Tall Cloud's younger sister. But she would sit there, no matter how much her back ached, for the length of time required to make Star more comfortable.

Looking down upon Star's tiny facial features, Christa could hardly recognize her now. In her pain, Star's face had twisted grotesquely and her eyelids had become swollen, so that now there were only slits for her to look through.

It pained Christa so, seeing Star's life ebbing away before her very eyes. And when Star began to scream as another pain grabbed her in the abdomen, Christa flinched and bit her lower lip in added frustration. Never had she felt so helpless. But she was doing all that she knew to do and could only look sorrowfully toward Tall Cloud who stood in a far corner with his head sadly hung in his hands and his shoulders sagging in a defeated posture Christa had never seen before.

Now looking toward the Indian midwife, Christa tensed, seeing that she had suddenly come out of her trance and was now spreading Star's legs apart and doing something between her thighs.

The midwife began to chatter loudly in Indian, causing Tall Cloud to rush to her side and kneel down beside her.

"What is it, Tall Cloud?" Christa asked, her heart beginning a hard pounding as she saw a red, liquid substance splash from inside Star. It was too thin to be blood. Yet, what . . . ? Christa wondered silently.

"The baby," Tall Cloud said anxiously. "It is coming. Soon we shall know its fate."

Star's head began thrashing about wildly. She reached and grabbed Christa by the hand and began tightly squeezing it. Tears formed in Christa's eyes when Star began crying out, pain thick in her words.

"Peshak," she cried, still tossing her head back and forth. *"Ah'tah lah 'tah lah! Peshak!"*

Tall Cloud gave Christa a forlorn look. "My sister now talks out of her head," he mumbled. "Comfort her as you can, *Nahkeeta*. Her spirit as well as her child is fighting to be released."

Christa dropped the deerskin cloth and took Star's other hand and now held on to both her hands as the midwife struggled to release the infant from inside Star's body. Christa felt a bitterness rise up into her throat as she watched the older Indian work a hand up inside Star while her other hand pressed down hard against Star's abdomen.

"Tyhee Sahale!" Star screamed as another contraction tore through her.

The baby's head finally appeared, and the midwife's hand formed around it, gently tugging, finally setting it free from Star's body. And then in one quick swoosh the baby's entire body was lying in the midwife's arms, but its dark purple color was evidence that it would never take its first breath of life.

Christa stared, mortified, at the discolored, lifeless figure of the child. And while staring, she discovered that Star had given birth to a son.

"Wakush tyhee a winna," Star said in a soft, quivering sigh, then her eyes closed peacefully and her body became lax.

"No!" Tall Cloud cried, gulping back a sob. "I give up the child of the wicked Haida but not my sister!"

He fell to his knees beside Star and drew her head upon his lap and rocked back and forth, crooning a song in Indian.

Christa's insides knotted with regret and with sorrow for the man she loved. Her eyes lowered, and she realized that she was still clasping Star's hands. With a throaty sob, she placed Star's lifeless hands on the abdomen which was no longer great with child, and then she rose to her feet and clumsily ran from the hut.

Breathless, she stopped only a few feet from the door and lowered her face into her hands, crying. Though she had never been given the opportunity to truly know Star, Christa felt as if she had just lost a sister. And the baby. The poor baby. It had never been given a chance at life, but had its . . . mother . . . either?

Having heard Star's wails and then the sudden silence, Tall Cloud's people appeared to know that she had died. All at once the air was filled with sounds from different musical instruments. Drums began to beat in unison; a sad tune played on a whistle sounded in the distance as did the booming noise made from a bull roarer, a flat stick whirled at the end of a string to make the explosive sound.

Tall Cloud had told her that each of these types of music represented the voices of supernatural beings. And standing there in the darkness, the eeriness of these unfamiliar customs surrounding her, Christa felt she was on alien soil. She was filled with an intense desire to flee, to return to the ways of the world familiar to her.

But when Tall Cloud emerged from the hut, his handsome face tear streaked and mournful, she knew that her place was at his side. With his outstretched arms a silent plea for her to go to him, Christa broke into a run and fell, sobbing, into his embrace.

"I'm so sorry, Tall Cloud," she whispered, clinging tightly to him.

Tall Cloud bent his back and buried his face in the thickness of her hair which lay across her shoulders. "Princess Star has paid the full price for her shameful ways," he said throatily. "My shame has even now been erased in the eyes of my people."

Christa winced, thinking that he sounded so heartless, still blaming Star for what Christa felt was a ridiculous custom. Star had behaved as most teenagers do, wanting to explore rather than be confined for a long period in a hut with so little space.

But the fact that Star had left the island and crossed the Sound had been the true cause of her brother's wrath. By her presence near the water, he had feared that she had placed a curse on his people and that the spirits would not allow them to catch enough fish as punishment for what Princess Star had dared to do. It seemed that the Haida's rape had been less in Tall Cloud's eyes than Princess Star's disobedience. It was as if Tall Cloud dismissed the rape as a punishment she deserved.

Could she ever truly understand these people? Christa forced herself to remember that it was these customs which caused Tall Cloud's words now and not the fact that he didn't care for his sister. If he hadn't cared, he wouldn't have let his tears be seen by his people; he was unconcerned that tears might make him appear weak.

Tall Cloud eased out of Christa's arms. "I must hurry,"

he said, turning his eyes back toward the hut. "My sister and her child must be readied quickly for the land of the dead. It must . . . be . . . done at once."

Christa sensed a strange urgency in his voice. "But, Tall Cloud, why must it be done so quickly?" she asked softly. "Surely you wish to see Star prepared slowly . . . lovingly."

With a jerk of the head, Tall Cloud looked down into Christa's eyes, his own eyes now dark and fearsome. "Never speak her name to me again," he said dryly.

"What . . . ?" Christa gasped, taking an awkward step backward.

"The Suquamish never speak the name of a loved one after his death," he explained softly. "We fear that by doing so, the loved one's spirit would be disturbed."

"Oh, I see . . ." Christa said. "I didn't understand. I didn't know."

Tall Cloud patted her gently on the shoulder. "I've much to teach you of the Suquamish ways. But for now, I'm too torn between grief at my loss *and* the fear of my sister's ghost. I must see to it that her body is removed from my dwelling as soon as possible, now that she is dead."

Christa gulped hard, her eyes wide. "Tall Cloud, will this dwelling now . . . be . . . our dwelling?" she asked, afraid to hear the answer. She couldn't bear to think of making love in a house—even on the same spot—where Star had given birth *and* died.

"No. This dwelling will be replaced by another," he said thickly. "Until then we will live in one now being prepared for us. My people know the customs. Soon we will go to the new dwelling, and I will forget my sorrows in your arms, *Nahkeeta*."

Christa moved her hand to the smoothness of his cheek "I'm glad I am here with you, to help ease the pain which I'm sure swells inside your heart."

"You are not angry for being forced to come?"

"I want to be here. Isn't that enough for you to know?"

"Yes. And now that you are, could you help me in preparing my sister for the land of the dead? If you were my wife, that would be part of your duty."

An involuntary shudder enveloped Christa, yet she forced a willing smile. "Whatever I can do to help . . . all you need to do is ask."

"Come. Follow me. I have lingered too long already."

Trembling, dreading to have to enter the hut again, with the bodies of Star and her child still there, Christa momentarily hesitated. Then she held her head high and followed Tall Cloud.

"Help cleanse my sister and her child of all foreign, impure matter, while I perform the duties required of the deceased's next of kin."

"What is it that you have to do?" Christa asked, noting out of the corner of her eye that the midwife was offering her the deerskin cloth.

"I must prepare a hole in the wall for my sister's body and that of her child to pass through," he said matter-of-factly.

"A . . . hole . . . in the wall?" Christa gasped, taking the cloth the midwife forced into her hand.

"All Suquamish believe that the body of the dead must be removed through such a hole so that the living will not have to follow the path of the dead as they pass in and out through the door."

Christa's face became flushed, and once more she felt a stranger to the ways of this world. Surely in time—

Her thoughts were interrupted as the midwife left the hut, and Christa realized she and Tall Cloud were alone with the bodies. "You cleanse while I labor here?" he said, already tearing shreds of rush matting from the wall.

Christa looked down with dread at Star and then at the baby now stretched out across her abdomen—mother and son reunited to spend their eternities forever together.

Knowing what was expected of her, Christa dropped to

her knees beside Star. She splashed the cloth into a wooden basin of perfumed water and began washing Star with it, starting with her face. It was no longer flushed with fever and the distortion had smoothed away, leaving her now peacefully beautiful, as if she were only asleep.

With her fingers, Christa swept strands of Star's hair back from her eyes and bathed her brow slowly and lovingly. She proceeded farther down her body, running the cloth across the loveliness of Star's long and slender neck and then, almost meditatively, bathing the thickened mounds of her breasts.

A renewed sadness rushed through Christa as she noted one of the baby's tiny, circled fists lying so close to a breast that would have been his thread of life if mother and son had survived. How ironic that her body had worked so magically to prepare this mother's breasts with rich, sweet-tasting milk and would never have the opportunity to offer this to the baby's tiny, hungry lips.

Almost unable to bear continuing and wondering why she must when so many Indian squaws filled this village who could have taken her place, Christa was quickly reminded of the reason when she heard a soft cry flow from between Tall Cloud's lips. He had finally torn enough rush matting away to provide a hole through which the bodies of his sister and her child could pass.

Lowering her eyes, Christa almost choked with emotion as she continued bathing Star and then her child. She sighed deeply when she finally completed the task which had left her drained and limp. She hadn't finished any too soon, however, for just then the midwife entered, carrying an arm load of animal skins and layers of cedar bark.

Rising to her feet, her face flushed, Christa eased next to Tall Cloud, and they both watched silently as mother and son were bound together with the skins and then an outer covering of cedar bark. When that was done, Tall Cloud nodded to the midwife, and, at his command, she hurried outside to stand beside the hole in the wall.

With loving, tender care, Tall Cloud lifted his sister's wrapped body and slipped it through the hole into the arms of the midwife, who gently placed it on the ground.

During this procedure, Christa's mind kept flashing back to that day when she had found the Haida Indian in the throes of a lustful passion which had filled the innocent Suquamish teenager's womb with his seed. She kept wishing, over and over again, that she had arrived at that point in the forest a moment sooner. There would have been no rape . . . there would have been no child . . . there would have been no death!

A vision of the Haida's tattooed face and body sent a sense of dread through Christa, and she wondered where he might be at this moment. She hoped he was among those Haida frightened back to their villages, perhaps forever. . . .

"It will soon be over," Tall Cloud said, once more embracing Christa. "Come. The canoe for my sister and her son has been readied."

"Canoe . . . ?" Christa whispered softly, wishing this horrible evening were over and relishing this brief moment in his arms.

"She will be placed in her personal canoe, which will be raised to the highest ledge overlooking the Sound and pointed west, to where the setting sun will be tomorrow, lighting her way to the land of the dead."

"You do not bury . . . your dead . . . ?"

"The spirit would not be free if placed in the ground."

Christa clung to his waist as they left the hut. Then she stepped away from him as he went to get the wrapped bodies. Tall Cloud carried them past Christa, now so immersed in grief he paid her no heed. And not wanting to interfere, Christa stayed far back from the crowd of Indians as they followed their chief to where Princess Star and her infant would finally rest.

It seemed an eternity of wailing and dancing before the canoe was lifted to the smooth surface of a wide rock. And after the Indians had disbanded, leaving only Christa and Tall Cloud standing in the gloomy, total darkness of night, she was finally able to breathe more easily.

Christa gave Tall Cloud a nervous smile when he came to stand before her, and his words surprised her, for she had thought that the burial rituals were surely over, even if they had been accomplished more quickly than she would have guessed possible.

"Now we, the principal mourners, must be purified to remove the contaminating influence of the dead before we can resume our normal lives," Tall Cloud announced hoarsely.

Christa's insides grew numb. What could she expect now? To be bathed by the Suquamish? The thought made her feel ill.

"How is this done?" she blurted.

"You and I will go to the waters of the Sound and cleanse ourselves there," Tall Cloud said, taking her by the elbow, already guiding her toward the steep steps that led down to the sandy beach. "Then we must part with all the clothes we now have on, because they can never fully be cleansed of their contamination."

Christa blanched. "Are you saying that we must . . . throw our clothes away?"

"It is required."

Christa looked back over her shoulder toward the activity of the village. "But, Tall Cloud, if my clothes are thrown away, how can I be expected . . . to . . . return to the village? I can't return there nude!"

"My people know the custom. They will retire to the privacy of their own dwellings. When we return after our purification, no one will look upon our nakedness. If one were guilty of doing this, my sister's ghost would forever haunt him for ignoring the final phase of the burial ceremony."

Silence prevailed as Christa concentrated on taking each step with caution, for their dampness was a constant threat. Thankfully the moon was full, lighting her way. Tall Cloud was proceeding ahead of her ready to catch her if her shoes gave way to the slimy substance beneath them.

Finally they reached the sandy, rock-infested beach where many canoes were moored, lining the shoreline. Tall Cloud led Christa to the smoothest, sandiest spot of the beach, away from the canoes. To her surprise, without any words he began releasing the buttons at the back of her dress. As her shoulders were exposed and then her breasts, Christa hugged herself, shivering from the damp, intense cold of the night.

She stared at the pounding surf and into the black of the water, knowing its icy temperature. The mountain stream continually fed the Puget Sound waters with their rivulets of melting snow, causing the temperature of the water to be near freezing.

Despite the cold, to please Tall Cloud and to show her strength and courage, Christa did not hesitate in doing what was expected of her.

"Now your shoes . . ." Tall Cloud said thickly.

He wadded up her dress and underthings and was about to throw them into the Sound, when he stopped as Christa grabbed him by the arm.

"Tall Cloud, if you throw my clothes away, what will I wear?" she asked, feeling quite vulnerable standing there totally nude except for her shoes.

"A soft dress of deerskin awaits your return to the village," he explained. "Moccasins will replace your shoes. Henceforth, you shall dress as an Indian."

He gently brushed Christa's hand away and proceeded to throw her clothes out to sea, as far as his strength allowed.

Christa stood as though in a daze, watching her clothes spread out in the moon-reflected water and then disappear beneath the surface as a wave swept over them.

"Now your shoes," Tall Cloud said once more, removing his fringe-trimmed shirt and then his breeches. "We must hurry. It's important to be cleansed of death's scent as soon as possible after becoming contaminated by it."

At this moment, Tall Cloud appeared oblivious to Christa's nudity, unlike times in the past when his gaze had scalded her bare skin as she revealed herself fully to him.

His indifference did not disappoint Christa. Instead, she felt relieved. Had he tried to make love to her then, she wasn't sure she would be capable of responding. She was still too disturbed by all that had happened, and she had to believe that he was also.

Yet, when he stripped himself of his last piece of clothing and the moon shone on the smoothness of his copper skin, displaying his broad chest which tapered to a flat belly and narrow hips, she couldn't deny the pleasure of her heart's nervous thumping against the curve of her ribs. Nor could she ignore the sweet pain that dared to rise between her thighs.

Her face became flushed. How could she think of sex at such a time? Tall Cloud's sister and nephew had just died.

Yet, it was her body that was betraying her, not her mind. And when Tall Cloud took her by the hand and guided her toward the water, she was glad, hoping that in its cold depths all her thoughts of desire would quickly vanish, for she truly believed that passion was the farthest thing from Tall Cloud's mind.

The water grabbed at her ankles like icy fingers, causing chills to crawl along Christa's flesh. But she forced herself to walk alongside Tall Cloud, deeper, ever deeper, until she tensed as even her breasts were covered by the cold wash of the water.

Then, to her surprise, Tall Cloud drew her quickly into his arms and embraced her, kissing her fiercely as waves splashed high and threatened to engulf them. As he cradled her body against his, his hands cupped the curves of her buttocks, his sex pressing against her abdomen, all thoughts of being cold or of stifling her desire were quickly cast aside.

Christa twined her arms about Tall Cloud's neck and locked her fingers together. His kiss transferred the heat of his body into hers. His molding hands, and the fire in his tongue as it parted her lips, melted the icy exterior of her flesh as a scorching flame shot through her.

"Help me to forget," Tall Cloud whispered as he pulled his lips only partially away from hers. "Love me, love me now, my *Nahkeeta*."

His hands glided over her body, arousing in her a passion she could no longer hold back. She pulled his head to hers and kissed him softly, then ran her tongue over his lips, tasting the saltiness from the seawater mingling with his own familiar taste.

His mouth opened and he sucked her tongue into it, the sensuousness of this act causing a small moan to surface from somewhere deep inside Christa. When his fingers traveled low over her body, touching her most sensitive of pleasure points, she lifted a leg and coiled it around him, shivering from ecstasy as his swollen manhood sought entrance where his fingers had just been softly kneading.

Tall Cloud placed his hands at her waist and lifted her body, easing her onto his throbbing sex. He sighed shakily and closed his eyes as he felt her softness wrap itself about his member, as if it had just been placed in a snug, protected velvet cocoon.

Kissing her ardently, holding her in place as waves crashed around them, Tall Cloud moved his body sensuously against hers. Then he lowered his lips, burying them into the soft curve of her neck where his teeth nipped teasingly at her flesh.

Giggling, Christa arched her neck backward, enjoying the feel of her loosened hair as it splayed out in all directions in the water. A splash of the waves caressed her cheeks and Tall Cloud's tongue licked the sparkling drops away.

Tall Cloud worked more feverishly into her, his eyes closed in rapture as his lips once more possessed hers. Christa writhed in response, unable to get enough of him. Then their bodies fused into one as their passions exploded, and the world melted away around them.

Trembling clinging, breathless, Christa buried her face into Tall Cloud's chest, feeling the feverish pitching of his heart as it pounded out its excitement of the moment.

"I love you so, Tall Cloud," Christa whispered against him. "Say it. Say that you love me as much."

Tall Cloud eased her away from him and urged her to stand on the sandy bottom of the Sound. His eyes seemed heavy as he looked toward her, yet he said nothing. Instead, he dove headfirst into a wave that crashed toward him and became lost to Christa's sight. With a fearful, pounding heart, she looked around her desperately, trying to find him beneath the soft splash of the moon. Yet she could see nothing.

Her hands went to her mouth. "Tall Cloud . . ." she whispered softly. "Good Lord, Tall Cloud . . ."

She wondered if he had been besieged by guilt for making love to her so soon after his sister's death. Was this the reason for his silence, for his swimming away from her so quickly after they had found paradise in each other's arms?

"No . . ." Christa cried, still unable to see him. Then she too dove beneath the surface of the water, her eyes burning in the saltwater as she tried to look about her. But the moon didn't fall beneath the surface. It was too dark for Christa to make out anything except the blackness which appeared to be swallowing up everything around her.

Feeling the need to get a breath of air, she surfaced, coughing and spitting saltwater from her mouth and nose. She fought the stinging of her eyes by wiping them with the backs of her hands. Then she felt Tall Cloud's arm about her waist, turning her. Crying out her joy that he was all right, Christa swung her arms about his neck and began laughing hysterically as she rained wild kisses across his face.

"Why . . . did . . . you . . . do that?" she asked then, imploring him with her eyes to answer.

"I . . . we . . . needed to complete the purification by cleansing ourselves fully beneath the water," he said hoarsely. "Now we are ready to return to shore. My sister will never be spoken of again between us. Remember that, my *Nahkeeta*. Her spirit will follow along behind our ancestors at tomorrow's sun setting. Until then, we will remain in seclusion inside the new dwelling prepared for us. And then, when the next day arrives, our future together will truly begin. My people will celebrate our wedding beyond any celebration ever held by the Suquamish."

Thoughts of David quickly entered Christa's mind. She so wanted this wedding with Tall Cloud, yet she didn't want to hurt her brother. She wondered what he might be going through with worry over her. Would he have assigned many to go in search of her? Might they even venture onto Pahto Island? Somehow, she had to find a way to get a message to David, to stop his worries and his search for her. She would convince David, somehow, that this was what she wanted.

Then she sickened inside as she remembered Harrison's body and how he had died. She could never hold Tall Cloud responsible and she couldn't let anyone else. Tall Cloud had acted in self-defense and, as it had turned out, in her defense as well. For Harrison Kramer had not hesitated to fire his pistol at them both, knowing very well that he could have shot and killed her along with Tall Cloud.

Was that what he truly wanted? she asked herself. When he realized he couldn't have me, did he decide to shoot us so that we would both pay for thwarting his plans?

Such thoughts had never occurred to her. Now she finally felt she understood Harrison's motives and, with this new understanding, she could dismiss his death completely from her mind!

But in remembering his death, she also realized that she could not send a message of her whereabouts to David. *She* understood Tall Cloud's innocence in Harrison's death, but no white man would even try. When an Indian killed a white man, that Indian was the same as dead in the eyes of the community.

Christa held on to Tall Cloud's hand as they waded out of the water. Immersed in the Sound and heated by passion, Christa had forgotten how cold the night was. Her teeth began chattering as the wind whipped her dripping, wet hair about her face. She welcomed Tall Cloud's arm as he began running with her toward the stone steps on the side of the bluff. And this time fearing freezing more then slipping, Christa rushed up the steps to the flat surface at the top, no longer caring if she was seen in her nudity by the villagers. She sought the warmth their shelter would offer her. She was anxious for the Indian clothes of which Tall Cloud had spoken. Anything to get warm again. She knew that her lips must be as purple in color as the skin beneath the nails of her fingers.

"We must hurry," Tall Cloud said, moving to her side. "The hour is late and the temperature cold."

The fire in the communal fire space still burned brightly, lighting their way behind a hut, around another, past several more, until they reached one which sat at the far end, isolated from the others.

Urging Christa inside, Tall Cloud drew her down beside a fire that had been prepared for their return. They knelt upon thick rush mats as they held their hands close to the fire. Christa hated the fact that she couldn't stop her teeth from chattering. Then she giggled when she heard that Tall Cloud's teeth were chattering also.

She gave him a sideways glance and laughed harder, seeing how he looked at her, his amusement etched upon his sculpted, handsome face.

"You are still cold?" Tall Cloud asked, rubbing his hands together briskly and moving even closer to the fire.

"I imagine as cold as you," Christa said, her eyes dancing, expecting him to deny it rather than show weakness to the woman he loved.

"Cold? I am not cold," Tall Cloud said, his face a mask of innocence.

"I expected you to say that," Christa said, giggling again.

Tall Cloud's eyes slowly moved over Christa, seeking her sleek, pink curves, feeling an ache in his loins to have her again. "And since I am not cold, let me show you my skills at warming your flesh," he said, turning to place his hands on her shoulders, gently lowering her downward.

"Yes, show me," Christa teased then grew serious when she found his lips so quickly on her breast. Her breath caught in her throat, and she felt desire washing over her anew as his tongue flicked out and wove its way around the quickening hardness of her nipple. He had known very well how he could warm her. His lips, tongue, and hands held the magic in them to do anything to her body that he desired. . . .

"I will pleasure you now as never before," he said huskily. "When I'm finished, see if you have a cold bone left in your body. This time I will love you. Don't worry about loving me back. This time is yours. Fully yours."

Christa didn't reply. She was already becoming dizzy from his manipulations of her body. Where his hands weren't caressing, his tongue or lips were. And when he gently opened her legs and his lovemaking centered on where the core of her desire lay pulsing . . . sweetly pulsing, his lips paid homage as never before. His fingers spread her apart; his lips sucked; his tongue plunged. Christa was carried away as if on a cloud. She tossed her head fitfully from side to side and desperately chewed on her lower lip.

Moaning, she curled her fingers through his hair and drew

his face even closer to her. She draped a leg over his shoulder and was lost to all but the sensations he created within her.

Closing her eyes, she let the rapture take hold of her fully and was bathed in such contentment that she was unaware that he had finished with her. Only when his lips met hers in a quivering gentleness did she realize that he was no longer pleasuring her. As he had promised, she was warm in every corner of her being, and she doubted she could ever be cold again!

"That was my gift to you, my love, for agreeing to be my wife," he said huskily, now looking down at her with passion-filled eyes as he leaned over her.

"But, darling, you didn't receive pleasure as I did," she worried. "That isn't being fair to you."

"You do not believe it is pleasurable for a man to give pleasure?" He chuckled. *"Nahkeeta,* you've much to learn about a man. The smell and the taste of you is payment enough for what I just did for you."

Christa blushed and turned her eyes away from him.

Tall Cloud framed her face between his hands. "Do not look away from me," he scolded. "Never be ashamed of what I might do or say to you. We are one, you and I. Always remember that."

His lips moved to graze the nipple of her left breast. "Your body—it feels warm." He smiled. "Was I right in saying that I could show you ways to become warm?"

Christa traced his facial features with her forefinger. "Yes"—she sighed—"to both your questions."

"And would you understand if I said that I must leave you alone for a little while, without explaining why I have the need to do this?" he asked, his eyes wavering as she openly stared at him.

How could he explain to her his need to leave the island, to ride the rivers in his canoe, to drown his sorrow and guilt over his sister's death? He had shamed his sister to death. He knew this, and though his *Nahkeeta* was with him and they had shared bliss together, he was still finding it hard to forget his sister and her dead infant, and it was even harder to forgive himself for their deaths. . . .

"If you have the need to do this thing, please do it," Christa said, rising up on an elbow. "Please never let my presence stand in the way of anything you must do. Trust is synonymous with love, Tall Cloud. Always remember that."

"Then I will go. I will try not to be long," he said, rising to his feet. He reached for his clothes which had been folded and placed neatly on a shelf along with others that were obviously for Christa. Tall Cloud chose to dress only in a loincloth. And after he had placed his beaded headband and a fresh, new feather on his head, he drew Christa into his arms and gently hugged her.

"Soon. I will return soon," he whispered then released her and made a fast, almost alarming escape from the dwelling.

Christa stood by the fire, stunned, feeling terribly alone. A tremor coursed through her as she slowly looked around, absorbing the interior of the hut. It was no different from the other huts she had shared with Tall Cloud, for it, too, was devoid of furniture and modern conveniences for preparing food.

"I'll grow used to it," she reassured herself aloud. "My love for Tall Cloud is so strong, the inconvenience will be overshadowed by the joy of being near him."

Growing cold again in Fall Cloud's absence, Christa went to the shelf and sorted through the clothes which had been placed there for her. Though it was time she retired for the night, something made her choose a dress. In it, she would feel more comfortable while alone. She slipped it over her head, admiring its fancy beadwork, then settled down beside the fire and stared into it thoughtfully. She was so alone. Silently she prayed for Tall Cloud's swift return.

Twenty-one

Growing drowsy, unable to keep her eyes open any longer as she awaited Tall Cloud's return, Christa eased her weary body onto a blanket which she had spread over the rush mats. She knew that she should add wood to the fire, but, expecting Tall Cloud at any moment, she didn't bother. She stretched out on her side, resting her head into the curve of her arm, and watched the remaining curls of fire in the fire space.

Slowly, lethargically, her eyes closed. Her breathing became quiet and peaceful, and her mind emptied of everything but her need to sleep. The fire popped and crackled, and the wind was a soft whisper as it blew outside the hut in which Christa lay.

And then another sound entered her consciousness, causing her eyes to fly open, and she became keenly aware of footsteps shuffling around outside the hut. She tensed then relaxed, sighing, for she expected Tall Cloud to step inside the hut at any moment now, returning from his strange, unexplained mission.

Yawning, Christa moved to a sitting position, trying to look alert for his return. She combed her fingers through her hair and bit her lips to fill them with color. Watching the door, she waited for Tall Cloud to enter. But her eyes widened in horror as someone quite different rushed into the hut and quickly clasped his hand over Christa's mouth to stifle her outcry.

Horrified, Christa began to scratch and claw at Striped Wolf, and it seemed the many designs of his ugly tattoos had become living creatures as he struggled to hold her at bay. His chest was bare, but fringed leggings covered his legs, and there was a pistol belted to his waist and a sheathed knife at the side of his leg.

Christa was fast becoming breathless. She eyed him with venom. Surely he wasn't foolish enough to believe that he could get away with this. Not on Tall Cloud's island.

Yet, Striped Wolf was winning the fight. Christa had no more strength in her arms or legs and she was forced to stop her struggles. But she did try to bite Striped Wolf's hand, which he still held firmly over her mouth. She succeeded more at getting a taste of his filthy flesh than at injuring him enough to cause him to set her free.

"It is good that Tall Cloud travels the river far from his Pahto Island," Striped Wolf said with a chuckle as he secured a piece of deerskin over Christa's mouth, sealing it. "I will get you across the Sound, and then we shall also travel by way of rivers. White woman with nerves of steel, you are to be my slave and mine to do with what I please. You will pay for shooting me and taking Princess Star from my possession. Yes, white woman, you will take Princess Star's place at my side in the Haida village, for all to see."

Christa's strength returned after hearing his declaration of ownership. She rose to her feet and began running toward the door but was stopped abruptly as Striped Wolf grabbed her roughly by a wrist.

"You cannot escape." He laughed. "You might as well go with me willingly. It will be much easier on you, white woman. If I have to render you unconscious to carry you from this island, I will do so without hesitation."

Christa cringed as his face moved closer to hers. He smelled of dead animals and perspiration, and in his eyes she could see a seething hatred for her. But she realized she had two things in her favor. She could understand his broken English, and she knew that Tall Cloud surely couldn't be as far away as Striped Wolf thought him to be. Striped Wolf would never get far with her. Tall Cloud wouldn't let this happen to her. He wouldn't!

"Now. We must go," Striped Wolf said, half dragging her from the hut. "Walk lightly." He took his knife from its sheath and thrust it close to Christa's side. "If you cause any noise, I will quickly kill you. If I must be discovered and die a slow death at the hands of the Suquamish for what I am doing here, your death will come before mine. Hear me well. What I say is true. Tall Cloud will not have you either way."

Christa half stumbled as she was forced to move away from the hut and then away from the village to the back side of the island, where she and Tall Cloud had at one time wandered, enjoying nature and each other.

When she saw that Striped Wolf had approached the island in this way, beaching his canoe where no others ever ventured, Christa's hopes waned. Yet she wouldn't let herself wallow in hopelessness, for she knew the waters of the Sound reached out in all directions, and Tall Cloud could, by chance, suddenly appear from nowhere to save her.

The thin soles of the Indian moccasins weren't enough protection for Christa's feet, since she was so used to the soles of her own shoes. When she was forced to step over piles of fallen limbs, their sharp points pushed their way into her feet. And the wetness of the scattered, dead leaves, soaked from the dampness of night, caused Christa to slip and slide as Striped Wolf pushed her on ahead of him.

Flipping her hair back across her shoulders, Christa panted, once more succumbing to the exhaustion she had felt even before her struggles had begun with Striped Wolf. This day had been a traumatic one to say the least, and it seemed that the full night ahead of her would be the same. Would it ever end? Would she ever live a peaceful existence again?

Tall Cloud, she thought over and over again to herself. Tall

Cloud, please hurry back to the island. Please find me gone and come for me. I'm afraid. This time I am sorely afraid.

The darkness of night made it impossible for her to see into the distance, but the splash of water and the smell of seawater told Christa that they were nearing the beach. She would soon be forced into Striped Wolf's canoe and carried off.

She jumped with fright when Striped Wolf once more grabbed her by the wrist and began running, half dragging her behind him, until they reached the beach and his canoe.

Christa's fear made her begin to fight him anew. As he set her free to prepare the canoe for travel, she rushed to him and gave him a hearty shove, making him lose his balance. When he fell into the water, emitting loud complaints in his Indian tongue, Christa turned and began rushing back toward the depths of the forest to hide herself. But all at once he was there, tackling her, causing her to fall against a tree. Her head hit with a crack and suddenly all that she could see was a slow spinning of Striped Wolf's ugly face as he leaned down into hers. Then she drifted off into nothingness.

Christa awakened with a start, aware she was traveling on water. She blinked her eyes nervously, now remembering Striped Wolf. She looked around her, seeing Striped Wolf's full figure on the seat of his canoe, his back to her, paddling.

Slowly pushing herself up from the floor of the canoe to get a better look around her and some idea of where they might be traveling, Christa saw the darkness of trees on both sides of her. They were in a narrow body of water which extended only a few yards from the canoe to the shore in either direction.

The water lapping at the canoe as it plunged through it appeared black in the total darkness of the night. Christa believed she would be able to swim to safety if she could manage to get over the side of the canoe without Striped

Wolf hearing her. But first she concerned herself with the
gag in her mouth. It had been there long enough. Had she
not been rendered unconscious by the fall back on Pahto
Island, she would have removed the gag sooner. While
Striped Wolf was busy paddling, there was nothing standing
in the way of her removing the nasty-tasting piece of deerskin material from her mouth.

A dull throbbing at the base of her skull caused Christa
to wince and her hand to fly to the spot. A knot pushed its
way through her hair, but she found that no skin had been
broken, for there were no signs of dried blood.

With determination, she untied the buckskin gag from
around her mouth and jerked it away, dropping it to the floor
of the canoe. Then she rose to a sitting position, barely
breathing lest Striped Wolf should discover what she was
about.

She watched him for a moment, afraid to move. Then sensing that the time was right for escape, fearing that the river
might stretch out to wider proportions at any moment, she
placed a hand on the side of the canoe and pulled herself
up.

She slipped over the top of the canoe and quietly eased
herself into the water, thankful that the canoe wasn't traveling at a faster rate of speed. She clung to the canoe for
a moment longer then released her fingers and sank deeper
into the water, feeling its iciness creep into her clothes and
then her flesh.

She began to swim away quietly in the opposite direction
of the canoe. Then she made a turn and headed toward the
shore. Her heart raced and the pit of her stomach felt hollow
from fear, for she had no idea where she would go once
she reached the land. She had no idea where the Haida had
already managed to take her, and she didn't recognize any
of the bends of this river.

Christa raised her arms in and out of the water, kicking
her feet only slightly for they were now heavy from the water

soaking into her deerskin moccasins. She trembled with the severe chilling of the water, yet her pulse raced with anticipation as she saw the shore now finally within reach.

Looking across her shoulder, she tried to find Striped Wolf's canoe. Then she took a quick second look when she saw that it was nowhere in sight. Had he traveled so quickly away from her? she wondered. Or had . . . he . . . circled around . . . after realizing she was gone . . . ?

In despair, she realized the latter was true. There was no denying the splash his paddle made. There was no denying the low, throaty laugh coming from Striped Wolf's throat as he now came into view on Christa's right side.

Christa's eyes widened as she saw the canoe coming swiftly toward her. Frantic, she quickened her strokes in the water and kicked her feet wildly, seeing shore so close, yet so far. She knew that Striped Wolf might decide at any moment to guide his canoe over to her and kill her.

Gulping air, her arms and legs aching from both the cold and her efforts to save herself, Christa turned her eyes away from Striped Wolf's canoe and thanked God beneath her breath when her feet reached down and made contact with a muddy bottom. She tried to place her feet solidly on the river bottom but only succeeded in slipping on the mud, which caused her to fall back into the water.

She gasped for air when she swallowed water, and her arms flailed about her. Then Striped Wolf's canoe was beside her. He lay aside his paddle and reached a hand to Christa, grabbing her by a wrist.

"Now you see, white woman, I have saved you from drowning." He laughed scornfully. "You will come willingly with me now, won't you? Or would you rather I let go of you and let you continue to fight the mud on the bottom of this river? It has sometimes even sucked a person completely into its depths. Either you choose to climb back into my canoe with me, or I will help the mud suck you up. I will give you a hearty shove downward, so that your ankles are quickly captured."

Christa looked anxiously about her despite the realization that she had no recourse other than to travel once more in the canoe with the dreaded Haida Indian. Perhaps later she would again find a way to escape. Perhaps Tall Cloud would soon appear to rescue her!

Her wrist aching from Striped Wolf's steady, tight grip, Christa nodded her head. "All right," she hissed. "You've won this time. But agreeing to board the canoe doesn't mean that I won't try to escape again."

"You won't get that chance," Striped Wolf growled, helping her into the canoe. "You see, white woman, this time I will not only bind your mouth. Your wrists will be tied together as well, to prevent you from any further escape attempts."

Christa's shoulders sagged in defeat. She trembled violently as she huddled in a sitting position on the floor of the canoe. There was no fight left in her when he placed the same gag around her mouth. Even when he tied her wrists behind her back she only watched in mute silence. With a shove, Striped Wolf made sure she was once more stretched out in the canoe, defenseless. And this time he faced her as he resumed his paddling.

Tears burned in the corners of Christa's eyes, yet she refused to set them free. This Indian had called her a woman who had nerves of steel. She had to prove to him that she still did, no matter what he did to her.

While lying there, Christa found her thoughts alternating between Tall Cloud and David, for both had been her protectors. If only one of them could save her! But would this be the one time that neither would . . . or . . . could? Perhaps she had traveled so far with the Haida that no one would ever be able to find her.

Christa watched the sky, seeing flakes of light appearing on the horizon, indicating that daybreak was about to occur.

A full night. She had now been with the Haida a full night. And yet he continued to travel onward. How much farther? Were they going into country unknown to the white man or the Suquamish Indian?

Yet, she had to believe that Tall Cloud knew *all* of this northwest country. He, his people, his ancestors, had hunted to survive all over this country of mountains and trees.

I have to believe that Tall Cloud will somehow know where to travel, she thought reassuringly to herself, concentrating hard on being positive instead of negative about all that was happening to her.

A sudden change in the direction of the canoe made Christa tense and raise her head up to see where Striped Wolf was now taking her. Then her eyes were drawn to him as he moved the canoe toward the shore and placed his paddle deeply into the river floor. He pushed the canoe even closer to the shore and beached it among many fallen branches which were piled in the water.

"We will travel by land the rest of the way," Striped Wolf said, grabbing her by the shoulder and urging her to a standing position. "We will be less vulnerable that way. But first we must find a white man's barn. We will steal a horse."

Christa half stumbled from the canoe as Striped Wolf yanked at her shoulder when he stepped out into the water. She forced herself not to cry out when her knee was scraped by a sharp twig jutting out from the pilings along the shore. She stepped high, then low, following alongside Striped Wolf, continuously losing her balance because of her bound wrists.

He didn't let up once they had reached shore. He shoved her ahead of him into the slowly fading darkness as they began their journey on foot beneath the tall shadows of the trees.

Spirals of light shone slowly through the trees as daylight became more of a reality. The birds began singing, and Christa caught glimpses of a deer in the brush and squirrels in the trees. The ground tangle impeded Christa's every step. The soles of her moccasins kept getting caught and the briars of blackberry bushes tore the skirt of her dress and sank deeply into the flesh of her legs.

But she continued to follow after Striped Wolf farther and farther into the forest for what seemed like hours, until her stomach ached from hunger and her throat was sore from lack of water. When would the Haida stop for nourishment? she wondered. Or would he not, for fear of Tall Cloud catching up with him?

Then Christa tensed when she saw a clearing ahead. Through the break in the trees she caught a glimpse of civilization as she had always known it, for she saw a cabin nestled at the edge of the woods. When Striped Wolf grabbed her arm roughly and swung her behind a tree, Christa realized despairingly that not even here—so close to this cabin which was surely filled with friendly people—could she expect to secure help to aid her in her escape. Striped Wolf wouldn't allow her even a minute alone. He was much too crafty for that.

Striped Wolf jerked her next to him and glared down into her eyes. "You will come with me while I find a suitable horse for traveling," he growled softly. He once more took his knife from its sheath and placed it at her throat. "One wrong move, white woman, and you will be dead."

Christa paled, looking wildly into his eyes, feeling the sharp point of the knife as he stuck it only slightly into her flesh as a reminder that what he was saying was true.

"I see that you understand," Striped Wolf said, chuckling. He lowered his knife yet kept it ready in case she let her bravery once more guide her into mischief, which could mean death to them both. He would kill her quickly, even if a bullet found its way inside his heart! He wouldn't allow her to escape. Never! Tall Cloud would not bed this woman again. No one would bed this woman again other than Striped Wolf!

Stepping to the edge of the clearing with him, Christa eagerly watched as a woman moved toward the barn with a basket over her arm. She was going to gather eggs, just as Christa had always done each morning. Then Christa looked anxiously toward Striped Wolf. Would he kill this innocent woman, she wondered, in order to get the horse?

Another movement caught Christa's eyes. It was a man—a man walking from the barn with a pitchfork. He thrust the pitchfork into the ground and stopped to give the woman—most surely his wife—a quick kiss, then he headed on toward the house.

Two people. Two *innocent* people. Surely Striped Wolf wouldn't—

"I will wait," Striped Wolf growled. "I do not care to leave a trail of dead people for Tall Cloud to follow. When the white woman goes back into the house, we will go soundlessly into the barn, lead their horse out, and soon be gone from this place."

Closing her eyes, Christa sighed with relief. At least this couple would be spared Striped Wolf's cruelty. If only she could also be spared. . . .

Jerking Christa down to a crouching position, Striped Wolf watched the barn, then the house. When spirals of smoke rose more steadily from the chimney, he assumed the white man was readying the fire in his strange fire space for the white woman to prepare their meal. While they were eating, the horse could be easily taken.

Christa never took her eyes from the barn, watching for the woman to leave with her basket full of eggs. And when she finally appeared then went on to the house, Christa knew that the time had come for Striped Wolf to steal the horse. Her stomach ached, her heart pounded nervously against her ribs, and her knees were weak as Striped Wolf roughly jerked her up and they began moving toward the back of the barn.

Praying that the couple would remain in the house,

Christa went with Striped Wolf inside the barn where they found two horses. She looked cautiously at Striped Wolf then back at the house, wondering if he would choose only one, or both.

"We will ride together," Striped Wolf said as though he had read her thoughts. "That way, you will have less chance to escape. Come. We will lead the horse from the barn and mount it once we get it far away from the eyes of the white woman and man."

Striped Wolf chose a tan mare with white spots on her lovely, brushed mane. He smiled, seeing that it was ready for riding, with reins in place, and he assumed that the white man had planned to ride out as soon as the morning meal had warmed his stomach.

Smugly Striped Wolf grabbed the reins. "Come. Follow me," he said to Christa, who stood, waiting.

Christa frowned, so wanting to break into a run toward the cabin, but afraid to do so. The pistol belted at Striped Wolf's waist was threat enough to make her think better of trying such a bold move.

Instead, she crept along with him into the bright sunshine of the blossoming morning as he made for the trees which lined this clearing. But loud shouts erupting from behind her made her turn with a start to see the man running from the cabin, swinging a rifle above his head.

Striped Wolf stopped, grabbed Christa by the waist, and swung her onto the horse's back. In one jump he was there also, sitting behind her. He didn't look toward the white man but instead urged the horse onward. A gunshot exploded. Striped Wolf ducked down low, pushing Christa's head down also, and thrust his knees deep into the horse's sides, urging it into the forest. He worked the horse through the trees in zigzags until he felt that he was far enough from the danger of the white man to stop.

Christa's chest heaved from exhaustion and anxiety. She searched Striped Wolf's face as he dismounted. There was no telling what his next move might be. But the look on his face, the anger in his eyes, caused her fear to surface once more. She flinched when he took her by an arm and threw her against a tree.

"I must return to the white man's dwelling," he growled. "And since I have no rope to bind you against a tree, I must think that you will not be fool enough to try to escape while I am away. You see, you couldn't get far. I would soon find you. You would then be spared from going to my village, for your death would come swiftly. Do you understand? Your life is getting less important to me. Only my life is of importance here. I can have any woman of my choosing from the Haida squaws."

A slow smile twisted his lips into a sneer. "But I would be sure to let Tall Cloud have you back," he said. "I would send you back to him . . . dead!"

Christa took a step backward. She wanted to tell him that she believed him and that she wouldn't try to run away. At this point in her captivity, she knew the evil of the man and was certain that he would indeed end her life if she did not listen and obey. Her will was slowly ebbing away to total surrender.

Mounting the horse, Striped Wolf gave Christa another lingering stare. "I will return once I have slain the man and woman," he said. "I didn't wish it to be this way, but since they saw us, they would be too much of a threat. They could tell Tall Cloud in which direction we are traveling. They have to die, but it will be swift. When they least expect it, I will kill them."

Tears formed in Christa's eyes as she slumped down to the ground. She turned her head away from Striped Wolf as he rode away, and she prayed that the white man would still be alert to the danger and kill Striped Wolf for her.

Twenty-two

Feeling refreshed and emptied of his guilt over the loss of Princess Star, Tall Cloud returned from traveling the rivers. A smile shaped his lips as he approached his hut, knowing that his *Nahkeeta* would be glad to see that he was light of heart once again. Today! The wedding ceremony would be held today! And then he would spread the word for everyone to hear and celebrate. The great chief of this band of the Suquamish married to an enchantress of a white woman! Surely this would gain him some attention that had been lacking of late. And what would the white men do once they heard? Would they think of him differently? Surely they would realize that a white woman would marry only a wise, influential chief. Perhaps they would reconsider the importance of the dreaded treaty papers.

But if he stressed the necessity of sending the news of their marriage to the Great White Father in Washington, he would have to convince *Nahkeeta* all over again that it was not the true reason he wanted her as his wife. For now, he would just be content to have her.

Striding silently to the hut as dawn edged its way along the horizon, Tall Cloud was impatient to slip into the blankets behind *Nahkeeta* and draw her against him, to let her wake up with the powerful strength of his manhood pressed against her. A sensual awakening on her wedding day! Yes, that would increase her eagerness to become his wife.

As Tall Cloud stepped through the entrance he tensed, seeing no fire in evidence in the firespace. His eyes moved quickly about the hut, noting with rising horror its complete disarray and the absence of his beloved!

"Nahkeeta . . . ," he whispered harshly, growing numb inside as he began to dash about, picking up strewn baskets and dishes, and knowing that she had been taken by someone, and by force!

"Her brother?" he growled, curling his hands into tight fists.

Then he shook his head. No, he thought, the white man would not take her this way. Only the Haida steal beautiful women in the middle of the night! Striped Wolf. This was the work of the Haida devil, Striped Wolf. Perhaps he had come in search of Princess Star, and, not finding her, had decided to take *Nahkeeta* instead!

A low growl rose to a howl as he looked upward to the ceiling of the hut. He closed his eyes and began chanting loudly, stiffening his body, thrusting his chest out as his arms folded rigidly across it.

A rush of feet outside the hut was evidence that his warriors had heard his war cry and had come to him to know the cause. Hearing the muffled sounds of their agitated conversations, Tall Cloud lowered his head, opened his eyes, and went outside to greet them. In brief words he explained what he had discovered and what was expected of them all. Then the war party began forming, and the proper rituals were performed, but this time Tall Cloud made it clear that none would be held at length. *Nahkeeta's* life was in danger. Speed was needed to rescue her before she reached the Haida village. Familiar with the customs of the Haida, Tall Cloud knew only too well the gruesome fate that awaited his beautiful, gentle woman.

Observing the same tradition that had been taught Suquamish warriors for generations, Tall Cloud led his men in the ritual bathing in the waters of the Sound, and once on shore they had rubbed their shins with brambles until they were bloody, believing this was a way to harden themselves for the coming battle with the Haida.

After returning to the village, Tall Cloud and his warriors joined the women in war songs that had been composed in a style different from their ordinary speech. These plaintive melodies were accompanied by box drums, rattles, and whistles.

The warriors painted and oiled their bodies while bundles of laths were brought to build the communal fire to much greater proportions than usual. There was singing and dancing, and there was a celebration of life to encourage the warriors to return home victorious.

Then the final dance was performed, the "Bringing Blood Into the House" dance. Hemlock wreaths carried by the performers were supposed to represent heads taken in battle. These they threw into the fire, calling out the names of the enemies they represented.

Tall Cloud had his own hemlock wreath and tossed it fierccly into the flames of the fire. As he watched it being consumed, his heart seemed to beat in rhythm with thc pounding drums.

"Striped Wolf!" he shouted, raising his eyes to the turquoise blue of the sky. "Soon your life will be no more. And if you have harmed my *Nahkeeta* in any way, your death will be a slow and painful one."

With his face painted black, while other warriors had chosen white or red as their personal war colors, and with his long rifle in one hand and a bow almost as long as himself in the other, Tall Cloud directed his men away from the village to their canoes. Before boarding, Tall Cloud thrust his rifle into the air and shouted: *"Nah! Skookum Kanaway!"*

The swift fleet of war canoes pushed away from the shore in unison while war chants rang out along the Sound. The beating clack of their paddles broke in on the sad tribal songs being sung by the women standing along the highest peak of Pahto Island, looking down upon their departing men. Tall Cloud sat stiffly erect in his own canoe, watching proudly as the huge, gently curved canoes of his warriors glided swiftly over the water. He was confident of their victorious return and of being reunited with his *Nahkeeta*.

Weary from the ride and the tension that he felt on the horse, David let his shoulders slump forward. He and the rest of the posse had stopped only momentarily for a quick meal. They had yet to sleep, and now they rode on again. Time wasn't on their side. If they had not gotten lost so many times in the forest, traveling in circles for long periods, perhaps they could have succeeded in finding Christa earlier. If this carelessness caused Christa's death, David would never forgive himself.

Leaning to rub the outside of his boot, David was once more reminded of the soreness of his foot. Not having had sufficient time to grow used to the pressure of the boot against it, his foot throbbed continuously.

But despite the discomfort in his foot, David was grateful that none of the posse had become discouraged. Not one man had turned back, not even after the fierce attack from the Haida. Most of the men seemed to have their own reasons for revenge. Some had lost their homes, some had had their cattle slaughtered, and others just hated Indians.

Their reasons didn't matter to David. His only concern was rescuing Christa. In his mind's eye, he could see his papa's soft, green eyes looking down at him, shaming him for not having been the kind of protector he should have been. If he had been, Christa would be with him now, back at the cabin, safe. . . .

Then a sharp pain circled his heart as he remembered that he didn't even have a cabin to return to. With hate fuming inside him, he thrust his knees more solidly into the horse's sides, and spurred it onward.

The morning had come and gone, and the sun moving lower in the sky indicated that it was midafternoon. The air had a soft warmth about it, and the buds on the trees were thick. On the forest floor, spring flowers were beginning to push their ways through the bed of brown, fallen leaves, and birds were busy building their nests overhead.

Then suddenly a different type of birdcall caused David to jerk quickly on his reins, halting his horse as he looked cautiously about him. When another rider came to his side, David saw the fear etched on his face.

"Indians," David said flatly. "I've never heard any birdcall like that before."

"Think they're close?"

David's eyes peered through the thickness of the trees toward the river, seeing only a slight twinkle of water. His shoulders tightened when he heard more of the strange calls echoing across the river and answering calls coming from the opposite shore.

"Yes, I'm sure they're close," David grumbled, lifting his rifle and loading it. "Too close for comfort, I'd say."

The rider swung his horse around and rode to the others to warn them. David now wished they had traveled by water. It would have cut their travel time in half, yet he had feared they would be more vulnerable in a boat.

"Hahh," he shouted to his horse, sending it into a gallop, trying to put space between the Indians and himself. He sensed that wandering Indians would not have his sister. These would be the ones ordered to observe and then return to the Haida village to warn of the white men's approach.

Thoughts of how he and the rest of the men in the posse might be greeted sent a shiver up David's spine, but he fought to put aside his fear. He had to be brave. His sister's life depended on it.

Then David's thoughts switched to Tall Cloud. Perhaps he should have gone to him to seek his help. Hadn't Tall Cloud fought proudly with the white men against the

Haida? And wouldn't he have fought even more fiercely against the Haida, if he had known that Christa had been abducted by them?

I just don't want to owe him anything, David reasoned with himself. But after struggling with his thoughts and his conscience, David realized that if he didn't succeed in finding Christa, he would have to go to Tall Cloud for help and swallow his pride in the process.

When he had ridden far enough from the river that he no longer heard the birdcalls, David slowed his horse's pace, lowered his rifle to its leather sheath on the side of the horse, then moved cautiously ahead, watching, always watching.

With extreme skill and swiftness, Tall Cloud and his warriors paddled their massive canoes along the waterway. Tall Cloud's canoe was in the lead, a symbol of command for his warriors to follow.

The air was refreshingly warm and the fish seemed to be dancing in the depths of the water as rivulets of sun reached down beneath the surface to urge them from the bottom of the river.

As they rounded a curve the river narrowed, and on both sides of them the forest lay deep and dark. Squinting his eyes, Tall Cloud tried to see into the distance through a break in the trees. Suddenly he caught a glimpse of a cabin nestled peacefully at the edge of the wood.

"Kopet!" he shouted, raising a doubled fist into the air. "Stop! I see a cabin. We will go there and speak with the white family to see if they have seen a Haida Indian with a white woman in his possession! Come! Follow my lead, my brave warriors."

With a racing pulse, Tall Cloud hurriedly beached his canoe and, along with his warriors, ran through the forest. At the clearing, they stopped to look cautiously about them.

Tall Cloud's gaze went to the chimney which extended from the side of the house. His brows arched. There was no smoke rising from the chimney. That was an oddity. Most white people as well as the Suquamish had a fire going from morning till night. He had observed in other white men's cabins that the women seemed to labor over the fire stove through most of the day.

He wondered why this cabin looked deserted. Then he remembered the brief Indian war caused by the Haida. Perhaps this family of white people had been too afraid to return to their dwelling.

But Tall Cloud observed that chickens wandered about the land, and cows and pigs were inside a fence, as if they had recently been fed. Then what could be the reason for the complete silence in and around the white man's personal dwelling?

Sensing that there was a great wrong here, Tall Cloud quickly led his men away from the protective cover of the trees and toward the cabin. He moved stealthily forward, keeping his rifle poised, watching for any sudden shine of a rifle or shotgun barrel that might be hidden close by. He gave his men a quick glance from over his shoulder then tensed, seeing the war paint they each had smeared across their faces. He also noted the shine of their bodies from the grease they had applied for fighting. All *nanitches* before had been done with clean faces. If the white people were in their dwelling, seeing the Suquamish in their war colors would give them just cause to panic.

But Tall Cloud would not be dissuaded from moving onward. This was the first dwelling that he and his warriors had seen since they had traveled away from the Sound, and Tall Cloud knew enough of the Haida ways to know that it would be hard for any of them to pass by a deserted white settlement without stealing something from the owners.

At the corner of the cabin, Tall Cloud cautioned his men

to stand behind him as he crept toward a window to peer inside. Reaching it, he inched his head upward and gasped when he saw the bloody remains of a man and a woman.

Turning his head and closing his eyes to the ravaged bodies, a bitterness rose into his throat. He clasped a hand over his mouth and gulped hard, feeling weak for being so affected by death. But the bodies were cut more horribly than if a crazed grizzly bear had attacked them.

Seeing their chief's reaction after looking into the window, low mumbling began among the warriors who had never seen their chief behave in such a manner. One by one they took a turn at the window and understood.

Tall Cloud walked away from the cabin, his hand clenched tightly on his rifle. He now feared for his *Nahkeeta* as never before. If Striped Wolf was responsible for these deaths, he was capable of anything!

A cold hand seemed to clutch Tall Cloud's heart as he remembered Princess Star's abduction and how Striped Wolf had taken advantage of her even before getting her back to his village. What if he had already done the same with *Nahkeeta?*

"We must hurry along!" he shouted, waving his rifle in the air. "Come. There is nothing anyone can do here. The spirits of the white men's dead frown upon our interference. Hurry. We must resume our travels in the canoes."

With a heavy heart, Tall Cloud once more boarded his canoe and headed north, to the land of the Haida. The muscles in his arms ached from the steady paddling. He kept his eyes straight ahead, trying not to imagine a picture of *Nahkeeta* being taken by the ugly, cruel Striped Wolf. Striped Wolf's death would be slow, Tall Cloud vowed silently. He would pay. He would pay over and over again for his evil deeds.

Tall Cloud's eyes moved suddenly upward as he noticed something rising into the sky from the distance "Smoke," he said in a bare whisper. "They see our approach. They send messages to their neighbors. Soon. I will get my vengeance soon."

Suffering from continuing fatigue, thirst, and hunger, David let out a loud cheer when he saw a cabin in the clearing ahead. No matter how much he wanted to continue north, he knew that a stop for nourishment had become a necessity. They could push themselves just so far before even the strongest men cracked beneath the pressure.

Turning and seeing that everyone else seemed to have the same thing in mind, David joined them in moving toward the cabin. The sight of scampering chickens made David's stomach growl with hunger. Perhaps the settlers would part with a few eggs. A well reminded him that his lips were parched from thirst, for he had not liked taking water directly from the river bed.

Shouting at his horse, he stormed ahead, yet the closer he came to the cabin, the more cautiously he looked about. There were no signs of life except for the chickens, pigs, and cow. No one worked in the garden and no signs of life could be seen about the cabin. His eyes moved upward and he noted the lack of smoke at the chimney.

Everyone seemed to notice at the same time the absence of activity about the dwelling. The horses were drawn to a halt and not a whisper was exchanged from man to man. It was David who decided to go ahead and approach the cabin, yet not without first pulling his rifle and readying it for firing.

David had not forgotten the settlers' concerns over another Indian attack. Perhaps this family hadn't returned to their farm, for fear of another uprising, he rationalized. Yet the animals didn't appear to be hungry. They most surely had been fed in the past day or so. . . .

With fear lacing his heart, David drew his horse up next to the cabin and slowly dismounted. He flipped his horse's reins over a low tree limb then moved soundlessly toward the cabin, his eyes darting about him, keeping watch on all sides. He jumped when he heard movement behind him, then he sighed with relief when he found that he was no longer alone. Several men had come to his assistance, armed and ready for anything that suddenly might happen.

Barely breathing now, David nodded his head to the men who had moved next to him indicating that he would now approach the cabin, to look through the window. He placed his finger on the trigger of his rifle and felt heat rise to his cheeks from the mounting tension. Then slowly he crept to the cabin wall and peered over the window ledge.

"Good Lord . . ." he gasped throatily, his gaze glued in place and his heart beginning to thunder wildly against his ribs. Then he stepped quickly away, shaking his head fitfully back and forth, still not believing what he had seen. He had never experienced anything like this in his life. The mutilation of each of the bodies was complete—so much so that he couldn't tell which limbs went with which body.

Turning abruptly, he ran to the well and quickly drew up a bucket of water. He grabbed the bucket and poured its icy contents over his head in an attempt to shock himself into releasing the memory of the two bodies from his mind.

Raking his fingers nervously through his wet hair, he blinked his eyes and swallowed hard. Had the Haida Indians done this as a group? Or had one individual Indian been the responsible party? It tore at David's heart that he didn't know if Christa was with the Indians who had done this terrible deed. And it had to be Indians! He was certain that no white man would be so cold-hearted, so savage . . .

"Think we'd better turn back?" a fellow rider asked suddenly from behind David.

David turned with a start, his face pale, his eyes determined. "The hell we'll turn back," he said bluntly, hardly recognizing his own voice, it was so deep and strained.

"But, David, who's to tell what we're heading for? We could all . . . get . . . massacred."

"Do you forget my sister, Christa? Don't you wonder about her fate after seein' inside that cabin?"

"She's probably already dead, David. I choose to turn back."

Rage rushed through David. Forgetting his usually gentle nature, he doubled up a fist and hit the man whose cowardice was too much for David to bear. A scuffle ensued, with David growling like an animal as his fists flew. And then the fight was brought abruptly to a halt as the two were separated and held apart.

"Let me at 'im," David hissed, his knuckles bruised, bleeding, and aching.

"This ain't the time for fightin' amongst ourselves," said a man with soft facial features framed by cotton-colored hair and long sideburns who held David back.

"He says we shouldn't search any further for my sister," David cried, panting.

"If he wants to return to Seattle, let 'im," another man broke in, raising a doubled fist into the air. "The rest of us choose to move on. No injuns are gonna get away with this."

"Let him stay behind and bury the bodies," another shouted.

"Yeah!" even another said. "Then he can ride back and warn everyone that the savages still are not to be trusted."

The soft-featured man gave David a look from beneath a lifted brow. "Sound all right to you, David?" he asked, releasing his hold and stepping away from him.

David straightened his shirt collar and cleared his throat. "Yeah," he said shallowly. "Let the coward go. I'm glad there's no more like him among the rest of you gents. We can't give up. We've got to find Christa."

"Then it's decided," the gentle-featured man said, slapping David fondly on the back. "David, we came to find your sister, and we won't return to Seattle until we do." He turned his gaze toward the cabin, his eyes wavering as he remembered what lay inside. "And now it seems we've other reasons urging us on. We must find and deal with the party or parties responsible for the slaughter inside that cabin. It can't be allowed to happen again. This time the Haida have gone too far."

"So you also believe the Haida are responsible?" David questioned, picking up his rifle and knocking dust from its barrel.

"Neither the Suquamish or the Duwamish have ever been guilty of such deeds," he replied.

David's thoughts went to Tall Cloud. Though David didn't like or approve of the Indian, he knew the chief was a gentle Indian, one who hardly deserved the term "savage."

"Then what're we waitin' for?" David said hoarsely. "Let's go. The longer we stand here talkin', the better the chances for the Haida to get Christa to their camp."

"We've a buryin' to do," the gentle-featured man said. "The rug the bodies are on can be used to wrap them. We'll bury them people, rug and all, in one grave." He gave David a solemn look. "But, David, you and a few men go on ahead. I know your concern for your sister."

David's gaze scanned the group of men who worked their way to his side, volunteering to ride on with him. David tried to ignore the doubt reflected in their eyes as he mounted his horse and rode out.

Christa's limp body shook painfully with each forward movement of the horse. Striped Wolf's breath was warm on her neck as he rode behind her, clutching her roughly about her waist.

Hardly able to hold her eyes open, Christa couldn't control her nodding head, but Striped Wolf grunted and purposefully stirred her so that she couldn't fall into a restful sleep.

Turning her eyes to him, Christa pleaded. "Please, stop for at least a little while," she begged. "I'm so tired. I'm . . . so . . . hungry."

She was at least thankful she was no longer gagged or bound. Because she had not attempted escape when he had gone to the settlers' cabin, he was confident that she wouldn't try it later. He was keenly aware of her complete fatigue.

Striped Wolf noted the drooping of her eyes, the curve of her back, and the disarray of her hair. This disturbed him. She would not be a presentable slave to show his people upon their arrival in his camp if he took her there in such condition, he mused. Perhaps a short rest was what she needed. And how could it hurt? There were now many miles between them and Tall Cloud's island. They had only a short distance to ride before reaching his camp. It appeared that all the Suquamish and white men had been left far behind. . . .

Christa tensed when she felt the horse coming to a halt. She looked slowly around her, seeing a cave partially hidden behind a cover of underbrush. She had begged him to stop, but now that he had, she feared what the next hour or so might bring. Would he rape her? And if he did, would he then decide against taking her farther and, instead, kill her?

She flinched when he removed his arm from her waist. With a pounding heart she watched as he dismounted then reached a hand to her wrist, jerking her roughly to the ground beside him.

"What are you doing?" she asked in a whisper. "Why have you stopped?"

"First you want to stop and then you don't," Striped Wolf said, shrugging. "White woman, you are hard to understand."

"I didn't say . . . that . . . I didn't want to," she said,

wincing as he gave her a rough shove toward the cave. "I just asked . . . why."

Bringing the horse with him, Striped Wolf looked cautiously across her shoulder then once more gave Christa a shove. "Just get inside the cave," he growled. "While you rest, we must stay hidden. Tall Cloud is a tricky Indian. He may be closer than I think."

Christa pushed back tightly woven morning glory vines and the fresh starts of trees that protected the cave's entrance. Then she stepped inside where a keen dampness greeted her along with the putrid odor of rotting vegetation. She curled up her nose and squinted her eyes briefly in the darkness, until suddenly a crack in the cave's ceiling admitted a faint stream of sunshine.

"This will do," Striped Wolf said, grabbing Christa and stopping her. "We don't want to go too far. It gets much darker the farther one goes. We will stay where the crack from above gives us at least enough light to see our way around. No fire can be lighted. Just sit down and rest, white woman, for we will not stay much longer from the camp of my people."

Christa sighed quietly to herself, relieved that rape was not his intention. Perhaps this Haida had more feelings than she had given him credit for. He did seem to be stopping for her.

Inching her way down to the cold, rock-covered floor of the cave, she cringed when her hands touched a slimy, wet substance. But it felt so good to be off the horse that she ignored these discomforts.

Leaning her back against the wall of the cave, she let her gaze meet his. In the dim light, she could see his eyes traveling slowly over her body, and the look of lust in their depths was very identifiable to her. Christa's insides did a strange rolling, and she began to think that she had misjudged his motives.

"What . . . are . . . you looking . . . at?" she asked, placing a hand on her throat.

"You are a beautiful woman, even if you are pale from the long ride from Pahto Island," he said, squatting as he pulled up his legs. He placed a forefinger on her cheekbone and began tracing the full outline of her face. "I could have you now, you know. You are my woman. You are even my *slave.*"

These words cut into Christa's heart like a knife. Her pulse raced from fear. "And what do you . . . intend to do about it?" she asked, brushing his hands aside, knowing that her brave act could be a foolish one.

"Later." He laughed, rising back to his feet. "Much later, white woman. First I must show you off to my people after you've rested. The waiting to have you as a man has a woman will only enhance the pleasure when I do make you my complete conquest."

He slapped the horse to get it to move farther away from him, secured its reins beneath a heavy rock on the floor of the cave, then sat down beside Christa, sighing heavily.

He closed his eyes and leaned his head back against the wall. "Rest. We will leave soon," he said. "The day has been full of many trials for Striped Wolf."

In her mind, Christa began sorting through the events of the day. This led her back to when they had found the cabin in the clearing. She gave Striped Wolf a pensive stare, then she spoke.

"The white settlers back at the cabin," she quickly blurted. "What did you do with them?"

A low, throaty laugh rose from deep inside him as he sat with his eyes closed. "Much blood was spread on white man's braided rug in that cabin," he said, boasting. "It will be a warning to anyone who tries to follow, white woman. I killed today as I have never killed before. It will be hard for them to tell man from woman." He laughed once more then let a peaceful sleep overcome him.

Christa's insides knotted, and she shivered at the thought of what he had just bragged about. She gulped hard then glanced hurriedly toward the cave's entrance. She was weak, but was she too weak to escape from this madman?

No, she thought not. She had to get away, for if she didn't, who knew what her fate would be once they did reach the Haida camp. It was obvious to her that the life of a white man or woman meant nothing to these heathen Indians. Oh, how could Indians be so different? she wondered. There were the Suquamish, peaceful with love in their hearts, and then there were the dreaded Haida . . . She closed her mind then to all but escaping.

Barely breathing, Christa watched Striped Wolf until his own breaths came in slow, even heavings of his bare, tattooed chest. Though her knees were weak, her stomach empty, and her head dizzy from lack of sleep, Christa's hand reached around beside her until it came in contact with the rock she sought.

She circled her fingers about it and waited a moment longer, making sure that Striped Wolf did not stir, which had to mean he was asleep.

Then she inched upward to her knees to face him, lifted the rock over her head, then brought it down upon his head as hard as she could.

The sound was that of a splat as she watched his flesh become blood soaked. He had only winced and groaned, yet now he lay crumpled on his side with blood gushing from his mouth.

Engulfed in heartbeats, trembling from her assault on another human being, yet feeling an overwhelming relief, Christa found the strength to rise to her feet. She backed away from where Striped Wolf lay so that he could not reach out a hand to grab her, she then turned and faced the horse.

Groaning with the thought of having to mount it again, she made her way toward the animal. Kicking the rock aside which held the reins, she led the horse quickly from the cave.

She looked toward the heavens, silently sending a prayer of thanks to God, then she mounted the horse and rode back in the direction from which they had just come.

She couldn't believe that she was free! She couldn't believe that the Haida Indian had become so careless that he hadn't thought she would try to escape again, especially after she had learned the fate of the white settlers at the lone cabin in the woods.

Aching, she took one fast glance back at the cave, wondering if she had killed Striped Wolf or had only stunned him.

Shivering, she pushed the thought of Striped Wolf from her mind. She urged the horse on more quickly now, knowing that she wouldn't be truly free until she had left this Haida country far behind her.

"Tall Cloud," she whispered. "Darling, where are you . . . ?"

Twenty-three

Knowing that the Haida camp was near, Tall Cloud directed his warriors to beach their canoes and to follow him on foot the rest of the way. With the sun dropping lower in the sky, Tall Cloud knew that his men must work with swiftness. He could not let one more sunset go by without having his *Nahkeeta* safe with him again!

With his head held high and carrying only his rifle with him for the fight, Tall Cloud trotted along the river's edge then made a turn, heading deeper inside the forest for cover. A thundering of hoofbeats drew him to a sudden stop. His face became shadowed as he looked in the direction of the horses then commanded his men to conceal themselves.

Crouching behind a tree, Tall Cloud watched as the men on horseback drew closer. He readied his rifle, for he could not yet identify the riders as Indian or white since the light in the forest was poor.

He squinted his eyes and tensed his shoulder muscles, still holding his rifle up, ready to shoot if they were Haida, the Indians who continued to sully the name of Indian. And would Christa be with this group of Haida? Had his search finally come to an end? A soft growl rose from his throat, his hatred a violent emotion eating away at his insides.

When Tall Cloud was finally able to see that the lead rider of the group was white instead of Indian, he lowered his rifle with a start, for he had quickly recognized his *Nahkeeta*'s brother, David.

Then once more he tensed. It was quite evident that David was not on a peaceful mission. He was most surely searching for his sister, and because David might now know which Indians were responsible for her abduction, Tall Cloud wasn't sure it was safe to show his face to the proud brother of his beloved.

Tall Cloud took a quick second look at David and glanced down at his feet. His wounded foot was now healed enough for him to wear the white man's boots! He was well enough now for a fight—a fight with any and all Indians he might choose to challenge. Then Tall Cloud also realized that it had not been the Haida who first abducted Christa from the streets of Seattle. It had been him!

But David didn't know this. Tall Cloud had to assume that David had suspected the Haida from the very first, or why would he and his many companions be traveling in Haida country instead of Suquamish?

Now certain that David sought only the Haida, Tall Cloud boldly stepped from behind the tree, confronting David and causing him to come to an abrupt stop.

David jerked on the horse's reins, his face draining of color when he saw Tall Cloud in front of him suddenly appearing as if he had dropped from the heavens. He studied the Indian, noting how Tall Cloud's face was painted and how his body shone with some sort of grease.

"Tall Cloud . . . ?" David gasped then pulled his horse back when many other Suquamish warriors stepped from behind trees with their faces varying colors of reds, blacks, and whites. David had to assume that they had painted their faces as Indians do when on the warpath. But why? he wondered. Why would they be in Haida country, ready for a fight?

Tall Cloud raised a hand in peace. "Proud brother of *Nahkeeta,* I am surprised to find you so far from the white man's settlements," he said, letting his gaze move slowly from David to the other white men who were with him, mentally counting how many there were.

"As I am surprised to find you, Tall Cloud, so far from your Suquamish people," David said dryly. "Why are you here? Have you had some sort of disagreement with the Haida?"

Tall Cloud realized that he should not mention *Nahkeeta's* name, for it was obvious that David knew nothing of his sister's abduction by the Haida. He lowered his hand, supporting the rifle against his palm.

David leaned forward in the saddle. "Tall Cloud, why are you here?" he persisted. "And why are your faces covered with war paint?"

"Why are *you* here?" Tall Cloud said, stubbornly refusing to answer David's questions.

"Then you don't know," David murmured, nervously raking his fingers through his hair.

Tall Cloud had to continue this deception or risk having to fight David if he revealed that Christa had been abducted first by him and then by the Haida.

"Know what?" Tall Cloud asked, forcing innocence into his voice.

David relaxed in his saddle, letting the reins slacken in his right hand. "Of course," he said. "You wouldn't know. How could you?"

"Tell me what you're speaking words around," Tall Cloud said, hearing the tired remorsefulness of David's speech and seeing the weariness in his eyes. Tall Cloud could see the love felt by this proud brother for his sister, and the hurt her absence had caused him. He was hopeful that when this was all over and *Nahkeeta* was found, David could learn to live with his sister's absence if he knew that she was with a trusted Indian—the proud Chief Tall Cloud? When Tall Cloud showed how valiantly he fought for *Nahkeeta's* safe release, how could David deny him anything?

"It's Christa," David said hoarsely. "She was abducted."

Tall Cloud didn't have to work too hard at pretending emotion. Just thinking about his *Nahkeeta* at the mercy of Striped Wolf and Striped Wolf's deranged followers made a hatred so intense flow through him that he let loose a loud roar, frightening even his own warriors who stood beside him.

Because so many of the Indians did not understand the white man's English, they saw Tall Cloud's sudden outburst as cause to raise their weapons, to secure the safety of their chief. It appeared that the white man with the pale skin and gold hair had said unpleasant words to their chief, or possibly even threatened his life!

David's breath caught in his throat when he saw the many rifle barrels now aimed toward him and the other members of the posse, and he wondered what had spurred the Indians to such action. No matter the reason, there was no denying the danger he felt himself in, but he knew not to lift his own rifle in his defense. He had neither the knowledge about weapons nor the speed required to fully protect himself, so he held his rifle down and away from him, afraid to move even one bone in his body.

"Tall Cloud, what are your men about?" he asked in a strained voice.

Tall Cloud turned on a heel and looked anxiously from Indian to Indian. A slow smile lifted his lips. He had trained his warriors well. It made him proud to see how even one outcry could send them into immediate defense of him, their chief. And he was wise enough to understand their alarm, since those warriors who looked the most cautious and concerned were those who did not understand the white man's way of speaking, so they had not understood the conversation here between their chief and *Nahkeeta's* brother.

Lifting a hand, Tall Cloud explained in Suquamish why no guns should be raised against the white men who faithfully follow behind *Nahkeeta's* brother. He explained that these white men were in search of her also. He asked that they be patient and assured them that there soon would be reason to raise their weapons, but only against the real enemy—the Haida.

As the Indians' rifles were lowered, David gained the courage to raise his, and now he felt he had the upper hand. His fingers shook as he placed one on the trigger, but he became braver when he heard the clicks of all the other rifles behind him, aware that they were also raised against the Indians.

Tall Cloud spun around then took a step backward when he saw the rifles pointed toward him and his warriors. He looked from man to man in the overwhelming silence that followed. He felt a fool for having placed his back to the white man and, even more so, for instructing his men to *trust* them.

Yet he straightened his shoulders, set his jaw proudly, and boldly faced David. "And what have we here?" he said dryly. "My back was turned for only a brief moment."

"Tall Cloud, only a moment ago your warriors were threatening us with their rifles. How do we know that they won't decide to do so again? Order them to hand over their rifles and then move aside so we can be on our way."

Tall Cloud stubbornly stood his ground, trying not to worry about the weakening of the sun's rays as it sank lower behind the trees. He had silently vowed to himself to have *Nahkeeta* with him before another night darkened the earth, concealing the evil that spread beneath its black velvet cloak. Would it be her own brother who stood in the way of her being found?

No. Tall Cloud knew he had to convince David of what must be done, and quickly, before it was too late!

"Proud brother of *Nahkeeta*, this is not the time for lack of trust between you and my people," he said firmly. "Did you not say that your sister has been abducted?"

"You know that I did."

"Then you must know how this knowledge lies heavy on my heart, the heart of the man who loves your sister."

"So? What are you saying, Tall Cloud?"

"Together we shall band together as one. Let us find *Nahkeeta* and make the one responsible pay with a slow, agonizing death."

David lowered his rifle and leaned forward in his saddle. He arched his brows. "You talk as though you know who is responsible," he said.

"I am sure I can point my finger at one man," Tall Cloud growled.

"Why would you accuse just one man when it probably is a group of men," David said then corrected himself. "Not men, but savages. It is the Haida camp that we travel toward. And you? Where were *you* headed? You never did say."

Tall Cloud's gaze raked over the rifles still aimed and ready to fire. "Have your men lower their weapons. Then we can talk further," he grumbled.

David nodded his head toward the men who in turn lowered their rifles. Then he once more directed his attention to Tall Cloud. "It is done," he said. "Now answer me. Where were you and your Indians headed with war paint discoloring your faces?"

"We also travel to the Haida camp," Tall Cloud growled.

David's eyebrows rose as he grew suspicious. It seemed as if Tall Cloud had somehow already known about Christa's abduction. But how? he wondered.

"And why do you?" David questioned blandly.

Tall Cloud knew he could not reveal the full reasons. The rape and death of his sister, Princess Star, would be enough reason to give at this time. Later all reasons would be spoken, but only after *Nahkeeta* was safe and had convinced her brother that she would not return with him to the settlement of Seattle.

"It is to avenge my sister's rape and death," he growled,

setting his jaw hard as his eyes reflected in their gray depths a fury that could not be denied.

David jerked his head back, his mouth agape. Then he said, "Your sister? The sister Christa defended and took to your Enati Island?"

"The same," Tall Cloud grumbled.

"You say that . . . she . . . is now dead?" David said weakly, beginning to understand.

"She only recently died as a result of that day with the Haida," Tall Cloud said. "She died while giving birth to a child conceived by the Haida. Even the child was born without taking its first breath of life."

David's fingers raked through the golden strands of his hair, as they always had when he was nervous or alarmed. "Good Lord," he gasped, involuntarily shuddering. "No wonder you've chosen to be on a warpath. You do this for your sister, just as I have come for *my* sister."

"So you understand, proud brother? We can band together as one?"

"You say you know the one responsible?"

"Striped Wolf. The same Haida responsible for my sister's death. If we find Striped Wolf, I can assure you that we will at the same time find *Nahkeeta.*"

"How can you be so sure?"

"Trust me, proud brother."

"On our journey here, we found two people slaughtered in a cabin," David said thickly. "Could one man do this?"

"We found the same cabin, I am sure," Tall Cloud said. "We saw the bodies. And yes, I am sure that only Striped Wolf is responsible. Now do you see why we shouldn't be wasting time talking when instead we could be searching? It soon will be dark. That is not good, proud brother."

"Then we must travel onward, now," David said, settling himself more comfortably in the saddle.

"Together?"

"Together."

Tall Cloud nodded toward the horse on which David sat. "We must leave all horses behind," he said.

"Why? We travel much more quickly this way. Where are yours?"

"We are canoe people. We do not use horses. We now go the rest of the way on foot. We don't have far to go. You must also travel on foot. It will be less noisy. Many horses' hooves echo like thunder through the forest and across the rivers."

"Yes. The sound does have a way of traveling out here in the wilderness," David agreed. "You're right. It's best to leave the horses behind."

After David's men had all dismounted, the journey onward was made in silence. The forest grew grayer and grayer with hastening nightfall. A loon's call echoed from far off, and cardinals fluttered in the brush, settling in for the night.

David and Tall Cloud walked side by side, united in spirit, united in heart. Neither looked to the other, but instead kept their eyes straight ahead, searching, forever searching. Suddenly the sound of a groan up ahead brought them to an abrupt halt.

Tall Cloud placed his outstretched arm in David's way. "I will go see," he said flatly.

"We should go together," David argued.

"One man makes less noise. I will move like a ghost in the night—soundlessly."

"What if it's a trap, Tall Cloud?"

"Then we will know soon enough, won't we, proud brother?"

David began to protest once more, but Tall Cloud was already creeping stealthily toward the area where the sound had surfaced. He stepped high over tangled ground cover then bent his back to go beneath the low-hanging limb of a stately elm. Another groan prompted him to hurry onward until through the semi-darkness he saw a body.

He stopped, peering more earnestly toward the body and then on all sides of him, definitely fearing a trap. But not finding anyone else there, lurking or waiting, Tall Cloud shouted to his Indians and the white men to come ahead, that it was safe enough.

Tall Cloud had immediately realized that the injured person was a Haida Indian. Even from the distance Tall Cloud could see the heavily tattooed chest and arms, and, as he drew closer, he even recognized the face. Striped Wolf! There was no mistaking the ugliness of his face and the heavily marked body that Striped Wolf always displayed as a proud Haida.

Rushing to bend over Striped Wolf, Tall Cloud's hatred for the Haida was set in his concern for *Nahkeeta*. If not here with Striped Wolf, where was she? Had she even been with Striped Wolf? Perhaps Tall Cloud had been wrong all along. . . .

Tall Cloud dropped his rifle to the ground, and, grabbing Striped Wolf by the shoulders, he lifted his head from the ground. Blood had dried at Striped Wolf's nose and mouth but was still wet and stuck thickly in his coarse, black hair. It looked as if someone had struck him over the head with a blunt object.

Hope swam inside Tall Cloud. Could *Nahkeeta* have been the one to have dealt the blow to Striped Wolf? Yes, it was something that she was quite capable of doing. She knew very well the ways of protecting herself. Was there another woman like her? No, Tall Cloud doubted that.

Striped Wolf moaned as he opened his eyes. Through a fuzziness he saw his enemy, Tall Cloud, looking down at him. Fear struck a chord at his heart. He knew to expect the worst from Tall Cloud, for surely Tall Cloud was here looking for his white woman.

"Where is my *Nahkeeta?*" Tall Cloud growled, pressing his fingers deeply into Striped Wolf's flesh.

Though he was afraid, Striped Wolf wouldn't let Tall

Cloud sense his fear. Striped Wolf knew that his death was imminent since it was Tall Cloud who had found him. Striped Wolf vowed he would die valiantly, appearing strong willed and brave to the end. He managed a low chuckle and a sneer as Tall Cloud continued to look down at him.

This was enough for Tall Cloud. He was now certain that Striped Wolf held the answers he sought. Striped Wolf *had* abducted *Nahkeeta*. But where was she now? He tightened his grip, yet Striped Wolf didn't flinch.

But Tall Cloud knew him well. He knew that Striped Wolf would die before ever crying out in pain in Tall Cloud's presence. And at that moment Tall Cloud would have liked nothing better than to test the Haida's endurance.

David came to Tall Cloud's side. His eyes widened as he saw the mass of tattoos on the Haida's body, and then the blood. He knelt down closer. "Is this the Indian you were talking about?" he growled, doubling his free hand into a fist and clasping his other more tightly onto the rifle. "His name, Tall Cloud. What is his name?"

"As I told you before, his name is Striped Wolf," Tall Cloud said, never taking his eyes away from Striped Wolf, his loathing for the Haida seething inside him.

David leaned down into the injured Indian's face. "My sister Christa," he said, trying to keep the tremor from his voice. "Are you the one who abducted her?"

Striped Wolf stared back blankly at David, his lips set firmly together.

David dropped his rifle to the ground and grabbed Striped Wolf by the hair, cringing when his fingers made contact with the wet, sticky blood. "My sister!" he shouted. "Where is my sister?"

Tall Cloud roughly dropped Striped Wolf to the ground and gently placed a hand on David's shoulder. "You will not get words out of him," he said. "But maybe I can. I may know a way."

David's eyes wavered, knowing that tears of frustration

were near. He rose to his feet and turned his back to both Indians, wiping his nose and mouth with the back of a hand. His breaths were coming erratically and his heart was pounding. He now felt that Christa would surely be found dead. He hung his head sadly. If only he and the posse had moved faster. If only they hadn't moved continually in circles in the unfamiliar forest.

Tall Cloud moved to David's side. Once more he placed a hand upon David's shoulder, to console him. "All is not lost here," he said. "There is a chance that *Nahkeeta* has escaped on her own. She may have been the one to have struck Striped Wolf. If so, she may be traveling from Haida country already."

David's eyes brightened. He looked up at Tall Cloud, seeing compassion in his expressive, gray eyes. David had never thought to expect anything from Tall Cloud but an elusive silence, since David had so flatly rejected any sort of friendship with Tall Cloud from the very first. But now Tall Cloud was being even more than a friend. He was an ally.

"Do you . . . truly . . . believe that?" David asked, wanting to grasp some ray of hope, yet fearing that Tall Cloud was wrong.

"It is only a possibility," Tall Cloud said, dropping his hand to his side. He looked at Striped Wolf over his shoulder, seeing how he still lay mute, staring blankly ahead.

"Should we head back to see if we can find her?" David asked, frowning as he realized that another day had almost finished its cycle and night was only a whisper away. "It's almost dark, Tall Cloud. I can't stand to think of Christa being out there . . . all . . . alone in the dark of the forest."

"I do not like to think of that either," Tall Cloud grumbled. "But remember, proud brother, it is only a possibility that she is. There is another possibility that I hate to consider."

David tensed. "And that is?"

"That another Haida stole *Nahkeeta* away from Striped Wolf," he said gruffly. "She is a prize any man would fight over. But I don't have to tell you that. You know of her beauty. You know of her sweetness. I would fight to the death for my *Nahkeeta*."

A flame of color rose in David's face. A part of him recoiled inside to imagine an Indian loving his sister so fiercely. Yet a part of him was glad, for David liked to think that if this man loved Christa, it was with a noble, sincere love. It gave David a sort of inner peace to know that Christa had chosen such a man to love in return.

His thoughts flashed back to Harrison Kramer and shame flooded him, for he had tried so hard to force her to marry him when all along he had known that Harrison wasn't the man for her. But there had been the security that would have been hers if she had chosen him for a husband. In these difficult times, when no one knew what the next day would bring, Harrison's security and wealth had so enticed David, that he wanted for Christa what she didn't want for herself.

Then David's head jerked around, and he once more faced Striped Wolf. "Harrison Kramer," he said thickly. "We've also got to question him about Harrison Kramer. He has to be the one who murdered him. I must take him back to face the authorities if he is the one."

Tall Cloud's eyes narrowed and his jaw tightened with the mention of the name Harrison Kramer. It still tore at his gut to remember the night that he had found that evil white man forcing himself upon *Nahkeeta,* and Tall Cloud was glad he would never be able to do so again. Harrison Kramer had deserved to die. But Tall Cloud had to be sure that David didn't question Striped Wolf about that death, for it was not the time for David to know the truth. It was only now that David had finally begun to treat Tall Cloud as a person, as a friend. At least until *Nahkeeta* was safely found, this friendship had to continue.

Once more placing his hand on David's shoulder, Tall Cloud stepped closer to David. "No. It is not the time to question this Indian about anything but your sister," he said flatly, as if commanding one of his own warriors. "We must forget everything except seeking answers from Striped Wolf about *Nahkeeta*. And we must do it now. We have waited much too long already."

Tall Cloud's face darkened with determination as he swung around, away from David, and went to Striped Wolf. He leaned down and grabbed Striped Wolf by the shoulders and half dragged him to a tree.

"A rope," Tall Cloud shouted. "Someone bring me a rope. We must get answers from this ugly Haida!"

David stood by and watched as Tall Cloud was given a rope. Then, assisted by one of his warriors, Tall Cloud used the rope to tie Striped Wolf to a tree, feet up, his head only inches from the ground. Because of his injury, Striped Wolf's head dangled lethargically. But his lips never parted and his eyes didn't waver.

Slowly David looked around him, into the depths of the forest, remembering the signs of smoke he had seen while heading this way. He took a step toward Tall Cloud. "What are you going to do?" he asked quietly. "Will it make any noise? What if the others of his tribe hear and come to rescue him?"

"There are many of us," Tall Cloud said, straightening his shoulders. "Do you forget how the Haida ran from the city of Seattle when Chief Tall Cloud's warriors came to help the white man? There are as many of us now as then. And you have quite a following, proud brother. Surely the Haida scouts saw this and ran back to their camp in fear."

"But should they—" David started, clutching tightly onto his rifle.

"Should they?" Tall Cloud echoed, lifting an eyebrow speculatively. "We will deal with them in the only way known to the Suquamish, when we are faced with the ugly Haida." He shrugged. "We will *kill* them."

Tall Cloud walked away from David and went to stand before Striped Wolf. He grabbed Striped Wolf's knife from its sheath then placed its point into Striped Wolf's face.

"It is this very knife that left blood and death back in the white man's cabin, is it not, Striped Wolf?" Tall Cloud growled. "There are traces of blood still on its blade."

Striped Wolf continued to stare into the space over Tall Cloud's shoulder. His insides felt empty. Fear was slowly growing inside him. He knew what to expect from Tall Cloud now that he held a knife in his hand. Death would be much better than what Tall Cloud planned for him. But he wouldn't struggle. He would take defeat like a proud Haida Indian. He would accept the castration, though deep inside him, he would, indeed, be the same as dead.

Tall Cloud laughed softly as his free hand reached to Striped Wolf's hair. He lifted one of his braids and yanked on it. "In one movement of my hand and knife, you will have lost your manhood, Striped Wolf," he said. "And when I remove the other braid, you will wish you were dead. Isn't that so? To lose your hair in such a way would make you wish you had the knife to fall upon. For in the eyes of the Haida, you would be forever shamed. Now what is it to be? Will you tell me the truth? Or shall I capture your braids and display them forever in the Suquamish village for everyone to mock and laugh over? Or will you tell me about my *Nahkeeta?*"

Perspiration laced Striped Wolf's brow, yet he refused to look in the direction of the knife. He set his lips more tightly when its blade scraped the flesh of his neck.

"Tell me!" Tall Cloud growled, yanking on Striped Wolf's one braid as a reminder.

Striped Wolf watched out of the corner of his eye as Tall Cloud moved the knife in the direction of the braid. In Striped Wolf's mind's eye he could see the maidens of his camp laughing and mocking him as he shrank away from them, devoid of his braids. Until now, he had been known for his virility, his skills at making love. Most women begged to be his wife, though he had yet to choose one since slaves had always been so easily taken from tribes of the Suquamish and Duwamish.

But to think that he would never be able to have a wife at his side to bear his sons. . . . Aie! It *was* a fate worse than death!

Tall Cloud placed the knife on the braid and tested Striped Wolf by yanking suddenly with a downward motion and acting as if he had already cut the braid from his head.

Thinking that the evil deed had already been done, Striped Wolf let out a loud howl then began a low chanting as he hung his head. Then he slowly lifted it again when he heard Tall Cloud's laughter.

"So you are too brave to care that you lose your manhood?" Tall Cloud mocked, showing Striped Wolf that his hands held no braid. "You have just proven how much your manhood means to you."

Tall Cloud stepped away from Striped Wolf, dropped the knife to the ground, and placed his hands on his hips, frowning. "Now you tell me," he said firmly, "where is my *Nahkeeta?* This is the last time you will get the chance. If you do not tell me, then I will give the white man—*Nahkeeta's* brother—the honor of removing your braid. That would mean even more shame for you having a white man castrate you. Isn't that so, Striped Wolf?"

With a pounding heart, Striped Wolf's eyes grew wild as he saw David take a step forward and stoop to pick up the knife. He looked desperately from David to Tall Cloud then began shaking his head up and down.

"Your woman has fled into the forest," he said excitedly. "She hit me over the head with a rock then left with the horse that I stole from the white settlers' barn."

Striped Wolf couldn't help but emit a soft laugh. "But

she won't go far. She was too weak to stay on the horse
for long. She was too sleepy. She would have been better
off had she stayed and traveled into the Haida camp at my
side. Now she will find death alone."

David recoiled, envisioning Christa falling from the
horse, lying unconscious, but then he breathed a sigh of
relief as he suddenly realized that she had had the strength
to escape from this ugly, devilish Haida Indian.

Tall Cloud's anger spurred him into action as he raised
a hand and viciously slapped it across Striped Wolf's face.
"You stole my woman and now you laugh over her fate,"
he growled. "Striped Wolf, your death will be slow and
agonizing, but not now. Later. Now we must leave this
place, to go in search of my woman. You had better pray
that she is all right, because if she is not, you will wish
that I *had* cut your braid and left you tied to this tree to
die."

David looked around him despairingly, seeing the total
darkness. "We'll never find her," he cried. "She'll surely
die out there all alone. Striped Wolf is right. She won't be
able to make it alone."

Tall Cloud grabbed David's shoulders and shook him.
"Calm down, proud brother," he said hoarsely. "We will
find her. Have faith. We will find her."

"But . . . how . . . ?" David said more weakly, tears
burning at the corners of his eyes. He felt weak and helpless
next to this powerful Indian chief.

"We will still travel by foot," Tall Cloud said flatly. "We
will comb every inch of land. We will spread out. Together
we shall find her, proud brother. Now go and instruct your
men as to what we have to do. I will instruct mine."

Tall Cloud cut Striped Wolf from the tree and tied his
hands behind him. He gave him a rough shove. "You had
better hope that I find my *Nahkeeta,* and *soon,*" he said.
"If I don't, more than your braids will be missing. It has
been many moons since I have taken a Haida scalp. It would

pleasure me, as much as being with a woman, to take yours, Striped Wolf."

He glowered more earnestly at the Haida. "And, Striped Wolf," he growled, "I have yet to avenge my sister's death. In time, that also will be done."

"Death . . . ?" Striped Wolf gasped. "Princess . . . Star . . . ?"

"Dead," Tall Cloud said coldly. "As is also the son . . . that . . . she bore you. . . ."

Striped Wolf's face paled. His heartbeat weakened. A son! A son. . . .

Twenty-four

The moon splashing through the trees was a welcome sight to Christa. It was lighting her way just enough for her to see what lay ahead. She came to a break in the trees where the land stretched out to a meadow. Clinging limply to the horse's reins, so weary that she could hardly keep her eyes open, she forced herself to stay on the horse's back. She knew that the farther she traveled away from Haida country, the closer she would be getting to Seattle. She had no idea how far she had already traveled. She only knew that she had willed herself not to give up, for to do so would most surely mean that death would have her in its clutches.

"Tall Cloud," she whispered. "David. Oh, I'm so alone. . . ."

She couldn't understand why Tall Cloud hadn't found her. She couldn't understand why a posse hadn't come in search of her. Surely . . . now . . . they would, she thought disjointedly.

Weaving, blinking her eyes nervously, laboring to stay awake, Christa moved her horse into the open country. Then she suddenly sat upright when in the distance she glimpsed a barn, and on, past that, a cabin. At last! she cried silently. Settlers! This could mean food . . . rest . . . water . . . and above all else, safety.

With all the strength that she could muster, Christa

nudged the horse with her knees and shouted a command to hurry it along. Her heart soared. She managed a soft smile. Then both faded away as she found the setting uncomfortably familiar. The closer she came to the cabin, the clearer her memory became. Could this be the same cabin she had seen with Striped Wolf?

Goose bumps rose along her flesh. She shivered involuntarily as she remembered the fate of the settlers who had lived in this cabin. Striped Wolf had savagely slain them to assure himself of their silence in the event that Tall Cloud stopped there to question them.

"No," Christa cried softly, lifting a hand to her dry, parched lips. She shook her head frantically back and forth. "Please, God. Don't let this be the same cabin. If it is, I am no better off than I was before."

Clearing her throat nervously, wiping a stray tear from the corner of her eye, Christa straightened her back and rode past the barn. Two mounds of freshly turned earth caught her attention as the moon played along the ground, and it was quite evident that fresh graves had been dug and filled.

A sob caught in Christa's throat as her gaze locked on the graves. "It is the same cabin," she sobbed. "I know it."

Then hope rose inside her. If it was the same cabin, someone had come and had found the bodies. The same person had been kind enough to take the time to bury the poor souls. Had it been Tall Cloud? Had it been a posse from Seattle? If so, in which direction had they then traveled? Could they even now be close?

Slowing the horse to a trot, Christa dared to venture on toward the cabin. She sniffed. There was no trace of smoke in the air, which meant that no fire was burning in the fireplace inside the cabin. Still she refused to give up that tiny hope that she might find settlers and that this was a different cabin from the one she knew had been the scene of a slaughter.

She peered through the darkness toward the windows. No. There was no lamp lighted. The cabin was most surely deserted.

A movement behind her startled her into a nervous shaking, and she turned her head quickly around only to see the lazy, dark eyes of a cow as it came lumbering toward her.

Movement on both sides caused Christa's head to move quickly back and forth, and she now saw chickens scampering toward the house.

"Are they hungry? Haven't they been fed?" she wondered to herself. "Why is the cow loose instead of barned for the night?"

All these things—no lights in the cabin, no fire in the fireplace, the unattended farm animals—forced Christa to conclude that she had indeed found the same cabin.

She once more studied the wandering chickens and cow. The one who had found the settlers must have hurried away as soon as the bodies were buried. But when? Who? How long ago?

Sorrowfully shaking her head, Christa directed the horse onward. Having been given the opportunity to find the cabin again, she knew what she had to do. Until morning, she had to take advantage of its shelter, its warmth, and what food she could find there. If she built a fire, no one passing by would know that it was a woman alone who occupied the cabin. For no one but she, Striped Wolf, and the one who had buried the settlers knew of the tragedy that had occurred here, or that she was alone, vulnerable. . . .

Striped Wolf! But, surely he wouldn't follow, she rationalized. And how could he? She had inflicted a severe wound to his head and had taken the horse. Yes, she would be safe enough.

Edging the horse next to a hitching rail, Christa glanced back across her shoulder to the graves and felt a deep sadness overwhelming her. This cabin had been built with hopes for the future . . . with love. She would feel quite the intruder while using it, but she knew that the settlers would have welcomed her with open arms, had they been there to do so. She vowed she would not let guilt become a part of the night. She had to think of herself, or she just might not survive another day.

Almost crawling from the horse's back, so tired that she hardly had the strength to move, Christa managed to get herself to the ground. Sighing, trembling, she flipped the reins over the post then set her sights on the cabin door.

In a weaving motion, dragging her feet, she moved toward the entrance. She saw that it already stood partially open. Lifting a hand, she pushed it open wider letting the moon spill into the room before she took her first step inside.

Christa's nose curled as she smelled a strange, offensive odor which stopped her momentarily. Then she inched her way into the room, feeling around, relieved when her hand made contact with a kerosene lamp. Not having the strength to lift it, she instead removed its glass chimney and placed it on the table. Then she felt around and found matches. Her fingers were so weak in the attempt that it took several tries to get a match struck. But when she finally managed and touched the fire to the kerosene-soaked wick of the lamp, she was rewarded as she watched the fire slowly take hold and spread a soft light about the room.

Too tired even to place the glass chimney back on the lamp, Christa left it on the table. She screwed the lamp's wick up higher, making the light blossom on all sides of her in wavering streamers which fell across the table, down onto the floor, and upward, along the ceiling and wall.

Wiping a stray strand of hair from her eyes, Christa began looking about her. Then she gasped when she discovered the red bloodstains spread out along the floor. Covering her mouth with her hands, she closed her eyes and quickly looked away. She took a step backward, thinking maybe it would be best if she left, not knowing if she could spend the night there, where the reminders of Striped Wolf's evil deeds were so evident. But she knew that it could have been worse. She remembered Striped Wolf had told her that he had slain them on a rug. Surely most of the blood had soaked into it, leaving only these splatters as a testament of sorts to what Striped Wolf was capable of doing.

Christa spied another rug at the far end of the room. That would be the answer to her dilemma. She would cover the stains with the rug and stay, to get her needed rest and, hopefully, some sort of nourishment before it was too late.

Picking up the oval, braided rug, she took it to the stained area and hurriedly covered it. A heavy sigh shook her body. She leaned heavily against the kitchen table, breathing hard. Would this nightmare ever end? What had she done in life to deserve this?

But she knew that she was no better than anyone else, to be spared hardships. The pioneer experience had brought both hardships and heartbreak to most who had ventured into these lands. She was quickly reminded of her dear mama and papa. Even they hadn't been spared, and no two people on the face of the earth had been as kind, as generous, or as loving.

Forcing herself to get hold of her emotions, Christa slowly raised her eyes and absorbed the room and its meager furnishings. It was evident that the settlers had probably been close to her and Tall Cloud's ages—young lovers, just getting a start in life. There was only a table and two chairs, carved out of rough-hewn cedar logs, and a shelf attached to the wall, which held only a few dishes, none matching. Two overstuffed chairs, with stuffing falling from each, had been positioned before the fireplace, and between these stood a table with another kerosene lamp which had a terribly smoked glass chimney. A Bible lay on the table beside the lamp alongside a squat, bulldog-shaped pipe, with tobacco half fallen from its bowl.

At the far end of this one-room cabin a bed had a prominent position, and on it had been spread a neatly embroidered, lace-trimmed white comforter with a stuffed animal in the shape of a bear resting peacefully between the two pillows. The pillowcases looked freshly starched, crisp and clean, as if they had not yet even been slept on.

Christa's eyes went to a closed storage cabinet inside the door. The painful emptiness in her stomach made her pray that food would be found there. Full of hope, she went to the cabinet, threw back the door, and smiled when she saw a dish of apples on the top shelf and potatoes and onions in a pot on a second shelf.

Grabbing an apple, Christa lifted it quickly to her lips and took a bite, chewing on it so heartily she almost choked in the process. Tears stung the corners of her eyes, so thankful was she to have found something to fill the void in her stomach. She ate away at the apple until she reached the core. Then she hungrily ate another one, pleasing not only her hunger but her thirst as well, for these apples grown in the state of Washington were known not only for their taste but for their juiciness as well.

Placing both cores on the table, Christa looked toward the fireplace. Should she start a fire? Could it draw attention?

She remembered her earlier thoughts, that a passerby would not think one way or another about smoke spiraling from this particular cabin's chimney. In fact, it would seem natural to have a fire on these cool nights just before spring.

Remembering a pile of wood she had seen next to the cabin, right outside the door, Christa went out and chose the lightest logs that she could find. The apples had given her enough strength to do what was required, and when she had carried in the wood and dropped it before the fireplace, she knelt on her knee and surveyed the fireplace.

A black kettle hung low over what had once been a fire. And once again the stench that had assailed Christa when she first entered the cabin tore through her nose, burning it.

She squeezed her nose closed with the fingers of one hand and lifted the pot from its hook with the other. When she looked down into it, she finally found the cause of the offensive aroma. It was apparent that a chicken had been simmering over the fire when the couple had been slain. It now lay rotten, swimming in a pool of cold, darkened grease.

"Good Lord," Christa said, taking the pot outside, and leaving it far away from the door. When she went back inside the cabin, she shut the door then went on with the business of building a fire.

Once flames took hold and began wrapping themselves like satin up and around the logs, Christa was finally able to feel comfortable enough to get some needed rest.

But first she would place a pot of potatoes over the fire to eat when she awakened. If she had enough strength upon arising, she mused, she just might go and gather a few eggs to fry before heading on her way back to Seattle.

Thirst once more suddenly plagued her. She looked about her and found that the opened door had hidden behind it a table and on it a bucket of water. She went to it and dipped a tin cup into it, drank her fill, then eyed the bed. After getting the potatoes over the fire, she would get that badly needed sleep.

As she hurried to peel the potatoes and quarter the onions, her thoughts seemed to grow more fuzzy by the minute. She could hardly hold her eyes open. After placing the pot over the fire, she went to the bed and crawled onto it. She looked toward the stuffed animal. Like a small child, she grabbed it, cuddled it against her chest as she lay down on her side, then drifted off into a deep sleep.

David and Tall Cloud's search led them to a clearing which seemed familiar to them both. David looked through the gray twilight, seeing the cabin in the distance. His shoulder muscles tensed as he observed the spirals of smoke slowly rising from the chimney. He gave Tall Cloud a questioning look.

"Tall Cloud, no one should be there," he said in a bare whisper. "We buried the settlers. No one would take possession of their house this quickly."

"Do you think it could be . . . ?" Tall Cloud started hoarsely, his heart beating faster.

"No. We wouldn't be that lucky," David scoffed. He gave Striped Wolf an ugly stare from over his shoulder. Ironically, Striped Wolf had been the only one to have ridden a horse across the long distance they all had traveled. This had to be done to ensure his return to Seattle for proper punishment. Striped Wolf's head wound had weakened him much more than they had at first thought, and he might not have survived the journey on foot.

"I will go to see who is in the cabin," Tall Cloud said, eagerly taking quick steps away from David.

David looked toward the cabin and then at Tall Cloud. "Wait. I'll go with you," he said, taking several long strides to Tall Cloud's side. Both broke into a slow run then moved more quickly as they came closer to the cabin.

Tall Cloud's throat had gone dry from anticipation. David's heartbeats inside his chest were so wild he felt he had ten hearts instead of one.

When they reached the door, Tall Cloud placed his finger on the trigger of his rifle while David crept closer and slowly pushed it open. Cautiously, they stepped inside together.

Tall Cloud squinted his eyes, trying to see through the dim lighting of the room. Then his mouth fell suddenly open when he saw Christa so peacefully asleep on the bed across the room from where he stood.

"*Nahkeeta* . . ." he said hoarsely. "My . . . *Nahkeeta* . . ." His feet wouldn't carry him to her fast enough.

He feasted his eyes upon her as he moved toward the bed, thinking that even in the disarray of her golden hair knotted with burrs and her deerskin dress ripped and soiled she was still just as beautiful.

When he reached the bed, he fell to his knees beside it and bowed his head in a silent prayer of thanks to his gods and spirits that he had found his woman and that she was still pink with the color of health.

David went to the other side of the bed, breathless. He sat down on the edge and started to grab Christa up into his arms, but he realized that he might startle her too quickly from her sleep. A low sob of relief rose from deep inside him and tears rolled from the corners of his eyes. "Christa . . ." he murmured softly. "Honey, wake up. I'm here. Wake up so you can go home with me."

A deep frown creased Tall Cloud's brow. He reached a hand to Christa's cheek then reconsidered and drew it back. *"Nahkeeta, I* have come for you," he said thickly. "Wake up. You are safe. We can now return to Pahto Island."

"Return with you . . . to . . . Pahto Island?" David gasped. "Tall Cloud, you sound as if you had . . . already . . . had her there, as if she had been living with you instead of with me in Seattle."

Christa stirred in her sleep, strangely feeling that she had heard David's *and* Tall Cloud's voices. Could she have been dreaming so realistically? The voices seemed to be so close . . . as though she could reach out and touch. . . .

With her eyes still closed, enjoying the peacefulness that sleep had given her, Christa moved a hand about her and felt someone on the edge of the bed with her. With her other hand she felt someone else, on the other side of her! Her stomach did a strange quivering and fear was once more her companion. She was afraid to open her eyes. She wondered if Striped Wolf had somehow recovered and had brought a companion with him this time, to double her torture.

"Nahkeeta . . . ?"

"Christa . . . ?"

The voices were real! One was David's and one was Tall Cloud's! Were they the ones who sat on the bed? Could it be truly possible?

Opening her eyes in a quick flutter, Christa let out a loud gasp then rose quickly to a sitting position and placed an arm about each of her loved one's necks. She burst into tears, kissing Tall Cloud and then David.

And then she moved fully into Tall Cloud's embrace as he rose from his knees and settled down beside her. She clung to his neck, sobbing against his bare chest.

"Tall Cloud, thank God you've come," she cried. "It's been so horrible. I'm even lucky to be alive. Hold me, Tall Cloud. Hold me. Convince me that you're real. Tell me that I'm not dreaming. I want to go home. I don't want to ever leave Pahto Island again."

David's and Tall Cloud's eyes met and locked. Tall Cloud could see confusion and then rising anger in the soft green of David's eyes. David could see caution in Tall Cloud's gray depths and then smugness, revealing that he knew he was the victor here. He had been the one Christa had turned to, which proved beyond all else that he was most important in her life, even above her brother, David.

Still under David's close scrutiny, Tall Cloud whispered into Christa's ear. "Did he . . . did he rape you, *Nahkeeta?*"

She snuggled closer. "No," she sobbed. "At least he didn't do that."

David began to speak, but a gunshot rang out somewhere outside the cabin, drawing him quickly to his feet. "What the . . . ?" he began, looking from Tall Cloud to the door.

"Striped Wolf," Tall Cloud growled, releasing his hold on Christa.

Christa's insides froze. "Striped . . . Wolf!" she gasped, recoiling. "Is . . . he . . . here?"

She pleaded softly with her eyes as she looked from Tall

Cloud and David, hoping not to hear that Striped Wolf was still alive and might have followed David and Tall Cloud.

Then her eyes widened as she now wondered for the first time how David and Tall Cloud happened to be here *together!* She glanced quickly down at David's foot. He was even well enough to travel! That was a surprise in itself. When she had last been with him, it had pained him terribly to place his foot into a boot. How was it that he had recovered so quickly?

"He's probably tried to escape," David said, rushing toward the door. "I'll go and see."

Tall Cloud glanced down at *Nahkeeta,* seeing the confusion in her eyes. "There is much to explain," he said hoarsely, placing a hand on her cheek. "But for now, I must go and see what is happening. I cannot allow Striped Wolf to escape. Though David's plans are to take Striped Wolf back to Seattle with him, my plans are much different, *Nahkeeta.* I just haven't yet told your brother."

He rose quickly to his feet and hurried toward the door.

Christa moved to the edge of the bed. "But, Tall Cloud, how . . ." she began, reaching a hand out to him.

Tall Cloud gave her a loving glance then left the cabin. He broke into a soft trot and hurried to where a crowd of both his warriors and David's men had gathered in a wide circle. His temples throbbed, for he feared he had lost his chance at vengeance.

If Striped Wolf should die . . . if Striped Wolf should die . . . , his mind echoed over and over again in time with each of his hastening footsteps. When he reached the crowd of men, he pushed his way through and stopped when he came to the clearing in the middle of the wide circle. On the ground lay Striped Wolf, a bullet wound oozing blood from his tattooed chest.

With a set jaw and anger flashing in his eyes, Tall Cloud looked accusingly from man to man, silently asking who was responsible.

David moved to Tall Cloud's side. "One of my men shot him. He was trying to escape," he said.

In the commotion, David had forgotten his anger at what had transpired moments ago in the cabin, when Christa had begged Tall Cloud to take her back with him to his Pahto Island. David's anger had turned into frustration that he wouldn't be given the chance to see Striped Wolf hanged by the neck in Seattle for what he had done to Christa and the two innocent settlers.

David had wanted to put Striped Wolf on display, to discourage any more of the same from any other Indians. From the moment the marines had landed at Seattle, things had begun to change for the better in the community. Now, David believed, even the Suquamish would not feel so free to enter the white men's dwellings for a *nanitch*. It seemed that the white men were not as outnumbered as they had been in the past. And soon the ratified treaty would show all of the Indians that the white men were indeed here to stay!

Tall Cloud's hatred had swelled inside him to proportions unknown to him until now. He went to his knees beside Striped Wolf and yanked his head up from the ground to glare down at him. "You deny me the pleasure of killing you slowly by dying now?" he growled. "You think you die without first being shamed? You are wrong, Striped Wolf."

Looking over his shoulder, Tall Cloud asked one of his warriors for a knife, and, once in his hand, he held it before Striped Wolf's eyes. "You will not be allowed to enter the land of the dead with your braids," he said, laughing throatily.

Tall Cloud's pleasure mounted when he saw Striped Wolf try to draw back away from him with fear in his wavering dark eyes.

"And, Striped Wolf, you should also know that my woman, my *Nahkeeta*, is safe," Tall Cloud said smugly.

"She is in the cabin, alive and well. So you see? Your vengeance was never fully reached. Your abducting her from Pahto Island gained you nothing but death. But before death will come your shame!"

David's insides did a strange rolling as he heard what Tall Cloud said about Pahto Island, alerting him to who had actually taken Christa from Seattle. It hadn't been the Haida Indian. It had been Tall Cloud. And had . . . Tall Cloud . . . even been the one who shot Harrison? Had he done this in the presence of Christa . . . ?

David tightened his hand more securely on his rifle, his trust of Tall Cloud suddenly gone.

But then he was reminded of Christa's behavior toward Tall Cloud. She wanted to return to Pahto Island with him. Had she gone with him willingly in the first place? Could she have shot Harrison? He closed his eyes and shook his head in confusion.

"And now your braids!" Tall Cloud laughed, clipping first one and then the other. He held them up into the air, chanting, proudly showing them to his warriors.

Then his laughter died as he felt the jerking of Striped Wolf's head. When Tall Cloud looked down at Striped Wolf, he found that Striped Wolf's eyes were locked in a death stare.

With his shoulders squared, Tall Cloud dropped the dead Indian's head to the ground and rose to tower over his warriors. "My sister's death is avenged," he shouted. "My *Nahkeeta's* abduction is avenged. Striped Wolf is dead, but his spirit is suffering, for his braids are in my possession, not his."

Loud chants rose into the air from the many warriors, but they abruptly ceased as Christa made her way into the circle of men. Soundlessly, she went to stand over the dead body. She placed a hand on her throat when she looked down at Striped Wolf. Then she looked up at Tall Cloud.

"He . . . is . . . really dead . . . ?" she whispered.

"You have no more to fear from that Haida Indian, my *Nahkeeta*."

"All of this," Christa said, looking from Tall Cloud to David then moving her arm in a sweeping motion around the circle. "I don't understand. How is it that you . . . you two are together?"

Tall Cloud thrust Striped Wolf's braids into the waistband of his breeches, gave the knife back to his warrior, then went to look down at Christa. "Again my warriors and the white men blended as one fighting force," he said in his deep, powerful voice. "Together we found and rescued you, *Nahkeeta*."

"But how did you meet? I never would have thought to see you two together under any circumstances."

"It was by accident, I assure you," David said, stepping forward.

David nudged Tall Cloud in the ribs with the barrel of his rifle. "And, Tall Cloud, I have some questions for you," he growled. "Explain to me how Christa happened to be on Pahto Island when—"

Alarm flashed through Christa as she anticipated David's next words. Wanting to protect Tall Cloud, she stood on tiptoe and placed a hand over David's mouth, sealing his words. "David, let's talk in private," she murmured, glancing about her, seeing the many eyes directed toward her.

She looked up into David's eyes. "Please?" she pleaded. "It would be best that way."

She spoke in an even softer tone. "I do not wish to reveal any private details of my life to all these . . . these men. Let us go to the cabin. Let us talk there."

She placed a hand on the rifle and lowered its barrel away from Tall Cloud. "David, for me?" she asked.

David's eyes wavered. "Oh, all right," he said, frowning.

"Oh, David, thank you," Christa replied, hugging him tightly. "Oh, how I've missed your bear hugs, my sweet big brother."

With his free arm, David hugged her back, then they walked arm in arm back to the cabin.

Christa's strength seemed to have returned with the knowledge that she was truly safe and once more reunited with Tall Cloud. This security, coupled with the full night of sleep and the snack of apples, had made her completely whole again.

As she stepped inside the cabin, she forced herself to ignore the braided rug which covered the bloodstains. Instead she turned to face David and Tall Cloud, who stood glowering at each other.

"How do you explain the fact that Striped Wolf abducted Christa from your island, Tall Cloud, instead of from Seattle, as we all believed?" David blurted. "And do you know anything about Harrison Kramer's death?" His gaze moved to his sister. "What do you have to say on the subject, Christa? Do you know that Harrison is dead—that he was murdered?"

Christa went to David, took his rifle from him and stood it against a wall, then placed his hands in hers. "I want you to listen very carefully to what I have to say to you, David," she said hoarsely. "You won't want to believe it, but everything that I will tell you is the truth. In the end, you will know that Tall Cloud deserves your respect. He is a good, loving man, a man who will soon become my husband."

David paled, and he gasped, "Christa, you—"

Once more Christa stopped his words as she reached a hand to his lips. "David, won't you listen?" she begged.

He slowly shook his head up and down, softening inside. He was so intensely glad Christa was alive that it didn't matter much to him any more that Tall Cloud had won. Everyone had won, for Christa had been found alive and well. Everyone except Striped Wolf. . . .

Christa went to Tall Cloud and placed an arm about his waist, looking up adoringly into his eyes. "It is true that I went to Pahto Island with Tall Cloud," she began. "It is true that Harrison was killed in Tall Cloud's attempt to take me there. And, yes, Tall Cloud killed him."

David took a quick step backward, alarm written all over his face. He reached for his rifle, but Christa was there, standing in his way. "You must hear the rest," she insisted. "You must hear *how* Harrison died and *why.*"

"You have told me all that I need to know," David grumbled. "Tall Cloud killed him. You know that he must be punished . . . that he will surely hang."

"See how quickly you wrongly accuse him?" Christa said, curling her fingers into tight fists at her sides. "Would you see him hung without first hearing that he saved my life?"

"What . . . ?" David gasped, glancing quickly at Tall Cloud.

"Now listen closely, David, to what else I have to say, or you will once more let your rage blind you to the truth," Christa continued.

"Go ahead, Christa. I'm listening."

"Tall Cloud was disappointed that the white men didn't sufficiently reward him after he had fought side by side with them to rid Seattle of the Haida," she said. "He had thought they would reconsider forcing the treaty papers upon the Indians. And when he found that what he had done hadn't changed anything, he came to Seattle to abduct me, to take me to his island to show the white men that he hadn't lost everything."

David's face grew red with rage. "So you abducted my sister not once, but twice?" he shouted at Tall Cloud.

Christa's chin rose proudly. "I went willingly," she said, smiling toward Tall Cloud. "I wanted to be with him. I couldn't marry Harrison. You see, the night of his autumn social function, he attempted to rape me. Tall Cloud came to my rescue. He is the reason Harrison took ill so suddenly at the party. Do you remember, David? Tall Cloud hit him over the head with his rifle, to get Harrison off me."

"Harrison . . . tried . . . to rape you . . . ?" David gasped, paling.

"He did. And when he knew that I wouldn't be his wife, he began watching me, to see if I was meeting a man, thinking it must be the reason I refused to marry him," she continued. "When he saw me with Tall Cloud and watched Tall Cloud sweep me up into his arms and carry me away on his horse with him, Harrison came after us, shooting at us both."

"He . . . meant to . . . shoot you?" David asked incredulously.

"He did."

"Good Lord, Christa."

"Tall Cloud carried me to safety then went after Harrison. He pulled Harrison from his horse. They wrestled. Harrison's pistol went off in the struggle and Harrison died. That's the way it happened, David. But who would want to believe it? One of Seattle's wealthiest men died that night. If word spread that Tall Cloud shot Harrison, do you think people would be fair? Do you think they would listen? And would you want me to have to go before the whole town and tell of Harrison's attempted rape—to be embarrassed and humiliated in that way in order to try to clear Tall Cloud's name? David, it would he much simpler if we let everyone believe that Striped Wolf is guilty of all that has happened."

David spun on his heel, turning his back to both Christa and Tall Cloud. His mind was swirling with confusion. He nervously kneaded his brow. One minute he had reason to hate Tall Cloud enough to see that he was hanged, and then the next minute he had reason to respect him and want him as a friend!

He tried to weigh all these facts in his mind, and he concluded that he wanted Tall Cloud as a friend, not an enemy. David knew now that Christa would marry Tall Cloud, and his heart told him to offer apologies and friendship to this Suquamish Indian, this chief who had stolen his sister's heart.

He swung around and thrust his hand out toward Tall Cloud. "I apologize for having wrongly judged you," he said thickly. "I would appreciate it if you would accept my hand in friendship, Tall Cloud. I have enjoyed traveling with you these past several hours. It proved to me that we could place all mistrust and anger aside when it was necessary to do so. I would like to continue with that friendship, if you'd like."

Christa's face grew flushed with excitement. Barely breathing, she placed her hands on her cheeks as Tall Cloud stepped forward and thrust his hand into David's. Oh, how she prayed for this moment. Could it truly be happening? Surely David understood what his offer of friendship to Tall Cloud meant. David had just, in a sense, approved of her marriage to Tall Cloud.

"My handshake seals the bond between us, proud brother," Tall Cloud said, his face stern, his shoulders squared.

David gave Christa a quick glance then looked unblinkingly into Tall Cloud's gray eyes. "We both love Christa," he said with emotion. "Of course, it is in different ways, but she is the main force behind our friendship, Tall Cloud. Don't ever forget that."

"My love for *Nahkeeta* is from the heart, not from my desire for alliance with the white man," Tall Cloud said dryly. "You must understand this, proud brother."

David's eyebrows forked. "You will no longer struggle to have the treaty papers destroyed?" he asked.

Tall Cloud eased his hand away from David and drew Christa next to him possessively. "There could only be destruction in trying to oppose the white man's treaty. And I have discovered that even though the treaty is soon to be ratified, it doesn't affect the friendship between the Suquamish and the white man," he said. "We, the Suquamish,

have twice proved only recently that we are still a strong
nation of Indians, and no papers will make us less in the
eyes of the white man. We will continue to prove our strength
when the need arises. On Pahto Island, the treaty will not
touch us. I feel assured of that."

Suspicions once more plagued David. "With Christa on
the island with you, you mean," he snapped. "You think,
still, that her presence will give you more power with the
white men—encourage them to leave you in peace?"

Tall Cloud stiffened. "Those are not words of a friend,"
he stated flatly. "Do you forget our bond so quickly? Where
is your trust, proud brother? At first I had wanted a white
woman in the hope that it would make strong ties between
our people. But when I chose *Nahkeeta* to *be* that woman,
she quickly stole my heart as well as my mind."

David lowered his eyes and raked his fingers nervously
through his hair. When Christa moved into his arms and
placed her cheek to his chest, the anger melted inside him.
Slowly he placed his arms about her.

"This is what you want, Christa?" he asked softly. "To
leave the white community behind . . . to live like an Indian?"

"Can I help it if my heart tells me that Tall Cloud is the
man I must choose?" she murmured. "My heart does not
see the color of his skin or the way he dresses. It led me
to feel emotions of sincere love for him the very first time
I saw him, David. I do love him and I do want to live with
him as his wife. Forever, David. Please wish me happiness."

David twined his fingers through her hair. "That's all I
ever wanted for you, Christa. Your happiness."

Christa leaned away from him and looked imploringly
into his eyes. "Then you will give me your blessing as if
you were Papa doing so?" she asked softly.

"Yes, as Papa would have done," David said thickly.

Christa threw herself into his arms, radiant. "Oh, David,

you've just made it possible for my happiness to be complete," she cried. "Thank you. Thank you."

"Soon you will come to Pahto Island for a *potlatch,* proud brother?" Tall Cloud asked, going to place one arm around Christa and the other around David, embracing them both.

David looked with surprise into Tall Cloud's eyes, while accepting the affectionate embrace. *"Potlatch?"* he echoed, wondering if it was similar to a *nanitch.*

"It is a celebration, a time for me to make the formal announcement to my people of my marriage with *Nahkeeta,"* Tall Cloud replied. "The marriage ceremony will then begin a day of feasting and gift giving. You must be there, proud brother, to share in the celebration."

Tall Cloud's words warmed Christa's heart. Her insides tingled with happiness and anticipation. Soon, she thought to herself. Soon. . . .

Twenty-five

Christa awakened in Tall Cloud's arms feeling as though the past several days had not even been real. Tall Cloud's tender embrace had erased all the ugliness from Christa's mind, and today was the day that their hearts would be sealed forever. The celebration was to be an elaborate one, but for now, in the quiet of Tall Cloud's hut, everything was sweetly peaceful.

Snuggling against the muscular expanse of Tall Cloud's naked chest, on a bed of piled blankets placed before a fire in the fire space, Christa watched night smooth away into morning, as rivulets of sunlight stole in through a window.

Christa smiled contentedly to herself, remembering that David and Delores were in a nearby hut, awaiting the full day of ceremonies ahead. It had taken much prodding on Christa's part to get David to agree to spend the night on Pahto Island. But with Delores's eager persistence, he had finally become a willing participant in what was to be Christa's wedding day. David and Delores had already had their special day. They had become man and wife upon David's return to Seattle.

A low giggle slipping through Christa's lips broke the silence in the hut, but she couldn't help herself. She was thinking how ironic it was that David had been the one to marry into wealth, when all along he had worked so hard for her to have it. It was also ironic that it was Harrison's wealth he had acquired by marriage, since it was Harrison's wealth that David had wanted for her. If Harrison had known, he would have given his riches away first, for it had been obvious at the end that Harrison wanted no part of either David *or* Christa.

Tall Cloud stirred. He opened one eye and looked lazily down at Christa. "Did I hear you giggle, *Nahkeeta?*"

"I was just thinking." She sighed.

"About what?"

"Everything."

"Everything? That must in part include me. Do you find me amusing?"

Christa leaned up and kissed him tenderly on the lips. "Never," she said seductively. "I find you fascinating."

Tall Cloud opened his eyes fully, letting his gaze touch her everywhere. "Everything about you is beautiful this morning, my *Nahkeeta,*" he said huskily. "You will make an enchanting bride."

"Today, Tall Cloud!" Christa sighed, glowing as brightly as a torch in her happiness. She placed feathery kisses along his shoulders. "It's finally going to happen. We're to become man and wife. Will your people truly accept me? There are no other white wives in your village of Suquamish."

"Haven't you seen it in their eyes . . . in their actions?" he said, running a hand slowly down her side, relishing the flower-petal softness of her pink skin as his fingers slid lower over the gentle curve of her hips. "They see your kindness . . . your warmth. They feel the love shared between us—their chief and his woman. You will never want for anything, *Nahkeeta.*"

He lowered his lips to the hollow of her throat and in a deep, throaty voice he said, "My people will treat you like a queen. Don't doubt that for a moment."

"And how will you treat me, darling?" Christa whispered,

trailing a finger down his chest, lower even, to where his need of her had risen to its full strength.

With a low growl, Tall Cloud rolled atop her. He scooped her into his arms, lifting her from the blankets so that her breasts were pressed hard against his chest. "How will I treat you?" he teased as he rained kisses along her face. "Like this, my *Nahkeeta*. Like this."

His lips found hers with a heated passion, his tongue a spear as it thrust between her lips to taste the sweetness inside her mouth. Without preliminaries this time, he entered her swiftly and surely then began to move inside her, causing snatches of her breath to sound throughout the small spaces of the hut. She clung to his neck, and she met his probing tongue with the softness of hers. As he laid her back down on the blankets, his hands moved sensuously over her body, arousing in her even more ecstasy and making her mind seem aswirl with a sweet dizziness. When his lips left hers to taste the taut tip of a nipple, flicking it softly with his tongue, Christa emitted a soft moan.

"I love you," she whispered, seeing him through half-lowered lashes, feeling the strength of his thighs in his every stroke inside her. She caressed the nape of his neck lightly with her fingertips as the flame of her desire leapt higher and higher.

Tall Cloud's senses reeled in overwhelming pleasure as his passion peaked. He placed his lips on the delicate curve of her throat, branding her there with a long, lingering kiss while his hands molded around each of her breasts, their softness reminding him of the springy, velvetlike moss that grew in the forest.

Tall Cloud's hot breath and kisses made Christa tingle with excitement. Then he once more gathered her fully into his arms. Their lips met with a gentle sweetness. Christa locked her arms about his neck and lifted her hips to meet his eager thrusts as he so wonderfully filled her.

His mouth absorbed Christa's outcry as she reached that

plateau of joy and fulfillment, and then Tall Cloud joined her as first his body stiffened then shook and quivered as he released his seed deep inside her womb.

Sighing, still trembling from the aftermath of pleasure, Tall Cloud gently released Christa and rolled away from her, onto his back.

Christa rose up on an elbow to gaze in rapture at him, still engulfed by her strong heartbeats. "Tall Cloud," she murmured, tracing his distinctive Indian facial features with her forefinger, "somehow I believe that we just made our first child."

Tall Cloud chuckled and reached for her, easing her up to lie atop him. His thumbs circled the stiff peaks of each of her breasts. "And, my sweet one, how could you know that?" he asked, his gray eyes twinkling as he looked up at her.

She shook her head, tossing her hair back from her eyes. "My mother was different from most mothers," she said, smiling down at him. "Mama made sure that I wasn't ignorant about such things. She prepared me for marriage and having children by explaining the monthly cycles to me. She taught me the time of the month when becoming with child would be the easiest."

"And . . . ?" Tall Cloud interjected, raising a brow inquisitively.

"It is *now,* darling," Christa said, softly giggling. She gazed intensely at the tiny tattoo in the shape of a raven on Tall Cloud's upper right arm, having grown so used to it that she rarely noticed it any more.

She placed a soft kiss on the tattoo, then asked, "Our children, when we have them—will they also carry your family crest upon their arms?"

"Yes," he said matter-of-factly. "And even you, my *Nah-keeta,* once the wedding ceremony is completed and you are my wife."

She was overcome with total surprise and wonderment.

Splaying her fingers against his chest, she pushed away from him slightly, her eyes wide, her lips parted. She was momentarily speechless.

"Tall Cloud, what did you say?" she gasped.

He laughed huskily, lifting a hand to run his fingers through the golden strands of hair which hung across her shoulder, partially covering a breast.

"Is the thought so distasteful to you?" he asked, his laughter dying.

In his gray eyes, Christa could see a trace of hurt. A knot formed at the pit of her stomach, for she never wanted to cause pain in the man who would soon be her husband. She sighed heavily as she worked herself back into his embrace, snuggling her cheek into the curve of his neck.

"I'm sorry, darling," she murmured. "I didn't mean to make you believe that I would dislike a tattoo placed on me. Why would I? It would be in the likeness of yours. It would be in the likeness of . . . our . . . children's. . . ."

In truth, she cringed at the thought, fearing the pain that being tattooed would cause. Yet, the tattoo was small. And she did have to appear strong at all times, to prove that she was worthy of being a chief's wife.

"It is the custom that all of my family bear the crest of the raven," he said thickly. He placed a soft kiss on her upper right arm. "It will be placed there. And the pain will be no more than that of a kiss."

Christa drew away from him, in awe of him anew. He seemed to know her so well. He had sensed her fear of being tattooed as if he had read her thoughts. But shouldn't this be so? she wondered. She could vividly remember the times her mother and father had begun to speak simultaneously. Afterward, they had laughingly revealed to each other that their thoughts had been identical at that moment in time. They had then embraced, saying it was a definite sign of true love when one stole the thoughts of the other and spoke them aloud.

Smiling smugly, Christa knew now more than ever that this union that would take place today was a rightful one. She and Tall Cloud would always be as one.

She looked toward the door, hearing the soft, plaintive notes of a flute being played from afar. In this sound was an aura of mystery, intermingled with romance. A shiver ran up and down Christa's spine as she was caught up in the magic of the enchanting song, never having heard anything quite so lovely, so stirring.

"What is it, *Nahkeeta?*" Tall Cloud asked, his gaze following hers.

"Don't you hear it?" She sighed. "Isn't it lovely? And everything else is so quiet, Tall Cloud. It's as though we and the flute player are the only ones who exist. It gives me such a . . . such a . . . strange feeling inside, Tall Cloud."

"The whole village pays homage to our special day," he said, reaching to pull her back into his arms. "Everyone remains in his hut until the songs of love no longer come from the flute. Then the air will be filled with the many sounds of drums, followed by laughter and shouts of excitement. It will be a day of days, *Nahkeeta.*"

He gave her a light kiss on the lips. "And it is *ours,*" he added, smiling warmly at her.

His lips once more found hers. While his fingers caressed her breasts, his kiss wove passion into Christa's heart. Her fingers traveled over the tight cords of muscle along his shoulders and down his back to where his bare hips were sleek and narrow. Her breath was stolen from her when he placed his swollen manhood inside her and once more they rode the waves of rapture together.

Their hearts pounded in unison and their lips burned against each other's. Then came their quiet explosion of love, and once more they lay spent, yet clinging, as they made that descent to a place where their minds were able to focus once more on the less erotic experiences they were to share this day.

Tall Cloud chuckled. "We must save a portion of ourselves for after the ceremony," he said, lifting her gently
from him and rising to his feet.

He stretched his muscles and ran his hands down the flat
smoothness of his belly. "But it can never be better than
now, can it, *Nahkeeta?*"

Christa rose from the blankets, flushed from sexual fulfillment and from anticipation of what lay ahead. She
started to go to Tall Cloud, to once more find a gentle peace
in his embrace, but she thought better of it. Today there
was some sort of excitement traveling between them, so
much so that their desire for lovemaking seemed endless.

Instead, she went to a basin and began pouring perfumed
oils into water, oils that were required of her ceremonial
bath before the marriage ceremony began.

"Each time with you is better," she finally answered, running a cloth up and down her neck, her skin tingling where
the oil penetrated.

Once more there was a hungry ache in Tall Cloud's loins,
making him wonder if some magic elixir had been cast
upon the air this day! He went to Christa and cupped her
breasts in the curves of his hands.

"Let me bathe your breasts with the oil," he said huskily.

"Tall Cloud, you probably shouldn't," Christa said, already overcome by renewed throes of passion as his thumbs
sensuously pressed into her nipples. She closed her eyes
and licked her lips hungrily, feeling wicked because of her
continued wanton need of him.

Tall Cloud took the cloth from her and began running it
slowly around first one breast and then the other. Goose
bumps rose along Christa's flesh and her eyes closed in
ecstasy. She trembled as the oiled cloth made a smooth path
downward, across her abdomen, along her thighs, and even
to her toes. The perfumed aroma was of jasmine, and it
clung to her skin as a babe does to its mother's breast.

Her breath caught in her throat when she saw Tall Cloud

on his knees, gently lifting one of her toes to his mouth. Her pulse raced as he sucked on one toe and then the others, and such heat rose inside her, she thought she would surely melt right down into the rush mats spread out beneath her.

"Tall Cloud, what you continue to . . . do . . . to me . . ." she said in a low rasp. "We shall never get on with the activities of the day if you don't stop."

Laughing lightly, Tall Cloud replaced her foot on the floor and rose to his feet. "It is not my plan to take you again, my *Nahkeeta*," he said, dropping the scented cloth back into the basin. "I wanted to arouse you just so much, then refuse you completion until tonight. This way, you will watch me today with stars in your eyes." He raised an eyebrow in her direction. "Is that not true, *Nahkeeta?*"

Christa smiled up at him bewitchingly. "You've never teased me in such a way before."

"I do not mean to tease now," he said sternly. "I am teaching you."

"Teaching? Teaching me what?"

"Restraint," he said, now sprinkling mica on his skin to make it shine. "While I am away from you, doing my chiefly duties or on the hunt for the rare albino deer, you will have to practice restraint. Sometimes I can be gone for many weeks. You will be without my embraces then, *Nahkeeta*, and will have to patiently wait for my return to have them again. You will learn that waiting enhances the pleasure."

Christa flinched, hearing the words "waiting enhances the pleasure." A memory stabbed at her insides as if cold icicles had been plunged through her flesh. Her face grew pale, her eyes haunted.

Tall Cloud saw her reaction. He went to her and framed her face between his hands. *"Nahkeeta,* what is it? Was it something that I said to make you take on the appearance of a ghost?"

"Yes, it was something you said," she murmured, swallowing hard.

"What? What did I say to put such fear in your eyes?"

"Your comment that waiting enhances the pleasure."

"But it is true. Just you wait. You will understand once we are separated for a time."

Christa brushed his hands aside and turned her back to him. She dropped to her knees to place a log on the fire and watched as the flames began to wrap themselves about it.

"What you said has nothing to do with us," she said throatily.

"Then what?" Tall Cloud asked, taking her by a wrist and gently drawing her up, into his embrace. "Tell me, *Nahkeeta*. Today is not a day for a sad face. You should be smiling. Your thoughts should be filled only with *us.*"

"Oh, Tall Cloud, I'm sorry." Christa sighed, hugging him tightly to her. "I shouldn't have let anything about Striped Wolf ruin our day."

Tall Cloud took her by the shoulder and pushed her away from him, holding her at arm's length. "Striped Wolf?" he growled. "Why are you thinking of him, *Nahkeeta?*"

"I said that I was sorry." She gulped, seeing the anger in his eyes and feeling it in the way he held her.

"Tell me why you spoke his name," Tall Cloud said hoarsely.

"It was something you said, Tall Cloud."

"Tell me, *Nahkeeta.* Tell me now. Don't you hear? The flute has stopped playing. The drums are now beating, stirring excitement in my people's hearts. We must join them soon."

"All right. I'll tell you." Christa sighed. "When you said that waiting enhances the pleasure, I was reminded of when Striped Wolf said the identical thing to me. He had threatened me, saying that as soon as we arrived at his village, he—" Christa's words broke off. She couldn't bear to say them. Instead, she turned her head and lowered her eyes.

Tall Cloud placed a forefinger beneath Christa's chin and forced her head around so that their eyes could meet. "Do you forget that those words are not owned solely by the Haida, Striped Wolf?" he said reassuringly. "And don't you remember that he is now dead and that he didn't gain that pleasure that he awaited at the end of his journey? Only I have been to paradise and back with you, *Nahkeeta.*"

"Yes," she whispered. "And we shall travel there over and over again, always, Tall Cloud."

"You are able to forget all sadness, all thoughts of Striped Wolf and the ugliness that he brought momentarily into our lives?"

"Yes . . ."

"Then let us prepare ourselves fully for the day ahead," he said, proud to see such strength in this woman who would soon be his wife.

Twenty-six

The sky was brilliantly blue over Pahto Island, and there were no clouds to inhibit the sunshine. The steady, rhythmic pounding of many drums reverberated from one end of the island to the other, and there was a hum of excitement as the Suquamish Indians sat merrily about a communal fire, feasting with their chief and his bride-to-be.

Large amounts of olachen oil had been poured on the outdoor communal fire, causing it to blaze up fiercely. Fish and meat were roasting over the fire. Shellfish, clams, and oysters had been collected in the shallow bays and on the beaches as part of the feast, and biscuits of dried, ground fern roots, baked near the hot coals of the fire.

Wooden trenches were filled with blueberries and white berries larger than blackberries, all of these having literally dripped from the bushes at harvest time which had only recently passed.

The dishes from which everyone was eating were large and spectacularly carved, with six to eight people seated at a single dish. The feast was fast becoming a high-pitched celebration.

Moments ago Tall Cloud had introduced Christa to his family of Indians, though, in truth, they had already known her for many months. But formalities were in order this day, for the Indians believed that the union between their Suquamish chief and his bride-to-he would be strengthened by these ceremonies and customs which had been practiced from the time the first Suquamish Indian had been born into the world.

Gifts given to Tall Cloud and Christa at this *potlatch* were spread out on display for all to see. There were many "button blankets," beautifully designed baskets, clothes, and furs. Silver bracelets had been presented to Christa as tokens of love from Tall Cloud's people, as well as kitchen wares, skillfully carved by deft fingers, and bark cloth for Christa's future use in making her own dresses and skirts.

Beaming, Christa sat beside Tall Cloud in a place of honor amidst his band of Indians. She had smiled so much and thanked so many people that her jaws were aching unmercifully. But she couldn't deny the happiness that filled her. She knew that she had won over the Suquamish, seeing their admiration of her in the way they continued to look at her and by the generous gifts they had given.

Looking at Tall Cloud who sat at her left side, her heart thrilled. Never had he looked so handsomely proud! His loincloth was accompanied only by a headdress made from a wide band of deerskin trimmed with the scarlet-feathered scalps of the pileated woodpecker, and arm and leg bands twisted and woven from shredded bark. He wore neither moccasins nor his necklace of animal dentalia. He wore only what was required of him on this occasion which was to be celebrated but once in his life. Christa was glad that the Suquamish didn't practice polygamy, for she would have refused to share Tall Cloud with another woman.

Christa sat up straighter, to be more comfortable on her legs which she had chosen to cross beneath her. Her hair hung long, appearing even more golden beneath the rays of the sun, and her face was pink with excitement. She felt she was truly meant to dress in buckskin, for her dress felt so natural as it clung to her gently and dipped in sensuously at her waist.

Looking around Tall Cloud to his left side, Christa caught

a glimpse of David and Delores. A smile curved her lips upward, for she had never thought to see David in only a loincloth. She now knew Tall Cloud's full powers of persuasion! Only Tall Cloud could have convinced David that he should wear a loincloth for the ceremony. David had always thought of a loincloth as being a shameful show of flesh.

Tall Cloud placed a hand over one of Christa's, squeezing it affectionately, then he released it and stood to tower over everyone. He raised a hand, causing a hush to ripple through the crowd, even to those who played the drums. All eyes rose to him and all dishes of food were placed aside.

"Nah! Skookum kanaway!" he said in his deep, commanding voice. "All things are connected like the blood which unites one family. Man does not weave the web of life; he is merely a strand of it. Whatever he does to the web, he does to himself. We know that most white men do not understand our ways. But there are those among us today who have proven that they do understand. As you all know, my *Nahkeeta* is the force behind this bond between the white man and Suquamish. With her and those who love and trust her, all of our lives will become one strand of the web being woven, and this strand will multiply into many, in the end becoming the strongest web of any between the white man and Suquamish!"

Loud shouts rose into the air, followed by low chanting from the most elderly of the tribe.

But Christa did not feel any pleasure from what she had heard. Instead, she was assailed by the same doubts she had had before. Was Tall Cloud still marrying her only to use her?

She gave David a concerned, questioning glance, which he returned with a frown shadowing his face.

"But, my people, understand me when I say that this web of life I am speaking of would mean nothing to me without the sincere love of my woman, my *Nahkeeta*," Tall Cloud continued. "She and you are the driving force of my existence—not an alliance with the Great Father who lives in Washington! He is a user and we are too proud to be takers. We shall keep Pahto Island where we should have made our residence many moons ago. This is where our ancestors prospered. So shall we!"

The drums once more boomed in unison. Dancers carrying beautifully flaked blades of red obsidian rose from the group and began performing, dancing in and around those who sat about the fire. Tall Cloud drew Christa up, to stand beside him.

Christa's anger had melted when she heard the final words of his speech, and she felt guilty for having momentarily doubted him again. She slid an arm about his waist, peacefully content, and together they watched as the dancing continued.

The dancers sprang into the air, turning rapidly on their heels in narrow circles. They chanted loudly with each and every movement to the rich, vibrant beat of nearby drums made of hollow boxes.

Tall Cloud once more showed his authority as chief by raising a hand to stop the dancing. "Now is the time for tribal games," he said. "Any of my braves who wish to participate, gather around!"

The younger men of the tribe rose quickly to their feet and began forming groups. "Games?" Christa asked as Tall Cloud took a step away from her. "What sorts of games? Tall Cloud, when will we exchange our vows?"

"We will join our hands when the sun dips lower in the sky, behind the great mountains," he said, smoothing a thumb over the curve of her jaw. "Now is the time for games. Some will wrestle, some will shoot arrows, and some will have foot races or tugs of war. Your brother and I, hopefully, will wrestle or have a foot race."

"You and David?" she questioned, glancing at David over

her shoulder, not knowing what David would think of such a suggestion.

"It will only be in fun, *Nahkeeta*," Tall Cloud chuckled, taking her hand to lead her to David. "Don't you know that your brother and I are now friends? We no longer challenge each other for anything."

Seeing Tall Cloud moving toward him, David took Delores by an elbow and helped her to her feet as he also rose to a standing position.

"I hope that you, proud brother, will want to participate even in this part of our celebration today," Tall Cloud said, placing a hand heavily on David's shoulder.

"And what do you have in mind?" David asked, clearing his throat nervously, wondering if either lost to the other would old resentments return? As it was, they now felt a mutual admiration.

A smile touched Tall Cloud's lips. "First we will participate in a wrestling match," he said, proud that the eyes of this man who had once been so stubborn had now softened, as had his mood when he was in Tall Cloud's presence.

David looked around guardedly, noting how the Indians had once more grown quiet and all eyes had centered on him. What could victory or defeat for either of them mean to these Indians? It seemed the repercussions could be varied, and David wasn't sure if he was ready to be the fool or the—

"What is your answer, proud brother?" Tall Cloud persisted, interrupting David's troubled train of thought.

David still couldn't give Tall Cloud his response. He looked down at the way in which he was dressed, now wishing that he hadn't agreed to wear the brief loincloth. If he lost to Tall Cloud, he would look doubly ridiculous!

Clearing his throat nervously, David finally offered Tall Cloud a handshake. "Wrestling it will be," he said tightly. "But I tell you in advance that I've never been a man of violence, so I have never witnessed or participated in such a sport as wrestling."

"This is no test, so it shouldn't matter that you've never wrestled before," Tall Cloud said with a shrug. "Come with me, proud brother," he continued, placing an arm affectionately about David's bare shoulders. "We shall choose a soft place of grass intermingled with patches of moss. There's no reason not to make our fun as comfortable as we can."

Christa walked beside Delores. She suddenly felt left out, and on her own wedding day! Tall Cloud shouldn't be separating himself from her—not even for a second! Surely this game that Tall Cloud wanted to play could as well been played another day.

"This is so exciting!" Delores exclaimed, covering her mouth with a hand to suppress a giggle.

Christa gave Delores a look from beneath raised eyebrows. Sometimes it was hard for Christa to believe that Delores was nearing her twenty-sixth birthday and was twice a widower. Delores was sometimes such a child, even though she voluptuously filled the bodice of the clinging, buckskin dress which she wore for this special occasion.

"Don't you think it's exciting?" Delores asked, looking up at Christa, her blue eyes sparkling.

"I would have preferred something different on my wedding day," Christa blurted. "A wrestling match between my brother and my soon-to-be-husband is not my idea of the sort of excitement I had anticipated."

Delores sidled up closer to Christa. "Oh, yes," she whispered. "Now I see what you mean."

Christa blushed and lowered her eyes. "Delores, not only that," she murmured. "I just don't think it's wise that Tall Cloud and David are going to wrestle in front of this audience of Indians."

She lifted her eyes upward and made a sweeping gesture with her hand. "Don't you see? Don't you hear how quiet Tall Cloud's people are as they eagerly follow behind him?

Tall Cloud must win this match, or he will surely be shamed before his people."

Delores tossed her head, making her auburn hair dance across her shoulders. "This is all in fun," she said dryly. "Christa, you're too serious about everything."

"Yes, Tall Cloud *did* say that it was to be done in fun," Christa said, watching now as Tall Cloud and David stopped in a clearing and were quickly circled by the Indian onlookers. She moved with Delores through the crowd of Indians until they were standing on the inner edge of the clearing, where they could get a much better look.

Christa tensed as Tall Cloud and David placed their hands on each other's shoulders; then both were in sudden combat. The sun shone down upon their bodies, which were a contrast of copper color and white. Now they entwined and twisted on the ground, sweat making their bodies slick, their muscles tightening as their holds strengthened.

First David was on his back and then Tall Cloud. The air was filled with grunts and groans. Christa looked away momentarily, closing her eyes. She gritted her teeth when she heard their bodies slapping against each other, for she wanted neither one to lose. She had loved David far longer than Tall Cloud, but the love she felt for Tall Cloud was a fierce, sometimes even savage one. Oh, what a savage heart she had for this Indian whom she loved!

Once more Christa watched. She was surprised to see that Tall Cloud and David were once again on their feet, pushing against one another, their muscles straining, as though every muscle in their bodies was being used.

And then suddenly a change occurred. Tall Cloud had managed to get a firm hold on David as he placed an arm about David's neck and seemed to lock it in place there, rendering David helpless. Sweat poured from David's scalp, his eyes were closed, and his face was a grimacing mask as his fingers dug into Tall Cloud's corded arm.

And then, just as quickly, David was loose again and had

Tall Cloud in the same position. Tall Cloud shoved his elbow hard into David's ribs. David flinched and groaned with pain, loosening his grip around Tall Cloud's neck long enough for Tall Cloud to regain the advantage, forcing David to the ground, and managing to pin both of David's shoulders at one time.

The eyes of the Indian onlookers reflected pride, yet not a sound was heard from them. Tall Cloud rose to his feet, the victor. His body glistened with perspiration. He turned and offered David a hand. "You wrestle well, proud brother," he said thickly, glad that David was willing to accept his hand.

David was proud of himself, and that he was capable of losing gracefully. He was also relieved that, so far, no resentment was forming anew between him and Tall Cloud. He smiled up at Tall Cloud and chuckled as he rose from the ground. "I wasn't so bad, was I?" he said, tightening his leg muscles as he placed his feet firmly on the ground. "But, Tall Cloud, you are the true victor here." He began shaking Tall Cloud's hand heartily. "Congratulations, Tall Cloud. I enjoyed it—truly enjoyed it."

Christa sighed with relief. Delores clasped her hands together, an expression of pride in her husband brightening her already lovely face.

"Then you are ready to meet my other challenge?" Tall Cloud asked, his gray eyes dancing as he saw David's smile fade.

"Good Lord, what's next?" David asked, releasing his hand from Tall Cloud's.

"A foot race," Tall Cloud said, squaring his shoulders.

Christa grabbed hold of Delores's arm, paling. "No," she gasped. "Has Tall Cloud forgotten that David's foot has only recently become fully healed?"

Delores patted Christa's hand reassuringly. "Don't fret so," she said, smiling coyly. "David will win. You'll see, Christa."

Christa measured Tall Cloud's height next to David's. Though David was tall and muscularly lean, Tall Cloud was taller and seemed to have the advantage here with his longer legs.

"But, Delores—" Christa began but was interrupted by Delores.

"David's foot is strong again," she said, looking adoringly toward her husband. "I guess you don't know that he's been exercising that foot endlessly, to strengthen its muscles for the spring planting ahead and for the building of our new house on the farm."

"He has been exercising?" Christa murmured. "No. I didn't know."

"He wants to prove to me that country living is better than city life," Delores said, laughing softly. "I think it will be exciting feeding the chickens and milking the cows."

Christa smiled to herself, hardly believing what she was hearing, unable to envision Delores in a cotton dress and apron tossing corn bits to chickens. But she had been willing to leave her diamonds behind this day, to dress in buckskin. Perhaps she *could* be converted into a country girl.

David studied the scar on his bare foot. It was quickly fading, and rarely did the gnawing ache return as it had so much at the onset of the healing. He moved the toes, stretching the muscle which had grown stronger as each day passed. But was the foot strong enough to accept such a challenge as this?

He remembered his earlier fears—of being left with a partially lame foot, being less a man, less virile. Couldn't this be the true test? He desperately wanted to prove to himself that he could do as much as before his injury. This was the time to rid himself of all his fears!

Gulping back a lump in his throat, he clasped his hand tightly around Tall Cloud's. "I accept," he said dryly. "A foot race it will be, Tall Cloud. Where? When?"

Tall Cloud smiled broadly. Out of the corner of his eye

he saw the thick scar that ran across the top of David's foot. "Where?" he said. "Here. When? Now."

David moved to Tall Cloud's side, seeing a space had been made for the race as Indians lined either side of the path. He didn't dare look at Christa, knowing that she would be concerned about his foot. Delores, on the other hand, was never a pessimist, and she had watched him exercise with a passion each day. David wished that he were as full of optimism as he knew Delores would be.

"One of my warriors will shoot a rifle into the air and then the race will begin." He gestured with a hand. "We will race to where the long line of my people ends." He offered David a hand. "Good luck, proud brother."

Tall Cloud and David then turned away from each other and stood poised, tensed, and ready. When the shot exploded into the air, they both bounded ahead, side by side, lifting their feet and running hard, their eyes directed toward the end.

David huffed and puffed, wincing as a slow ache began in his foot. Tall Cloud grunted as he pushed his body forward, yet he didn't push as hard as he could. It was important, he realized, that he let *Nahkeeta*'s proud brother also have a taste of winning this day. Tall Cloud had planned carefully. This could make a stronger bond between soon-to-be brothers. And with David's weakened foot, it was only fair that Tall Cloud didn't put all his effort into his running. David must win to make things even. David *would* win!

David lost sight of Tall Cloud from the corner of his eye. He didn't want to take the time to look back, to see where Tall Cloud was. Could it be true? Was it possible he could win this foot race against Tall Cloud?

He ignored the stabbing pain in his foot, pounding instead with more energy against the ground, running harder and harder. Perspiration streamed into his eyes, blurring his vision. His heart beat erratically, thundering inside him. He

wiped his eyes clear and broke into a nervous smile as he
finished the race and knew that he had won!

Thrusting a doubled fist into the air, David shouted with
glee then spun around on a heel just as Tall Cloud ran up
next to him, panting.

Wiping his brow, Tall Cloud laughed between pants.
"Seems . . . you're . . . the winner, proud brother," he said.

David's response was only a nervous laugh, for he still
could not believe he was the victor. He offered a handshake
to Tall Cloud. "Sorry about that, Tall Cloud," he said. He
looked across Tall Cloud's shoulder, seeing that Tall Cloud's
people didn't seem at all unhappy over Tall Cloud's loss;
in fact, they were gazing toward David with looks of affec-
tion, pride, and, most of all, sincere friendship. David now
understood that not only had he won the foot race, but also
the respect of Tall Cloud's people!

"You ran like a deer," Tall Cloud said as he chuckled,
shaking David's hand vigorously. "Congratulations, proud
brother."

Two Indian maidens approached, each carrying wooden
basins of water. One basin was placed on the ground before
David and the other before Tall Cloud.

"Cleanse yourself," Tall Cloud said, nodding toward the
basin of water. He looked toward the sky, anxious when he
saw that the sun had moved lower toward the mountains.
"Soon the ceremony will take on a more serious note. We
must be refreshed before we stand beside our women."

David was relieved to see that the crowd of Indians was
thinning and moving back in the direction of the communal
fire, leaving only Delores and Christa to observe the sponge
baths.

Willingly, David stooped to a knee and began splashing
water on his face and then his chest. He smiled toward
Delores as she came to him and knelt beside him.

"I'm so proud of you, David," she said, helping him now

as she cupped water into her hands and lovingly bathed his back with it.

Christa stood over Tall Cloud, full of love for him, sensing that he had just done a noble deed, though she would never be sure. She somehow knew this would not be something ever spoken of between them—this victory of David's.

"Darling, are the games now over?" she asked, seeing how the Indians were settling down around the fire. Slowly her eyes rose to the sky. She thrilled inside, seeing the orange streaks in the sky as the brilliant circle of the sun dipped lower, toward the mountains in the far distance. Soon her dreams would be a reality. Soon. . . .

"The games are over, the victory shared equally," Tall Cloud said, giving her an easy smile. "And now the time is almost ripe for us to become man and wife. This is a day of days, my *Nahkeeta.*"

A sensual shiver ran across Christa's flesh. Seeing that Tall Cloud was sparkling clean and smelling refreshed, she reached a hand toward him. "Then let's wait no longer," she murmured. "Let's do it now, Tall Cloud."

Tall Cloud took her hand warmly in his and together they walked toward the waiting Indians. Christa watched as David and Delores moved arm in arm ahead of them and she saw their love reflected in their smiles and embraces. Christa felt secure in the world she had chosen and was certain now that the future would be filled with happiness.

Settling down on a blanket beside Tall Cloud, Christa tensed slightly, not knowing what to expect next. Her eyes widened when the crowd of Indians began singing tribal songs while wooden cups designed in the shape of the raven were passed around so that everyone would have one. When Christa received hers, she looked down into it and at the white, milky liquid that partially filled the cup.

Tall Cloud urged Christa up beside him as he rose to his feet, held his cup into the air, and spoke in full Suquamish to his people, even as the songs continued softly.

"Drink," Tall Cloud whispered to Christa. "Then others will follow our command."

Christa blinked her eyes nervously then placed the cup to her lips. Tipping it slightly, she sipped at the liquid, recognizing clam juice, and something more. A bitter substance had been added, which gave the drink the sharpness of wine. Then she remembered that Tall Cloud had once told her that whale oil was sometimes used as wine, and she now believed she had just taken her first taste of whale oil. The taste curled her tongue, but she stood proudly erect as the Indians, one by one, emptied their own cups.

Christa's heart warmed when she saw that the sky had become completely inflamed with the color of burnt orange as the sunset now was only a half circle above the long range of mountains that spread beyond Mount Rainier.

Tall Cloud took Christa's cup and placed it with his on the ground at their feet. Slowly he turned to her, his eyes a deep gray and truly mirroring his soul, for his love for her was revealed in their depths.

The sky's glorious glow of color was reflected on Christa's upturned face. She smiled almost bashfully at Tall Cloud as he offered his hand to her. She remembered how he had talked so often about the joining of hands at the marriage ceremony, and she thrilled as she lifted her hand, slowly, to meet his.

Delores snuggled closer to David, feeling a hushed tension in the crowd of Indians as their songs suddenly ceased. She took David's hand onto her lap and squeezed it. "Happy, Darling?" she whispered.

"Never happier," David said, watching Christa, radiant in her own joy. This day had proven much to David, especially one very important fact—Tall Cloud was a fair, very likable person. Though Tall Cloud was an Indian, David no longer harbored regret in his heart that Christa had chosen him for a husband. David now knew that he had been so wrong about so many things.

As the sun dropped from view, Tall Cloud clasped his hand fully around Christa's. She was engulfed by warm, delicious feelings as his eyes branded her as his. Her insides glowed warm as he took her other hand and affectionately squeezed it.

"With the joining of our hands, also comes the joining of our hearts," Tall Cloud said with deep emotion. *"Nahkeeta,* you are now my wife. I am your husband. My people as well as your brother and his wife are our witnesses. We are joined as one, forever, my *Nahkeeta."*

Christa's heart soared as Tall Cloud swept her up into his arms and began carrying her away from the crowd of silent onlookers. She twined an arm about his neck and placed her cheek on his splendid, muscled chest, oblivious to anything but her husband. She had waited too long to let anything other than him enter her thoughts at this magical moment. And the moments ahead—how rapturous they would be! She knew that no part of her would be left untouched by the ecstasy that he would bring to her. She closed her eyes, already dizzy with the passion building inside her.

Tall Cloud's heart raced as he felt the warm pressure of her body against his and heard her uneven breaths, knowing that the love potion added to the clam juice was already having its erotic effect on her. Lovers they would be, as never before!

As he began a soft trot toward their hut, he glanced down at Christa, the sight of her gentle loveliness inflaming his heart. The moonlight spilling over her fair body gave her a luminous glow. She seemed a lovely apparition in his arms.

The fire burned low in the fire space, casting its soft glow and lighting Tall Cloud's entrance as he carried Christa into their hut. In their absence, great bear skins had been spread on the floor by the fire, and clusters of roses in wooden vases were scattered about the room, emitting a sweet, heady aroma.

Christa's eyes opened drunkenly, and she saw the prepared bed and smelled the roses. It couldn't have been more perfect if she had been carried into one of Boston's finest hotels and offered the grandest bed, she thought happily to herself. Even the most expensive champagne couldn't replace the delicious feeling swimming around inside her.

"My wife . . ." Tall Cloud said huskily, gently placing her on the soft fur of the skins. "You are now truly mine. No one can ever take you away from me. Our love is sealed forever by the joining of our hands."

Christa reached her arms out to him, beckoning for him to come to her. "Not only our hands, but also our hearts, Tall Cloud," she murmured. "Love me, Tall Cloud. Love me."

Tall Cloud knelt over her, bracing himself with a hand on each side of her head. His eyes revealed the flaming passion scorching his insides, and his face was a hungry mask of desire.

"My *Nahkeeta*," he whispered, lowering his lips to hers. The kiss was at first soft and gentle then became demanding, hot, frenzied. Tall Cloud's hands crept up the skirt of her dress and found the waiting softness between her thighs. Slowly he caressed her there, while his other hand wandered eagerly down the lines of her voluptuous body.

He then drew his lips from hers and watched her drugged passion grow as she writhed in pleasure and tossed her head.

Christa let out a soft cry of sweet pain as his fingers brought her closer to the brink of joy. Then she emitted a quivering sigh when his fingers crept down and away from her to busy themselves at releasing her from her confining dress. And when he had freed her body, he worked with her hair until it was spread out beneath her head like a golden halo.

Slipping his loincloth off, Tall Cloud let his gaze take in the loveliness of her—the gentle, sweet curve of her hips, the tiny taper of her waist, and the magnificent swells of her breasts. Her eyes were a soft, hazy green, her lips seductively parted. And as he positioned himself over her, he felt she would swallow him whole with her sweetness.

"My love . . ." Christa whispered, her hands wandering over his perfect body. "Take me now. The waiting has become pure torture."

Chuckling, Tall Cloud eased his man's strength inside her, feeling her sensual shudder at his entrance. He began gentle strokes, his loins hot, his loins full. His lips sought a breast and kissed its taut tip, and his tongue flicked out to tease and torment her even more. His hands were like hot coals traveling along her body, firing her insides with each added touch.

Then his lips went to hers, and he kissed her passionately and long, while his strokes became fevered inside her. She clung to him. Her fingernails sank deep into the flesh of his buttocks. She was soaring, dizzy with rapture, and she met each of his thrusts with wild movements of her hips.

Mouths pressed. Tongues probed. Fingers sought and captured. Christa was mindless with the pleasure. She savored Tall Cloud's closeness, her breasts tingling hot as his hands kneaded and fondled.

With a soft cry she sensed her complete release take hold and felt she was being swept away from herself, so filled was she with ecstasy.

Tall Cloud could feel the sweet wetness of her pleasure coil around him, and knew that she had once more experienced and enjoyed the ultimate of ultimates. Then, being so close to the edge himself, he stopped his thrusting for a moment to catch his wind.

Once more he bent his head and flicked his tongue over one of her breasts, then, when she urged his lips to hers, he kissed her ardently. He once more began his strokes inside her until sweet lethargy began to sweep his mind clear of everything but this moment, and he welcomed the soaring mindlessness that overcame him. . . .

Tall Cloud gently embraced Christa. Their possession of each other had been so blissfully sweet, they trembled together with the ecstasy.